The Year 5865

The Year 5865

by
Hippolyte Mettais

translated, annotated and introduced by
Brian Stableford

A Black Coat Press Book

Visit our website at www.blackcoatpress.com

ISBN 978-1-61227-100-2. First Printing. July 2012. Published by Black Coat Press, an imprint of Hollywood Comics.com, LLC, P.O. Box 17270, Encino, CA 91416. All rights reserved.

Introduction

L'An 5865, ou Paris dans quatre mille ans by "le Docteur H. Mettais," here translated as *The Year 5865*, was published in Paris by Librairie Centrale in 1865. It is a re-markable novel in several ways, the bulk of it consisting of a first-person narrative related by a character living 4000 years hence, after various disasters have obliterated almost all the documents relating to the world with which the readers of 1865 were familiar. In consequence, the narrator's knowledge of the reader's world is severely limited and densely clouded by myth; in his world, archeological investigation is in its infancy, and has only just begun to provide corrective evi-dence allowing some slight penetration of that fog of myth.

In the latter respect, there is a crucial similarity between the world of 5865 A.D. featured in the book and the world of 1865 A.D., in which archaeological endeavors—particularly those in Egypt sparked by the legacy of Napoleon's Egyptian campaign—were beginning to cut through the fog of myth clouding the past of several millennia before, creating a heady combination of intellectual excitement and threat to en-trenched belief. For that reason, the project of writing such a novel must have seemed both exciting and challenging—but it posed extremely awkward technical problems for whose po-tential solution there was virtually no literary precedent in 1865. The establishment of a first-person narrative viewpoint that is both radically different from that viewpoint of the read-er and ignorant of huge amounts of information known to the reader creates obvious problems for a writer in transmitting information to the reader, because of the considerable disso-nance between what the narrator knows—especially the things he takes for granted—and what the reader knows and takes for granted.

L'An 5865 was not the first work to make the heroic attempt to cope with such problems, but in 1865 it was by far the longest and most complex, and its endeavor was unprecedented in some significant ways. Previous novels providing elaborate descriptions of the future, including the landmark examples Louis-Sébastien Mercier's *L'An deux mille quatre cent quarante* (1771; rev. 1786; tr. as *Memoirs of the Year 2500*) and Émile Souvestre's *Le Monde tel qu'il sera* (1846; tr. as *The World as it Shall Be*) had employed protagonists from our own time who were able to observe the future in visions, and were thus able to transport the reader's awareness into the future with them. Even the handful of much shorter works that had attempted to do away with such artifice and offer straightforward accounts of future reality, the most important of which were Charles Nodier's "Hurblubleu" and "Leviathan Long" (1833)[1] and Félix Bodin's *Le Roman de l'avenir* (1834)[2] had used an omniscient narrator able to serve, at least to some extent, as an interpreter ready, willing and able to explain to readers what is happening in the future being described, in terms of their own experience.

Mettais scorned the use of both of these explanatory crutches; even when he interpolates fragments of texts supposedly originating from the 19th or 20th centuries into his story, as he occasionally does, they only make information available to the reader slightly and elliptically, and even though he equips the principal first-person narrative with a documentary frame, that too is strictly limited in its assumed vision. Given that the unreliability of remembered history and the vagueness of transtemporal understanding are important themes of the novel's didactic endeavor, this essentially fractured viewpoint—which requires the reader to deduce many

---

[1] combined in translation as "Perfectibility" and included in the Black Coast Press anthology *The Germans on Venus*, ISBN 978-1-934543-56-6.
[2] translated as *The Novel of the Future*, Black Coat Press, ISBN 978-1-934543-44-3.

things that cannot be explicitly stated in the text, and almost always leaves such deductions open to doubt—is perhaps uniquely appropriate to the project, but that does not make it any less difficult for the writer, as a methodical project, or for the reader, whose attempts to make complete sense of what is happening are likely to feel slightly frustrating throughout.

This problem is further complicated in the present translation because its 21st century readers are significantly removed from the context of French readers in 1865, aware of an extra century and a half of actual history and no longer immediately aware of many facts and issues that seemed familiar and urgent then. I have tried to compensate for the latter deficit by including footnotes that point out some of the items of information known to French readers in 1865, whose remembrance would have been triggered by names and other clues included in the text, but I doubt that I have been able to catch them all, and there is much, in any case, that Mettais either intended to remain mysterious or never quite got straight in his own mind. By way of compensation, the spectacular development of futuristic fiction in that interim has given 21st century readers much greater expertise in negotiating text akin to *L'An 5865*, but the fact remains that to modern English readers, as well as to its contemporary French readers, the novel retains certain indissolubly puzzling aspects. That is by no means entirely a bad thing, however, adding to the sum of the book's interest rather than distracting from it.

In the context of early French futuristic fiction, *L'An 5865* belongs to a curious and fascinating set of texts that might be called the "Ruins of Paris" sequence. The sequence was initiated by a brief text by Joseph Méry, "Les Ruines de Paris"[3] which first appeared in book form in 1856 but had almost certainly appeared in a periodical earlier than that date (but no earlier than 1848). Méry's story is essentially an in-

---

[3] translated as "The Ruins of Paris" and included in the collection *The Tower of Destiny*, Black Coat Press, ISBN 978-1-61227-101-9.

flated joke, which mocks the habit of equipping Parisian monuments with Latin inscriptions liable to confuse future archeologists. In the story, amateur archaeologists living in a Phalanstery in North Africa in the year 3844 play a flying visit to the chilly northern climes that civilization has long since deserted in order to inspect what survives of ancient Paris; they blithely draw absurd conclusions by misinterpreting the inscriptions on various familiar Parisian monuments, sometimes mangled by their slapdash reconstructions. Méry's idea was then considerably elaborated in Alfred Bonnardot's novelette "Archeopolis" (1857),[4] which combined a similarly farcical account of archeological misinterpretations with a more earnest account of the historical processes that had caused the ruination of decadent Western European culture and the subsequent shift of the forefront of civilization and progress to the heart of Africa.

Mettais—who was almost certainly personally acquainted with Bonnardot, as was Méry—took up the argumentative thread where Bonnardot's visionary fantasy left off, and elaborated it vastly. Further developments of the theme, in Alfred Franklin's *Les Ruines de Paris* (1875),[5] Léo Clarétie, in the final sequence of *Paris depuis ses origines jusqu'en l'an 3000* [Paris from its Origins to the Year 2000] (1886) and Edmond Haraucourt in "Cinq mille ans, ou la traversée de Paris" (1904)[6] reduced the scale again and reverted to a documentary style of narration that was much easier to handle, leaving Mettais' Herculean endeavor isolated in its magnitude and distinction. Although most of the other inclusions in the series had serious points to make as well as, or by means of, their

---

[4] translated in the anthology *Nemoville,* Black Coat Press, ISBN 978-1-61227-070-8.

[5] to be translated as "The Ruins of Paris" in the anthology *Investigations of the Future*, Black Coat Press, ISBN 978-1-61227-106-4.

[6] translated as "A Trip to Paris" in the collection *Illusions of Immortality*, Black Coat Press, ISBN 978-1-61227-075-3.

jokes, they were all essentially light-hearted; Mettais was the only contributor to the series to attempt to substitute melodrama for humor, thus contriving a very different compound with his earnest arguments.

To some extent, those earnest arguments are peripheral; like most of the French futuristic novelists of the day, Mettais had a strong interest in social reform, and his recipes for desirable reform are interpolated with the story-line, sometimes forming lumpen obstacles to the progress of the plot and the pace of the narrative—although the complexity of the work does have the effect of producing a ragged spectrum of utopian possibilities rather than a single focused image. One serious issue is, however central, and that is the one he took over from Bonnardot: the notion, common at the time, that 19th century French society, along with the rest of Western culture was fast approaching an irredeemable decadence, and was then bound to collapse, as so many other civilizations (including monumental Egypt, glorious Greece and Imperial Rome) had collapsed before, having passed inexorably from triumphant grandeur to ignominious decay and ultimate oblivion.

Mettais' primary purpose, throughout his exercise in viewpoint gymnastics, is to undermine arrogance: not only the arrogance of historians, who overestimate the reliability of their own narratives, but the wider arrogance of a culture that believes itself not only to be progressive but immortal in its progress. *L'An 5865* is, in essence, a cultural *memento mori*. Mettais is well aware, of course, that the job of whispering "Remember thou must die" in an Emperor's ear traditionally devolves to a Fool, but he is not afraid to don motley for the purpose. If his preface is a trifle defensive in that respect, beginning with the claim that what he is doing is neither a joke nor an assault, it is also unrepentant, pleading necessity as well as correctness. Like many of the writers of the period, Mettais dates the effective collapse of Western civilization to the temporal environs of the year 2000, but the fact that we have contrived to reach 2011 while still teetering on the brink is, of course, no cause for self-congratulation, and that part of

9

his argument still remains relevant, in spite of all the recent technological advances that make his account of and attitude to mechanical progress seem distinctly quaint.

One of the curious side-effects of Mettais' innovative literary method is that in attempting to interpolate his didactic material into a melodrama rather than a travelogue—following the example set and fervently advocated by Félix Bodin—he provided an anticipatory echo of a future subgenre of popular fiction: the "lost race" story. In conventional ventures of that sort, of course, it is present-day explorers who find relics of ancient civilization rather than futuristic explorers who find echoes of ours, but it is noticeable that the displacement in time does not affect the plot-structure that seems somehow to arise naturally from the theme. Thus, significant elements of the story-line of *L'An 5865* are strangely echoed, undoubtedly by coincidence, in such classics of the lost race subgenre as H. Rider Haggard's *She* (1887) and A. Merritt's *Dwellers in the Mirage* (1932), which are themselves echoed plangently in Romantically-inclined works of modern science fiction, including *The Legion of Time* (1937) by Jack Williamson and *The Dark World* (1945) by C. L. Moore and Henry Kuttner. Given that it was the advent of labeled science fiction that paved the way for the standardization of the kind of immersive futuristic fantasy pioneered by *L'An 5865*, the repeated echo is intriguing.

Another factor that needs to be taken into account in looking back at the text from a 21st century viewpoint is that the issues inevitably raised by futuristic fiction in 1865 were highly sensitive in both a political and a religious context. The use of a first-person narrator allows Mettais to mask his own political affiliations, giving him what is nowadays called "potential deniability," but his protagonist is a Republican who is sympathetic to radical ideas—a stance that had had got many writers into serious trouble in the aftermath of Louis Napoléon's *coup d'état* of 1951, resulting in the exile of such prominent figures as Victor Hugo and Alexandre Dumas. The Second Empire seemed much more secure by 1865 (an arrogant illusion, as it transpired) so Mettais was no longer at risk of bringing the wrath of the censors down on his head merely by treating Republican ideas sympathetically, but his awareness of the political sensitivity of what he is doing is very obvious in his text, especially in the section dealing with the penitentiary of "Tahiti."

The religious sensitivity of Mettais' ideas is equally obvious in his text, albeit mostly in terms of the determined omission of any direct reference either to Christianity or (given the importance of Morocco and the Sudan within the story) Islam. He does hint, very diplomatically, at a potential misinterpretation of Christian iconography that was to be much more fully developed (in much less hostile circumstances) by Edmond Haraucourt, but does not press the point. The danger of offending entrenched religious beliefs—much sharpened in the context of the archaeological and paleontological discoveries of 1865 by the determination of many believers to cling rigidly to Archbishop Ushher's chronology dating the creation of the world to 4004 B.C.—probably seemed more urgent to Mettais than the danger of offending Napoléon III's censors on political grounds, in that he was a physician in private practice, whose livelihood would be at stake if he became publicly embroiled in religious controversy.

In this context, one of the most remarkable arbitrary interpolations in the text is the protagonist's brief visit to the island of the "Androgenes" and his subsequent debate about the origins of humankind with a mysterious individual who might or might not be an Androgene. Just as the protagonist cannot believe that his interlocutor means his argument seriously, the reader has to interpret the whole episode as a fable akin to Aristophanes' apologue regarding the androgyne in Plato's *Symposium* (which Mettais must surely have had in mind) but as a veiled comment on the debate about the evolution of humankind, as it stood in 1865, it is as striking as it is peculiar. It was, however, the argument by omission that was most likely to cause offence to Mettais' contemporary readers: the assumption that the entire theological and ritual heritage of

Judaism, Christianity and Islam might be something temporary and arbitrary, cable of being lost and forgotten without any consequent damage to moral philosophy, is something that was bound to give pause to believers, however covertly and diplomatically it was presented.

L'An 5865 therefore qualifies as a daring text in more ways than one, in terms of both its literary method and its innate convictions. For those reasons alone it would be worthy of the attention of modern readers, but it is also notable that, in spite of its self-imposed obstacles to easy reading, the narrative does built up a certain pitch of dramatic suspense as well as a teasing pattern of mystery, which is, in the end, rather engaging. Even those readers who will think the melodrama's ultimate denouement sneakily evasive will surely be unable to deny that it has a certain eccentric and provocative charm.

Hippolyte Mettais was, as his by-line indicates, a physician who practiced in Paris from 1834, when he left his native town of Blois, until the 1870s. His birth date is given in the first edition of Pierre Larousse's *Grand Dictionnaire* as 1812, and that datum is reproduced in the catalogue of the Bibliothèque Nationale, but he was not considered important enough to warrant inclusion in subsequent editions of Larousse and the date of his death is unrecorded in any of the standard sources. None of the easily-available sources indicate whether or not he was related to the roughly-contemporary illustrator and portrait-painter Charles Joseph Mettais, but it might be relevant that the latter also had literary connections, once having collaborated, in 1845, with Paul Féval on a dramatic production.

Although he had previously published a medical treatise, Hippolyte Mettais' first manifest literary endeavor was in the early 1840s, when he published two novels of his own, *Rupert* (1841) and *Le Portefaix, roman de moeurs* [The Street-Porter; a novel of (contemporary) mores] (1842) and one in collaboration with the prolific but now-forgotten writer of popular fiction Georges Touchard-Lafosse (1780-1847), *Un Lion aux bains de Vichy* [A Lion (i.e. a social "lion") at the Vichy Spa] (1842). Touchard-Lafosse also contributed an introduction to *Le Portefaix*, and the fact that he published nothing more after his collaboration with Mettais suggests that he had recruited the latter to help him complete a project imperiled by ill-health. Mettais might well have been his doctor. Although the subtitle of *Le Portefaix* suggests that it was affiliated to the reaction against the supposed excesses of Romanticism stigmatized by Charles Asselineau as "the novel of common sense," it may be worth noting that the term *roman de moeurs* had previously been used, and perhaps coined, by another of Touchard-Lafosse's occasional collaborators, Étienne Lamothe-Langon, a writer who delighted in deception and fakery, and rarely removed his tongue from his cheek.

That first foray into literary publication was presumably unsuccessful, because there was a long gap before Mettais resumed that aspect of his career, publishing another naturalistic novel, *Le Père Thuillier* [Old Thuillier], in 1857. His next publication was, however, a reformist pamphlet, *Des Associations et des corporations en France* [Associations and Corporations] (1859), whose propagandist argument in favor of the elaborate development of trade-union-based insurance and pension schemes is summarized in one of the more arbitrary chapters of *L'An 5865*. He then published *Souvenirs d'un medécin de Paris* [Memoirs of a Parisian Doctor] (1863), which is a novel rather than an autobiography, but claims in its introduction to be factually based. The literary ambitions of the young doctor who is its protagonist, and the similar ambitions of his friends in Paris in the late 1830s and 1840s, are peripheral to the plot, but the story does feature walk-on parts by Alexandre Dumas, Alfred de Vigny and Émile de Girardin, and places the young protagonist very firmly in the Romantic camp.

It was, perhaps understandably, after his excursion into autobiographical fiction, recalling his youthful hopes and ambitions, that Mettais cut loose and soared away into uncharted literary skies in *L'An 5865*. He followed that novel up

13

with an inverted companion piece, *Paris avant le Déluge* [Paris Before the Deluge] (1866), whose title is a trifle misleading, as its primary concern is the hypothetical lost continent of Atlantis. It was one of the earliest modern fantasies of that subgenre, predating the repopularization of the Atlantis myth by Ignatius Donnelly's magisterial scholarly fantasy *Atlantis, the Antediluvian World* (1882) and Madame Blavatsky's mystical extravaganza *The Secret Doctrine* (1888). *Paris avant le Déluge* has links of its own with subsequent lost race fantasies, which provide a further complement to its predecessor, and I hope to translate it at some time in the future.

Following the publication of *Paris avant le Déluge*, Mettais wrote a further fantasy, *Simon le magicien* [Simon Magus] (1867), but reverted thereafter to more conventional literary fare, after a further gap in his production, with *Docteur Marat* [Dr. Marat] (1874) and *Les Amours d'un tribun* [The Love-Life of a Tribune (i.e. a popular spokesman)] (1876). He published two further novels, one of which—*Le Secret des catacombs* [The Secret of the Catacombs] (1877)—has an intriguing title, and a one-act play, but information regarding their contents is not easily available. Following his unremarked death, his works appear to have been completely forgotten, even by specialists in the history of imaginative and speculative fiction—although *L'An 5865* is mentioned in passing in Charles Richet's essay on futuristic fiction "Dans 100 Years" (1891-2)—until the Bibliothèque Nationale's *gallica* website and Google Books made the text of *L'An 5865* available for reading on-line or downloading, thus paving the way for a reignition of interest in what is undoubtedly an fascinating text, long ripe for rediscovery and celebration of its pioneering spirit.

This translation is taken from the version reproduced on *gallica*.

Brian Stableford

THE YEAR 5865

PREFACE

I would be very sorry if this book were to be taken for a humorist's jest; I would be even sorrier, however, if I were believed to be a social critic. I am serious, and I am not a mud-slinger. If my opinions regarding history do not have the orthodoxy that certain people would like them to have, I beg pardon from those people, but I humbly retain my opinions, convinced that they are the orthodoxy of a good number.

I would not like it any more if I were to be accused of offending anyone's religion, by virtue of having cast doubt on the antiquity of our globe, and I shall never regard myself as impious for believing that the world is older than it is said to be—that before the creation from which our era dates, there might have been, and probably was, an existent world: a world that must, like all worlds, have passed through its various periods of birth and barbarism, growth and civilization. And if this world has been preceded by other worlds, even indefinitely, why should I not say more? Why should I not say that it is illogical to deny it, simply because we have no memories of them, no facts and no traces, extending back to that epoch of chaos in which God, according to *Genesis*, created our world?

Oh, I know full well that there are arguments extending as far as the eye can see on the part of scientists; I know full well that there are theories which calculate the epoch of the birth of our Earth and the term of its duration—but those arguments are so subtle and contradictory, and those theories are so conclusively annihilated by one another, that one really only has the right to believe whichever one of them one pleases, and I do not believe any of them.

For me, the world is very old—much older than anyone can say, even though I admit a commencement. Who would dare to seek out that commencement, however, in the darkness of its impenetrable antiquity? Let us therefore be content to conclude...yes, can we even conclude the perenniality of the world? In view of its imperfection, the mobility of its beings, the intestinal fermentation that perverts or destroys incessantly, have we not the right to conclude at least that unexpected changes are produced in all its parts, that the globe of today is not the globe of old, and that the globe in several thousands of years will no longer be that of today?

Will the air, the seas, the rivers, the continents, the cities all be changed, in their essence? No, for water will still be water—but everything will have changed its location, everything will be changed in its relationships, in its appearances, in its very qualities.

And it will be thus with humankind.

Do I mean than human beings will have changed their nature? Certainly not—even less in their passions. Why? Because that has never changed—but civilization, mores and laws will change.

So, may I, without being a great prophet, foresee today what human beings will be in 4000 years, giving their passions the colors of the future?

That prospect might be rather gloomy, in my opinion—although my opinion might be wrong, I admit, for every question has at least two faces, one cheerful and the other sad.

The France of today, which still has a free and light-hearted spirit, and which has its civilization, with which it is content and of which it is proud, never fails to laugh at the civilization of our ancestors. It is probable that if it could read the future, it would laugh even more at the civilization of its descendants. It holds its strength and its science in such high esteem that it is far from thinking that they will ever be equaled, and especially that one or other of them might be in the hour of its decadence.

It is to be wished by every good patriot that France is not mistaken; that it will stay as it is; that it will progress even further, and forever. Moreover, I would take infinite pleasure in seeing it painted in the most beautiful and vivacious colors, not with its vestments of the past, but with those of the future—the future that I wish for it with all my heart. But who can say that it will not be otherwise; that in 4000 years, France will not have the decrepit face of old age and animality? Who can say whether, instead of the luxury that renders it so beautiful, the science that raises it so high, the valor that renders it so redoubtable today, there might not be nothing then but pettiness, ignorance and misery? Who can say that its palaces, so luxurious, might not be replaced by huts, that its squares, so splendid, will not be forest crossroads, that its streets, so magnificent, will not be thorny paths, its rivers miry marshes? Who can tell us whether its population, so powerful, proud and numerous, might not be a petty tribe of slaves, fallen under the lash of barbarians?

May God will that it shall never be so!

But when I see the enemy sowing tares in the field of our civilization, have I not the right to dread that our civilization might one day be stifled? When? I have no idea…in 50, 100, 200 years, perhaps. What do I know?

When I see so many vices weighing everywhere among us, with egotism at their head, I am afraid for our society, because I know that a building never crumbles as surely as when its foundations are undermined by insects.

When I see the God of the wise dethroned from his altars by the God of the foolish; when I see virtue set beneath knowhow, poverty beneath money, for what can I hope?

Then again, what do all these discords between great and small, all these incredible disputes of rich and poor, and all these contradictory pleadings with regard to the social contract signify?

What do all these clashes of arms signify that can be heard from one end of the world to the other; all these prideful pretensions of strong people against weak; all these massacres, futile unless there is an objective to which a large number are obedient; all these pillages by means of arms?

There are no longer any laws than those of the strongest, no longer any logic to regulate common interests than the logic of cannon. There is no longer anything but an all-out war of all against all, some to seize and others to defend.

Are these not the symptoms of the dissolution of society?

Could any of the peoples that have fallen in the past have done so in another fashion?

Am I not then authorized, without wishing to paraphrase the words of a great man, to believe that France in 4000 years might be Cosaque?[7]

"Cosaque! Why?"

History is done; I shall not remake it here; but why not Cosaque? If I wanted to dabble in political philosophy I could prove that it is possible; if I wanted to dabble in politics, I could prove that it will happen. In order to convince ourselves, we have only to look hard at what is going on around us.

"Utopias!"

---

[7] The literal English equivalent of the French term *Cosaque* is Cossack, a similar remolding of the term Kazakh, but the French term is more frequently used familiarly to refer to any coarse and brutal individual; its usage here is metaphorical as well as literal. The notion of "Cosaques" in Paris has a particular resonance throughout 19th century French literature because Tsar Alexander's cavalry were among the first troops to enter Paris in March 1814 after Napoléon I's defeat, and the sight of them riding along the Champs Élysées administered a sharp shock to the Parisian psyche—as well as giving the mistaken impression, seemingly held by Mettais, that "Cosaques" were actually Russian, rather than conscripts from an ethically and culturally distinct region of the Russian Empire. I have retained Mettais' term partly for that reason and partly to avoid having to translate *Nouvelle-Cosaquie* as New Cossackia or New Kazakhstan, neither of which seems appropriate.

If they are utopias, so much the better. But is it not with that name that speakers in Nineveh, Babylon or Carthage would have been castigated if, in the times of the greatest splendor of their countries, they had predicted the physiognomy that Nineveh, Babylon and Carthage present in the year 1865 of our era?

There too, huts have replaced palaces, and barbarism civilization.

No, these are not utopias; this is what will happen. Peoples only ever change their laws and habits; their nature is always the same; their lives always move in the midst of a sea of passions, and the end of every one is similar.

The life of a people, like its civilization, is a mountain that each one must climb without ever stopping. Having arrived at the summit, there is no longer anything to do but descend.

Is France at the summit of the mountain? In the year 5865, will it not have descended therefrom a long time ago?

One may pose that question, but never in jest. It is always seriously that one watches one's fatherland set foot on the downward slope.

But if, in the year 5865, France has descended the mountain, to find itself in the ruins and forests of the New Cosaquia, if Paris has then exchanged its palaces for the huts of Figuig,[8] the mountain of civilization will not have disappeared in consequence; it will be occupied by other peoples.

But what peoples?

That is the question I ask myself. To resolve it with probability, I have looked back, and, according to what I have seen, I believe I can say that civilization and life will be dis-

---

[8] The publicity given to French colonial achievement and ambitions in the Second Empire press would probably have ensured that Mettais' contemporary readers would have known that there is a place called Figuig in Morocco, and perhaps also that it was noted for the neolithic rock-paintings found in its vicinity.

placed in the world; that where we see activity and social sciences today, we shall see barbarity, and that where we see barbarity, the sages of the time will see civilization, and perhaps a civilization more advanced than our own, whatever we might think of it.

Is that improbable?

I have not lost sight for an instant of this important philosophical point, which my savant Caucasian traveler, Daghestan, has been able to bring out in his various peregrinations, either in the most civilized countries of his time, such a Borneo, the Sudan, the Congo, Caucasia and Zeeland, or in the most deserted and primitive, such as France, which has even lost its name, in order to take that of New Cosaquia.

If, furthermore, the mores of the peoples of that time resemble ours somewhat; if we see them getting drunk in the cups in which we steep out lips, let no one reproach me! What is astonishing about human beings, who only have a narrow circle of passions to indulge, being devoured in the year 5865 by the same passions that devour them in 1865?

In any case, I do not accept responsibility for the opinions of my characters, and I can no more guarantee the historical veracity of the peoples they pass in review than the historians of our day can guarantee the veracity of their accounts. I am only a historian, like all the rest, and a very humble one— but I am an impartial historian who is trying to do his best to paint an accurate picture of the mores of peoples he has seen in the mirages of the future.

EDITOR'S NOTE

Caucasipol, 15 Ventose 5002[9]

The immense popularity obtained in the past year in the *Caucasian Gazette* by the publication of *The Year 5865* by Citizen Daghestan demands that its disparate sections be combined this year in a single volume.

We dare to hope that the patrons of the publishing house will give the publication the same welcome as the subscribers of the periodical. This edition, reviewed very carefully by a friend of the author, perhaps ought to been given a different form in losing the effect of its periodicity, but we thought it best to reproduce it as it originally appeared, to conserve its sap and primitive savor in leaving it all the frankness of a journal, and, what is more, not even removing a few journalistic appreciations, which only serve to complete his friend's thoughts.

It is, in brief, the *Caucasian Gazette* that we have adjusted to the size and appearance of a volume, with all the respect owed to conscientious works.

Editor Guriel

---

[9] Ventose was the sixth month of the Republican calendar briefly employed in France after the 1789 Revolution, which named months after aspects of climatic change. Its use in this "French translation" of a story presumably told in "Caucasian" thus carries an implication regarding the kinds of names that the Caucasians attach to the months in their calendar, which is evidently different from ours—a presumption further emphasized by the enigmatic figure attributed to the year of notional publication. Mettais has no way of explaining this himself, and thus has to leave such matters to the reader's inferential skills.

I. THE CAUCASIAN HUNTER

Caucasian Gazette
Caucasipol, 5 Prairial 5001

There was nearly a terrible accident yesterday on the shores of the Black Sea. One of our friends, a hunter who is fortunately as maladroit as he is intrepid, had launched himself into the rocks of the Caucasus on the track of a hind with such ardor that he had not noticed dusk falling, and had gone astray in the mountains a long way from any habitation. That was not a matter of considerable anxiety for such a hunter. Our friend's decision was soon made; he took shelter beneath an overhanging rock, which far-sighted nature appeared to have suspended there expressly for him, and went to sleep with one eye open.

At dawn he was up and about, perched on the highest point in the vicinity on the scent of the previous day's prey—but the previous day's prey had not waited for him, and no other appeared.

Our friend then descended the mountain slope far enough that he soon had nothing below him but the waves of the sea and the little tongue of land that separates them from the foothills of the Caucasus, which is so small that the smallest village could not be accommodated there—although it was once so large, so it is said, that there were cities there, the cities of the warrior tribes of the old Abasges.

It was early morning, as we have said, and a thick mist covered the mountains and their surroundings—which did not prevent the ardent eye of our hunter glimpsing a black mass some distance away, standing almost immobile on the sea shore. Either his eye was fatigued by the night's poor sleep, however, or the daylight was still too weak, for he could not distinguish the nature of the prey. It was nevertheless volumi-

23

nous—perhaps a group of hinds, asleep or bathing in the cool waves. Perhaps, however, it was a more redoubtable prey.

Being in doubt, our hunter carefully loaded his rifle, stealthily drew nearer, as close as possible, and then aimed and fired.

When the smoke had dissipated, he saw that the group was still perfectly immobile. Our friend is a hunter devoid of pride; he did not blush on seeing the immobility of his prey. So, reloading his rifle with all the precaution of a man intent on success, he took a few further steps forward, since the prey did not seem timid, and prepared to fire again.

At that moment, the sun's radiance dissipated the morning sun and clarified his vision—but he did not fire. The rifle fell from his hands. His heart was gripped by an indescribable sentiment, and he nearly fell off the rock on which he was perched.

His prey was none other than a woman sitting on a boulder, holding on her knees the discolored head of a young man lying at her feet. She appeared to be a young woman; whether she was beautiful our friend was unable to judge from where he stood. It seemed to him that her hair was ash-blonde, plaited and forming two graceful curves around her cheeks. On her head she wore a conical hat ornamented with white feathers, in the fashion of the high society of the savage lands of the west. Her costume was also clearly indicative of a foreign woman. She was not wearing the ample and chaste peplum that serves the modesty of our Caucasian women so well; her upper torso was enclosed in a corsage perfectly fitted over the breast, all of whose contours it outlined, and then extending to the knees, or very nearly, in two skirts with large loose pleats. She also wore loose-fitting trousers, tightened at the bottom of the leg by ribbons whose knot was formed externally as an elegantly-expressed rose.

In one of her hands she held the limp hand of the man whose head was sustained by her knees; her other hand was placed on the breast of the dead or dying man, doubtless in order to study his chances of living. Her eyes were anxious;

her face, bleak with anguish, was only awakened at intervals by the stimulus of some hopeful thought. A moment later, however, it was illuminated and stirred by relaxation; a palpitation had doubtless made itself felt in the dying man's breast. Then, laying him gently down on the ground, she ran to draw water from the sea, and returned to inundate the face of the man she was doubtless yearning to bring back to life.

Her hope was not betrayed. His breathing became more abundant; the moribund man opened his eyes, and then raised his head. He looked around, bewildered...

He was alone.

His companion, so anxious and attentive, had just fled, as nimbly as a desert gazelle, gliding over the water with the rapidity of a seagull, with the aid of wings of a sort that had suddenly spread out around her arms. By that means she reached a boat that seemed to be waiting in the distance, and on which she stood up to her full height, contemplating with an indefinable sentiment the place she had just quit and, doubtless, her protégé—who, completely conscious, had got to his feet and was standing straight, motionless on his boulder, trying to make out with his as-yet-feeble gaze the vision of that boat, in which he seemed intensely interested.

Our hunter, profoundly moved by this scene, which he only understood in part, had gradually and instinctively drawn nearer, but discretion and respect for the misfortune kept him at a distance. When he saw the poor injured man alone, he came to offer him sympathetic assistance.

"Thank you, sir," the latter said to him. "There is only one person I need at the moment."

The hunter bowed without replying, and turned to go.

"I beg your pardon, sir," the shipwreck-victim continued, calling him back. "My heart and mind are numbed; excuse an unfortunate who could not yet comprehend the generosity and graciousness of your offer. I was wrong. I shall not refuse your services; I have need of them. Merely grant me the favor of allowing me to remain alone for a few moments more. I will wait for you here."

Our friend slung his rifle over his shoulder, went hunting for an hour, and came back.

The castaway was sitting on his rock, holding a writing-pad on his knees, in which he was scribbling. When the hunter arrived he raised his head and smiled; then, sealing the letter that he had just finished, he gave it to him.

"Are you going to Caucasipol?" he asked.

"I live there."

"Could you deliver this letter to the office of the *Caucasian Gazette*?"

"I have a friend there," the hunter replied. "I'll give it to him."

"Thank you, sir," the castaway said, effusively, seemingly not desirous of a longer conversation.

His interlocutor was enthusiastic to continue but he kept silent, took the letter, put it in his game-bag, and left. Scarcely had he taken a few steps, however, than he came back again.

"Would it be indiscreet, sir," he said, "to ask your name?"

"What! Have I not told you?" exclaimed the confused castaway. "My name is Daghestan."

It was Daghestan, our friend, our intimate friend: our illustrious colleague Daghestan, the glory of Caucasia!

"Daghestan!" cried our friend the hunter, in amazement—but he said no more; Daghestan seemed absorbed by a profoundly intimate sentiment, his eyes still motionless and staring out to sea.

The friend of the Caucasian hunter was us. Daghestan's letter was therefore given to us yesterday.

Too profoundly moved to preface it with any commentary, we are publishing it immediately, enclosing in our heart all the veneration that one always experiences for a great misfortune.

The Shore of the Black Sea, 4 Prairial 5001

Have you forgiven me, my dear fellow? On seeing my fatherland again, shall I still find my best friend? If I have sinned, oh, forgive me, in view of the sufferings I have endured! How many times since my departure I have regretted having deceived your friendship, of not having told you about the voyage I wanted to undertake, of not having made my final farewells, since I would not be able to come back!

But what can you expect? I was so full of desire and hope; how could I sadden my friends by showing them the will-o'-the-wisps of my illusions, in taking up before them the staff of the traveler and the writing-pad of the delirious chronicler, yearning to launch forth beyond the sea, to go explore the most distant lands, the least known and perhaps the most inhospitable of all, alone with the dreams of a young man and a passionate lover of science?

Finally, here I am, returned! But how? In truth, I have no idea. Who has thrown me here at the threshold of my fatherland, on the shore of the Black Sea? Was it a loving hand or the fury of an enemy? Was it the waves or human beings?

It seems to me that yesterday…my God, but where was I yesterday?

My friend, I no longer know whether I have been dreaming, or whether I am dreaming still. Yesterday, however…no, I don't know any more; I no longer remember anything...

All that I know is that I've just woken up from a profound and dolorous sleep, that I'm alone and helpless, that my traveler's staff and my writing-pad were here beside me, stained with blood. A sad scene to strike my first gaze! Well, what can I tell you, my friend? My first thought, my first sigh—alas!—were not for them, and, forgive me, my dear friend, were not for you either, nor for the fatherland.

Sitting on a Caucasian rock, whose foot I see immersed in the water, I turn my back to the fatherland and my friends, while my eyes full of tears search in the distance, in the far distance, beyond our sea, for heartbreaking memories, which I can as yet only glimpse as in an obscure mirage, which never-theless cause my heart to palpitate violently, like a dream...

Oh, no, no, my friend, it is not a dream that I have had! The hand that is writing to you, and is having so much diffi-culty holding the pencil between its bloody fingers, the feet that refuse to carry me, agonized by wounds that are still gap-ing, and my body, all covered with wounds, which can scarce-ly stir upon the rock, all tell me that no, I am not dreaming, I have not been dreaming.

I have come from a savage land; I have crossed vast de-serts inhabited by ferocious beasts that have not done me any harm, and by humans that rushed upon me as if to devour me...and yet, I confess, I weep sensuously at the memory of those lands. My mind, my heart, my soul—everything is there. If you only knew what emotions I have experienced there, what happiness...

In sum, I wanted to die there, far from the fatherland. Poor fool! The fatherland, that beautiful jewel of civilization, that abode of happiness and glory, no longer speaks to my heart. I would prefer a dead glory, an extinct happiness, bar-barity—perhaps the most ignoble barbarity of the countries of the west.

Oh, there too, my friend, there was no longer for me any disorder or chaos...and yet I was in the bosom of New Cosaquia, the France of antiquity, that beautiful France, it is said, where despair, desolation and death now reign. I aspired through all my senses the perfumed memories of the ruins of Paris, the great capital of the earliest ages of the world; I dreamed of happiness on the debris of the palaces of such proud kings, such renowned works of art, which is covered now by the huts of a few savages, the descendants of the un-civilized Cosaques who once inhabited our beautiful land, and whom the hand of God drove so far away, doubtless to hide from the world of today the degradation and ignominy of barbarism, and punish a people who, according to the Sacred Books, deserved to be punished...

And today, here I am, injured, thrown upon our shore, my heart broken by dolor.

Oh, no, that was no dream; the memories are coming back to me...

And then again, out there, that vessel out there, bobbing on the waves...I would rather not believe my eyes, and yet I can see it, I can see it clearly, so long as I remain motionless, lying on the rock where I was doubtless deposited; and the vessel also remains motionless in the midst of the waters. I have seen it stir, as soon as I was able to raise myself up a little, and instantly, its life became more active; it is balancing itself on the waves as if to take flight; human beings have reappeared on its broad back; its machinery is rotating in the air and in the water, alternately, like the wings of a bird. It is about to launch itself into the distance; there is no doubt about it.

One man—just one—is standing, motionless, his arms folded over his chest and his eyes turned in my direction...

Before ending the letter I am writing, my friend, I shall stand up on tiptoe one more time. in order to see as far as possible, finally to determine who that man is...that man who is staring at me so fixedly and waving at me so graciously from his vessel...

Ah! The vessel is leaving...like a flash of lightning...

Alas, my friend, my friend...that vessel...is taking away my last hope, my last affection, my last illusion...

Oh, what frightful separation! That man...but it is not a man, my friend! Have you not guessed...?

Forgive me, my dear friend, all my divagations. I believe I'm still dreaming: let me wake up. Later—yes, later—I shall take my courage in both hands, I shall exert all my strength to remain impassive and bring out the truth of the traveler's tale. My eyes will tell you then what they have seen, and my soul what it has felt, its pleasures and its anguish.

Until then, Adieu!

II. DAGHESTAN

Caucasian Gazette
Caucasipol, 6 Prairial 5001

We shall not recapitulate here the entitlements of Daghestan to the admiration of our fatherland and the entire world. That eulogy, which it would be impossible for us to make with equanimity, would appear suspect to those who know what good friends we were. Everyone is familiar, in any case, with his important and very curious publications on ancient history. The entire Caucasian press was enriched thereby twenty years ago. Our journal, more than any other, tried its utmost to extend their distribution as far as possible, even beyond our Caucasian tribes.

If I do not want to say anything about him at present, however, I cannot resist the temptation to recall his last observation on history, which summarizes so well, in my opinion, the spirit and range of his important works, and which raised such a clamor.

"Ancient history," Daghestan wrote, "is a fine puzzle handed down from olden times, to exercise the sagacity of scientists and the verve of novelists..."

"So you deny the existence of ancient times and peoples?" he was answered from all sides. People doubtless forgot, in saying that, the neat little fable that we find in the works of the illustrious writer.

Reni, according to this fable, had been cast away by a shipwreck, with his father and mother, his brothers and sisters, on an island lost in the immensity of the ocean. The father kept silent about the shipwreck, in order not to make his children regretful, and arranged a life for them there as best he could. Reni therefore grew up without knowing anything except the soil of his island, the sky and the sea—nothing beyond. Having hunted and fished for a long time, he grew bored. He then wrote down, doubtless for posterity, his impressions of boredom, and then his history, and that of the island. The world, of course, began with his father, whom God had surely created in order to perpetuate a species hitherto unknown...

One day, however, he discovered a means of venturing over the water, and soon perceived other islands, inhabited like his own, and even more than his own. This gave him to reflect; he reread his impressions and his history...and then began to laugh wholeheartedly at the naivety of his tales.

"As we should also laugh," Daghestan added, "if we were able to cross the sea that conceals the past from us and hides islands perhaps more populous than our own—we who fix the precise moment when the world was born with so much precision!"

It was, therefore, far from Daghestan's mind to want to deny antiquity. He meant that its books, if it had any, and its monuments, if it built any, had been so utterly ruined or so well hidden from us, that even our imagination is at a loss to say anything about it. Historians who want to be known as serious historians are content to call those times barbaric, and those people, to whom they only accord a near-vegetative life, barbarians. On the other hand, other, bolder historians place in those times and those people their monstrous illusions, their phantasmagoric dreams and their cherished ideals.

It was a time of gods, demigods and genies. It was China before Sione-Fine, Egypt before Mehmet Ali; it was New Cosaquia before Nhoel I. Happy times! Our poetry lives on it, our most graceful literature stems from it. It was the time of legends, of heroic songs, when men were giants, ogres and slayers of armies. It was the time of our Sheikh Mansour the Invincible, who destroyed a whole army with a single sweep of his scimitar.[10]

---

[10] Mehmet Ali was, of course, the actual founder of Egypt as we know it. It is unclear whether the reference to "Sheikh

31

That is ancient history.

Perhaps, someone will say to me: "But after all, even if Daghestan is right to incriminate the veracity of ancient history, he ought at least to respect modern history, which can be seen, felt and touched, which crushes us with its reality. And yet he has also said that he only approaches that history tremulously. Why?"

Why! Because, unfortunately, a man who wants to write history cannot see everything; because he is obliged to rely on documents drawn from all over, which are entirely foreign to him. If, therefore, these documents are taken from one of those peoples whose society is divided into twenty separate parts, twenty opposed camps, who watch one another with weapons in hand, who tear one another apart with deceitful reportage, which slander one another all the time—and there are many such peoples, peoples in which truth is silent, in which a biased and all-powerful press reigns, whose voice speaks as it wishes, so loudly that it alone can be heard—how can he write its history?

Thus, I tremble with anxiety like Daghestan every time I try to form an accurate idea of that which I have not seen. Were those heroes of which history speaks to me really heroes? Was that brigand really a brigand?

I only know what my historian tells me; I see through his eyes, I think via his mind. But has he seen clearly? He is human; he has passions. Might he not have seen too distantly, or at too close range? Did he not have an interest through which he gazed, if only the interest of self-esteem?

Poor history!

Given this, who can tell me that ancient history has been engraved with a different chisel than our own, that the ancients did not also look at facts through the naivety of their beliefs, under the mirage of prejudices suckled by the mores of a time

---

Mansour" refers to the man our history recognizes as the ancient founder of Bagdad.

when civilization was far from being advanced? And after all, when they are silent, who has spoken for them?

Everyone knows that horrible catastrophes have disrupted our globe several times; science says so.[11] Tradition speaks to us of universal deluges—is that impossible?—of frightful conflagrations, of irruptions of barbarians that have decimated, or even annihilated, civilized peoples. Who held the chisel then to transmit these important facts to us? And where are the original writings, the monuments, the documents of every sort? Annihilated—swallowed up by the corrupting waters or burned by the flames.

Let us, then, bow down. We know nothing...nothing but what amiable storytellers have wanted to invent for us, perhaps aided by a few historical crumbs that they have plucked from the air, by a few distant and deceptive echoes that have reached them in their solitude.

And we, because we are a trifle incredulous, because we attribute to olden times legends and ingenious poetry edited by a legion of unknown rhapsodists...

---

[11] In 1865 scientists had not yet developed any reliable yardstick for dating the phenomena that were being revealed by geology, palaeontology and archaeology, and there was still an ongoing debate between "uniformitarians" and "catastrophists" regarding the time-scale according to which the geological record of past upheavals had to be measured. The most prestigious Frenchman in the former camp, the Comte du Buffon (1707-1788) had favored a long timescale in which the principal forces remolding the world's surface worked very slowly, but his ideas had been partly overtaken in public consciousness by those of the catastrophist Georges Cuvier (1769-1832), whose account of "epochs of nature" suddenly and violently reshaped by floods and volcanic eruptions was inherently more melodramatic, and far more appealing to anyone with any sympathy for Biblical chronology, which placed an all-consuming flood only a few thousand years ago and also included the fiery destruction of the Cities of the Plain.

Sacrilege!

Oh, what I mean to say, I shall not retract, in spite of all my respect for your Hang-Fo, the most ancient Chinese writers, for your Bulbul, the illustrious Persian, whose imagination is so cheerful and so fecund that it surpasses ours, for your Parawendo, the glorious poet whose genius elevated him, it is said, to the presidency of the glorious Republic of Siam, for your Nasreddin, the pearl of Egypt, for your Chari, of the old kingdom of Sudan, whose work is in everyone's hands.[12]

Those men were men of olden times, it is said; their talents are beyond reproach, their eloquence admirable, their narrations gripping—but as to their veracity, who will certify that for me? Have not a few indiscreet individuals been saying for a long time that the works of these men are of doubtful paternity, attributed to sonorous names to make them heard more clearly and further away? Has not even more been said? Has it not been said that these men, no matter from what country and what time they hail, were graceful writers who, to please their compatriots, wrote historical romances that have had the good fortune to reach us without encumbrance.

Thus, perhaps, it will one day be with the ingenious and brilliant works of our fecund Kazbek, whose lively and colorful imagination is so adept at dressing up history. We smile at them ourselves, and taken pleasure in them—but who can tell us that the history in question might not be the only one that reaches posterity, which will not smile as it reads it? Poor posterity!

---

[12] All the names cited here are presumably intended to be fictitious, although Nasreddin is known to us as a legendary Sufi philosopher, who figures in so many fables, anecdotes and jokes that it would not be entirely surprising if the name were to survive the extinction of our culture. Mettais surely knew that Bulbul is Persian for "songbird," and probably also knew that it is Hebrew for "penis"—a coincidence that has given rise to many a colorful joke.

I do not know, in truth, why Daghestan is the only historian of our days who has had the courage to speak so frankly about times past. It seems that people are happy to sleep in tranquil belief in the elementary history learned at school, and take pleasure in plugging their ears in order not to hear the reportage of science, which speaks to us every day and which, even in isolation, is sufficient to make us doubt the past.

Does not science, and science alone, without the aid of fallible history, tell us that vast transformations have overtaken our globe? Valleys have been filled in, mountains have collapsed, rivers have vanished, while others have changed their course or been given birth, and all that often under the terrible impact of volcanoes. Under the impact of volcanoes, islands of great extent have emerged from the depths of the sea. On the other hand, the earth has opened up and swallowed entire countries. Perhaps the interior of the Earth is as extensively populated as its surface. Our daily excavations demonstrate it to us. Oh, if we could only excavate beneath the seas!

All these catastrophes are undoubtedly rare within a human lifespan; they are less so within the lifespan of a people; are they not frequent within the lifespan of a world?

Everyone knows, besides, that the sea has changed and continually changes its location; that it invades one shore to retreat from another—but people do not think about that. You do not think that today's land is not the land of old; you do not think that our ships are sailing placidly over the ruins of old cities, old peoples whose remains you want to find in your fields. With your compasses and measuring devices, you steer where your imagination directs you, and you say: it was here; here are its ruins. That city was on the edge of the sea, on a mountain or in a valley, here it is. And if, in fact, you find an old cornice, an old potsherd or some rusty medallion there, oh, you are triumphant then, you load your vessels, you cross the sea full of the enthusiasm of the scientist who has solved a difficult problem, and you cry: Glory to me, to my wisdom! Reserve a place for me in your Academies! I have found ancient Constantinople, the great city of the earliest ages of the

Orient—because you have found on the edge of the sea, where you know the great city was, some petrified slipper or the broken pillars of some wretched caravanserai.

But you do not ask yourself whether the sea might not have retreated, whether the Bosphorus might have been filled in, whether the Sea of Marmora might not have been that beautiful verdant valley we all know, whether the famous strait of the Dardanelles that has exercised the imagination of novelists to such an extent might not have been that deep and delightful ravine at the bottom of which you can walk with dry feet, alongside the canal that we have dug there. No, you still want to find Constantinople on the sea shore.

With the same eyes you will doubtless also search for London, the capital of the England of the earliest ages of the world, which you will try to find in one of those bastard islands that rose from the depths of the nearby seas only a few centuries ago, and close your mental vision to the narrow English Channel that you can no longer see, on those rocks and mountains that a volcanic eruption has evidently heaped up, in order to make the familiar solid road that extends into New Cosaquia, the France of olden times—the road that science has discovered.

These are facts—well-authenticated and very important facts—but no history has seen these changes...

I apologize to the readers of our newspaper for allowing myself to get carried away involuntarily by the charm of the critical novelty that no longer wants to believe in the classical axiom: the master has spoken. What I have just said, moreover, is not mine; I have only reproduced the thoughts and writings of our friend Daghestan, as anyone can see. I therefore claim no honor for myself, but I am honored to belong to his school, to the school whose skepticism, I hope, will enable our history to make great progress.

Far be it from me to ask forgiveness for my boldness, but I will say to those who are less sympathetic to us: do not judge us lightly. Peel off the old man, renew yourself, and then, like

Daghestan, depart courageously for the difficult conquest of the truth; follow him, if you dare.

He is one of the first to have had the courage to let himself down to the bottom of the sea, with the aid of the prodigious apparatus created by our immortal Danielo Raviel, and to scrutinize the depths of submarine valleys and mountains, strolling there, staff and notebook in hand, writing as calmly as if he were in the middle of the most beautiful garden in Caucasipol.

It is because of those submarine excursions that he brought us such clear and precise considerations of ancient history. For, after having climbed the mountains that rise up from the sea-bed to breathe our air at the surface, or extend on to on land in long chains, with which we are all familiar without knowing their origins; after having traveled through the moist valleys in which so many unknown trees grow, and where so many plants lie rotting or petrified that have disappeared from our countries; after having sounded and interrogated the deep rocks that we have never seen, and on which are found imprints of the human hands and human genius, and the unknown but gaping volcanoes that allow the sight, around them and in the depths of their roaring craters, of the debris of cities; what could he think of the enormous efforts we make to find on land the cities and provinces that have lain dormant on the sea-bed for centuries?

So, since that time, he has written: "Let us bow down before the mysteries of the past; let us only admit with extreme reservations the traditions of olden times. Ancient history is a trackless forest, in the bosom of which we see at intervals a few fleeting facts, like will-o'-the-wisps, that lead us astray, because we see them emerge and die without knowing where...

"The human mind is like an eye; it can only see within a limited horizon; but as its curiosity is boundless, it wants to see beyond, and the efforts it makes to see only provide illusions.

"This counsel is not that of the despair that says to us: do not seek, for you will not find anything; but only: be circumspect. Search the sky, the land and the sea, and do not kneel down before any debris without knowing whence it comes, without turning it over a thousand times in your hands, before judging its origin."

That advice is wise, and it had proved its worth to Daghestan, who had made so many discoveries—but that was not yet enough for that worshiper of science. His mind looked even further; he cast covetous eyes upon the immensity of the skies, where he divined another life, another nature, other peoples aspiring toward us as we are toward them, but discouraged by the immensity of space and doubt.

To that aspiration we shall soon owe, I feel sure, a discovery presently unknown, which will complete all the improvements that Daghestan has already brought to aerostatics, and will, perhaps deliver us the most curious secrets of the universe. No one is unaware of all the prodigious ascents that have been so often carried out in recent times; but only one of his friends, perhaps, knows the result of his most recent ascent—the one that he made some time before the voyage from which he has just returned. In that aerial experiment, which succeeded so perfectly, our friend made use of a hitherto-unknown gas light enough to transport the balloon to a height that no one, including himself, had yet attained, while surrounding himself with an atmosphere dense enough to breathe easily. He then arrived close enough to the stars, and especially to the moon, to see incredible things there, which he will one day reveal to us, when he has completed his observations by renewing them. He will then give us his last word on the difficult problem of steering at will the vagabond aerostats that have, until now, only followed the various and hectic flow of aerial currents. There is no reason, we can admit without indiscretion, why that problem cannot be solved.

Oh, the power of humankind is great today—who knows where it will end?

What is the point, I have also been saying for a long time, of the mysteries of nature that God had set around us? Why would he have hidden such a large part of his magnificence from our adoration? No, God has made nothing that is inaccessible to us, but he wants us to search for the paths. That is why he has given us intelligence.

III

Caucasian Gazette
Caucasipol, 8 Prairial 5001

Daghestan has written to us:

Caucasipol, 7 Prairial 5001

Come to see me, my friend. I have just arrived in Caucasipol, and will not rest until I have embraced you—but I shall tell you nothing, because I have nothing to tell about my voyage. All my ideas are in chaos; my mind is not free and knows nothing. There is nothing in me for the moment but an immense sentiment, which absorbs me entirely. Sentiment is a poor traveler, a poor judge and a poor storyteller. Ask nothing of it. Later—perhaps tomorrow—we can set off together, quietly sitting in the corner of my hearth or yours, if my dolor will allow it!

Adieu, my friend—I await you.

IV. PÈRE FRANCO'S BOOK

Caucasian Gazette
Caucasipol, 20 Prairial 5001

Today we are beginning the story that our friend Daghestan promised us. We do not want this story to be told for us alone, in a low voice, in the corner of the hearth, as our friend desired. His recent arrival has provoked a lively sensation in all the tribes of Caucasia, and has excited such sympathetic curiosity, that we have persuaded him to write the story of his voyage for us instead of imparting it to us orally.

You know, my friend, that my dominant passion, perhaps my only passion, is curiosity.

It is, therefore, for the sake of curiosity that I have devoted myself, with the avidity of which you are aware, to the study of ancient history. I merit, perhaps more than anyone else, the reproach that one makes to the idler who becomes ecstatic before the debris of a cornice, provided that it is black and dates from long ago, provided that it does not seem to belong to our era, or before a mollusk-shell found several feet underground, provided that there is nothing similar in the nearby river, or before an old broken seal, corroded by rust and worms, if it seems to belong to a family with the crown of some old king.

In sum, I have a folly for the history of olden times—and, what is worse, I feel inclined to increase it further. But as that kind of history does not reveal itself to us by the fireside, I have become a cosmopolitan in order to go in search of it. I have descend to the beds of seas, as you know, and truly thought I heard voices in my hallucinated ears which told me to search for a ladder long enough and a fireman's armor sufficiently incombustible to go and ask the sun if it had anything to tell me.

Do you remember, my friend, the last evening we spent at your home?

There were several good comrades present who asked for no more than to be distracted from the gravity of the day's labors than launching themselves randomly into any domain that was not that of ancient history. The joy was at its peak, and threatened to go on for some time, when someone brought me a letter, which I read as seriously as I could, and which intrigued you greatly, for, contrary to my habit, I did not read it to you, and left immediately, without saying anything to you except "Goodnight."

The handwriting of that letter was magnificent, and it seemed to me that I was not reading it, but that it was speaking to me. I was carried away, and something that I still cannot explain is that at the end of the letter there as a little head, whose eyes were looking at me and whose mouth was smiling at me. That head followed me everywhere. I was to see it again later, my friend, on the body of a woman.

Well, I have that letter in my hand now. This is what it says:

Monsieur, old Père Franco, so well-known since your last voyage throughout the Caucasian Republic for his eccentric pretentions, has just died at the age of 196 years in the hamlet of Copenhagen on the shore of the little Baltic Lake. It is said that he possessed a precious book, known to no one, which no one had ever seen and which is as old as the world. As I am aware of your liking for books of this sort, I am informing you that a sale will be held at his home on the second day of next week.

I knew that old man—Père Franco, as he was called, although that was not his name—very well. He had been given the name because of the claim he made to be a descendant of the ancient French, who have been sleeping underground and in forgetfulness for so many centuries. According to him—and why should it not be true?—when the last catastrophes that had wrecked the ancient West, and which a few of our historians, on no authority of which I am aware, have described to us so singularly, but which must have been as terrible as an avalanche of mountains to have ruined such a people and wiped them off the face of the globe, a part of the royal family of France had escaped and settled in Denmark, in Copenhagen, which was then a brilliant city and the capital of a kingdom.

Thus, the royal family of France had not been massacred, as was generally believed, but had retired to Copenhagen, from which it had witnessed all the various evolutions through the centuries, remaining firm in the midst of their debris and never contracting a misalliance. Père Franco would have been the last drop of that pure royal blood.

Whether or not Père Franco's story was merely an extravagance, I did not know, but what did the old man's extravagance matter to me at that moment? I knew that he had an old book, older than anyone could say. I had glimpsed that book one day. It was in a box, securely locked and sealed, in a glass case so blurred by dust and decrepitude that it was almost invisible. The old man had not wanted anyone to touch it.

"On my death," he said, "buy it, and pay off my debts with its price, if I have any."

My greatest desire was to possess that mysterious book, and from then on I took every measure possible to ensure its inheritance for myself. So, when I learned of Franco's death, I did not hesitate for a moment. The letter advising me of it had arrived on the day of rest; the sale was to take place on the second day of the week; I only had two days to prepare for and make my journey. My departure was therefore urgent, and I left immediately.

To talk to you about it, my friend, would have been to open the door to all possible objections, to all the obstacles that brains hallucinated by a zest for pleasure could imagine. I thought it wiser to remain silent and hasten my preparations; then I mounted my most powerful and fastest mechanical charger...and two days later I as in Copenhagen, the little village in question, which you will not find on the map of the country, but which I can indicate to you as adjacent to the frontier of our tribes and forming the most remote extremity of the powerful kingdom of Zeeland.

I had only visited that little village once in my life, on the day when I had made the acquaintance of Père Franco, so I had largely forgotten my itinerary. Even so, I set off boldly without any other guide than my compass and binoculars, alone and confident. It seemed to me that an invisible hand was guiding my steps. My assurance never faltered for an instant, and although I did not recognize any of the places through which I had traveled before, I went straight to the village and, better than that, to Franco's house, which opened before me as if I were expected.

If I was expected there, however, it was not to give me the book without a contest. I immediately took cognizance of Franco's debts and presented my money in order to pay them off in memory of what the old man had said—but the debts had been paid. When I asked for the book, it was shown to me in the hands of a person that I had not noticed when I arrived, and who appeared to be contemplating me avidly from the back of the room, where she was seated.

That apparition astounded me, my friend, for those eyes that were staring at me so obstinately were the eyes of a young woman, beautiful, imposing and…forgive me for this pusillanimous observation, but I believe those eyes were the ones that I had seemed to see, doubtless in a momentary hallucination, in the letter I had received before my departure. Oh, if I had believed in the occult sciences and the magic that are presently so controversial but were, it's said, so powerful in remoter antiquity, I would have been afraid—but I'm a strong man, and I didn't believe in anything, in spite of the strangeness of what I was seeing. The woman was evidently an enchantress, but her charms were in her eyes, which fascinated me, on her lips, which had an unusual grace, and in her pure and melodious voice, which caused an unknown agitation to vibrate within my senses.

It was, therefore, with considerable reserve, but a warmth of unknown origin, that I informed her of the conversation I had once had with Père Franco, and the promise he had made me and making me the possessor of his book after his death.

That did not persuade my charming adversary, who argued that she had every right—rights unknown to me and which she could not communicate to me—to keep the book. I was in despair; the more I had desired Père Franco's book, the further I had traveled in order to obtain it, and the more difficulties I had experienced in acquiring it, the more burning my desire had become. It seemed to me that my life and all my happiness were therein.

I honestly do not know, my friend, whether there were tears in my eyes. Imagine therefore, how precious that book must have been whose possession was being disputed which such strange tenacity. Oh, if I had only been dealing with a man...but in the presence of that woman, what could I do?

I was thinking about that when I saw my adversary direct her gaze at one of the walls of the room, and then to me, with a superhuman interest, and hand me the contested book herself.

That change of mind appeared to me to be so strange that I immediately looked at the wall myself, and saw...this is incredible, my friend, and astounding for a strong man...I saw a hand, a shadow, an illusion—what do I know? But I saw something like a hand writing on the wall words that I did not understand: *Donnez-lui ce livre pour l'honneur de la Patrie.*[13]

When the book was in my hands, the hand did not write anything more; it vanished, but the letters remained there, flamboyant, speaking to me in a language that stirred me, even though I did not understand them

I was fascinated, motionless, aspiring the unknown of the prodigy through all my senses; my eyes seemed to have been

---

[13] Unlike the rest of Daghestan's story, which must be assumed to a translation from some unknown tongue, these words really are in French, although the original text could not make that obvious as I can. Their meaning is: "Give him the book for the honor of the Fatherland."

45

fixed for an eternity on those mysterious words, whose power I wanted to divine, when they suddenly vanished.

I turned round then to interrogate my divine sorceress—but she had disappeared. I was alone…alone! But not entirely, for I soon perceived on the threshold of the partly-open door a face as hideous as that of the young woman had been dazzling with beauty. The apparition did not scare me, though; I did not even seek to understand it. What could that ugly face do to me, since I had my book—the book that I had been on the point of not having, the book for which I had come so far?

That book, my friend, was indeed very enviable; it was a treasure, a veritable treasure. Unfortunately, however, that treasure was closed to me. It was a precious diamond in the hands of a blind man, a melodious music in the ears of a deaf one. I turned it over and over in my hands; I examined it from every angle; I raised it to my mouth, my nose, my eyes, my ears and the top of my head; I was mad. I interrogated it everywhere and in every sense, but it as mute—or, rather, I was deaf. Its language was unknown to me—its words, its letters, its numbers—and I could not read anything at all.

Undoubtedly, it was in the French language. That was really the French language, for which our savants had been searching for centuries; the language of which nothing remains to us—nothing at all, not a syllable: the language that had died with its people, their books and their monuments, and which some of our boldest savants have thought they could divine in the hieroglyphic symbols they have found in deserts—beneath ruins obviously, but which ruins? French ruins, they say.

At any rate, that language, the cause of so much argument and dispute, so utterly unknown, I had in my hands. "Oh, if I could only understand it!" I cried, like a madman. It would then be me who would judge, in the final analysis, that great controversy of the ancient world. I alone would be able to speak, to confirm or destroy with a word the reputations of our antiquarian savants!

Who could tell? Perhaps Père Franco had not lied. Perhaps he was not a maniac, a madman. Oh, what a mistake it had been not to have interrogated him more seriously! Perhaps the man had custody of traditions unknown to anyone else, related to the history of France. Perhaps...

Poor fool, like everyone else I had laughed at the man. That very book, which I had desired so much deep down, without daring to admit it to myself, that book which I had only glimpsed through the dust, and for which I would nevertheless have given anything in the world, but in secret, with a hand that would have been hidden from the other, that very book, I would have laughed at aloud...and yet, it was a treasure. That treasure, I had had beneath my hand, and I had disdained it.

After that, Père Franco had perhaps behaved mysteriously with me, as with everyone. Everyone! Undoubtedly—no one wanted to take him seriously. When the wind blows, the traveler lowers his head and gathers his cloak more closely about him. The wind of doubt and irony does no less. But if I had only listened to the presentiment that was whispering in my heart, if I had believed what the poor old fellow had said, and if he had seen that I believed it, oh, he would not have given me his book—certainly not!—but he would at least have given me the key to its treasure; he would have taught me to understand the language in the book that he destined for me, whereas now...

Now, I could still discover an important truth: I could resolve a great and difficult problem that no one had yet been able to solve; a problem that had given birth to volumes, caused great disputes, divided schools, by finding out whether its printing was of recent date.

V. THE SCIENCE OF GROS MATHIEU LAENSBERG[14]

Printing does not go back more than 800 years, say some of our scholars, and yet its inventor is unknown.

"I beg your pardon," the reply is made a trifle bitterly, in Caucasia, "but everyone knows, provided that he has a little education, that printing was discovered in the year 2000 of our era by one of our compatriots, the renowned Gori."

"That is a gross error," reply some of our neighbors, bluntly. "The inventor of printing was a Chinaman named Ké-Chan, who lived 500 years ago." Before that epoch the ancients wrote with pencils very similar to ours, on an unknown species of paper, but nevertheless on paper. They probably had copyists occupied in reproducing in a fair hand the works they wanted to distribute in considerable numbers. It even appears to have been a lucrative employment, some scholars say, for it was a position of trust and it was necessary to pay dearly for it."

---

[14] Mettais' readers would have recognized the name "Gros Mathieu Laensberg" as the ostensible signature routinely attached to a number of provincial almanacs, most significantly the *Astrologue Normand*. Mathieu Laensberg (who was not initially charged with obesity) was the notional author of one of the most famous astrological annuals, the *Almanach de Liège*, published from the 1620s to the 1797, and his name had been borrowed by several of those who took up the dubious torch. Contemporary readers would thus have understood, although Daghestan cannot, that Laensberg's "science" is astrology, and that the book's contents would be a mixture of calendrical information and dubious predictions. As things turned out, a new version of the *Almanach de Liège* was still being published in our 1998, although the *Astrologue Normand* had vanished by then.

Ultimately, though, the same scholars add, everyone admits that this prodigy of the human mind was not revealed to the old world. One could, if one wanted to say everything that can logically be said, find evidence in recent excavations that have been made on the site of old Moscow. Has not an entire cabinet been found there filled with papers and books, perfectly bound but written by hand? They were books of laws, regulations and administrative orders, undoubtedly very precious for our history but, once again, handwritten.

"That cabinet must have belonged to a man of law, probably an advocate," our savants always say. "His library is there, everyone can see it. How can one suppose than an advocate would not have had a printed book in his office, if there had been any in that era?"

"What? Why? My friend, all this fine reasoning is false. A cabinet has been found, it's true; I've seen it—but I won't take responsibility for explaining why is does not contain printed books. It's a matter that remain inexplicable for us, in that we do not know enough about the ancients' habits."

Printing was known in the most remote antiquity. My book has told me that, and it does not lie. Its age is very respectable, and its authenticity cannot be doubted for a single moment. If I'm not mistaken in taking for numbers symbols that resemble them, its date is 1998. 1998! The figure will only speak to my mind when I know exactly when the French era was, and, thank God, I shall know that, my friend, for I hold at this moment part of the secret of that glorious people of our old globe, and you shall know by what stroke of luck.

Père Franco, a far-sighted man who wanted his book, which had reached him intact, to be preserved indefinitely, had copied it exactly in his own hand, and then translated it word for word into the Zeeland tongue, doubtless for posterity, with the minutest care. But he had hidden the manuscript of his translation in the double bottom of the box in which his little book lay, perhaps by reason of eccentricity or perhaps to hide the key to his treasure from profane hands. Well, I have discovered that secret, after having investigated the box as I had investigated the book, and I have it here, in my hand. I am, therefore, as knowledgeable now as a savant of the olden times. So I can tell you now, my friend, what my book is. I have read it. Its title is *Le Gros Mathieu Laensberg, Paris, 1998.*

And all that is in beautiful printed characters—on very mediocre paper, it's true: gray, soft and easy to tear; which is far inferior to ours, but nevertheless on paper, whose invention certainly denotes a knowledge of very advanced arts.

What will our scientists say about that, who for some years have had their binoculars focused on antiquity in order to see it, some as large as a mountain and others as small as a grain of sand?

My book, my friend, very small as it is, very humble as its origin might be, will speak to us more clearly than all our scientists; it will speak to us more clearly than the whole world. I shall study and caress it as much as necessary in order to extract its secrets. I shall certainly not ask it to tell me that entire history of the old world it will doubtless not even tell me the life of the France or Europe of its time, but it has already told me so many things that I do not despair of obtaining immensely more from it.

If our scientists have had enough imagination to bring worlds to life on the basis of a mollusk-shell found a few feet underground, if their ears have been keen enough to hear the language of an old jaw buried deep in the mountains, for what might I not hope, from the clear and specific language of my book? Let it tell me only a few words, and with those few words I shall find all of antiquity!

Don't laugh at my pretention, my friend. Many things have been said about ancient France and its neighboring peoples. There has been much debate about their kings, their geographical situation, their civilization, their institutions, their size, their cities, their populations—well, my book tells me that we know nothing. Our novelist Kasbek and his school are people of great intelligence, for having rendered plausible the historic lies they had told us about antiquity, for having given the color of reality to scenes of the imagination, for having picked up here and there formless scraps with which they have built such magnificent palaces; we all know that there is much merit in thus captivating the interest of savants and the curious. But have patience! My book, which, for the moment, aspires to no other favor than that of pleasing you, will tell us more, I hope, with fewer words and less artistry, for it will give us numbers and proper names. Numbers and proper names often have an eloquence above all eloquence.

Do you know, my friend, after all our historical disputes, what the French government was in the year 1997 of the ancient era? No, you don't.

Well, my book knows. France had kings; it had twelve of them, and my book gives the names of those kings. They were:

Mathurin I: Nicolas-Pierre-Mathurin Bonnet, born in Argenteuil, 10 August 1960. Acclaimed Emperor of France 31 December 1997. Resident in Paris.

Thomas I: Jacques-Thomas Percepied, born in Patay, 2 September 1959. Acclaimed King of France 15 December 1997. Resident in Orléans.

Jean-Louis I: Jean-Louis-Urbain Legras, born in La Guillotière, 15 May 1961. Acclaimed King of France 1 December 1997. Resident in Lyon.

I shall stop there, my friend, for you will read my book yourself. You will then see all these names, which it would take too long for me to list here, and you will have a better understanding, I think, of all the disputes we have had for such a long time in classifying all these kings, almost the only ones of those times whose names have reached us. Alas, none of us has had the wisdom to say, on that question: "I don't know." We have all preferred to say stupid things rather than stay silent.

The names of all these kings we knew, and we were very proud of it, and strove with them to speak at length and knowledgeably about ancient history. We specified the dates of their reigns, recounted their important deeds. And yet, my friend, we knew nothing.

How long did they reign? For centuries, say our most erudite historians, obstinate in giving them an impossible order of succession. Centuries! Perhaps only a few months, my little book responds to them, mocking our savants by revealing to them the dates of birth of these kings and showing them the seats of their government.

Poor history!

Who can say, my friend, that it will not be thus in several thousand years, if the world still exists, in our Caucasia, which is divided into twenty little independent states, each with its private government? Serious historians will doubtless then strive to arrange the presidents of each Caucasian tribe in a sequence, to put them at the head of the whole of Caucasia. Oh, happy then will be the man who finds in the home of some Père Franco a Gros Mathieu Laensberg to rectify the historical errors that will then be current.

That first revelation of my Gros Mathieu is not, in my opinion, and as you can see for yourself, of such minimal importance, and yet it is not the only one that he will give us. He has another datum—a single datum, but a very important one—to tell us, and that is the almost certain date of the fall of France. None of us is certain of that, and, in truth, it is quite excusable for us to be reduced to conjectures, for no very certain or definitely authentic monument remains to us from that epoch.

The territory of France has never been excavated; it has become an inhospitable desert since it has fallen under the sway of the barbarians of Cosaquia, Morocco and all the other various peoples that have rushed upon it from all directions. We therefore know nothing about that country except what has reached us by way a few of our old historians, who were writing a long time after its ruin on the basis of traditions that were probably incomplete, perhaps erroneous and perhaps even ridiculous and utterly false.

How can you expect, given that, my friend, that we can know the truth about that terrible catastrophe? My book itself, which was printed in 1998, under the eyes of the authority of the day, would tell me nothing and would allow no suspicion, if an indiscreet hand, doubtless betraying its ill humor, had not attached a note to the name of each king in the margin of my almanac.

That note is handwritten, in letters quite similar to those of the printing, tightly-bunched, firm, perfectly and even equally accentuated. If one can judge the man by his handwriting, I can say that he is an honest man, full of energy, educated and ashamed of his kings. He must be an honest man, for he has, in a few words, stigmatized the powerful individuals who dishonor society.

To the name of Maturin I this note was appended: "Acclaimed emperor by 2000 drunkards. Everyone knows that the illustrious Bonnet was a rich proprietor of cheap eateries at the barriers, from which he conceived a desire to be named emperor, as so many others had done before him. One day, therefore, he invited 2000 Paris gutter-prowlers to dine in his immense halls, gorged them on meat and wine, and then presented himself to them, smiling, glass in hand, and, at an agreed signal, they all shouted in chorus: 'Long live Emperor Mathurin I.' It was also dinner time in the Tuileries. The guards on duty had just gone to sleep of casks of Champagne. The drunkards from the barrière had no difficulty sweeping away the brave defenders of the Tuileries.

"Paris, bewildered, like a man who, falling asleep, continues to sound a note, and as indifferent as a dying man, willingly cried: *Long live Empereur Mathurin I*…while waiting for someone else to come along and make him utter another cry."

To the name of Thomas I was appended another note…which you shall see in due course.

Now, this is the reasoning, my friend, that enables me to say, boldly, that we can place the great catastrophe that destroyed France in the year 1998, or very shortly thereafter. Let me expand my thesis somewhat; it will perhaps be more tedious, but it will be more convincing for it.

A throne, whether one calls it an Empire, a Kingdom or a Presidency, can evidently either be inherited or seized. When it is inherited, one can assume that a people is wise, full of energy and can exert its rights; it is, in consequence, likely to endure.

On the contrary, when a throne is seized, love of public good and the fatherland is extinct in the people; the people has forgotten its rights its duties, its social contract. There is no longer anything in its heart but weakness, apathy and stupid egotism. It is a man who shuts his eyes in order not to see, his ears in order not to hear; he wants to sleep in order that no disagreeable noise will torment his tranquility. That people is not yet dead, but it is sick, suffering from a mortal malady. If it still has life in it, it is only a breath, a death-rattle.[15]

What can we say, then, if a throne is seized with gold, seized as Mathurin I seized it? Oh, then the fatherland is dead; its remains have been displayed, its purple put up for auction. Assuredly, the people is dead...or perhaps only rendering its last sigh, for one has seen bold rogues buying the remains of a dying man expiring on his bed, or a dead man whose corpse is not yet in the tomb.

Well, the throne of France was seized in 1998, perhaps even being sold—my Laensberg does not say so, but the note says it, and it is easy to suspect. Evidently, therefore, the people was dead, or at least dying. The birds of prey, the ambitious, were already falling upon its cadaver, while waiting for other birds of prey, the barbarians of neighboring or distant lands to descend upon it, to devour it in their turn.

---

[15] There must still have been a certain risk in penning this paragraph in 1865, even though Napoléon III's censors had relaxed their grip considerably since the years immediately following the *coup d'état* of 1851, as the Second Empire came to feel more secure.

We also know, or at least have the right to suppose, according to tradition—and a tradition that we have no reason to deny—that France formed a single kingdom for a long time. In my book, however, we find several kingdoms in the land of France in 1998. How had such a major change taken place? Unfortunately, Laensberg says nothing about it, but is it not good reasoning to say that what had happened to the France of that time is what happens to all peoples in their decadence? The single throne has gradually collapsed, undermined by luxury, indolence, shameful and mortal passions, while the corruption of mores weakens the people in parallel. A few bold hands will then reach out to seize the scraps of the royal purple and rig themselves out in it, without anyone having the strength or the energy to oppose them, as we can see so clearly in the elevation of Mathurin I.

Now, what one bold man can do, two, three or twelve men can also do. But if unity gives strength, disunity brings ruin. Each king has his ambition, his pride, his private interests, doubtless irreconcilable with those of others, and isolates himself. There is, in consequence, no more strength thereafter in France, and thus no more hope of reviving the stricken fatherland.

Thus, the France of 1998 surely crumbled. All its divided thrones had to fall by virtue of weakness, first to the auction of the ambitious and drunkards, then to the huts of the savages who sweep away the debris. Nothing, my friend, can prevail against that opinion, or it would be necessary to suppose that France fell in a different fashion from other empires.

Do you understand now, my friend, why I had reason to call my little book a treasure, and what honor it can do to my science? I would not trade it for the richest library in Caucasia; I would not even trade it for all the treasures of an empire of old.

VI. THE HOUR OF DEPARTURE

That is sufficient to tell you, my friend, what price I attached to that diamond, how happy I was to possess it. My happiness was not perfect, but I think that it would have been if I had been able to interrogate my divine enchantress as I wished, to ask her what the rights were that she had mentioned, and what power had traced on the wall the few words that I had read there, the statement of which had changed her inclinations with regard to my book.

If I could no longer addressed myself to the divinity as I desired, however, nothing prevented me from speaking to the big fellow with the ugly face who was standing motionless in the partly-open doorway, whose eyes never had left mine for a moment. The man, whom I then considered attentively, seemed to me to be about six feet tall. He was frighteningly ugly; his face, with its ragged and bushy beard, was red—which did nothing to detract from its ugliness—and furthermore, his goatskin garments, which retained the full length of their hair, were laden with iron-tipped arrows, yataghans and other weapons, which made the monster in human form an ambulant arsenal, and scarcely reassuring.

I advanced toward him nevertheless, in order to speak to him.

"Sir," I said to him, "I am a stranger and do not know the lady..."

I stopped suddenly, perceiving in time, before employing my rhetoric to improvise a fine speech, that the man did not understand my language; for, at the first words I pronounced, he opened the door fully, stepped aside and indicated that I had free passage. He obviously thought that I was asking him for permission to go out.

At that moment I cursed the diversity of languages, and swore to write a little book at the earliest opportunity, to prove to my peers how much more fortunate we would be if we were all able to understand one another, in every corner of the world to which hazard might take us. I then recalled that the proposal had already been developed by some poor devil of a writer from one of our tribes, who had doubtless also traveled—but I had laughed at it like everyone else, as one always does at everything that does not affect oneself, however wise one is. Oh, I would not have laughed then.

I therefore bowed deeply and went out, without paying any more heed to the bear, who no longer seemed to be at all concerned with me; he did not even make the slightest gesture of politeness. But I did not want to leave Copenhagen without having exhausted every means of seeing the angel or demon I had met in Père Franco's cabin again.

My search could not take long, I told himself, to give me a positive result—at least, I hoped so. Copenhagen is only a poor village composed of half a dozen huts, which I had soon investigated and interrogated—but there, where I could make myself understood, I learned nothing. No one knew the woman I described; a few admitted to having seen a stranger as beautiful as the sun, but no one could tell me what had become of her; no one had seen her in his house or talked to her.

She was a foreigner, then. A foreigner! My God, what use was that information to me? A person coming from three or four leagues away had to be a foreigner to these poor people, who had probably never been as far from their village in their lives. Fishing for the poor fish in their lakes or the Great Baltic Marsh, hunting birds or other denizens of the neighboring forest sufficed for their livelihood and their commerce with one another.

What astonished me greatly, however, was to perceive on several occasions, some distance away, the ugly apparition in Franco's half-open doorway. Every time I went into a hut the man stopped dead, like a stone fixed in the ground; he only moved on again with me, always keeping the same distance. I approached him twice to question him, convinced that his conduct in my regard had some motive important to him, and doubtless for me, but his face remained impassive to my questions, and his great ugly body did not budge an inch. He listened to me as a tombstone must listen to the unfortunate it crushes.

I gave up on him, therefore; he definitely did not understand me—but he did not give up on me. That was his obsession—doubtless the obsession of a savage who wanted to study the actions of a civilized man.

I continued my research without taking any further notice of him, but I no longer carried it out in the village, where I had learned nothing; I ventured into the countryside.

The environs of Copenhagen appeared to me so scarcely alive that I could only understand how anyone could live there by invoking the intimate sentiment that links a man to his native soil, or the indomitable force that binds an oyster or a sponge to its rock.

That corner of the continent, moreover, so completely abandoned by nature, also appears to have been completely abandoned—O happy village!—by the government to which it belongs. It certainly figures on the map of the country; it is the frontier, on our coast, of the vast kingdom of Zeeland, but I am quite sure that it does not figure in the state budget, either in the matter of owing anything or receiving anything, and it seems more than probable to me that when the country's king says "my subjects" he has no thought of the poor wretches of Copenhagen. It is a forgotten point on the globe, which I only discovered by the greatest freak of chance. I have discovered it, but I shall not give it my name. Too bad, my friend, if you do not find its own as beautiful.

I shall not tell you, my friend, about all the old and new thoughts, all the sighs I uttered in that corner of the Earth—which does not seem, however, to be in ruins. One sole thought, one sole sigh, overshadowed all the rest. I was in despair; I had not found the lady I thought—but everywhere, I saw the big fellow for whom I was not searching, and whom I could not avoid, I assure you.

I therefore suppressed the urges and ardent desires of my soul, and resolved to leave the next day. I was curious to know whether my diabolical guardian would follow me all the way to my homeland, and whether he could travel as rapidly on his long legs and I could on those of my charger, and whether he might then deploy bat-like wings presently concealed beneath his goatskins.

Night had fallen and I could no longer search in the fields. Before leaving Copenhagen, however, I resolved to visit Père Franco's grave, in order to say my farewells there, and thank him for his book, which I kept constantly in my hands, fearing that in that land of sorcerers, some enemy magician might spirit it away from my pocket.

VII. THE MAID OF TREVIG

I therefore went to Copenhagen's cemetery—a fortunate cemetery in which perhaps only one dead man is deposited every half-century. It ought not to be very difficult for me to find the grave I sought. There, were the earth had been freshly dug, I would pray.

A word of explanation here, my friend, to enable you to understand what I am saying. Copenhagen cemetery, like all those in that country, is not like the cemeteries of Caucasia. There, a burial is very simple. They treat humans in the way we treat animals. A ditch is dug as long as the corpse. The ditch has to be several feet deep, not out of respect for the memory of the deceased, but in order that in rotting, it will not harm the living.

That was, I believe, the custom of several peoples of antiquity. That does not surprise me, for barbarity does not assist the development of affectionate sentiments—but among modern people, I cannot help being astonished by it. It is true that the civilization that each people displays is very diverse—which makes one think that perhaps not all of those who claim it possess it. I shall never understand, personally, a civilization that does not say to a person: your father, your brother, your son, your friend is the dearest thing you have in the world after God—and you hasten to hide them all from your eyes! You hide those features that you cherished so much, and which you could see again every day, if you wished! You could still preserve the features of your beloved daughter; her mouth could smile at you until your dying day; but you don't want that; you dig a hole in the ground, and, with tears in your eyes, you say: "Rot in there... Adieu, face so beautiful and so dear! Decompose, be devoured by worms, and filthy insects. Decay..."

Don't think, my friend that that manner of forgetting the dead is an anachronism in the life of Zeeland; that it is an idiosyncrasy of the semi-savage village of Copenhagen—no.

The entire country conserves that outdated custom, excusable at the mot among our forefathers, among those whose sentiment of the beautiful was weakened by egotism and the harshness of mores...[16]

What I just said, my friend, is not entirely accurate, however. The harshness of the inhabitants of Zeeland is perhaps not as bad as I was able to believe on examining the little charnel-house in Copenhagen. So, to put the record straight, I shall tell you here what I was able to observe later in their cities.

There, doubtless, sentiment is more cultivated, and people have realized that it is ignoble to reduce the beautiful machine that we call the human body to a dung-heap by burying it in a hole. So the burial-pit is lavishly coated with stones and mortar, and surmounted—according to wealth—with more or less beautiful slabs of stone raised above the ground. Some even embalm the bodies—but not, it is true, in order to see them for longer; no for everything is locked away and sealed, so that it can never be seen again. It can, however, be seen, and that is sufficient for the Zeelander heart. Poor heart!

---

[16] This diatribe is bound to sound odd to modern readers, but burial practices had become controversial in the mid-19th century and the modern vogue for cremation did not begin until the 1870s. Writing in 1865, however, Mettais must have been aware of Jeremy Bentham's eccentric legacy, and might well have been aware of the progress is embalming made during the American Civil War (although he had probably completed the novel before Abraham Lincoln's body made its long journey home, which was only made possible by embalming). Mettais was writing before the discovery of formaldehyde in 1867, but his anticipation of improvements in the technology of embalming was not unreasonable, even though its widespread adoption as a method of keeping dead bodies available for permanent family consultation remains an idiosyncrasy of future Caucasia.

How very different, my friend, from our Caucasian in-humations! How loudly the religion of a good heart and the gentle piety of memories are proclaimed among us! And yet, would you believe that I have seen Zeelanders laughing at us, that I have heard them calling us cry-babies while giving their impiety the noble name of philosophy!

Poor philosophers!

Be patient, my friend, while I describe to you right away a burial that I witnessed in Zeeland, a few days after leaving Copenhagen, and you will see a little corner of that civilization about which our neighbors make so much noise. We can thus finish at a single stroke with this lugubrious question of funerals, which one does not like to raise too often on road to be traveled.

It was in the capital, Trevig.[17] A poor young woman died, while still very young, dear to and adored by her family—and virtuous too, it was said, as pure and innocent as a virgin of our mountains. The grief was heart-rending, inconsolable. To lose suddenly, in a matter of days, the object of the happiest and sweetest dreams, an entire happiness!

But the young maid was dead; she was no more than a cadaver on which the law was about to lay its hard, icy, pitiless hand. For the family, it was all the consolation of their lives that was vanishing; it was a divinity returning to the heavens; it was a jar of precious perfume that a hostile hand had broken. For the law, it was no longer anything but filth that it was necessary to remove from an inhabited house, for fear of infection.

I do not blame the law, my friend; the law has neither tears nor a heart; it is a machine that runs continuously and whose mechanism is unstoppable. But the men of law! Oh, my

---

[17] Daghestan does not, in fact, get to Trevig until much later in the plot and only touches down there for a matter of seconds; there are a number of similar errors in the story, suggesting that Mettais was improvising it as he went along and did not write a second draft.

friend, if those in Caucasia were like those I saw in Zeeland, I would cry: "*Vengeance!*" until my voice gave out.

I do not ask that a man of law should commiserate with my pain, but I want him to be serious when I come before him to register my misfortune. Let him recall, the wretch, that the role that I am presently filling before him, he will one day fill himself, and let him sound his heart, if his heart is not harder than rock, in order to ask himself how, on that day, he will see the man of law laughing at his memories of debauchery as he inscribes in his register the great pain that has just been declared to him.

I am indignant, my friend, at all that I have seen. From that poor child's last sigh to her inhumation in the fatal hole in the cemetery, the family heaped dolor upon dolor. A flock of birds of prey unknown in our homeland fell upon her. Death in that country has to nourish a legion of vampires. Religion measures out its prayers, counts its honors, its hymns, its candles, its ceremonial vestments. The more one pays, the more prayers are offered for the deceased. Poor deceased! Poor family! Poor country!

Oh, and they laugh at us, whose religion is so gentle, whose religious rites so simple, so serious and so disinterested! For us, a dead man that we place outside our dwellings is a friend for whom his friends weep, gravely and religiously saluting the unknown, while there...well, here is the conclusion of the scene.

When it was necessary to lift the inanimate maid from her own bed in order to place her in the death-bed, dear and pious hands rendered her that service, covering that poor stricken angel with perfumes and virginal crowns. Oh, my friend, my friend, I saw that heart-rending scene...those hands clenched in pain, those foreheads streaming with the cold sweat of despair, those sobs...oh, I saw it all, understood it all. Tears came to my eyes—but indignation dried them up as a north wind dries the dew in the meadows. Behind us there were the men of law, laughing in pity, regretting in loud voices not having to do work that ought to bring them gratifica-

63

tions. Gratifications! These men demanded them, however, in front of me, exacting, haggling…it's ignoble, ignoble, ignoble!

Well, my friend, let's get out of this. If these people are civilized, what do they understand by civilization? If they are civilized, they have the hearts of savages. No, I'm wrong— they have viscera in their breasts that, instead of blood, transport through their bodies a river of desire…desire for money, and nothing but the desire for money…

I beg your pardon, my friend, for thinking out loud with you. I could have spared you my funereal and funerary impressions, but I am so pained by these memories that I feel relieved in pouring that pain into the heart of a friend who, I am certain, will sympathize wholeheartedly. Then again, I swore an oath to tell you about all my thoughts in keeping you up to date with my travels. Your kind heart will forgive me if mine sometimes overflows and gets carried away.

It is, in any case, quite natural that these thoughts occur to me as I remember the cemetery of Copenhagen, where I went, as you will recall, to pray at Père Franco's graveside and bid him adieu.

That cemetery is a little corner of fallow ground, where all the grasses grow that nature sows there, and a few meager and paltry trees planted by human hands. It had not been necessary to build any wall around it to defend it from the approach of the few animals that lived in the little village with their owners. Rocks, stony debris blackened by the rain, lichens and time surrounded the little cemetery on all sides. A tree-trunk placed across an opening contrived in the circle of rocks indicated where the entrance was, and was its only closure.

VIII. THE VISION IN THE CEMETERY

When I approached, the tree-trunk was lying on the ground; someone must therefore have preceded me. I looked behind me; no one was following me now, as the ugly devil had been all day, but ahead of me, in the cemetery, on a small mound of freshly-moved earth, I saw something vague, less dark than the shifted earth and motionless. It wasn't the shadow of a tree; the trees weren't casting any shadows in the dark night.

Was it the big fellow? I drew nearer; it wasn't him. It was...O my friend! That pretty hair, so neatly put up, so gracefully pulled back around the ears; that white dress; that figure, so supple and amorously rounded, although slightly disguised by her posture—I recognized it all. It was the lady from Père Franco's cabin, the mysterious woman that I had desired so much a few hours ago. She was kneeling there, squatting on her heels, with her hands on her knees, her face hidden in her bosom.

She doubtless did not see or hear me, for she remained as motionless as a corpse. She was not dead, though; I could hear her respiration, which was sometimes jerky and halting, at other times calm and child-like. I contemplated her, standing behind her, folding my arms over my chest and trying to divine the prodigy that I had before my eyes, and which had disrupted all my thoughts. I was yearning to speak to her, to talk to her, alone together in the religious silence that enveloped us, but an indefinable dread restrained me—perhaps respect for a profound grief, for how could I know whether the young woman might not be beside her father's grave?

I waited. I waited for a long time; she remained on her knees, while I stood in the field of the dead. I stood still, not making the slightest noise, scarcely breathing, in order not to lose the sound her respiration.

Suddenly, she raised her head and turned abruptly toward me, as if someone had alerted her to my presence. I couldn't make out the expression on her face, but I saw the hand she held out to me. I moved toward her precipitately and seized it avidly, as a sign of alliance offered to me, perhaps a pledge of the beginning of a friendship that might last forever.

She got up immediately, sat down on a nearby block of stone and drew me gently to her side. I sat down on the stone; my knee touched her knee; my shoulder supported her shoulder, and her hand remained in mine.

"What do you want from me?" she asked, in a soft tone, speaking to me in pure Caucasian.

"I beg your pardon, Madame," I replied, "but I spend my life in learning and seeking information, and I am, in any case, naturally curious. Since this morning I have found myself in a situation so strange, and so many things have happened to me that are inexplicable to my intelligence, that I wanted to speak to you to find out where I am and…with whom I am." I stammered slightly in adding the final phrase.

There was no immediate response.

"I'm in Copenhagen, I know that," I added. "I'm with a woman that a man with a heart could not help but adore—but that's all I know." And I stretched my neck and cocked an ear with an anxiety that is difficult to describe.

"You would like to know Franco," was the response to my question. "I'll tell you who he is."

That was certainly not all that I wanted to know, but it had already piqued my curiosity, for I was beginning to believe that the old man must have been something other than what he had appeared to the world and to me, for a creature as charming and mysterious as my neighbor to hold him in such great veneration. Instead of immediately commencing the revelation that she had announced to me, however, my gracious Pythoness pressed forcefully upon me with the hand I held in mine, and which I was trying hard to retain indifferently, then placed her head on my shoulder and remained silent—

infiltrating a fire into my entire being, O my friend, which burned me.

But that happiness was only momentary, for she suddenly raised her head again and pulled away, trembling all over, by means of a movement that violently separated our hands and pushed me a few paces away from the block of stone on which I had been sitting. I wasn't frightened; on the contrary, my courage was galvanized, and thinking that some anger was threatening to surge forth nearby, I spun around promptly and most heroically…to find myself in the presence of the ugly face that had been following me all day.

"Is it, then, written," I said, "that this man, if he is one, will be my damnation?" His heavy hand was laid upon the shoulder of my pretty companion, who was held motionless in his grip, lowering her head like someone guilty of a crime. I put my hand instinctively to my belt, where I had lodged, along with my map, a fine pair of revolvers. That demonstration was probably perceived, for the man, without showing the slightest concern, and without taking a single step, extended his arm toward me, holding some weapon or other.

All these demonstrations were futile, though; the mysterious lady had thrown herself between us so rapidly that we could only put away the instruments of our wrath if we did not want to sacrifice her to our stupidity.

She made a gesture and her tyrant drew away; then, sitting down again on the block we had just quit, she showed me a place by her side—but I was no longer holding her hand, and could not feel her knee, her shoulder or her soft breath.

"Speak, Madame," I said to her then, "for I am eager to learn…" And I added, in a voice full of menace that was certainly not addressed to her: "And even to avenge, if necessary."

I thought myself proud and worthy, my friend, when I was merely stupid. No one challenged my boast.

"Franco," said the soft voice of my companion, "was the last survivor of a royal family of ancient France." She hastened to add, in a reproachful tone; "Oh, don't doubt…"

In fact, I had experienced a flicker of doubt, but only in thought. How had she grasped it? That was alarming.

"Since the men of today," she continued, "are the descendants of the men of the earliest ages, since every son has a father, since human life, from the first day of creation to us, is a chain whose links are firm, why do you want Franco to be a son without a forefather? And if he was not a son without a forefather, why not admit that his forefathers was a king of the olden days?"

"I don't doubt it any longer," I told her.

"I shall force you not to doubt it," she replied, swiftly, "for I shall show you his genealogy."

"You, Madame?" I exclaimed.

"That king I mentioned," she replied, very calmly, "that ancestor of Franco signed is name in a family book, which each member has signed, from him to us."

"And that book, Madame...?" I said, anxiously.

"Franco only had two books; one will remain my property..."

"You're a member of his family?" I said, interrupting her.

"Of those two books, then," she continued, without paying any heed to my interruption, "one will be by my property; the other, I abandon to you, since I must."

"You must? Ah! That's fair...but why?"

"It's a secret I don't know; the instruction is strict."

"I respect and admire that instruction, Madame," I said excitedly, "for my book, in my view, is a treasure."

"A very precious treasure," she replied, in an emotional voice, "since it is the only one that Franco's ancestor was able to take with him into his exile, after having been expelled from the throne of France. It's the only souvenir, the only fortune, that he had in his misfortune, to console him for the absent homeland."

"And...that ancestor...was named?" I asked, hesitantly, for fear of a refusal.

68

"Antonin I, the illustrious chief of the family of Blanquets."

"So Franco..."

"So Franco was a Blanquet. He would have been noted in the history of France under the name of Antonin the 820[18]. Antonin I was dethroned by an infamous caterer by the name of Bonnet, who called himself Mathurin I—but the usurper's reign was brief. In his time, Russia, which had become all-powerful in the world and stifling in its immense empire, unleashed hordes of Cosaques, which surged into Europe, flowing like a torrent descending from the mountains after a violent storm, drowning in their impetuous waves all the kingdoms that were in their path, including France, which crumbled in its turn and has been buried for 4000 years beneath those filthy waters.

"Having escaped France with one of his sons, Blanquet hid for a long time, sometimes in one kingdom, sometimes another, taking up any craft that came to hand in order to make a living, One of his descendants eventually retired to the extremity of the kingdom of Zeeland, many centuries later, and remained there, as did his descendants, until Antonin the 820th, living in the strictest incognito under the name of Franco…and as the last of the Blanquets left no posterity, his heritage reverts to me."

---

[18] This figure is surprising, all the more so given the earlier assertion that Franco was 196 years old when he died. If there have been 819 more "kings" following in the footsteps of Antonin I during the 3867 years that have supposedly elapsed since 1998 within the context of the story, that implies that they have "reigned," on average, for less than five years, which is obviously inconsistent with their being succeeded by direct ancestors. The lady must surely be confused as to the nature of the "reigns" in question, which might have been more akin to presidential terms when uninterrupted by death— but Mettais ultimately leaves the judgment to the reader's powers of inference.

"So you, Madame, are also a descendant of some royal family of France?" I said, with a hint of pride.

"The head of my family was a leader greatly celebrated in history," that poor fallen queen replied, with considerable modesty. "Except that historians have distorted his name. He was Emperor of France, or rather of Paris, for in his day, the Emperor of France was only master in Paris. That empire, so great and so glorious, was confined within the walls of a city. The rest of France was divided into a dozen principal king-doms and a host of secondary kingdoms that had taken the titles of Baronies, Earldoms, Duchies and Principalities, ac-cording to their size. Our ancestor, an honest man ashamed of the abasement of his homeland, and a hero, got up one day and gathered his people, and was able to inflame them so well with courage that is a matter of days he reconquered the Duchies of Montrouge, Vaugirard and others, and finally reached the great principality of Sceaux—which, frightened by so much valor, capitulated without a fight.

"And what was the name of this illustrious warrior?" I asked, admiringly.

"Nhoel I, the chief and most illustrious of the family of Merlhukeck. He only reigned for 28 days. After his return from his great and noble expedition he was found one morning dead in his bed. He had suffered a fatal apoplexy during the night. He left two sons, the elder of whom died of grief on the day of his father's death; the other, being too young to bear the burden of government in such difficult times, could not reign. It was his uncle Blanquet, Antonin I, who took the reins of the Empire, until the crime of the infamous Bonnet. By right, the Empire belonged to the son of Nhoel I; it is from the son in question that I am directly descended."

"You're the rightful heir to the French Empire; Blanquet was the emperor in fact. Doubtless you have amalgamated with the Blanquet line."

"We have amalgamated."

"The throne belongs to you, then."

"Undoubtedly."

"It's your right."

"It's my right."

"And a well-established right; 4000 years of pretention, if I'm not mistaken.[19] But it would probably a little difficult to exercise that right without soldiers, perhaps without money— which is to say, without heaps of gold and silver, without any strength—with adorable hands, but the hands of a weak woman, against the savages, or near-savages, who inhabit ancient France, today's New Cosaquia."

"But my right, my right..."

"That's understood," I replied feeling a fire rising to my head that was buzzing in my ears. "Nothing is more respectable than right; right is everything. Since your illustrious ancestors reigned over France, France belongs to you; all the more so since you have amalgamated. Two rights to an empire since then, for the fact is also a right—two forces united. The people of Cosaquia will understand you, I hope. Except Madame, you will need at least a few soldiers, a few cannon, and a few of the engines that we have invented, with which your illustrious ancestors were probably unacquainted." I lowered my eyes modestly to add: "And you will also need the firm, robust and intelligent hand of a man."

"I have one."

"Ah!"

"Here it is," she said, quite seriously, taking my hand in hers and squeezing it with and affectionate sentiment that competed within me with the confusion into which the unexpected statement had thrown me. I soon collected myself, though.

"You're charming!" I exclaimed, hotly. "Yes, I'm all yours, body and soul—soul especially. I am at your disposal, Madame; my arm will sustain you until my dying day. Command me! What must I do?"

---

[19] This must be a slip of the pen—Daghestan has no basis for this estimate, and, it will ultimately transpire, every reason to cite a different figure.

"I don't know yet," she replied, very coolly. "Our orders will come from the other world, from Franco."

That name was a drop of cold water thrown on to milk on the point of boiling over. It rendered me more serious. For me, it's true, Franco was no more than a Blanquet—which is to say, a curious memory of olden times, or a petty joke of our day, and yet the name, evoked thus in the midst of my most cheerful hopes, suddenly reminded me of that hand writing unknown words on a dead man's wall.

What was this charming woman, then, receiving orders from him from the other world and divining my secret thoughts? Was that hand inscribing mysterious characters the hand of some ferocious god? Was the soft voice that had been talking to me for an hour the voice of the priestess of that god? Might I be a the victim destined to appease that bloodthirsty god?

I was in a distant, savage place, in a graveyard—and, in the final analysis, I was completely ignorant of the mores of the people in whose homeland I was. Although the Zeelanders pass for perfectly civilized folk—which is to say, not devouring their fellows—it would not have been wise for me to judge that little corner of their empire lost in the desert sand and rocks by the same standard. Even in the least cannibalistic cities, it is not rare to find a family, a few people with ferocious prejudices, who kill casually and without remorse—cheerfully, even—and out of religious duty. Who could tell whether I was not at grips now with one of those prejudices?

A covert glance darted behind me betrayed my anxiety, but reassured me, for what I dreaded the most at that moment was a powerful sacrificer: an executioner against whom it would have been risky to fight; an executioner like the man who had followed me all day—and I did not see one. My companion was only a woman, and such a gentle, graceful woman…and I saw no weapon in her hand.

I therefore said to her, with the perfect ease of a servant knight yearning to earn his spurs from his lady: "Well, Madame, evoke the soul of the venerable Franco, if you have that power, and let us find out forthwith what his orders are."

"Oh, his orders," she replied with an adorable smile that pierced my heart. "You'll know them in Paris."

"In Paris!" I cried. "Oh, you're jesting cruelly, Madame. For thousands of years there has been no Paris, if Paris ever existed—for some of our most erudite savants doubt it. If it did exist, it must be so deeply buried today in gulfs, volcanoes or bottomless seas that I would require all the sagacity and piercing sight of the sorcerers of olden times—of whom history has transmitted marvels incredible to us and to our scientific civilization—or of the somnambulists who are said to have infested the later ages of the peoples of antiquity."

I added: "There is, I know, in a corner of the Earth over which our savants have been debating for centuries, but perfectly unknown, a very tiny village, a few abandoned huts on inaccessible crags, called Figuig, which is said to be the ancient Paris, but..."

"Well, what does the opinion of your savants matter?" said my companion, authoritatively. "You're young, you're curious, you're even more savant than your Caucasian savants—go to Figuig."

I was astounded. My priestess fell silent, doubtless to enjoy the magical effect that her words had just produced on my face, which was gazing at her avidly.

Whence came that knowledge? Who had told her that I was a citizen of Caucasia, a man known as a savant in that land—I, who had traversed so many cities, so many deserts alone, resident for only one day in a region unknown to me and where I was completely unknown? Franco had said nothing about me to anyone while he was alive, and he had been dead when my adorable sorceress arrived at his house.

"Well?" she added, after a momentary pause, during which she plunged her gaze into the depths of my heart.

"But Madame," I replied, "To search for Paris on the Earth! I would rather try to find a drop of water that you had cast into the sea." Resignedly, however, I added: "If that is your desire, however, your desire will be a command for me. I shall go, I shall always go, everywhere; I shall march until the last day of my life; I shall use every possible instrument to dig in the earth and to find Paris; I shall dig with my fingers, if I must. I shall precipitate myself into every gaping gulf, to the bottom of the sea, in order to obey you. Speak, Madame—I am yours, entirely yours..."

My voice was trembling with emotion; my respiration was staccato, suspirious, my eyes full of tears—the sweet tears of the heart.

Oh, my friend, if you had seen her then! How her breast was also palpitating! How her lips were trembling with desire, hope and love...yes, love, my friend...yes, yes, with love. Of if you had seen her, if you had seen her!

Avidly, I seized her two hands, which I covered with kisses. I threw myself at her knees, without being able to utter a single word, but squeezing her knees frantically with both my arms—which she did not seek to escape...

Suddenly, an iron crampon caught hold of me by the neck, lifted me up to I don't know what height, and threw me away, to the other side of the cemetery, where I fell unconscious.

IX. THE DESIRE FOR VENGEANCE

When I awoke, I was alone and furious. Everything came back to me in memory; I cursed the coward who had seized me unexpectedly and from behind. Oh, if he had said to me: "*En garde!*" If I had only had him in front of me! But who was that monster, that wretch, that torturer, that torturer of a woman? I would find out; I wanted to know.

Fury gave me strength, and I got to my feet. How long had I been unconscious? I don't know, but I was damp; my limbs were all aching, my arms numb from being unable to move, and I could still feel the claw of the ferocious beast that had taken me by surprise upon my neck.

I walked toward the village; I went through all the surrounding fields; I looked in every covert, all the rocks, the slightest nook that was in my path, a weapon in hand and rage in my heart. The demon of vengeance was transporting me. But nothing! I saw nothing, and learned nothing of what I wanted to know.

I was not dishonored, my friend, any more than an honest man maltreated by a cheat, but I was vexed. What humiliation, too! A civilized man overcome by savagery! And unable to avenge himself! Oh, vengeance is such a soothing balm, though. Vengeance is justice; it is for the individual man what prison is for the State, and Hell for God. "Oh, I will avenge myself," I said... "No I shall punish that man; I shall bring down the blade of my justice upon him."

I therefore bestrode my mount, and said goodbye forever to Franco's grave and the village of Copenhagen—but I did not take the road to Caucasia.

I dare not tell you, my friend, that I was setting out in search of Paris. What was Paris to me at that moment? I was in search of something less or more than that; I was in search of satisfaction for my righteous anger.

I ventured, therefore, at hazard, in the direction opposite to that from which I had entered Copenhagen, although there was nothing in that direction but a frightful desert, a sea of sand, dominated here and there by the sharp point of some arid and bare crag. No road, or even a path, was traced there. One might have thought that one were walking on the bank of a river or the shore of a sea, so dry and mobile was the sand, if the eyes had not been able to see the same aspect everywhere, as far as they could see. It was frightful.

In spite of the conviction, firmly established in my mind, that all the parts of the globe, even those that are the most deserted and uncultivated today, had once been inhabited, I confess that was quite unable at that moment to say that any cities had covered that inhospitable sand in antiquity. The Zeelanders, more occupied with the present than the past, had never carried out any excavations in this region. Had they even suspected that there were once cities similar to their own here?

A few of their historians, the most serious and those fondest of antiquity, have supposed that the Baltic Sea, whose name recurs in a miserable local marsh, extended as far as there; others have claimed that it was the sea that the ancients called the North Sea that has left its sand and rocks on that ground. The latter are very bold, and have been pilloried for avowing that the North Sea that we see today, a few hundred leagues from there, once covered this region.

For myself, I do not refuse to believe that the sea or some great lake once inundated this region with its silt and its sand, since I can see them there, but nor can I doubt that there were cities there too: the general aspect indicates as much, and I am perfectly sure that the man who digs in these sands will find beneath their thick layers the debris of forgotten palaces.

I went on for a long time, and very slowly. My mount continually sank into the sand, and my weak arms were almost impotent to help it out of the profound ruts that it traced underfoot. I could see nothing over my head and beneath my feet but the sky and the arid sand, devoid of all vegetation.

It was thus for I don't know how many leagues, but I was sure of advancing westwards; I was making progress. The route I was following was difficult, it's true, but it offered no danger. In any case, I am not very fearful, and I was well-armed. In the evening, however, an enemy presented itself against which I had no weapon.

Of all the monsters that inhabit the terrestrial globe, especially deserts, there are none more terrible than hunger and thirst. They loomed up before me, bristling with menace. Not having taken such an encounter into account in my desire for vengeance, I had departed without arming myself against those redoubtable enemies, so I was afraid then, in truth, my friend. A cold sweat passed over my forehead; my ears were ringing and I saw a mist before my eyes. Phantoms appeared to me in the distance, dancing in the middle of an oasis that alternately appeared and disappeared.

My legs weakened under me; I collapsed to the ground and lay alongside my charger. I waited there for the coolness of the ground to give me back some strength. The strength did not come, but I soon felt a well-being that made me drowsy.

Was I asleep? In truth, I don't know. If I was asleep, I had a very agreeable and very useful dream. If I was not asleep, the course of my ideas, it must be admitted, was mysteriously embellished.

I saw around me a kind of beautiful oasis populated with cooked poultry, with an exceedingly succulent odor. They were pecking at little gilded loaves of bread hanging from all the trees. Streams of wine and milk were running around me and coming to moisten my dried lips of their own accord. I reached out my hand toward the bread and the birds; I brought them to me mouth and ate; I made a delicious meal…and then I woke up.

Oh, my friend, believe me if you like—I don't ask you too, for the fact is too marvelous and too far beyond the possibility of our habitual beliefs—but in my hand there were still the remains of bread and fowl, which I finished with a excellent appetite before reflecting on the singularity of their welcome presence. I had not, therefore, been dreaming entirely. And yet...

Finally, I got up; I was strong; I took a few steps forward. Suddenly, a human arm appeared at my side, which seemed to emerge from a cloud, in order to point me in the direction of a magnificent oasis a short distance ahead of me.

That sudden apparition chilled me with terror. I took a few steps backwards, staring at the being who had so suddenly surged from the entrails of the earth. Oh, I recognized him, my friend—so I rapidly put my hand to my revolver; for that arm belonged to the savage for whom I was searching.

"*En garde!*" I shouted at him, in a voice strangled by fury, aiming the gaping barrels of my weapon at his breast. "I want to kill you, but I don't want to murder you."

"Drink," he said to me, with terrifying self-composure, offering me a bottle. "You've eaten, but you haven't drunk. It was *her* who sent me to you." All that was said in a rather coarse language, but which I was able to comprehend.

What should I have done, my friend? I lowered my weapon. If I was obliged to kill the man, I put it off for another day. *She* had sent him; *she* was, in consequence, thinking about me! Besides, *she* was saving my life; I could not be churlish. Then again, where was she? My desire to know that was greater than my desire to kill her huge devil of a servant or master.

"Where is she? I want to know," I said, in an imperious and ill-tempered tone that perhaps did not sit well in the mouth of a man who had nearly died of hunger, in the presence of his savior, but which gave some satisfaction to the pride of a man who had consented to disarm himself at the moment of combat. "Where is she?"

"There," he said to me, pointing at houses that I was beginning to glimpse some distance away from us. "It's the oasis of Lining, one of the largest in this desert. It's part of the kingdom of Zeeland. Lining has a reputation for civilization in the cities of the kingdom, which doesn't prevent it from being grossly lacking in humanitarian duties. In my barbarous land, you kill men who insult you but women are sacred. Here they're put in prison."

"What are you saying? *She*'s in prison?"

"I think so, at least."

"And you haven't got her out?" I exclaimed, sneering at him. "Oh, so you can't sneak up on her cowardly jailer without being seen, to grab him by the neck and throw him over a cemetery wall?"

My eyes were burning, they should have been emitting fire at that moment. Evidently, I no longer knew what I was saying. I was confusing the prison in Lining with the cemetery in Copenhagen—such a sad memory for me. The dart that my wit had just let fly with so much pleasure fell upon my interlocutor like an arrow on a marble wall; he didn't turn a hair. But I was content; my pride was satisfied; the civilized man had vanquished the barbarian in his turn, with a sarcastic remark.

We walked side by side. I felt lighter, since I was no longer bearing the heavy burden of anger. He told me about his unfortunate arrival in Lining.

I don't know whether they had found a shorter route than the one I had followed, or whether they had had a more powerful means of locomotion at their disposal than I had, but they had arrived the oasis in the morning of that same day. I was greatly impressed by the speed of that journey, of which I thought only I was capable with my mechanical mount, and I interrogated him about it as clearly as I could. He understood me perfectly, but it was not the same for my part; it was impossible for me to grasp the awkward explanations he gave me—perhaps by design.

What I understood very well in what he said, though, incomplete as it was, was that his companion had known about—or, rather, had divined—my journey, my fury, and the weakness I had experienced under the empire of hunger. I was astounded by that intuitive knowledge, that supernatural divination,

"So the woman is a witch!" I exclaimed.

A frightful grimace, in the guise of a smile, strayed over my guide's lips.

Witch! That word has always been ignoble and fearful, my friend, among all peoples at all times; no matter what the era or conditions of life, witches have always been accursed. Some, wiser or more stupid, have laughed at the word. At that moment, I confess, it gave me a chill in the heart, for I was confronted by a fact, an irrefutable fact. Today, in my study, I can weigh the word coldly, analyze it and say to myself: "Witch! What does that word matter to me? It has been turned to ridicule in my mind in showing to me what it showed to our ancestors: the witch departing at midnight for the Sabbath, riding a broomstick. It has also been rendered terrible, in showing witches exercising atrocious vengeances at every hour of the day, on their own behalf or that of others. A witch is not that for me."

To me, it is evident that there are two worlds, the visible world and the invisible world, the world of Bodies and the world of Spirits. When I say "to me," that's wrong; the belief is not particular to me, it's general, and no more contentious than the light of the sun. But where I am perhaps too weak and too credulous, and perhaps alone, is in the faith I have in reciprocal communications between the two worlds.

To arrive at the world of Spirits there is a road that I do not know; but it evidently exists. So I am not surprised that there are humans who have divined it, have seen it and have followed it. The world of Spirits! My God, but that world envelops us; it is only hidden from us by a curtain that the hand can lift, by a cloud that the light can pierce. I do not have that hand; I do not have that light—but I would be very reckless to deny in others a power that I do not have.

That power is that of certain humans of our days, and the prophets, sibyls, somnambulists, diviners and witches of the ancients. There is, in consequence nothing risible or frightening about it, and it is an inexcusable pusillanimity for science not to dare to take it seriously enough to study it in depth.

I did not know whether I was dealing with a prophetess, a sibyl, a somnambulist or a witch, but according to a statement I was able to grasp and recall perfectly, the science of my guide's companion was mingled with the name of Franco. She doubtless knew the way to the spirit world where Franco was living, or Franco, for his part, was perhaps able to make himself manifest in the material world.

X. THE CADI OF LINING

Our travelers had, then, arrived that morning in Lining, by air or by land, but before me. More fortunate than me in another respect as well, they had been able to participate in a celebration that had taken place in the morning.

In one of the town's squares, a wooden statue had been erected, perfectly sculpted and an exact likeness, it appears, in honor of a citizen of Zeeland hailing from Lining. The citizen was a courageous man—even courageous enough to witness the inauguration of his statue.

I could suppress a malicious smile when I learned that the statue, so skillfully sculpted and so proudly erected in the middle of a large town of recognized civilization was the recompense accorded to the probity of a poor devil who, having found a bag containing several million rubles, had returned it to its legitimate owner. *That's good*, I said to myself, *but it's good in the sense of accomplishing a duty. Woe betide the nation that sees virtue in the negation of theft! This man did not steal, let's raise statues to him! Poor nation!*

The crowd at the celebration was large, it seems; the entire oasis was there. Our two travelers, on learning the object of the celebration, did not make the reflections I have just made about the morality of a town where it is considered heroic not to be a thief. They mingled with the crowd, without mistrust and without guarding their pockets, the lady still in the lead and separated from her mentor or jailer by a fairly considerable gap, which the crowd gradually increased.

Jewels that I had not noticed were covering the lady's breast, arms and fingers—but others had seen them clearly and, insensible to the fine example of probity that the statue was preaching to them, they maneuvered in such a manner as to enclose in a narrow circle the exotic jewels they planned to steal.

82

The lady soon found herself too narrowly confined in that human circle and instinctively appealed with her gaze to her colossal guardian, who only had eyes for her, and was beginning to growl dully at seeing her almost swallowed up by the crowd. That gaze electrified him; with a jackal-like bound he launched himself toward her, seized her in his arms and, lifting her above the crowd, carried her away.

The maneuver was magnificent; the lady and the jewels were safe and sound—but cries of pain and insults rose up on all sides. The courage and skill of the savior had shone at the expense of those nearby. The frustrated and bruised thieves shouted loudly and made a deafening racket, which made no impact of honest people, but to which they raised no opposing chorus, doubtless in the hope that a statue of Moderation would one day be erected to them.

The jewels were saved, therefore. That was good for the poor voyager but annoying for those who coveted them—and as, after all, the men were honest, since they had never been condemned by the law, they had the right to demand justice. So they spoke loudly, and, addressing themselves to the police, demanded as compensation a portion of the wealth that they had failed to steal. The hero and his companion were, therefore, taken to the Cadi.

In Zeeland, my friend, a Cadi is a magistrate who has no analogue in our homeland. Here, justice is always rendered in public, by several people, our peers, whom we know, and are always competent in the matters that are submitted to them. In Zeeland, the Cadi's court, to which one often has recourse at any time of day, is a tribunal held in his office, where he renders justice in private, in his own fashion, according to his views, his appreciations and his prejudices—which he has, being human.

Personally, I have always been fearful of a man who passes judgment alone, with the confidence of a man who has authority and brutal force at his door. That man might be a very dangerous tyrant; he is a king in his town, a despot armed with redoubtable weapons. But the government of Zeeland has

83

not anticipated that, for it has installed its Cadi in Lining to deal with disorderly individuals, thieves, swindlers and murderers, to see to the maintenance of good order, to encourage people to be good, to frighten the wicked. Of, that was a fine mission, a well-conceived idea well worthy of a civilized government like that of Zeeland—but Zeeland ought to have completed its institution by petitioning Heaven for a few angels, because humans...there are humans for whom the wicked are those who get in their way, or whom they envy.

The Zeeland government also appears to have forgotten its principles in this instance, for all its tribunals with one or two exceptions, are composed of several judges. Why several? Can several men judge more competently than one alone? If they cannot judge more competently than one alone, then why have tribunals of several judges? If they can judge more competently, then why have tribunals with only one? Might it be, by chance, that they think one judge sufficient for minor cases?

A minor case! Oh, poor legislator, who has not understood that what is important to me is not the object contested, but justice, the consecration of my right. Justice is our wealth, often the sole wealth that we have on earth. Why not render it incontestable, by surrounding it with every guarantee? Why put it in the balance of your appreciations? Why measure it in the number of your rubles?

The Cadi of Lining is a short, stiff man, marching gravely and uniformly, always perfectly coifed, gloved and shod. One might think that he considers himself a very important man. If he speaks, it is aphoristically, savoring his discourse at his leisure; if he judges, it is softly, slowly and ceremoniously. He has, moreover, nothing over his eyes but spectacles that have been put on without him seeing them, nothing in his mind but thoughts that infuse him without him knowing it, nothing in his heart... Ah! He has something in his heart that is not easy to recognize, but which perhaps emerges in his little glittering eyes, in which the fires of lust burn.

The man is not wicked; he is stupid and conceited.

Outside the door of his intimate tribunal stands a bear with a human face, always grumbling, always threatening to devour. The Cadi calls him his secretary. That is, in fact, what he is, and better still: he is the Cadi's master, his genius, his god. He it is who inspires and directs the Cadi. A magnificent mission, my friend: to redress the wrongs of an idiot; to direct to its target an arm that deviates therefrom! But the man in question has not understood his mission.

Slender of fortune, he has all the appetite of a starving man. His needs are great. His stomach is voracious; he would like, at any price, to have large pieces of gold to bite down on. The philosophy of the sage and modest is for him merely the idea of the dupe. Anyone who is rich, honest, reputable and honored is his enemy. His friend is the man with nothing. His friend? I'm mistaken. He has no friend. I mean that the man he protects is the man with nothing, while he makes every effort to soil, diminish and bring down the honest man whose honor cries vengeance against him.

His face...I've seen it, my friend, that face, and I shall never forget it. It has something wild, uncertain and sinister about it, which frightens you. At the sight of him, a good man trembles; a wicked, guilty man is reassured, in recognizing in his features the veiled features of his fellow convict.

On their arrival in the lair of the justice of Lining, the two foreigners had been separated. The lady had been introduced into the Cadi's office; her companions stayed in the waiting room.

"Madame," said the Cadi to his lovely visitor, bidding her to sit beside him with a hand gesture full of grace and urbanity, and with an amiable smile that she was far from expecting, "I beg your pardon. I believe that my men are mistaken in bringing you before the Cadi of Lining to answer an accusation. Such a lovely person, a person of such accomplished manners, could not have disturbed our town festival. There's some mistake."

"There has, indeed, been an error, Your Honor. I have not disturbed your celebration."

"But with you," he went on, moving his chair closer to the lady's, lowering is voice slightly and placing his hands very close to those of the accused, "was there not a man...a big, ugly man, frightful of face, costume and manners?"

"That's true, Your Honor," the lady replied, smiling.

"Aha!" the Cadi went on, raising his head and fixing his little glittering eyes upon the poor woman, who was trembling with shame on finding herself in the dock, accused and suspected, when her heart was so pure... "Ah! You were with a man...far from your homeland, no doubt, since no one here knows you...with an exceedingly ugly, brutal man, who has thrown you into the hands of the police!"

The poor woman was trembling in every limb; her eyes were moist with large tears. Perhaps, however, she did not understand anything of that scene except the humiliation of being accused. Her tears moved the Cadi to pity; he got up suddenly, consoling the poor afflicted woman with gentle words. Then he took her hands in his, and drew them to his breast in order to bestow the kiss that was already wandering over his lips upon her beautiful forehead.

The accused seemed to wake up suddenly then, and, raising her head proudly, displayed two dry eyes flamboyant with anger, which changed the Cadi's voluptuous kiss into a bewildered and confused smile, still pleading—which gave the judge an indefinable expression of ignominy. Then she took an abrupt step backwards, so badly calculated that her chair fell over with a noise that was audible in the waiting room— for the door opened, and the ugly and brutal man precipitated himself toward his lady, demanding his orders with a gaze that she understood, but to which she made no response. Perhaps she did not have time, for a fourth person appeared on the heels of the giant, and the scene immediately changed its aspect.

"Write," said the Cadi, to the newcomer, who was none other than his secretary. "The accusation has been found perfectly warranted by me. These people are vagabonds who will have to account to the law for their recent misdeeds, and others, if necessary. Let them be placed under guard within view of here until I have considered the matter."

As he spoke, he draped himself magnificently in his robe, crossing his legs, folding his arms over his chest and lowering his head with a little grimace of intimate reflection, which he would have liked to seem very serious but which only seemed spiteful. The secretary wrote with unparalleled animation, while the lady remained motionless, profoundly wrapped up in herself and appearing to pay no heed to what was happening around her—no more to her judges than her unfortunate knight, who did not miss a single one of her movements and tried to divine whether there're might be an instruction in her attitude that he could carry out.

That instruction soon came; the lady suddenly raised her head and, looking at hr traveling companion, said a few words to him that no one else understood. Without taking any notice of anything but the order that had just been given to him, the latter went out precipitately.

"But Madame?" said the Cadi then, in a tone of voice and with an interrogative gesture that demanded to know why the man was escaping thus.

"He will come back, Your Honor," the lady replied, with a smile full of bitterness. "I have just received an order, which I have transmitted to him: the order to save me, my friend. Have no fear; while I am in your custody, he will not be far away."

"That's good," replied the Cadi, bowing graciously and leaving his office. "Oh, by the way," he added, retracing a few of his steps and addressing his secretary, "interrogate Madame to the extent that the needs of the affair demand. Ask her for her name, her age, her profession and her homeland. You know, at any rate, what I usually do. Treat Madame with re-spect. I shall see her again, I hope."

He repeated his graceful bow and went out majestically, like a theatrical king.

When the Cadi had left, the secretary put his pen down on his desk, gathered together a sheaf of papers, some written and others blank, which he put in a pile and considered, seeking with a skillful eye to assess their volume. Then he stood up, went to close the door, and, coming back to sit down with the accused, with whom he found himself alone, said: "Madame, your situation is bad. The laws of our county are very severe. In your case, there is prison and a heavy fine, and compensation to various parties. You'll be dragged before the courts, vilified by the public prosecutor, harshly questioned by the judges, sentenced, condemned..." Looking his victim in the face to judge the effect of that word-which produced no emotion, as if she were certain of the contrary—he added, slowly: "Condemned..."

Still looking at her with a profound gaze, which demanded a response that was not forthcoming, he added: "Then again, if you're rich..."

He got up again, holding the papers he had just written in his hand, along with those which he doubtless proposed to write, and continued: "Look, Madame, I can see that you're not made for such ignominies. You've fallen into a hornets' nest, from which it will be difficult to get out safe and sound." Slyly, he went on: "I don't know why, but Cadi is angry with you—but I can soothe that anger as easily as you excited it, Madame. He only sees through my eyes, only hears through my ears; he's a fool and a pedant, as you've been able to see. Well, I can get you out of this uncomfortable position. I can throw this procedure on the fire, open the door of this office for you and bid you farewell, without anyone paying any more heed..."

The secretary, his neck stretched and his mouth agape, cocked his ear anxiously on the lookout for a response—but the accused looked at him with wide, dazed eyes, not understanding the language that seemed so disinterested—for, being still young, the man had not advanced either his hands or his lips toward her.

She made no reply. She was, therefore waiting for him to say something else.

"Madame," the shrewd secretary continued, hastening a denouement that seemed too long delayed, "I confess to you without shame, here I do the work, almost gratuitously, of an incapable man who is well-paid, as if I had no merit and no...needs." He lowered his voice. "So, I swear, if you care to leave here only a fraction of the fines to which you will infallibly be condemned, you can leave immediately. I'll take care of the rest."

Wasted eloquence, my friend! The lady remained insensible to everything that had been said. What was she waiting for, then? The secretary thought he could guess; he thought that it would be good politics, in order to attract the lady's attention, to make a generous gesture. He therefore burned the papers of the procedure, and then looked at his prisoner. "It's done," he said to her. "You may leave...in total security..."

Evidently, the mind of the prophetess was elsewhere. She did not budge, and made no reply. The secretary, standing before her, was beginning to fear that his heroism had not been understood, when he saw her suddenly emerge from her state of torpor and advance hurriedly toward the office door, which immediately opened...

We were there, my friend. Guided by my enemy of the day before, my savior of today, I had come to the aid of his companion, who threw herself upon my breast, where she shed abundant tears. Her heart as heavy with anguish; her lips, taut with dolor and emotion, were unable to articulate any sound.

The Cadi had just come in through the opposite door. Bewildered by that ender scene, he stood there while his secretary bit his fingernails, dreading that his confidence had been deceived.

As for me, my friend, I was full of zeal for my lovely protégée, who was and whom I believed to be, entirely innocent of the charges brought against her. What I knew about her gave me the highest opinion of her heart, and I would have sworn, at the expense of my life, that that kind and beautiful face could not be the mirror of a vile soul. But what could I do? What could I say?

I knew very little about the Zeelanders' laws, and not much more about their mores. What I had heard said in our contemporary accounts was so contradictory that I had preferred not to take any notice of it. Oh, if it had been a matter of high morality, of a capital fact that public consciousness appreciates in the same way everywhere. I would have been able to speak loudly and firmly—but in this case, my friend, there was only a petty matter that everyone might appreciate from his own point of view, which is good for him, indifferent to another and bad for someone else.

So, I frankly admit, I would have been greatly embarrassed if I had not sensed by my side a human providence in which I might hope.

At the door to the court, in the street, my companion and I had been accosted by a man with a kind face, still young, who had said to me with perfect ease, redolent with his nobility but especially his honesty and energy: "Are you a stranger, sir?" He pointed at my giant. "Seeing you with this man, I believe that you're going to see our Cadi, to bear witness in favor of someone in whom you're interested. I'm a native of the region, and I enjoy some consideration here; furthermore, I have a considerable advantage over you, in that I saw the incident with respect to which you want to render you assistance to a lady who is, in my opinion, very interesting. Let me speak in her favor; the Zeeland language is my own. It's understood, of course, that although I speak my own language better that you, I won't refuse the favorable arguments that you would like to suggest to me."

And we went into together to the office of the Cadi, to whom my advocate made a profound bow, which was not reciprocated. That coldness took away a little of the confidence that he had initially inspired in me; I feared that he had overestimated his own power. I turned toward him, however, after wiping away the tears of the poor accused, and my gaze demanded the aid that he had promised me.

"Your Honor," he said to the Cadi, "your people have brought this lady before your court, accusing her of actions of which she is entirely innocent. To judge her as I do, it is sufficient to look at her. If there is a guilty party, it is certainly not her."

The Cadi listened coldly and distractedly. Leaning his elbow on his desk, with his chin in his hand, he appeared to be reflecting profoundly—so profoundly that he did not even reply to our advocate. It was the secretary who took responsibility for that.

"Who are you, then?" he said, brutally, in a hoarse voice, with an oblique haze that did not augur anything good.

"I am, sir," our advocate replied, politely but firmly, "an honest man who has seen, and who has come to say what he has seen."

"There's no need—and besides, we haven't asked you for anything," the acolyte replied.

"I believe, sir, that an honest man always has the right to speak in order to enlighten justice," our advocate relied, very softly. "Justice can always listen to me, and evaluate hereafter. I have no intention of forcing the Cadi's conviction, and what I am saying and want to say, I am saying and want to say politely. You may reply to me in the same way."

"Shut up!" cried the impudent secretary, shrugging his shoulders and turning his back on his interlocutor. "You're nothing here."

"Shut up yourself, sir!" cried our advocate, in his turn, very energetically. "You ought only to speak here when the Cadi instructs you to do so."

"You will observe, Your Honor," said the secretary to the Cadi, furiously, "that this man is speaking too loudly in our court on behalf of suspect individuals whom you are going to send for trial, and put in a secure location in the meantime, because they are strangers, because they are subject to fines and indemnities, and have no guarantee to give us."

The Cadi still remained silent, only intervening in this heated debate by means of a slight grimace that the most expert of men would have been unable to divine. Our advocate, whom I had seen so mild-mannered and polite thus far, raised his head proudly, darted at our poor judge a commanding glance that reassured me slightly with regard to our case, which seemed considerably compromised, and then let his anger overflow.

"Your Honor," he said to the mute judge, with a smile of cruel pity, "you are failing in your duty in not imposing silence on this fanatic who is playing the role of devil's advocate here, while assuming that of the Cadi, which he has no right to do. It is, therefore, up to me to call him to order. In the meantime, however, listen to this, and nothing but this: I give you my guarantee for this woman and her actions, and I expect to be believed. If, however, indemnities are necessary, here they are." He threw a well-rounded purse on to the Cadi's desk, disdainfully. "Would you please give me a receipt."

"What is your name?" asked the secretary, in a milder tone, casting a covetous glance upon the money, and a gaze of repentance and gratitude upon its owner.

"Here it is," our unknown man replied, writing a few words on a piece of paper, which he presented to the Cadi—who read it from the corner of his eye, and then immediately stood up with the greatest urgency.

Our advocate, however, nailed him to his chair, into which he fell back, struck by the terrible stare of the man he had allowed to be insulted so benevolently. "Stay there, Your Honor," he said to him. "Our renown is not deceptive. Tomorrow you shall hear the will of your superiors. In the meantime, send these people away from your court..."

We all went out, my friend, leaving the Cadi and his secretary distraught.

XI. THE UNKNOWN FRIEND

You can understand, my friend, how satisfied I was with that unexpected denouement. To begin with, it seemed to be to be a fine act of justice, and then…my God, in truth I don't know, poor philosopher than I am, whether I did not rejoice more in having so fortunately recovered a woman who had become for me an entire happiness, an entire future—a future, of course, that Franco, his book and his stories had caused me to glimpse.

I was happy, therefore…but with some anxiety however—the anxiety, perhaps, after all, of ruffled self-respect, for in the midst of all that, my sagacity had been direly lacking. Who was that man, whom hazard had sent to Lining as we were passing through, at the moment when we had such a great need for him, and had handled a difficult business so well? Where did he come from? He was certainly not from Lining, for the Cadi would have known him, at least slightly, and if the Cadi didn't know him, how did a man come to be in his town what had a talisman sufficiently magical to do what the name of our advocate had done?

That problem was insoluble for me for the moment, my friend, but I hoped that it wouldn't be for long. I therefore didn't part from the unknown protector immediately. I followed him without affectation; I talked to him without any express desire—but he was an intelligent and observant man, and he saw through me.

"You're a stranger, sir?" he asked me, again.

"From Caucasia," I replied, forthrightly, hoping that he might do the same if I asked the same question. I added, obligingly, as if it were a mark of illustriousness: "From the tribe of Caucasus, from Caucasipol itself."

"And you're going…?"

"Oh, I don't know," I replied, looking at the lady of my thoughts. "I don't know where I'm going."

"To Paris," she replied, matching my gaze with a gaze that fascinated me.

"And you're a man desirous of knowing the mores of all countries," he added, without appearing to have understood the reply that had just been made to him. "You would have much to learn in our Zeeland if you had the time. Perhaps I can be of some use to you, if you wish. For now, permit me to leave you; I'll meet you tomorrow morning at nine o'clock in the square in front of the courthouse."

Then, bowing to us with infinite grace, he left us abruptly, without my being able to thank him for his fortunate intervention in the business with the Cadi and his generous offer of assistance the following day. I followed him with my eyes for as long as I could. He was soon joined by another man who linked arms with him, and they disappeared together in the distance, without giving me the backward glance that I almost expected.

The next day, I couldn't wait. Well before the appointed hour I was in the square in front of the courthouse, for I was entirely free. I was staying in the same hotel as my new allies, but the lady had told me that morning not to try to see her, that she needed rest after the journey. I had told her, for my part, that I hoped that her message was not a message of farewell, that we could not separate in that fashion, and that I had a heart full of thoughts that I wanted to communicate to her. I went out, after making my recommendations—fruitfully, I hoped.

I strolled around the square while waiting for my cicerone, reflecting sadly on the miseries of human society—which, founded with a goal of utility for all, could not attain that goal with tribunals and prisons. Men, I said to myself, bitterly, are merely rebellious schoolboys, only obedient to the cane, when they are not dangerous lunatics that it is necessary to cage. Was that the aspect of Zeeland mores that my cicerone wanted to show me, in meeting me in the square in front of the courthouse, doubtless to introduce me to the tribunal?

On seeing the crowd that was going in and coming out continuously, like the bees of a well-populated hive, one could only consider the people as a people in difficulties. The tribunal had already been open for some time; the judge—for it was still a tribunal occupied by a single judge—was sitting and passing judgment. I went in several times and came out with everyone else, in order to see and hear, but I understood very little. I therefore ardently desired my advocate of the previous day, who was a little late. The last time I came out of the courthouse, he spotted me and came over to me, holding out his hand.

"Forgive me," he said. "I was delayed—you became impatient and went in without me."

"So it is in there that you wanted to take me?" I replied.

"Yes," he said, "but we won't go in right away, for the most curious aspect of justice, for someone like you, who is doubtless something of a philosopher, is to be found here, in the square."

I opened my eyes wide in astonishment to look at my interlocutor, who gestured with his head toward a number of men who were strolling around the square, as I had strolled myself, and said: "Look; study those faces. Follow those men with your eyes, without them being aware of it; that's enough to tell you to be prudent. The spectacle interests me, too, and I'd be upset if we did not follow it through to the end."

While chatting, therefore, and without affectation, I looked at the men he had indicated. In the crowd I saw three of them, especially, who, with their hands in their pockets, as if they were merely curious amateurs, were going to the people coming out of the courthouse one after another. They were preferentially accosting those whose contracted features attested to their discontentment.

Some gave the three men a sideways glance without replying; others seemed very animated and furious, and doubtless recounted their dissatisfactions with all sorts of threats against their adversaries and the unintelligent or corrupt judge who had refused them justice. I saw little pieces of paper slipped into the hands of a very few.

"Well," said my cicerone, "did you see?"

"Perfectly. Those three men are benefactors, generous benefactors of suffering humanity, who have come here, where there are grievances to soothe and consolations to give. To give bread to someone who is hungry is a virtuous action; to wipe away the tears of those who are in pain is perhaps even better."

My interlocutor burst out laughing, and looked at me attentively. "Caucasians have noble souls," he told me. "I don't suppose they're quick to suspect evil."

I looked at him in bewilderment. I thought myself a man of sound, even clear-sighted, judgment, but I saw myself surpassed by a man I had not suspected of having eyes as keen as mine. My naively interrogative gaze did not interrupt his train of thought or his conversation.

"What I find singularly touching," my interlocutor continued, "is to see kind faces, the faces of honest men, among the people that are coming out of the tribunal with rage in their heart, probably having been found guilty."

"That's true," I replied. "I noticed that too, and I examined those faces so closely that they will not be soon erased from my memory."

"And some received those little pieces of paper," added my cicerone, uttering a profound sigh.

"Yes, I saw that."

"Those pieces of paper, sir, are assuredly addresses given by conspirators who have come here to recruit soldiers for their army."

"What!" I exclaimed. "What are you saying, sir?"

"I'm saying that I now understand what I have never wanted to understand," my new friend replied, sadly, "which is that governments make thousands of enemies every day without knowing it, and without concerning themselves with it. I'm saying that there are anthills under thrones that are incessantly at work, at which one laughs, but which eventually hollow out an abyss deep enough to engulf them. I'm saying that I've always believed that people love justice and those responsible for rendering it...oh, but what am I saying? Let's go into the tribunal, and we'll see whether those responsible for rendering justice are rendering it with gravity, verity and moderation. Afterwards, we'll judge for ourselves whether the kind faces we've seen emerging were those of honest men."

"Do you doubt it, sir?" I asked.

"Do you?" he replied, with a thin smile.

"I don't doubt it at all," I riposted, swiftly, glad to joust with such a stern competitor. "The face never lies. The features of a thief don't resemble those of a good man. Their ensemble might sometimes deceive you at first glance, if you're not on your guard, but go closer, look harder, and you'll soon find the disorder that you didn't see at first: the broken lines, a threatening question mark that stands up here and there're on the face of the fraudster and the hypocritical trickster..."

And I looked at my cicerone, who had stopped on the steps leading to the tribunal, and looked at him with eyes full of fire.

"Go on," he said, mildly.

"Well, sir," I went on, more calmly, "I was going to say that if our kind faces don't have that malevolent question mark, then it's possible, in my opinion, in spite of the ill-temper to which they testify, that those who are rendering justice do not always render it, as you put it, with verity and moderation."

"Do you believe, then, that a discontented man is never mistaken?" my interlocutor replied, with a smile of heart-rending bitterness.

"Pardon me," I said, "but, if he is mistaken, make him see it with verity and moderation, and his face will not become chagrined—or, at least, you will never succeed in slipping little pieces of paper into his hand."

"Ah! That's precisely what I wanted to get back to," my interlocutor went on, excitedly. "An honest man who receives those little pieces of paper from a conspirator..."

"I don't know what the morality of Zeeland is, sir," I replied, "but I know that a good man, who doesn't find justice in a court of law, might, despairing of finding it anywhere, demand it of his conscience. If his conscience—which is to say, the intimate torch that God has given to everyone, which lights up before our social conventions, causes him to see a breach of the contract of his rights; if his conscience orders him besides to punish any beach, wherever it might be, what can one say to that man? He has rights and he has duties; his rights, you have scorned; why complain is he misconceives his duties? Besides, what are his duties? Would you care to tell me?"

"To obey."

"To obey the law, yes—but the judge is not the law."

"Oh, the distinction is so difficult for many, my dear sir," my cicerone said to me, gravely, "that the best thing is to obey."

"The interested say so," I retorted, smiling, "And I am perhaps somewhat inclined to the same opinion, but what will the government gain thereby, even if the city gains the maintenance of good order? The good order of the city cannot be sufficient for the government; it also requires affection to defend it. How can you demand affection from people whose rights you have offended? You're unjust; why do you expect them to be good? Social duties are reciprocal; there is a contract. Whoever breaks it with respect to his own duties, therefore, breaks it with respect to those of others. Thus, I have seen perfectly good men whom an injustice has caused to reflect severely on tribunals, and hence on the government that employ them—for a master, the law says, is responsible for his servants' actions.

"Thus, if a judge is hated, do not ask for his government to be liked, for you are demanding a superhumanly heroic abnegation. And once again, if the government is not liked, how can it survive? Who will defend it in dangerous times?

Poor government—it doesn't even have the virtue of egotism!"

"You're a charming man," my cicerone said to me, graciously, shaking my hand affectionately. "We'll talk about all this again, later; let's go in."

And we went in.

The judge was on his bench. In front of him, two advocates of a sort were raging like two fanatics, pleading for two poor devils who were standing there silently, listening to the various arguments that were being offered for or against them, but in either case with unparalleled fervor. One of the two defenders, in particular, talked and talked and talked, assiduously interrupting his adversary, who, as a polite man, only wanted to speak in his turn. The judge allowed it, and seemed strongly influenced by the verbiage of the inexhaustible defender. The case was concluded; I have nothing to say about it, but the polite man lost.

The spectacle did not see very interesting to me, but it impassioned my cicerone considerably, who listened with the attention of a conscientious judge.

Several other cases unfolded before us. As the mores of Zeeland were unfamiliar to me, they might have concerned matters very important to interested parties, but were of little interest to me, and I began to do as the judge was doing, yawning to the full amplitude of my jaws. My new friend remained as motionless as a statue. Once, however, I saw him become agitated, as if he were ill at ease; his face contracted with impatience, perhaps even discontentment. Evidently, it was the case being heard that had produced that emotion, so I listened. This is what it was about.

There were two men before the tribunal, who were not advocates. One of them was short, fidgety and embarrassed, seemingly very ill-assured, whether because of fear of justice or because he was naturally timid. Timid! That was not my opinion, though. There were on his face a few traits of bold effrontery, of stupid and ridiculous pride, and of a slyness that was not suggestive of honesty.

The other had a calm and open face, which inclined me in his favor. The case was reaching its conclusion, and I was only able to hear a few words, which gave me to understand that the man with the honest face was there against his will, and that he had done everything, even sacrifice his right, to appease his pestiferous adversary. Whatever he said, though, his case was settled by the opinion of the judge, who was not favorable to him, and I saw with some chagrin that the opinion in question came from beyond the court-room, by virtue of the bitterness of a few words that lacked the gravity of justice.

"Forgive me, Your Honor," said my cicerone, them, advancing toward the bench, "But would you care to postpone your definitive judgment for a week? It will be very easy for me to prove that the guilty party is the one you deem to be innocent. I am well-acquainted with the affair; moreover, I know the two adversaries who are here. After investigation, Your Honor will be astonished by the clarity of the affair, which seems somewhat confused today."

"The case has been heard," said the judge, sharply. "I shall pronounce judgment, if the two parties do not want to accept my advice."

"I understand the little pieces of paper better than ever now," my cicerone said, between his teeth, as he returned to me. "I shall take one of the little pieces of paper myself."

"Bailiffs, throw that insolent fellow out," said the judge, pointing at our discontented advocate, whom he had not heard, but to whom he attributed all the other murmurs.

"Don't touch me, sir," my friend, who was growing in my esteem, riposted hotly to the bailiff. "I shall leave, but of my own accord, as I came in. I am not guilty of any insolence, nor am I causing a disturbance; you have no right to expel me." He scribbled in pencil on a page in his notebook, which he then tore out. "In any case, here is my name and my address; if you wish to drag me before your bench to be enlightened as to the law, you may."

The judge, having read it, got up immediately, bared his head, and was doubtless about to speak when an usher came into the court-room very hurriedly and, addressing himself to my friend, handed him a large envelope, which the latter opened as he went out, drawing me along with him.

In the middle of the square he stopped and looked me up and down attentively, from head to toe, and then burst out laughing. "The idiots!" he said, in a low voice, before addressing me. "My dear Daghestan, he said, you are an honest man?"

"No one has ever doubted it, sir," I replied, a trifle piqued.

"No one who knows you," he said. "I believe it—but not everyone knows you. You are accused of being a Republican."

"I'm nothing in Lining," I replied. "I'm a Republican in the Republic of Caucasia."

"You're an honest Republican," he said, shaking my hand, "but the idiots want you to be a dishonest man sent to disturb the peace of Zeeland."

I protested; he closed my mouth.

"Let it go," he said. "Don't protest. I'm as good a physiognomist as you are. I know your face, and your heart into the bargain." With a vague hand gesture, he added: "The idiots are over there." Pointing to the court-house and the public square where the suppliers of the pieces of paper were still strolling, he continued: "The dishonest men are here and there." After a moment's reflection, he tapped his large envelope. "All the same," he went on, "I'm curious to know where this advice came from, and who has sent it from there to here."

"Is *there* Trevig?" I asked him.

"Yes, Trevig."

"Well, it isn't so far from Lining to Trevig, if one can admit that such a long distance can be traversed in such a short time. As I am only aware of one enemy, the Cadi or his secretary, I suggest that the advice came from one or other of them."

"You're right," said my unknown friend. "That is where it comes from. The Cadi wanted to harm you or me. He has been quicker than me, and perhaps better informed. He evidently found out who you are immediately, and where you come from. After my admonition he immediately sent a vengeance to Trevig, which has come back to us by telegraph."

Telegraph! Do you know, my friend, what kind of telegraph he meant? It's nothing other than the electric telegraph—our electric telegraph. Oh, I can laugh at it wholeheartedly! What would our scientists, our immortal scientists who have invented the telegraph, say to that of Zeeland, which has existed, it seems since time immemorial—as a phantasmagoria, it's true, among the local witches, and then, for a few years, as a secret means of transmission for the government, but for the government alone. When one wants to invent something new, one has to contend with the science of everyone else.

Well, it was the electric telegraph of Zeeland that was working against me. I bless it with all my heart, since it caused me to find and appreciate a friend in my cicerone, whom I was yearning to know better, but who was in any case a man of rare intelligence and rare good will.

I had hardly left the public square when I learned about the destitution of the Cadi and his secretary—a fortunate and new effect, I thought, of the electric telegraph! I immediately set out in quest of my mysterious friend, to tell him the good news, but I could not find him. I therefore resigned myself to wait patiently for the hour of a further rendezvous that he had given me, and headed in all haste toward my hotel and my other traveling companions, to whom I had a great deal to say.

Alas! They had just left the hotel, and were not coming back.

Oh, my friend, I was in despair. I, who had done so much to find *her*, who ought to have been so dear to *her*, since I had rendered her such a great service, who was hoping not to be parted from *her* again for a long time, perhaps forever…had lost her.

A domestic handed me two letters, which I opened avidly.

The first was from *her*; she wrote:

My friend...

I shivered with pleasure and sweet sensations at that name, which she had never given me.

My friend. I am leaving Lining today, at eleven o'clock in the morning, but without breaking the promise I gave you, because I am not leaving freely. I have not even been given an hour to wait for you; I have only been given a few minutes, of which I am taking advantage to tell you this and to remind you of the promise you have made to go to Paris. I shall meet you there...

The second letter was conceived as follows:

Farewell, my dear Daghestan! I have so little time that I cannot go to shake your hand. It is necessary that I be on my way to Trevig at eleven o'clock. Give me the pleasure of coming to see me there someday...

And it was scarcely and hour since I had left him! I was downcast. Alone! Alone in Lining, when I believed that I had two friends there, whom I had lost without having spoken to them, not knowing whether I would ever see them again, with a doubtful rendezvous offered by each of them, in countries utterly unknown to me. But why had they gone?—both of them so precipitately, at the same time, both of them virtually compelled to depart.

My state of mind was frightful. It was, however, necessary to resign myself to the loss, to think seriously about what to do next. Go to Paris...? But where was Paris? My heart, however, urged me strongly in that direction... Go to Trevig...?

XII. A DREAM IN A BALLOON

While my mind was shaken up by those contending thoughts, a man came into my room.

"Sir," he said to me, handing me a piece of paper, "I was commissioned to deliver a package to you, which I have deposited in the courtyard of the hotel."

I went down with the man, while reading the note, which was also from the woman who had called me her friend. She informed me that my presence in Lining was suspect, that an order had been given to arrest me, and that it would be difficult for me to escape the consequences of that order; that she saw only one means, and that was to flee, and that the only flight that would get me out of danger was the one she indicated to me.

She was in fact, my friend, indicating a singular kind of flight, the nature of which you will never guess, and which was far from inspiring any great confidence in me.

The man who had handed me the warning note pointed to a mass of silk and ropes confusedly heaped up in a corner. It was a balloon—yes, my friend, an authentic deflated balloon, lying at my feet and offering me a precious hospitality. A balloon! A balloon brought out from the lair of some savage! Oh, and we are so proud of having discovered the balloon! We praise so highly the genius of the Caucasian who invented it!

Patience, though! That isn't all. Listen to me, my friend, with all ears, for here is another marvel. Having indicated to me a simple, reliable and almost instantaneous means of inflating my balloon, the note added: *you have, my friend, a compass and a telescope in order to reconnoiter the road that you want to follow, so I have not sent it to you—but I have sent you instructions for steering the balloon at will.*

That was not a joke, my friend; the instructions did, indeed, accompany the warning note.

And I had been searching for that knowledge for such a long time in my beautiful land of Caucasia! I had studied so hard and carried out so many experiments trying to discover the art of steering balloons at will; I was so proud of almost having found it, had promised myself such glory for myself and my country in demonstrating that art to my compatriots!

My balloon was inflated in a matter of moments. I was very glad of that, for the hotel was surrounded, and I had not risen above the roof of the building when I saw a squad of armed men irrupt into the courtyard—only to stand there open-mouthed as they watched their prey soar into the sky with a rapidity that left them desolate.

When I saw that I was out of range, my first concern was to examine my balloon carefully, to see whether I could entrust myself to it. The gondola was remarkably simple, but nevertheless offered the aerial voyager every comfort. It was not made of wood, nor metal, nor fabric, but of a substance that was malleable, flexible at will but as form as one could desire, stretching if the aeronaut required it but contracting according to his needs. That material was utterly unknown to me. The gondola was attached by asbestos cords to a large principal balloon surrounded by several small balloons, which the art of the voyager consisted in maneuvering by means of an electric machine in order to steer at will.

All of that was perfect in its simplicity and organization, and occupied so small a volume that while he was on the ground that the voyager could carry under his arm, without being overburdened, the enormous machine that, in its turn, carried him through the skies. It was admirable.

Before going any further with the inspection of my balloon and all the curious objects it possessed, however, I set about studying its mechanism of propulsion. That study was neither long nor difficult; what I had done previously on my own account in Caucasia during all my aerostatic experiments was extremely useful to my understanding and my skill. I was able to see—and I saw it with astonishment mingled with amazement—that I was fully in control. I only had to orientate myself with the aid of my telescope and compass, and take whatever direction my heart or me mind indicated as that of Paris.

I cannot describe to you, my friend, the sensations that assailed me in my gondola. Can you imagine my situation? I was the master of a secret for which I had been searching for ten years: a secret that all serious aeronauts had always sought; an immense, immeasurable secret; a secret whose effects are incalculable. Oh, you're proud at present of your tortoise-like carriages, your expensive wagons, heavy and bruising, your mechanical chargers that are stopped by the moving sands of the desert, water and steep mountain slopes. The intelligence of the thinker can stop now; there is nothing beyond aerostatics, master of distance and the entire world. No more roads to pierce, at great expense of men and money; no more gigantic bridges to extend over the waters or the mountain abysses; no more squandering of land in roads and constructions, no more long hours lost on the traveler's road; no more limits at which a neighbor's hand says: "pay, or you shall not pass!" No more strangers for any people. Fraternity! Fraternity!

How do I know what I thought and said in my gondola? My heart was overflowing with sensations, my voice trembling with emotion. I allowed myself to stretch myself out at full length, no longer saying anything, no longer looking at anything, but enjoying an ineffable joy, while my balloon made endless progress.

I don't know, my friend, whether I went to sleep then, but as I made a movement on the floor of my gondola it seemed to me that a small rod that I had not yet noticed made an effort to get into my hand, which I opened and closed immediately.

Oh, then the door of dreams opened wide in front of me. I was no longer dreaming only about the little wand, but the divine enchantress who had sent me her balloon, and the friend of a day—of a few hours, even—whom I had met in Lining and from I had been so abruptly separated. My mind followed them from afar; my eyes saw them both—all three of them, in fact; the third you know—heading for the capital of Zeeland, where I was arriving with them.

All minds were excited in the city, although the greatest calm reigned in the streets. The entire population, like the active population of a beehive, was incessantly going in and out, following the normal course of its affairs. No one seemed to see or divine the subterranean fire that was seeking to explode beneath their feet.

And yet, an immense conspiracy, long in preparation, fomented by a few fervent leaders, reinforced by the immense army of the actively discontented whom governments call revolutionaries, rendered more terrible still by the inertia of honest people, who never revolt but sometimes fold their arms to make governments expiate their incessant harassment, was rumbling dully in a few coverts of the city.

My attention was first attracted to a group of conspirators who were lying low in a wretched and dilapidated apartment on the sixth floor of a house of mean appearance. They were silent and thoughtful, listening attentively to a hot-headed orator who was speaking in a low voice and trying to infiltrate into their souls the venom that his own distilled. His words were those of a thief and a murderer; he was trying to prove that wealth only ought to belong to them, and that it was necessary to cut off heads that had risen too high with a single blow of an axe.

The opinion seemed welcome, and caused the listeners to smile frightfully.

"It's better," said one of the conspirators then, raising his head proudly, "to kill ten men who threaten us today than leave in their hands the scepter-stumps with which they will one day kill millions of our brothers."

"Bravo! Bravo!" they cried, in whispers.

The soothing orator, who only wanted ten heads for his share, was…guess, my friend! I wasn't surprised, myself. It was the Cadi's envious secretary from the Lining tribunal.

Relieved of his functions, he had found nothing better to do than become an assassin.

That man will go far, I said to myself. *Much further than his simpleton of a Cadi*—for whom my eyes searched everywhere, and whom I thought I glimpsed sitting quietly on the threshold of a house, in which I saw more conspirators, from whom he doubtless expected his daily dog-food and the hope of a better future for which he was incapable of working.

Men of that sort aren't birds of prey that kill; they're crows that devour carrion. Oh, I had judged the Cadi accurately in his court; I could have prophesied accurately enough what he would be until his dying day. The life of such men is an open book; it's sufficient to leaf through it to know their destiny.

While I was looking at the Cadi and his secretary my gondola seemed to experience a sudden shock. Thick darkness covered my eyes; it seemed that the houses and monuments of the city, which I had seen so clearly until then, were lost in a cold, penetrating fog...

Then I opened my eyes; I was awake. Awake! I think so, at least, since I recall having seen my balloon still cleaving the air with its usual rapidity—but it was doubtless only for a moment, for I felt my eyes close again immediately. Clarity seemed to return over the city of Trevig, but the city was no longer as peaceful as I had seen it previously.

All the houses, doors, windows and shops were closed, and there was a threatening agitation in the streets that frightened me. The streets were crowded with men in rags, hideously decked out with weapons and tawdry ornaments of all sorts, which made them resemble pillaging savages. Inside the houses, on the contrary, the greatest calm reigned; other men could be seen there lowering their heads and sitting down by their hearths, their arms folded over their chests, quietly waiting for the denouement of the drama that was playing out in the street. They were the honest people letting things take their course. Through all the gates of the city, meanwhile, I saw disarmed soldiers escaping, seemingly fearful of hearing the rallying cry, running away, doubtless to deafen themselves and forget the oath of fidelity they had sworn.

The spectacle seemed strange to me, but it soon disappeared from my eyes, which were absorbed by another spectacle that interested me singularly and gripped my heart with an unspeakable pain. Jeers suddenly rose up, and I saw a dense crowd emerging from a narrow street, chasing a few breathless men whose garments had been ripped to shreds. One of them went to hurl himself into a house whose door was open, to seek refuge there, but the door was slammed shut in front of him, in the midst of the mob's joyful cries.

That man, my friend, I recognized immediately: it was the judge from the tribunal in Lining, and the person who had just delivered him thus into the hands of his executioners was one of those honest faces whom he had cheated of justice a few days before.

The judge had his punishment, therefore—but the punishment was frightful, for he was knocked down and his body dragged through the streets. *God is just!* I cried, putting my hands over my eyes in order not to see any more. Perhaps the man had committed many injustices, either by virtue of incapacity, carelessness or malevolence; he had been punished— may God have mercy on him!

I opened my eyes again, quivering, but it was written that my heart would drink the chalice of bitterness to the dregs. In the middle of the square where the unfortunate judge had been struck down I saw a scaffold erected, in the middle of which a few somber men placed a block, and then an enormous axe whose like I had never seen before. The crowd was held back, and men hideously decked out in military garments and rags were guarding the scaffold with weapons in hand, gravely — with dignity, even—as if some great act of justice were about to be carried out. The executioner, who climbed up to his funereal platform at that moment, took the heavy axe in both hands and struck the pose of a man awaiting his victim. I had no more doubt then: a capital execution was about to take place.

A few cries, which were immediately suppressed, were soon heard in the distance; the crowd opened up and I saw a double line of soldiers suddenly form up, all the way to the foot of the scaffold. A man marched between them; his stride was noble, grave, devoid of arrogance; his head was bowed, as if his eyes dreaded encountering accursed faces. When he arrived at the foot of the scaffold, he raised his head in a dignified fashion, to examine the place of his torture...

Oh, my friend! A piercing scream escaped my mouth. I woke up, and was very happy; I was bathed in sweat, but I saw with pleasure that I was still in my gondola and that my balloon was making good progress.

I smiled at my dream and went back to sleep. I don't know whether the atmospheric altitude at which I was traveling was making me drowsy or whether there was some other reason, but scarcely had I woken up than I felt my eyelids closing, as if by a hand that was simultaneously heavy and gentle.

My dream recommenced; it was strange. I still found myself in Trevig, but at least I could no longer see the scaffold or the murder. The spectacle had changed completely. The city was joyful; the houses were all decorated with flags; the streets were filled with emblems of celebration, and triumphant arches had been erected in all the public squares. The king's palace was being decked out with splendid and cheerful illuminations.

My heart expanded with relief; I was finally able to breathe. While I was enjoying within myself the pleasure and joy that I saw in preparation for everyone, a brilliant and spirited cavalcade of mounted men suddenly emerged from the king's palace, some on mechanical chargers like ours, others on red deer or reindeer, as in the lands of the West. Embroideries, jewelry and decorations of all sorts ornamented all the riders.

A deafening cheer went up in honor of the king, who was at the head of the cavalcade, waving and smiling graciously at all the curiosity-seekers waiting for him to pass by.

To his right was a man strangely clad in a long white robe with broad sleeves, with a large collar falling over his shoulders, secured at the waist by a sort of hairy leather thong. His ugliness was phenomenal, capable of frightening the most tolerant with respect to the possibilities of human ugliness. He was short and thickset, his head half-hidden between his shoulders, which did not appear to be attached to his torso but to his ears. He had no neck. His face was in keeping with the rest, the face of a bull, entirely composed of a snout and a mouth; but there were also two eyes: two large eyes set beneath the brow like two craters emerging from beneath a large rock.

In the individual was not tall, by way of compensation, he was immeasurably broad. His limbs had incalculable proportions; they seemed to be designed to sustain and serve a colossus who had assuredly been forgotten.

If that man had reproaches to address to the creator of all things, however, he had compensated himself amply by covering his disgrace with sumptuous clothing, decorated with diamonds and rubies. His breast, like the walls of our civic temples to which we attach the decorations of those to whom the fatherland has granted them, was covered with insignia of origin unknown to me. An enormous scimitar, under which it would not have been good to fall in battle, hung from his belt. His head was covered by a sort of skullcap surmounted by a spike. From the summit of which sprang, like a foaming cascade, a flood of white feathers that fell to his shoulders. It was wonderful. I don't know whether the man could speak, but I saw him open his mouth several times as if to bellow. That was his manner of smiling at the people surrounding him.

I was trying to figure out who that man might be when the rumble of a raucous voice, when a contained by very energetic oath that made itself heard in my ears informed me that it was the illustrious Rhaman X, the Emperor of New Cosaquia.[20]

That ill-timed oath, which was audible to others than myself, gave me a high opinion of the swearer's courage, and I looked at him. It was the secretary of Lining's Cadi. Oh, I fully expected to find him there, proffering curses of envy and covetousness.

To the King of Zeeland's left was, in a grand official costume—guess who, my friend! The king's brother, my cicerone in Lining, to whom I sent an amicable salute—which he returned without affectation, as if without constraint. That man would have been a worthy citizen of Caucasia.

I was certainly dazzled by the splendors of so much magnificence, but I was not satisfied. What is the point, I asked myself, of all this phantasmagoria of command, this carnivalesque procession, this infantile demonstration? Would there not have been a more honest, more generous and more grandiose spectacle, to celebrate the arrival of a foreign prince, to show the prince who had come to see and the people who were looking at him?

Perhaps I was wrong, and perhaps my gibe was unjust, but I was pained to see serious men displaying so much pettiness, in wanting to show off their strength and grandeur. So I smiled, and my smile was sad. We are so unused to such parades in our worthy, severe and great Republic.

I was about to turn my eyes to the heavens, to see whether there might be a pitying smile there to reply to mine, when a final glance darted at the body of the procession fell directly upon my great devil from the cemetery in Copenhagen, my ally in Lining.

---

[20] Mettais probably borrowed the name Rhaman (but not the description offered here, which does not tally with later appearances of the character and is presumably tinted by the dream) from an 1845 painting by Eugène Delacroix of Muley Abd-ar-Rhaman, Sultan of Morocco.

At first, I was stunned by surprise; then my heart beat faster at a pleasant memory. I had no doubt that his lady, and mine, must be there. He was standing up straight, rigid and attentive, appearing only to have eyes for a carriage that was moving slowly ahead of him. I had no difficulty discovering therein the woman I desired so much to see. She saw me too, and graciously blew me a kiss. She was stunning in her beauty, clad in a costume that was unfamiliar to me, but which was simple and exquisitely tasteful.

To my great regret, that costume was stained by a few insignia of honor unknown to me, of which I could not divine the merit or the significance. I thought however, that they were indicative of a high status, and not, as I had been able to believe, a gracious adventuress or a divine witch.

Whatever she was, she had not forgotten me, and I was charmed by that. So, I was about to launch myself toward her carriage in reply to her kiss and take her in my arms, when I awoke...

I saw then, to my inexpressible surprise, that I was not in Trevig at all, but lying on the floor of my gondola. I had a little ivory wand in my hand, trivial in its length and breadth; I had no idea how it came to be there, but it did not seem to me to have either the strength or intelligence to have introduced itself without my being aware of it, even in my sleep. Had it played some part in my dreams? I am, my friend, too strong-minded a man to believe that. However, I cannot help pointing out to you that ever since my first encounter with the legitimate heir of the throne of France, I had not ceased, at every step I took, to run into some significant manifestation of witchcraft.

I uttered a deep sigh of relief when I acquired the conviction that everything I had seen and heard had only been a dream. What was not a dream, though, was the progress—the regular progress—of my balloon. Having slept for so long, I felt the need to consult my telescope and compass. It would not take me long to find out whether I still had a long way to travel before arriving at my destination, in Paris, where I ought to and wanted to find the woman who had promised to meet me there.

Alas, my friend, a thousand times alas! An evil genius was pursuing me doggedly, that was very evident. I was not heading in the direction in which I wanted to go. While I slept, a hostile wind had obviously driven my balloon in a direction other than the one in which I had initially steered...or was I the victim of my stupid credulity? Like a fool, I had believed in the solution of the great problem—the problem of the intelligent and controlled direction of aerostats—on the word of a savage; it was nothing of the sort.

I almost smiled with pride, my friend—for the problem remained to be solved, I told myself, and who could tell whether that honor might be reserved for me?

However, I reread the written instructions that I had in my pocket, and then examined the steering mechanism, and...I burst into laughter: strident laugher that was certainly undeserved. Was it a reproach addressed to my stupidity, or an outburst of anger over the time lost? No, my friend, no! It was because I had just recognized that my problem really was solved, and that I alone was culpable. I had operated the steering mechanism ineptly; I was, therefore, not heading westwards, in the direction I wanted to go. I was somewhere else—but where?

XIII. THE SUDANESE PENITENTIARY

Being uncertain as to where I was, I felt an urgent need to communicate with the ground. I therefore stopped my balloon and looked in all directions, in order to ascertain my position. I was over a vast extent of water, obviously the sea. My eyes did not take long to distinguish a black dot in the middle of that vast liquid expanse, which grew as I fixed my attention upon it. I took my balloon lower; the black dot was still growing, allowing me to distinguish vague masses that changed, as I drew closer, into houses, trees and rocks. Eventually, I saw that it was an island, and an inhabited island.

I had been seen. I steered my descent in such a way as to land in the middle of a field, in the idle of a host of laborers, who hastened toward me, bewildered by my singular arrival. I was not afraid, for I could not see any hostile expression in any of the visitors.

One of them, who was some way behind the others, parted the crowd, advanced toward me and bowed politely. His costume told me that he was a dignitary. He wore a long robe, as in our homeland, and had a woolen bonnet on his head—but the robe was checkered by embroidered along all the seams, and there was a gold tassel hanging from his bonnet. The others, except for two or here who accompanied the dignitary, equipped with metal arms and armor whose African origin I immediately recognized, were only wearing simple jackets buttoned over the chest, enclosing the waistband of trousers made of the same fabric, in the same color.

One might have taken them for a religious order at work, a college on vacation, or prisoners in a penitentiary. I did not recognize either the penitentiary or the country that had established it, for I had never seen any establishments of that sort or any of their employees—but I soon had confirmation that I was in a penitentiary.

"Sir," said the dignitary who had greeted me so civilly, "You are in the great penitentiary of Sudan, on the island of Tahiti, at the extremity of the great Ocean, about 3000 leagues from Timbuktu.[21] Your arrival here is doubtless involuntary, for I know that aerostats do not travel at the whim of those they transport, but while according you the hospitality you require, the administration of the penitentiary must appeal to your sound judgment in begging you not to be offended if it sets before your eyes the law that forbids landing on the island and abiding there without express orders."

The employee was, as is evident, exquisitely polite—which did not surprise me; I knew that such is the rule in the Sudan. An employee who acted otherwise would immediately be sacked and recognized as incapable of possessing any public employment. That people has understood how despicable the functionary is, who, being paid out of public funds—which is to say, funds amassed by the people—is insolent in his treatment of the people, which is his master, although it only commands him on great occasions, on days of revolution.

I declared then that I, as a citizen of Caucasia gone astray in the air, through which I was seeking a land that seemed to flee before me, and that I had only descended on the island, without knowing where I was, to recover somewhat from the fatigues of a difficult voyage.

No suspicion appeared to welcome my narration, and I became the guest of the functionary, who accommodated me with all graciousness that could have been extended to a friend. I was very touched by that fine welcome, which put me entirely a my ease, so I had no fear of seeming indiscreet in

---

[21] A French league is five kilometers, so this estimate gives the distance from Timbuktu to Tahiti as 15,000 kilometers, which is not far off the actual distance. It implies, however, that Daghestan's balloon has flown at least 17,000 kilometers since setting off from Zeeland, seemingly in less than a day: a prodigious speed for an aerostat.

asking for information about the penitentiary, which was given to me with all possible cordiality.

My host was not a dignitary of the highest rank, but he was an intelligent man, who did not think that he as lowering himself in accepting secondary functions. Moreover, he had confidence in the justice of his nation, and confessed without arrogance and without shame that the only hierarchy consulted in the administration of the Sudan was that of merit.

"I once traveled in Caucasia, sir," my host said to me, after the light meal that he had offered me, "where I learned to admire and love its citizens—but I believe that if you had also lived for a while in the Sudan, you would similarly have learned to admire and love us."

"I have lived there," I replied, "and I know your admirable nation slightly. After the government of Caucasia, yours is the one I would like the best, if it were set on a base more solid than the life of your Sheikh. In your country today, your government is the Sheikh; he is your happiness, your wisdom. When he dies, what will come after him, and what will your government be? Your right of inheritance is regrettable. Woe betide the nation that only has one man to sustain it! Woe betide the government that is entirely invested in one man."

My host replied: "My government—and I am not speaking as a man who hesitated to voice his thoughts for fear that the walls might hear him or the air might carry his words to tyrannical ears; liberty is so great among us that it only remains for us to take advantage of it—is, as you say, rare and admirable in its wisdom. So you will not be surprised when I tell you that the Sheikh has probably thought as you have about our base and our future, for he has provided for that eventuality. But we shall talk about that later; for the moment we have only to occupy ourselves with the penitentiary, about which you do not know and wish to know.

"It has existed for twenty years, since the second year of the reign of Fittri, our present Sheikh. It is rather well populated, as you see, but its population is not excessive for a country as large as ours. In any case, we all recognize and loudly declare that this is one of the finest results of our sheikh's philosophy.

"When Fittri came to the throne, the whole Sudan quivered in anticipation. His pure mind and sublime philosophy were well-known. There was only one dread, which was that he might renounce his inheritance, so little did he seem to care for the honors and advantages attached to royalty. Personally, I believe that he only accepted his position in order to do the good that he would not otherwise have been able to do.

"The first two years of his reign were employed by him in studying the needs of those who are called his subjects, but whom he himself called his brothers. But how do you think he carried out that study? Do you think that he could be content to ask for statistics from all parts, opinions and information from all the particular administrations of the kingdom? No: he set forth, not with a numerous escort and couriers advertising the coming of the king along his route, nor with a deceptive incognito shouted from the rooftops a month in advance, but with a few intimate and devoted friends, perfectly familiar with his projects, without any fuss, and unidentified to the extent that he needed in order to conduct his business. He went to knock on the doors of all the administrations; he interrogated the great, the rich, the poor, the people of all parties—and he did so for two years. Then the reforms were made. The legal code was erased; the old customs that were still appropriate to the new ores of Sudan were reinscribed there, along with the new decrees that the present civilization demanded.

"It was in that era that the idea of our penitentiary germinated, and an important question was resolved—that of the right of death that all governments believe they have over those submissive to their society. I can still recall the royal edict issued at that time; it is in my opinion, the work of a great philosopher. This is what it said, or very nearly:

"*Inhabitants of the Sudan*, our Sheikh said, *called by the hazard of my birth to the honor of representing and guiding our society in his corner of the earth through the miseries of life, I have carefully weighed the laws that our forefathers have handed down to us. What they have done, I believe that they have done well; it is not for us to judge today the necessities in which they found themselves formerly; but our situation is different—at least, I think so—and our laws ought therefore to be different. You will accept them if you wish. Those who are unsympathetic to them, if they are in a substantial minority, will be free to create a new state in a corner of our fatherland and live there as they wish; we shall facilitate that with all possible means. Those who accept them, will have done so seriously, and they will be punished seriously for their infraction.*

"Among these punishments, however, I do not believe I have the right to insert capital punishment. That is my conviction. Human beings, I am told, have rights and duties of two kinds, as no one can contest: the natural rights and duties that they obtain from God, which cannot be alienated; and social rights and duties, which they accept by remaining in the societies that have adopted them.

"Against the former, I can evidently do nothing; I cannot arrogate to myself the right to undo what God has done, to prevent on my personal authority the execution of an order that God gave to humans when creating them: go forth and live! But I believe that I do have the authority to protect the society to which we consent by expelling from its bosom those who wish to destroy it, and making it impossible for them to do so. I shall therefore inflict on them, instead of death, a grave and frightful penalty, which will punish the guilty and serve as a lesson and deterrent to ill-disposed natures...

"That sir, is the origin of our great penitentiary.[22] We have no more scaffolds over there, no more gibbets, no more

---

[22] In presenting this argument, Mettais is obviously deliberating on the controversy surrounding the French penal colony in the Caribbean that came to be known as Devil's Island, which had been set up in 1852. He was well aware, of course, that Napoléon III had founded the colony primarily in order to accommodate 237 hard-line Republicans who had opposed his

executioners, but we have here labor of every sort, hard for those indomitable natures that have always existed and always will exist, more or less gentle for others, according to the sentence passed on them. Everyone has his corner of the island; we even have the corner of repentance, from which the justice of the Sudan occasionally extracts a convict to return him to society, where his crime, perhaps excusable in many countries, is not in our own.

"A murderer, therefore, comes here. He comes here firstly to be subjected to his punishment, and then to serve as an example to those excessively facile hands which are always ready to satisfy their slightest caprice with dagger-thrusts. He may leave, eventually, if his crime is remissible, but there are guilty men on the island who will never leave. Their evil nature is incorrigible, their crimes so atrocious, so coldly cruel, that they leave no room for indulgence. I do not even know whether repentance can count for anything other than to reduce the harshness of their labor. Society needs severity, in order not to be troubled in its existence."

I was listening to my host with an attention that encouraged ardor, and he continued: "Punishments are not spared here; the labor is incessant, the corrections severe, but without cruelty. The prisoners are given what they need to live, nothing more. There is no consolation for them, nor hope; only repentance and good conduct bring a few ameliorations to their punishment."

"But your convicts seem to me to be free," I said to my host. "Can evil natures not abuse that freedom?"

"A man who commits murder," he replied, "is chained like a ferocious beast to some rock, which no one goes near." My host looked at me with horribly interrogative eyes. "Do

---

coup d'état, and that its employment as a dumping ground for thieves and murderers was something of an afterthought. Mettais could not know that the Second Empire would fall in 1870, and that the leaders of the short-lived Paris Commune would also be shipped off to the prison colony.

you understand how frightful that punishment is? In consequence, no one commits murder here.

"As for revolt, if ever the convicts were to think of it, behold the cannon aimed at the island, which form a wall of fiery mouths. The order is to fire without pity, for that is a case of legitimate defense, in which it is impossible for the slightest doubt to infiltrate. If the men want to kill us, joining forces, taking up arms and hurling themselves upon us to kill us, we shall kill them; every one of us has received the order to guard and defend the life that God has given us. Society does not want to punish an unarmed man, but it defends its life. It is, in any case, a life for a life; it's better to protect that of the innocent that that of the guilty.

"That, sir, is how we reason in the Sudan, since the great penal reform," my host said, trying to read my approval in my face, "and I do not think we have any murderers among us than elsewhere. It is always regrettable to kill a man, in whom there is not often a hopeless perversity, and we give him the means of returning to society while punishing him. For the hardened murderer, the professional assassin, is it best to punish him by death? Our island is harder for him, I assure you."

"Your logic is admirable, sir," I told him. "It is astonishing that it has gone uncomprehended for so long."

My interlocutor smiled thinly. You're young, sir," he said, "and you have the inexperience of your age. People talk for centuries about the necessity of abolishing an article in their code, and never get around to it. The article will only be abolished by a bloody revolution...always provided that the eye of the revolutionaries is focused upon it; otherwise, it will require another revolution, perhaps a third or fourth for its abolition. Governments proceed like tortoises; it is only revolutions, which always do immense harm, that have the knack of attaching machines to them and making them go full steam ahead...unless, they chance to find a Sheikh like ours, in order for the revolution to occur gently and without catastrophe."

I had been hearing talk for some time, my friend, about that great Sudanese penitentiary. I had always wanted to see it and discover whether it's renown as justified—but I also knew that one could not land there, and that the government had taken all the precautions suggested by science to make sure that no vessel could even arrive within some distance of the island without permission. I don't blame the government for that. Its Inferno should not, under any pretext, become a place of hope for the pitiless murderer that justice has imprisoned there as in a tomb, to await the day of divine justice. An unexpected hazard had granted my wish, but I now knew all about the penitentiary that I desired to know, so I got ready to leave be the same route that had brought me here.

On broaching that subject, my host laughed at me with all the politeness of which he as capable, and confessed his incredulity. I had but one means to convince him, albeit a excellent one, which was to release my aerostat, steering it as he wished, and I was about to propose that when he said to me: "If you assure me that your balloon can progress as you desire, I will believe you, sir; but I pray you, in the light of that confession and its demonstration, to consent to visit the governor of our island. You have landed here without his permission, but you ought not to leave without it. A stranger has arrived among us, where no one has come before; our governor ought to see that stranger and learn from him what I have learned from you, sir."

The functionary had a duty to fulfill, and the last thing in the world I wanted was to cause him to fail in that duty I therefore accepted the invitation to pay my respects to the governor of the penitentiary, to reveal to him the reasons or my presence there, and then to depart immediately.

The governor opened his eyes wide with astonishment on seeing me arrive, and opened them wider still when I had explained to him how I had fallen into his empire and how I intended to leave. He had the discretion not to laugh at my pretention, but he proposed a surer means, which was to take me by boat to the nearest island, where his government had a small fleet stationed, to maintain communication between the region and the motherland, passing via various ports of other realms, in any one of which he could set me down as I wished.

The offer could not have been more obliging, but did not serve my purpose. I did not want to go to the Sudan, or anywhere else in that direction. I had made a mistake in my itinerary and fallen into the Sudanese penitentiary, but I wanted and was able to rectify that itinerary by steering my balloon better, and I replied gratefully but firmly that my balloon was at least as sure a means and, in any case, quicker and more agreeable than a boat and a ship, that the surprise and incredulity of the governor did not hurt me at all, for my balloon was probably the first that progressed under the control to the traveler, and that I would offer to take one or two people up with me to demonstrate the truth of what I as saying.

"Since you are speaking seriously, sir," the governor replied, "I will respond in the same fashion. I believe you, admire you and will accept your proposal. I have an urgent dispatch to send to my government; by boats and ships are fast, but certainly not as swift as your aerostat. Would you consent to deposit the bearer of the dispatch in Timbuktu?"

I could not refuse; one does not refuse a service requested in that manner. For me, moreover, it was only a few days' journey, if I hurried my little balloon slightly. I saw no great inconvenience in delaying my voyage to Paris by a few days. I therefore accepted the governor's proposal, while smiling at a private thought. My smile was slightly ironic, and did not escape the governor's notice.

"Speak, sir," he said. "You have an idea to communicate to me, and I think that idea is biting down on us slightly with an uncharitable tooth. No matter! Speak."

"This gentleman and I have discussed the Sudan," I said, pointing to the functionary who had welcomed me on my arrival, and who was still there, "and many good things have been said about it—enough to give me pause for thought. I have thought about it so much that I am even wondering whether our Caucasia, which I am accustomed to regard as a model of government and civilization, is not inferior to yours in certain respects."

"Aha!" sighed the excellent governor, in satisfaction.

"But..."

"Oh—a but!" the governor said, sarcastically. "I expected as much."

"But you told me just now, Governor, that you have an urgent dispatch to send to Timbuktu."

"Yes, very urgent."

"And that your ships are not as fast as my aerostat."

"You've said so."

"And it's true. Well, do you know how our urgent dispatches traverse our republic in a few minutes, with neither ships not balloons?"

"Pardon me, my good sir, but I shall tell you that in six months," the governor elide triumphantly. "Come back in six months, when out electric telegraph will be established between Timbuktu and Tahiti. We began laying the submarine cable that will produce that marvel a few days ago." Bowing graciously, the governor added: "The honor, moreover, is due to you sir, for it is to Caucasia that we owe the prodigy—the immense, incommensurable prodigy—that suffices in itself to give our epoch the superiority that it has also acquired by so many other entitlements, but that no one here disputes in the name of past centuries. The past never suspected that a day would come when people would be able to speak to one another over fabulous distances by means of a iron wire, privately, without any interruption, for several minutes. In fact, it confounds the human mind." With an enthusiasm I admired, the governor cried: "Oh, why can we not invite all the peoples of the old world to the banquet of our civilization?"

"Since it is a Caucasian who has invented the electric telegraph, Governor," I replied, "that is enough to tell you that we established it there some time ago, in all our provinces, cities, villages and even hamlets—it is, in a word, our postal service."

"Well, sir, we shall follow you," the governor replied, with a gracious smile. "But in the meantime..."

"In the meantime," I resumed, understanding my interlocutor's thought completely, "I shall deposit your man and your dispatch in Timbuktu in a few days."

I saw with pleasure that the dispatches were put into the hands of my host, the functionary, who climbed into my gondola confidently. I took my bearings then with the aid of my usual instruments, and allowed my balloon to rise slowly into the air; then, giving the steering mechanism the required force and direction, I waved to the governor, whose eyes were following us with the greatest interest, and we departed with the rapidity of an arrow.

I don't know whether the confidence of the governor of the penitentiary had been entirely won over, but I have no reason to think that he sent the same dispatches simultaneously by ship.

XIV. TIMBUKTU

Our journey was unremarkable. We completed it in less than two days. Dusk was falling when we arrived at Timbuktu—with the result that we were able to landing the city without attracting overmuch attention from the curious. I was not displeased by that.

My traveling companion left me immediately in order to deliver his dispatch, then came back to find me. He seemed to like me a great deal, and wanted to be of use me, as much as he could, in the immense capital of the Sudan. I did not refuse his services, because I knew that capital more by renown than experience, and I knew no more of its language than I had been taught in school—which is to say, enough for an educated man to follow what I said. In the ordinary course of a day, however, I could not rely on only encountering educated people.

The Sudanese, my friend are one of the most civilized peoples of the modern era. They are the head, the mind and the heart of Africa. All their neighbors render them that homage in sending their children to learn or improve themselves in the Sudan's schools. Governments themselves do not disdain to ask advice as to the organization of its private and public institutions, in order to establish good order and prosperity in their own lands.

I do not know how ancient the Sudan is; it is said to date back much further than other countries, but I think the same principle applies there as elsewhere. Every people dips its pen in the ink of vanity to some extent, in order to write its history, and thinks itself more respectable the older it is. Not only is the Sudan as old as the earth, but it has always held the place that it occupies today in Africa, always dominating its neighbors. Its star once shone with a brilliant gleam, which extended as far as the most distant lands...they say.

126

Poor vanity! There are historians of contestable merit in the Sudan, however, men of superior intelligence. I am astonished that none of them has given consideration to an old popular legend of unknown origin that runs around the streets, Perhaps a less brilliant origin or antiquity can be found therein. Would you permit me, my friend to say a few words about it? You can judge it thereafter as you wish. It is the first verse of a song that has no less than ninety-five. It goes:

Would you like to know, my friends (repeat)
The legend of the black man? (repeat)
The Peuhs say, lamentably.
That the black man is the Devil;
When we all know full well
That the black man is Sudanese.[23]

This popular song is included in a charming collection of antique naivety, among the legends. A long dissertation that precedes it proves, however, that not all the historians of today look at it indifferently.

According to the author of the dissertation, the black man is the enemy demon, or...but forgive me, my friend, I will spare you all the suppositions, which are not few in number, about the black man of legend. As I am not involved in the pride of the Sudan, however, I shall feel free to wonder, outside of all interested supposition, whether, by chance, the black man might simply be the ancient inhabitant of the Sudan, as the song says, even though that variety of the human species appears to be extinct today. The idea in question is strongly reinforced, for me, by the account of a few travelers

---

[23] I could not retain the rhyming couplets of the original without distorting the meaning too much—which is, of course, of the essence. I have also left Peuh as it is because it is here being used as the name of a tribe, as the English equivalent of the identically-spelled French scornful expression (Pooh) never was.

who have assured me that they have encountered individuals with black skin in a few remote islands belonging to the Sudan—completely black, of a shiny, oily black, if it they had been painted or varnished. Their hair, it seems, is frizzy or wooly, their forehead low, their noses flattened, their lips thick and their cheekbones vey prominent—worthy ancestors of the Sudanese, in fact, for these characteristics are precisely those of the present day Sudanese, although modified and embellished to the degree we see today. Their present manifestation has always led the Sudanese to be considered as a variety of our white race, from which they only differ by virtue of their swarthy, slightly coppery tint.

The Sudanese, moreover, although they are not cited for their beauty, represent a type that is not without grace, in being exceptional.

Anyway, my friend, I have given you these ideas for you to make of them what you will, and I certainly do not take responsibility for answering all questions on that variety, the primitive type of which is, apparently, extinct. Where does it come from? Why is it different from the others? I do not want to sustain the above thesis, not seek to explain one of the thousands of mysteries that nature has taken pleasure in sowing around us, to exercise the sagacity and patience of scientists—unless it intended to set us in contention against one another...

My traveling companion doubtless allowed himself to be pressed by the minister to whom the dispatch was addressed to tell him the details of our journey. Nor had he omitted to lavish eulogies upon me and my vehicle.

The Sudanese are no strangers to progress. Any science or at that is unknown there, but is suspected, is researched. Aerostatics is no more unknown there than in our own land, and there too, for a long time, as everywhere else, the capital question of the voluntary direction of balloons has been addressed. What my friend said thus appeared so marvelous that the minister conceived the desire to see my balloon and its owner.

In more than one country, even civilized ones, the inventor of such a marvel would have spent a long time soliciting his government for the honor of donating it to his nation. Perhaps he would never have obtained anything from his communication but laughter, mocking gibes, or, at most, a smile of incredulity or indifference. It is not like that in the Sudan. The king wants to see everything and assess everything, and if he cannot do it himself, he still wants everything to be seen and assessed—woe betide anyone who refuses without looking, and looking seriously.

In many countries, too, if some highly-placed individual had consented to investigate a useful discovery and to interrogate the inventor, the first duty of civilization, politeness, would certainly have been lacking, in favor of the pretensions of pride; under the pretext of dignity, I would have been summoned by the minister, to demand a service from me. In the Sudan, however, there is none of that pride; the minister came directly to me, to my hotel, where he had himself introduced by my traveling companion. He was admirable in his frankness, amiability and grace. My reasoning with respect to my balloon convinced him; an experiment then followed. I had come from Tahiti in less than two days, and directly, at will. He invited me not to leave Timbuktu without seeing and being presented at the Court, however little I desired it.

The proposal was quite appealing to me, for I had no greater desire than to see the Sheikh of Sudan, the philosopher-king who had no subjects, but brothers, no kingdom, but a vast family to render happy. My friend had told me so many good things about him that, in truth, I was glad of the opportunity to discover whether he had not exaggerated slightly, and whether there really was a worthy citizen of Caucasia on the throne of Sudan.

The next day, I had to return the visit that the minister had made to me; my presentation at Court was therefore postponed until the day after. I could not go any faster without being impolite. In spite of the desire I had to leave Timbuktu promptly in order finally to reach the goal of my voyage.

As that arrangement of my official visits left me at least two full days of liberty, therefore, I resolved to take advantage of those two days to study the city and its mores a little, and in order not to waste such precious time, I immediately set to work in the company of my new friend. I set about touring Timbuktu with him, opening my eyes as wide as possible in order to listen attentively to my cicerone.

The city of Timbuktu is the largest, the most beautiful and the most flourishing in Africa. Situated on the Nigerian Sea, an immense lake that does not communicate with any other sea, it is enclosed in a peninsula formed by a branch of the lake and the river Tabou, which flows into it. That situation is admirable.

Whether Timbuktu was always there is a serious question at present, my friend. The Sudanese savants are debating it keenly. They are in agreement on one point, however, which is that the present-day Timbuktu is not the original Timbuktu—but some claim very insistently to have discovered the foundations of the ancient city in recent works carried out on the Timbuktu peninsula, while others deny it and affirm with equal assurance that wherever it was, the Timbuktu of yore was not there. The latter base their opinion on a colorful dissertation that is not without interest for a lover of ancient civilization. It runs as follows.

The Timbuktu of old, they say, was not, like that of to-day, the largest city of the Sudan; it was called Sankore. Taken and retaken several times by nomadic tribes that pillaged it, then rebuilt it at their convenience, that city flourished by virtue of growing large enough to seem important It was adventurers from Morocco who established themselves there most solidly and created the famous quarter of Sane-Songu, so celebrated for its wealth in the old legends. It was also that quarter which most tempted the greed of a few neighboring tribes, especially the Touaregs and the Berbechs, who mounted armed attacks on its alternately. The Touaregs were even strong enough to install themselves and maintain possession of one of the city's quarters, which they fortified. It is generally believed that it is to that time that it is necessary to credit the sovereign power of El-Bakay, one of the most famous Sheikhs of the ancient Sudan.

If that prince was brave, slightly civilized and the fortunate founder of the Sudanese monarchy, we should not demand too many virtues in order to glorify, for he was in reality little more than a bandit chief. But let us not blush too much, my friend; more than one of our present celebrities, in all genres, have similar forgotten origins. What do origins matter, after all? Every man for himself. Do I think about the source of a river when I find the abundance of water that I need at its mouth? In the same way, I do not make a habit if estimating a people, or an individual, by what their ancestors were; it is by what they are today that I need to judge them.

At any rate my friend, the Moroccans, the Peuhs, and Sour'eyens, the Berbechs and the Touaregs who partially invaded that poor city of Timbuktu—or, more correctly, Sankore—being unable to live there in peace and not finding it comfortable, while fighting among themselves and persecuting the indigenes, resolved to abandon their old and unfortunate fatherland. They were able, to that effect, to take everything that was most precious to them into the peninsula, where the new city is located today, which then contained only a few poor fishermen's huts. They fortified it in a redoubtable manner, and then, on an agreed day, they all escaped from the city, which was, at that moment, in a state of complete anarchy. The anarchists who remained behind continued to fight one another, so effectively that the city was completely destroyed after a relatively short time and rendered utterly uninhabitable.

The new city on the peninsula was given the name Timbuktu; the other never rose again from its ruins.[24]

_____

[24] The city referenced here as "the other" Timbuktu, on the Niger River, was still a mysterious place in the early 19th century—so much so that the Societé de Géographie offered a 10,000-franc prize in 1824 to the first non-Muslim to get into the city and report back on it; the prize was claimed in 1828

131

The Sudanese of Timbuktu, whether they be Peuh, Touareg or anything else, bear no resemblance today to the sons of a brigand. They are the most civilized and polite people in the world. I think, though, that their character is more acquired than natural. Their politeness contains too much benevolence for it to be fundamental to their nature.

Nature is in them as it in all humans, my friend; I shall not make an exception of them. It is nothing but pride and malevolence—let that be said without flattery, as without hatred; it is my conviction, and would be yours too if you cared think about it a little. It does not matter; their pride and malevolence are in chains for the time being.

How can you expect, in fact, my friend, that people who lack nothing, not even pleasures, would allow themselves to be governed by evil passions, and not be amiable toward their brother—in sum, polite? And that is the work of a powerful genius, the preset Sheikh, who has been able to create laws, not for himself and is favorites, but for everyone. His favorites, in any case, are not a coterie or a caste, a few fortunate individuals, but everyone.

His Code, unlike ours, is very complicated, even intricate. The prince wanted to anticipate everything, conciliate everything, obviate everything. I don't blame him for that, since he thought he was doing good, and although I don't like

---

by René Caillée. By the time Mettais was writing, it was known that Timbuktu had once had a reputation for wealth, and had been repeatedly conquered in the previous 500 years, more than once by the Touaregs, at least once by the Songhai Empire and at least once by the Moroccans, who had briefly made it their capital. Its one real claim to distinction was its possession of the Sankore Madrassah (i.e. University), which at one time had the largest book collection in Africa since the Great Library of Alexandria. Although that Timbuktu was not annexed by the French until 1893, when it briefly became part of "French Sudan," it would have been squarely in the sights of their colonial ambitions in 1865.

a code to be a dense forest in which the path of the law is difficult to find, I shall not rebel against him. It is up to the man who does the work to assess the difficulties of the work and the means of overcoming them. Perhaps it is as well, after all, to leave nothing to the free appreciation of the judge, whose intelligence is no always equal to that of the legislator.

When one examines that Constitution closely, one cannot help being struck dumb with admiration in the presence of the profound philosophy and the profoundly practical reasoning established there.

Making a law is easy; making a good law is difficult; making a perfect law is impossible—but the most impossible thing of all is to make that law work. That achievement is sublime, when it approaches most closely the justice for which the law was made. The law is a dead good, we say in Caucasia; what that means is that it is not the legislator but the judge who gives it life.

But the judge! Oh. My friend, you know what I think of that poor man, whose nature is made of the same clay as everyone else.

In the Sudan, however, the position of the judge is simple, for it is the law that reigns and governs. The Sheikh himself is inevitably submissive to the law, and a judge can condemn his acts freely and conscientiously, without having anything to fear. The Sheikh has foreseen all that in advance; he is the one who wanted the judge no longer to be dependent on anyone but his conscience. But a conscience, although clear, might fail one day. Who can say, in fact, whether, beneath that healthy and vigorous bark, there might not be a gnawing worm that will appear when its time comes?

The Sheikh has also asked himself that question, and it is quite natural that he did, since he put himself, like everyone else, under the dependency of the judge. The problem is not easy to resolve, and yet he has resolved it. How? For that, he descended into the depths of the human heart, fathomed the motives of all its actions, and finally discovered two powerful motors, as powerful as conscience in almost everyone and more powerful in a good many: self-interest and fear. He has, therefore, made appeal to those two motors, which he has suspended over the judge's head, not as a menacing sword but as a pleasantly-perfumed flower, sufficiently odorous and sharp to impregnate all his thoughts.

The self-interest for the judge who judges well is considerable in the Sudan, for all honors and social advantages will one day be awarded to him. That is good—but that motive was still not sufficient for the Sheikh, who reinforced it with that of fear. Yes, my friend, fear.

Why shouldn't fear, in fact, command a judge with its salutary voice, since it certainly commands the accused, and often the innocent? Before the accused sit severe judges, brutal force, the menacing code, anxiety and public opinion, always so terrible; in sum: fear. Why should fear not also come to sit beside the judge—not to trouble his conscience, of course, and not to threaten his words and judgment, but to say to him softly and benevolently: "Take care! Don't go to sleep on your seat; summon all your attention to the case you are judging; learn, if you do not know; abstain, if you cannot learn; forget that you are a human being in order to recall that you are justice. Take care, in sum—or else...or else your judgment and your future will find themselves facing a very redoubtable judge, facing public opinion..."

The Sudanese judge, my friend, sitting on his official chair, must indeed tremble for his future, for if honors are waiting for him one day, he will only have them on the day in question on the judgment of the public voice, at the bar of the people, to which the Sheikh has determined that he will be deferred in his turn.

All that is very good, in my opinion, and yet the Sheikh decided that it was still not enough. He wanted to ensure that fear would not cease to clarify the conscience of the judge for a single instant, and for that he wanted an eye to be continuously open on the least of his judgments. To obtain that excellent result, a judiciary newspaper is published every day; it witnesses all the preliminary conciliatory meetings as well as the judiciary and definitive meetings. The newspaper has its subscribers; in addition, it has a subsidy sufficient for it to be sent to all the localities that have not subscribed and posted in public places in sufficient numbers.

Do you see, my friend, how the judge might then be judged himself, by everyone, and the condemned rehabilitated, if the sentence imposed upon him is unjust? Do you see how careful the judge must be to bring in a decision as sound as he can make?

I shall not tell you anything about judiciary appeals, which are multiple there, as they are everywhere else, but are without expense and harassments, even for the smallest cases. I forgot to mention that the law is free of charge in the Sudan. In that fortunate land, there is no desire to sell a right that is natural and one of the principal bases of the social contract. That which is sold, they say, is not accessible to everyone, and justice is everyone's right.

That principle, fortunately, is no more scorned among us as in the Sudan, and is older, for it dates in the Sudan from the present Sheikh, who might have borrowed it from us, as I believe I can say that he has borrowed several other institutions from us.

One institution that he has not appropriated, however, which I would be glad to see functioning in Caucasia, is that of corporations.

XV. THE CORPORATIONS OF THE SUDAN

The present Sheikh of the Sudan, Fittri, appears to me to have but one passion, that of the public good. To accomplish that good, he thought that the political association of which he was the head was insufficient, that it only protected his subjects against violent dangers from without and within, and that it would be good if there were another, more intimate more everyday and more efficacious, association to defend them from poverty.

He would certainly been able to obtain that result by drawing upon the government purse, as we do in Caucasia, to bandage all social wounds and provide for everyone's needs. He did not want to. More profoundly philosophical than our legislators, he thought that mutual aid would produce other benefits than that of the relief of poverty—and he was right for it also encourages civic dignity and self-respect, and tightens the bonds of fraternity.

The citizens of the Sudan thus have a special bond that links them in groups to the bosom of the fatherland and gives them the strength of family union. It is the professional association, the corporation. Everyone, therefore—even those who seem the least occupied—is placed in the category of a profession, either according to his work or according to his inclinations. To be a member of a corporation, moreover, it is not necessary to be rich or to be a skilled worker; it is sufficient to prove that one is competent in the work of the corporation or that one can pay a sufficient membership fee. All the advantages of the corporation, however large it might be, are then assured to the associate.

The Sheikh himself is a member of a corporation.

Membership of a corporation is not a matter of caprice, which can be arranged and broken at will. The law in severe in this respect; it has anticipated everything.

The organization of these corporations is remarkably simple, so they function effortlessly. Every corporation, of course, is independent, but if it has its own particular rules, that does not hinder in any way the common action of corporations and the functioning of the governmental association. On the contrary, every association is intimately attached to the social unity by general laws that affect everything in their life.

Perhaps, my friend, I have gone more deeply into the idea that gave birth to these corporations and the objective they attempt to attain—the extinction of poverty—than I have studied their statutes, but this is what I think I have learned.

Their mechanism, in brief, appears to me to be that of our tontines,[25] our life insurance, but with a few differences, especially in the creation of capital.

The associate, while he works, is bound to contribute—and does so automatically, everything being arranged for him—a certain percentage of his wages: five per cent, I believe, for those with an annual income below 2000 francs, ten per cent above that. These capitalized sums only serve the associates in instances of illness, unemployment or old age. The pension or assistance, of course, is in proportion to the deposits.

---

[25] A tontine is nowadays imagined as a kind of wager, in which a group of individuals pool and invest all or part of their wealth, with the last survivor to scoop the compounded pool—thus giving rise to incentives for murder that novelists have often found useful in plotting—but when first envisaged, at the end of the 18th century, tontines were envisaged as a primitive form of life insurance, at a time of high and uncertain mortality. The insurance and pensions industry had made some advances by 1865, but had not attained anything like the sophistication they subsequently acquired in the 20th century, with the result that most of the ideas that seem fresh and ingenious to Daghestan and Mettais are perfectly familiar to us, although experience has taught us to see certain drawbacks that they could not.

These subscriptions do not appear to be an inconvenience to anyone, and everyone considers them to be an advantageous investment of his funds—a safer investment than any other he might imagine. Thus, one sees wealthy society-members paying well above the basic subscription, in order to obtain a more considerable pension in future.

In sum, my friend, the advantages of these associations are, in my opinion, immense. I cannot tell you everything about them at the moment; I hope to be able to compensate you at a later date. I cannot, however, resist telling you briefly about another marvel they produce, which is that with the subscription, however small it might be, every associate can, if he wishes, give a complete education to his children from their earliest youth to the age when they choose a profession. To that effect there are perfectly-adapted institutions possessing all the desirable comforts, which are maintained by the general purse of the association. It's quite simply admirable...

The statues of these associations generally seem to be very wise, but I have found one severity that our sensibility would certainly criticize, although it is logical. They grant all that it is necessary to grant, but only in accordance with right and duty; they are pitiless with respect to the idle and the unwilling, who receive, I believe, just enough food not to die of starvation, and are continually subject to a surveillance that would weary and recall to duty those whose hearts are not entirely dead.

Every corporation, as I have said, my friend, has its rules and funds, but by virtue of an admirably extensive foresight, there is another association between the funds, like the one between the members of the same profession. Every fund therefore contributes a determined annual sum to that association, and the sum of all those contributions constitutes a general fund that comes to the aid of funds depleted by unforeseen accidents and those whose revenues are inadequate to their habitual needs and to the maintenance of educational institutions. That fund also serves to maintain the unfortunate disabled individuals whom no corporation could admit to its bosom without eating into its budget inordinately.

Do not believe, my friend, that this professional enrolment takes away any of the liberty of the associates. Every associate may move as he wishes within his profession, increasing or diminishing his affairs, working or resting, doing this or that without hindrance or espionage. As, however, there is a solidarity between himself and his corporation, even if it is only a solidarity of honor, the corporation keeps an eye on him and can inspect his affairs from above if necessary. Thus, any associate who has not succeeded in his enterprise is subject to judiciary monitoring by the corporation; his conduct is carefully examined, his business severely but impartially scrutinized. If he is guilty of recklessness, bad management or incompetence he is punished, and the penalty might go as far as declassification from the corporation. His debts—his legitimate debts, at least—remain the responsibility of the corporation, but primarily his own. Payment is only withheld when it would compromise the society's services and that of the culpable associate.

The severity of the corporation in this respect, which is far from being a bad thing, is, moreover, largely compensated by another ingestion of the society in the affairs of the associate. An associate brought before a tribunal for a misdemeanor or a crime is always assisted by the corporation's counsel, who lends him the support of his advice and moral strength.

All that is very good, in my opinion, but what I found even better is the disinterest of the Sheikh, the primary instigator of the establishment of these corporations, who, instead of seeking to retain them in his hands, has left them independent of government. The government has no other leverage on them than they have on their members; it affords them protection from above, and nothing more. In exchange, they furnish it with all the subjects it needs. It is rare for the Sheikh to choose a servant directly; when necessary, he addresses himself to the committees of the corporations, who send him a list of the most capable people, from which he makes his choice.

The committees, who are in daily contact with all their members, are. He says, much better able to judge people than he is. It is unusual for the government ever to have cause for complaint about this mode of recruitment, which also has the advantage of closing the door on favoritism.

The fact is that since my arrival in Timbuktu, the few contacts I had had with various employees had only given me a high opinion of their capability and good will. I was genuinely amazed by one governmental action so rare that it is necessary, my friend, for me to tell you all the details so that you might admire its wisdom. I shall only tell you briefly, saving discussion for later.

One morning, which I was strolling with my gracious cicerone, I saw a middle-aged man with a grave expression pass by, with a portfolio under his arm.

"He's a physician," my new friend told me. "He's going to visit his patients. He writes his notes in that portfolio; they'll probably be checked in the course of the day by a competent inspector, who is at liberty to observe the patient himself to monitor the treatment the latter is receiving."

My friend added: "That's because we take the health and life of our fellow citizens seriously here. We don't abandon them to the caprices and possible errors of one man. We think that it's not sufficient, in order to be a wise, far-sighted and enlightened physician, to have received a diploma after passing a few miscellaneous examination. Here, therefore, the law never abandons a physician to his own devices, or the life of a patient to the uncertain calculations of a single individual.

"That man has every right to our confidence, however, for he only obtains his title after rigorous trials. He can only aspire to working alone after having spent five years under the tutelage of a experienced man, to whom he serves as an aide, while acquiring alongside him the skill and surety of judgment that make a good practitioner. But don't think that he is then abandoned to himself—oh no!

"Firstly, he has for our guarantee, and for his own too, that portfolio you saw and its notes, and the daily inspection.

Furthermore, he is obliged, for years, to give a public demonstration every three months, which is very similar to an examination, forcing the physician to keep his knowledge up to date while revealing incapacity if, by chance, an incompetent has been artful enough to snare a diploma.

"All that is arduous, but you'll agree, too, that nothing is more important to people than health and life. Physicians are, moreover, handsomely recompensed for all this study and surveillance by the respect accorded to them and the honoraria they receive. These honoraria are levied on the funds of each corporation that contributes to the funds of the medical corporation, which takes responsibility for its remunerations. Those remunerations always take the form of a annual salary. The patient owes nothing to the physician himself but gratitude for a benefit.

"Physicians are only required to make two visits per day—one in the morning and one in the afternoon—if necessary, for bedridden patients. Those who can travel to the doctor's domicile ought not to summon him to theirs; for them there is a consultation office open every day in every district at the same times. It is not the visiting physicians who man that office. We also have medical posts open day and night, for accidents and emergency cases that cannot wait for the visiting physicians.

"These different services are not always maintained by the same individuals; the wise corporation does not overload its members and does not make their work too burdensome. Physicians are human; like all people, they need relief in their labors and have a right to the distractions of social life.

"In thus directing the occupations of all its members and ensuring work and wellbeing to each, the medical corporation does not intend to infringe anyone's liberty. The physician who wishes to extend his labors and so more than the regulations demand of him has that right; but if does not owe those services, they are only partly remunerated.

"We thus have physicians who broadly manage their own affairs. They are not always more learned or more zealous that the others, but they are more desirous, and I cannot blame them for that." My cicerone smiled and shrugged his shoulders slightly. "And after all, ought we not make some concession to prejudices? There are people who always prefer the smile of the ignorant to the grim face of the scientist; what can you expect? Let them. It will always be thus; it is perhaps only in the other world that there are no prejudices.

"To tell the truth, that activity of a large number of physicians is far from being a bad thing; it maintains a competition between them that works to the great advantage of society and science. It is very rare that the competition degenerates; the corporation keeps an eye on all its members. There, as in all the other corporations, there is a tribunal of honor, to which any member who thinks himself injured in his rights or merely in the reputation to which he can lay claim, can make a complaint. The case is examined, discussed and judged in house, and it is rare for the two adversaries, after a frank explanation, not to be reconciled, if there is an infringement of rights, or satisfied, when it is merely a misunderstanding. Such tribunals are among the most useful institutions of any corporation.

"The life and duties of the medical corporation are no concern of the government. The corporation provides for all, and assigns to each his labors, nominating medical employments even with respect to those concerned with public administration. The government wisely considers that no one is better qualified than the professional committee to know the aptitudes of the individuals its controls. At any rate, the committee in not free to yield to any caprice; statues establish the rights of the individual, which cannot be forgotten without incurring public criticism."

What a difference there is, my dear friend, between those strongly-established corporations and our own ghostly corporations! Like the Sudanese, we have understood that the millions we spend in feeding the shameful poor, the brazen poor and the idle poor will never cure the ugly wound of pauperism that corrodes today's societies. Like them, too, we have extolled and encouraged associations, welcoming them into our midst in the form of tontines and retirement funds, but we are not convinced of the efficacy of the remedy; we do not impose, we recommend.

Recommending good to the ill-willed, work to the idle, thrift to the prodigal, and honor to the degraded is a waste of effort, my friend! We are talking to the deaf. The Sheikh of the Sudan does not recommend; he has founded the corporations, and they work.

Do you think that they would not work here too? How many larger enterprises have we mounted, though? How many more complicated mechanisms have we set to work? And here, what would we have to do? What would we have to create? Nothing. We would not have to change anything in our routines; there would be no laws to abolish, no institutions to torment; we would only have to fill the frames that we have, since we already have corporations; we would only have to enlarge them and generalize them.

Imagine it, my friend: no more poverty, no more beggary, and hence less crime! Oh, the Sudan stands very high in my esteem, I confess that to you in all sincerity; its Sheikh is a god to me, a god more worthy of worship than any conqueror, for the latter destroys and the former builds. How I desired to see him, in consequence!

Two days after my arrival in Timbuktu. I was introduced to him, with my guide the prison officer, by the minister who had already received me in his home. I cannot tell you, my friend, how much pleasure that introduction gave me. To me, the Sheikh was an old friend, a brother. His frankness, and the clarity of his thought, his affections and his desires are unequaled. He is a perfect human being, who enthused me to the utmost, with the result that if I were not Caucasian, I would become Sudanese, in order to live near him.

I hope to make you think as I do, my friend, when I am able to tell you everything that I learned about that extraordinary man. You only know a small fraction of his merits, the renown of which has been brought to you on the wings of newspapers, appreciated from the viewpoint of the reporter and disfigured in consequence, after having traversed the immense lands that separate us and muffle the Sultan's admiring echoes.

If I was made welcome by the Sheikh, I certainly owe that to the keen curiosity that he has always had to talk to travelers, wherever they come from and whatever opinions they hold, but I owe it perhaps even more to my status as a citizen of Caucasia. It appears that Fittri holds our nation in great esteem, and that his keenest desire would be to introduce our laws and constitution to his own country, even though he is the head of a monarchy.

During my first visit he talked to me about my voyages and my incredible balloon, but I was obliged to promise another visit for the following day, in order to talk to him about the Republic of Caucasia.

The next day, I was awaited impatiently at the Royal Palace. The Sheikh came to met me, and, taking me by the hand, he was kind enough to say: "I know, Daghestan, that you have made a particular study of the history of Caucasia, about which you have written, with new insights worthy of a true philosopher; would you be kind enough to tell me something about it, and especially to talk to me about your divine Schamyl?"

That question did not displease me, nor did it embarrass me, for my mind was thoroughly steeped in that history, of which I have, as you know, published so many fragments in your periodical. But what you might perhaps not know, my friend, is that I have revised that work and prepared it for publication. It's ready, or very nearly so—with the consequence that I had it entirely, not only in my files but still in my head. Thus, I was fully able to recite to the Sheikh, without faltering, my thesis regarding the origins of Caucasia and our Schamyls, which he was so desirous of hearing from my own mouth.

XVI. THE ORIGINS OF CAUCASIA

"It is not easy, Master," I said to the Sheikh, "to discover the truth in the historical accounts of the antiquity of my homeland. Everyone has spoken according to his own inclination, and so diversely, that I can confess to you without shame that we know little or nothing about it—nothing very certain, that is. We do not even know where the cradle of Caucasia was; we do not know from what departure point it spread out into neighboring lands, or how it was able to appropriate them to become what it is today.

"I shall not, therefore, linger seriously over those primitive times of gods, demigods and heroes, whose noble fats are furnished to us so graciously by epics. For me, our history only dates from the time of the Schamyls, with which our era begins. I say Schamyls, although our historians only recognize one. Personally, I believe—and my opinion is well-founded—that there were at least three of them, whose reigns were separate from one another, extending over a period of about 300 years, as we shall see in due course.[26]

---

[26] Subsequent history has not been favorable to Mettais' choice of Schamyl as a legendary hero, because he has almost been forgotten since his death, although he certainly seemed to be shaping up to be the stuff of legend before then. Mettais' readers would have been perfectly familiar with the name, as that of "the lion of the Caucasus": a Circassian resistance fighter who was credited with holding back the expansion of the Russian Empire into the Caucasus for many years by means of what would now be called guerrilla warfare. Born in 1797, Schamyl was still alive when Mettais wrote *L'An 585*, but he had suffered his final military defeat in 1859, having been soundly beaten twice before, in 1839 and 1845 but miraculously escaping capture each time. He was the subject of a eulogistic book, *The Life of Schamyl*, written in English by

"It would certainly be posing an insoluble question to ask whether Caucasus, the father of Schamyl I, came from the far West, from ancient France, as is believed with some plausibility, with his entire family and various friends—fleeing some say, from the tyranny of kings, or fleeing, as others say, from the general and profound catastrophe that swallowed by his fatherland and all the nations of the West—or whether he was born here of parents whose ancestors had lived here for a long time.

"Recently, I found a rather singular book in an obscure old library, which no one else has read, for sure, and which might perhaps throw some light on this question, if its authenticity were demonstrable. It's a poem in twelve parts; each part contains a thousand lines that are not to be disdained from a poetic viewpoint. I don't know whether the poem has ever been printed; it was in manuscript, and no one could give me act, or even satisfactory, information as to its origin. It was in the Russian language.

"My objective for the moment, is not to render an account of it; I shall probably do so eventually, or perhaps publish it in its entirety. It sings the praises of the indomitable valor of Russia, against which the entire ancient West was allied: France, England, Poland and Italy, which had just joined their forces with those of Turkey. For twenty years the waters of the Black Sea and all others had been covered with ships, but all the allied ships were sunk, to the extent that a few seas were encumbered. The Russians triumphed everywhere and permanently. The West was depopulated of its warriors, and it only remained for Russia to take possession of the entire world.[27]

John Milton Mackie and published in 1856, while he was yet to be defeated; the book has recently been reprinted, but that has not prevented the name from slipping out of the annals of popular legend.

[27] Mettais' readers would have had the memory of the Crimean War of 1854-56 fresh in their minds, in which the Russians

"Thousands of episodes are disseminated throughout this curious poem; the most interesting episode for us is undoubtedly the one in which we see Caucasus, the general-in-chief of the French army, retreating amid the intrigues of the other generals to the mountains of the Caucasus, with his entire family and a large number of warriors, who did not want to abandon him.

"It is true that other poems held in great honor among us, offer us alternative accounts of our origins, and scarcely even mention Caucasus. At any rate, we find Caucasus securely established among us, in the year 6600 of the world according to vulgar belief,[28] with his two wives, Ymirette and Mingrélie, and his three children, Schamyl, Danilo and Béchir. The last-named was by a third wife, whose name we do not know.

"Caucasus was so beloved, it is said by our earliest and most naïve historians, that when he died, his peoples wanted to build him a tomb such as had never been seen and would probably never be seen again. They placed the body of their beloved leader beneath a pyramid that they erected on the shore of the Black Sea. Then, fearing that the tomb might one day be profaned, they resolved to hide it under a mass of earth and rock, so broad and so high that no one would ever dare to touch it, frightened by the immensity of the labor...

"That is how the Caucasian chain was formed, say our old writers—and what supports our opinion, they add, seriously, is the immense extent of the Black Sea, which had until

---

were, of course, defeated following their capitulation at Sebastopol in 1855. They would therefore have seen the much later war featured in the epic in question as an ironic turnabout.

[28] Mettais' readers would have been perfectly familiar with the world chronology proposed by Archbishop Ussher, and would therefore have been tempted to decode this date as 2596 A.D., but that is not consistent with the other tentative and deliberately confused chronologies suggested by the text, for reasons that are never explained and can only be partly and dubiously inferred.

then only been a small lake. Doubtless it was the removal of the earth of the Caucasia Mountains that created the sea we know...

"Although that tale of our ancestors reeks of fable, the principal fact is nevertheless true; for me, at last, the existence of Caucasus and the names of his children is firmly established. For me, therefore, there is no more doubt: Caucasus was a good father and a good prince. On his death, he divided up the Caucasian regions—Ymeretia, Mingrelia and Caucasia properly speaking—between his three children.

"Schamyl received Caucasia. He was the eldest and the most enterprising as well as the bravest of them all. Like his father Caucasus he became the idol of his people. He was not that of his family; his glory and prosperity made his brothers envious; they joined forces against him and made war on him relentlessly until they were finally vanquished and dethroned. That was the first enlargement of Caucasia, which was rounded out by the conquered provinces.

"Schamyl did not enjoy his prosperity for long, however, for his brothers, having fled to Russia, reanimated the war against him, and he was killed in a bloody battle, which his own side nevertheless won. No one had seen him fall; the fury was so great that none of his soldiers had perceived it. Only his eldest son, who was fighting by his side, had witnessed it, and had hidden it from everyone else.

"As no one had seen Schamyl's death, some thought he had gone away in the interests of the fatherland, while others claimed to have seen him flying in the sky, from which he was watching over Caucasia. His son, alone and with no witnesses, had deposited him on the summit of the Caucasus, at the base of a rock, as Schamyl had instructed him to do before dying. Schamyl the younger continued his father's reign, always commanding and acting in the name of his absent father. That is probably the origin of the opinion that there was only one Schamyl.

"Schamyl I died in the year 30 of our era. He is the one that we have put into our calendar, numbered among the saints. Schamyl II, whose reign ought to be dated from the time of his father's death, governed Caucasia for ninety years. He was only forty when he took possession of the throne. That long interval of time was filled with battles and victories. Caucasia was further enlarged by provinces seized from Russia and Persia.

"Schamyl II left twenty children by various wives, but as none was in any condition to carry the enormous burden of affairs of State, he summoned one of his nephews to his deathbed, to whom he confided his empire and his family. That nephew was Shamyl III, our Schamyl the Great. It was during his reign that our nation acquired the great glory that set Caucasia above all the nations of the world. It was also during his reign that Russia finally understood its inferiority relative to us and, fatigued by its numerous fruitless struggles and the enormous losses that we caused it to experience continually in its battles against us, decided to leave us in peace and turn its weapons against less redoubtable neighbors, which it defeated.

"It took possession successively, on the one hand, of Sweden, Norway and Denmark, and on the other of Turkey. It then believed itself to be a colossus. It had indeed become a colossus in extent, but not in power, and it soon met the fate that overly vast empires whose population is not homogeneous always meet. No one any longer had a fatherland; there were no more bonds, no more fraternity. Everyone obeyed the same laws, but everyone had his own affections, predilections, desires, language, mores and memories, and bore the yoke of the conqueror impatiently.

"To govern such an empire requires more than a human hand. The Emperor of All the Russias had recourse to the governmental science of some of his favorites, with whom he shared the burden of a crushing administration. He set all of them at the head of kingdoms, of which he had made as many provinces, with the title of Viceroy. Soon, however, one of his favorites rebelled, then another, then all of them; the example had become contagious. To subdue them, the Emperor sent his armies on campaign, but the rebels knew the axiom that there is strength in union; they made an alliance in order to sustain the impact of the powerful Emperor, who was defeated. The allies were satisfied then, and by virtue of a residue of kind memory toward their former protector, they let him keep his throne—but Russia had shrunk, and had been dismembered.

"I know that there are historians who offer different accounts of the expansion and abasement of Russia. Personally, for the moment, I hold to the opinion I have just proffered. At any rate, Russia only fell after a long and devastating struggle. During that struggle, Caucasia kept its weapons in hand, its eyes attentively fixed on the relentless conflicts that weakened Russia to its own advantage, as will soon be seen.

"The victors' moderation was only temporary. Intoxicated by their success, they became arrogant with their neighbors, and especially with us, although our distance from their frontiers ought to have preserved us from their bad temper. It appears that our glory offended them. Russia, for its part, ashamed of its defeats, was seized by vertigo and dared to behave unjustly toward us, evidently in the hope of repairing itself somewhat at our expense.

"They were all wrong, however, for they were exhausted, and we were intact and vigorous. So, attacked by all of them, we were able to beat all of them, and beat them so convincingly that proud Russia, Sweden, Denmark and Turkey, gripped in our powerful claws, expired in order to be reborn under the name of Caucasia, and to form the Caucasia of today, minus a few distant provinces such as Demark and Sweden, which subsequently experienced revolutions to which we abandoned them.

"We were great from then on, and greater than the Russia of old. Too well instructed by the example he had before his eyes, however, Schamyl did not want to reign everywhere and over everyone. He was strong enough to trample underfoot the pride and ambition that so often lay siege to the powerful, and to forge of his own accord the memorable and unprecedented revolution that was the commencement of the long and fortunate prosperity that our tribes still enjoy today.

"Schamyl cast down all the thrones that he had conquered, and then divided his vast empire into tribes, which he established in submissive circumscriptions, as far as was possible, with the same mores, in similar geographical latitudes, and said to them, in words more worthy of a philosopher than a warrior:

"'Friends, God has not made me to reign over you, nor you to obey me. He has created me to live, that's all, and you too. He has given me a body like yours, needs like yours, and there is probably an intelligence greater than mine among you.

"'It is, therefore, chance that has determined what we are in respect to one another. As we cannot live in isolation, however, and it is necessary for us to live in society, well, let us live in society. What, then, is it necessary to do? It is necessary that there are some of us who watch while others work or sleep. Let us, therefore, regulate all that! We shall all come together to make laws for out use, and then we shall appoint people to make sure they are observed...'

"Schamyl was a great warrior, but he was also a great philosopher. He understood the human mind, which willingly returns that which is allowed to fall into the hand. His words were therefore greeted with enthusiasm, and, as he had doubtless foreseen, he was charged with organizing the society that he had conquered.

"His laws were few in number, simple and appropriate to the needs of society and each of its members. As for the question of governmental organization, we have seen that the immense empire of Caucasia was divided into a large number of tribes. Warned by the example of the past, however, attributing pride, arrogance and the spirit of domination and invasion to great empires, and knowing full well, in addition, that the stronger people feel, the more wisdom they require in order not to abuse their strength, and that it is not prudent to allow strength even to the wise, he gave scant extent to each tribe. He thought, too, very wisely, that a state restricted in its

151

limits will develop its interior administration all the better for it. The activity of an energetic man is not expended for or against his neighborhood, but for the increase of his intimate wellbeing.

"Schamyl was too wise, however, not to think of holding in reserve the strength that he did not want to abandon blindly to its nation. Although it is good that people who are constantly struggling against their evil instincts cannot find brutal force to hand, at the behest and command of their passions, it is nevertheless necessary that they know that when danger threatens, there is a weapon to hand that wisdom might put at his disposal at any moment.

"That weapon, he found in a strongly and cleverly organized confederation of small states. The common and indissoluble bond that kept them all together was nothing other than a superior and independent administration, which had no other force than that of justice and reason, no other support than that of the states from which it emanated, no other mission that receiving communications interesting to the wellbeing of the States and their members, in order to submit them to general assemblies for appreciation, and to act as an advance sentinel whom nothing can distract from his orders, always ready to cry: 'Who goes there? Look out!'

"It is evident that our Schamyl's plan was a good one, since Caucasia is today what it was in that epoch, and that we do not feel any need to change our constitution. It is true that the constitution in question is not entirely the work of Schamyl alone, not of his time. Sages came after him; aided by experience and the counsels of peace, they have achieved what the warrior Schamyl could not, in improving our social relationships, and they have succeeded to such an extent that they have fortunately contrived to satisfy the command that God issued on creating humans—'Go forth and live'—well enough that we have had no need o touch those laws since.

"That is also because those laws are not the work of a self-interested individual, not of egotistic legislators; they are the work of the wisest in the nation.

"Now, when a nation organizes itself, it counts its miseries, its needs, its desires and it provides for them; but if its laws are the work of a single individual, then private interests, class interests and family interests are always there; the proletariat is forgotten. That man thinks of the nation in the same way a sculptor thinks of the pedestal that will support his statue..."

The Sheikh smiled at that little sally, and said to me, holding out his hand: "I don't hold that against you. If I wanted to converse with you, it wasn't to receive compliments; it was to hear the truth."

"You told me that, Master," I replied to the Sheikh. "Which doesn't prevent me from begging your pardon if the last words might have wounded you. I did not think that you were the sole organizer of the Code of the Sudan; if I had thought that, I would certainly not have made the reflection I made, for, in my opinion, the constitution of the Sudan approaches human perfection so closely that I admire it wholeheartedly."

"Go on!" said the Sheikh, with a burst of Homeric laughter, striking my familiarly on the shoulder. "The Republic of Caucasia is in its decadence, for its philosophers have become flatterers of kings."

And at that point, my dear friend, we exchanged gibes for a few minutes, launching as much with a one another as we could. Then I took my leave of the Sheikh, who shook my hand cordially, wishing me a good journey, for I was to depart the next day. The brilliant and warm reception I had received in Timbuktu had not made me forget my goal. My objective was double, and attracted me forcefully: it was to locate Paris, and it was also to go to Zeeland; for I had to find friends there who were making me neglect those in Timbuktu.

XVII. THE SHEIKH'S FAREWELL

The next day, I was pleasantly surprised to see the Sheikh entering my lodgings, just as I was about to leave, accompanied by a single friend. I had not expected to see him again; I had said my farewells to him, but he wanted to shake my hand one last time, and to see my balloon being prepared.

"I am interested to witness the strange preparations for your voyage," he told me, "but that was not the motive that led me to surprise you thus." After a moment's silence, full of emotion, during which he took my hands in his, he added: "I have come because I believe that I might have found a true friend, and that he is going away..."

That assertion touched me deeply, my dear friend. It would have kept me in Timbuktu if anything could have retained me—but it was written that my destiny would not conclude there, and that it was necessary to go on."

"Then again," the Sheikh added, "if you have need of a recommendation for any neighboring state, or even any distant state where I might have credit, I am putting myself at your disposal, since I was stupid enough not to do so yesterday. Yesterday, in fact, you left more abruptly that I had hoped..."

I savored those words lovingly; I made to reply.

"We are in a relationship of amity," the Sheikh added, in a voice that seemed to me to have taken on a greater pith of benevolence because my silence had allowed him to hope that he might convince me. "We are in a relationship of amity with the powerful Sultans of Darfur, Oaidai, Barnouh, Egypt, Feuta-Dhiallon—the Feuta-Dhiallon whose capital is so beautiful, its mores so polite and civilized, that one of our proverbs says that if God wanted to dwell on earth be would take up residence in Timbo, the beautiful capital of Feuta-Dhiallon..."[29]

---

[29] Timbo is a town in Guinea in the Fouta-Djallon highlands

The Sheikh's eyes were expressively interrogative; they were seeking to read the depths of my soul—but I made no reply.

"Or," he continued, "if you do not want to go so far—and there I will accompany you, since it is at our gates—go to Bornou to visit Kouka, the city of a hundred gates, the city of a thousand marvels, where the genius of invention sits in all the public squares in the guise of a tall and prodigious sandstone statue. The statue in question is that of a man who immortalized himself by covering the soil of Kouka with small sandstone paving-stones, which replaced the thousands of more or less ingenious attempts that had been made for centuries to sanitize the streets. That paving, which we are going to adopt here, is truly admirable in cleanliness and elegance—so, may we not go to thank Bornou, which has endowed us with so many fortunate inventions, and which a philosopher could not fail to admire and study fruitfully...?"[30]

The Sheikh was becoming increasingly animated. "Why, my friend," he went on, "don't you also visit the celebrated and sage Republic of the Congo, where it's said that there are still a few tribes of black men to be found—the most astonishing rarity of our modern times, which never ceases to excite our academies and their most boldly utopian savants? The Fezzan, whose capital, Mourzouk,[31] you must surely know by name, at least, will show you thousands of serious men seriously occupied in tailoring and retailoring new garments every six months, to establish what they call high society fashions. Why...but where do you want to go?" The Sheikh fixed his eye attentively upon my silently thoughtful face. "I'm at your disposal."

I made no reply.

---

[30] The plain of Bornou, in which Kouka is situated, is now located in Nigeria.

[31] The Fezzan, in which Mourzouk is located, is now a region of Libya.

He went on: "Would you like to go to the great empire of Ghat, the vast Republic of Asben, where you'll find Tintelloust, a marvelous capital, where the houses are so beautiful and luxurious that only millionaires can live in them, and in order to become a millionaire, everyone has become a thief..." The Sheikh immediately exclaimed: "Oh, don't tremble, sir, they don't use daggers or revolvers to accomplish their thefts. The inhabitants of Tintelloust are very mild, very disciplined; everyone robs you in his own manner, with so much honesty, and even gentleness, that my own prime minister, who is not lacking in joviality, recently said on returning from Tintelloust that he was going to advise the government of Asben to put all the good folk in prison in order to keep the honest thieves whom the law protects in the city..."[32]

I was still listening to the Sheikh's gracious verve, but making no reply. What could I say? My decision was made, and I remained absorbed in profound thoughts of nascent amity.

"You're a philosopher of the first order," the Sheikh added, gallantly. "It isn't possible that you're voyaging only to see nothing. You certainly haven't come here to inspect houses, streets, hairstyles and the cut of our garments. No, you came to study more than that. Well, if you want to study the moderation and wisdom of a government, go to..."

"Timbuktu," I said, swiftly, suddenly recovering the power of speech.

"No," riposted the Sheikh, smiling. "To our neighbors, to Oualata in the Birou.[33] There—as among us, for modesty ought not to make me unjust—the sovereign has the wisdom not to believe that he is different in kind from those he administrates. Like us, he has always devoted himself to the com-

---

[32] Asben is nowadays more commonly known as the Air Mountains; the town of Tintelllust is now in Niger.

[33] Oualata (or Wilata) in the Biru, now in Mauretania, was once an important Saharan oasis, whose importance as a crucial caravanserai was overtaken by that of Timbuktu.

mon cause, only taking from power hat which he needs in the public interest. The throne is not his, nor for him; it is the signature of the people at the foot of an edict, and the people of whom he is the first member is not, for him, merely a flock that one may encumber or shear at will, under the eye of a menacing soldier.

"Oh, if I'm telling you this, my friend, it is because that system is beginning to prevail in the majority of today's states. Sovereigns have an unfortunate tendency to believe themselves gods to whom all honor and incense is due, or masters for whom entire peoples must live and die. In Birou, it is not like that..."

"Nor in Timbuktu," I said to the Sheikh, squeezing his hands.

"Nor in Timbuktu, thank God," the Sheikh agreed. With a supplicant gaze he went on: "If you wish, stay with us for a few more days, and I will take you myself to Oualata, for the sovereign of Birou is my close friend."

"I suspected as much," I said, "given the conformity of ideas, but..."

"But you won't accept, will you?" said the Sheikh, with a sadness that affected me. The scenes I have presented to you can't seduce you. You want to go; your plans summon you far away. If they were calling you to the extreme confines of Africa, my friend, I would be able to be useful to you; I can give you a passport to the great and distant island of Tripoli, a vast and curious kingdom, the last of the civilized lands of our hemisphere—and also the most voracious, it must be said, for it is in the process of devouring all the petty states that surround it. At least, after that feast, it will have to ruminate alone on its isle, for there is nothing but the sea beyond, and beyond that, the barbarity enchaining the former Europe and its ancient civilization. But neither Tripoli nor anyone else has any desire for those conquests; only scholars now desire, at a distance, from their firesides, to make fine speeches about a extinct civilization and a reigning barbarity, to philosophize loftily about a France that was once, it's said, as civilized as

157

the Congo of our day, or an England whose ancient renown could equal that of today's Tripoli, and yet have been so utterly annihilated today that we do not even know where they were located." The Sheikh looked at me profoundly. "Ah, history, history, my friend—is it really worth the trouble that scholars devote to it?"

"Don't expect too much of history, Master, and don't ask it for the impossible," I said to the Sheikh. "History is respectable when it only says what it knows, and when it works to discover what it doesn't know. Then it gives the savant indescribable joys. So, to obtain those joys, I would like to learn, to interrogate antiquity, not in its splendors, since they're extinct, but in its decadence, which can sometimes speak so loudly. It's for that reason, Master, that I cannot accept all your gracious offers at present." I looked at him with a gaze full of regret. "That's why I don't want to go to Tripoli, where I would only see the present, but beyond, beyond its seas, where the civilization of the olden times, where the most hideous barbarity of modern times reigns, to France...to Paris, in fact..."

"To Paris!" cried the Sheikh, in terror. "But how will you find Paris?"

"I shall search for it."

"But where? Have not a host of scholars and voyagers searched for it already?"

"Yes, and fruitlessly, I know—dangerously, even, for not all of the voyagers came back."

"Poor fellow! You'll perish too, for these people are savages, and savages whose ferocity is proverbial. I'm not even certain that they aren't cannibals."

"No, no—that's an error that prejudice and fear have spread abroad."

"They're still a poor people."

"As to that, yes—so it's said, at least."

"And that's where you're going?"

"Yes, that's where I'm going...and one day, I'll tell you why."

The Sheikh bowed then, and shook my hand one last time. I climbed into my gondola, activated the machine that would steer it, then rose up slowly, in order to be able to see my good crowned friend for as long as possible, and also to let him see the movements of my balloon, while simultaneously investigating the air current into which I was about to enter, in order to travel more easily.

Then I waved goodbye, and launched rapidly into the sky, taking the direction I had declared to the Sheikh.

XVIII. A CITY IN THE SEA

I had only been traveling for a few hours when I felt my balloon gripped and buffeted by the turbulence of capricious winds that seemed to be playing with it. I had never experienced similar shocks and found it very difficult to resist them. My knowledge of aerostatics was inadequate to the situation in which I found myself at that moment. I didn't know, therefore, how to make my steering mechanism combat that aerial profligacy.

My mechanism was soon out of order, and my entire balloon suffered damage. I then decided that the safest thing to do, if not the most courageous, as to surrender to the air currents that were overwhelming me while descending to the lower layers of the atmosphere, resolving to go down all the way to the ground if necessary.

I was still in Africa—at least, I assumed so, by calculating the time that had gone by since my departure from Timbuktu. Indeed, it didn't take long for me to perceive towns whose appearance indicated to me that I wasn't mistaken. How I regretted then not having accepted the passports offered by my friend the Sheikh! Perhaps I was in one of the countries he had mentioned to me, and where I would be able to find shelter and protection, even help in repairing my aerostat. Those belated regrets ended up making me understand that I still lacked the foresight that skillful voyagers exercise in stuffing their pockets with recommendations of every sort.

I decided, in spite of everything, to descend to the ground, and did so slowly. I was fortunate enough to encounter in the course of that maneuver a gentle air current, easy to follow, which my balloon did indeed follow in such a reassuring manner that I allowed it to do so. I was no longer thinking of anything but continuing my route, since I could no longer see and urgent danger threatening me.

I went on in that way for some time, glad to have escaped my battle and smiling at an agreeable perspective, when a frightful thought suddenly chilled my joy. Imprudent as I was, I had not thought to check the direction of my flight and determine whether or not it had changed during my atmospheric struggle—I had only thought of making progress. I therefore consulted my compass. Alas, it had been broken by the violent shocks that my balloon had experienced.

Where was I, then? Was I really in Africa? I didn't know anything for certain, for at that moment I could no longer see any towns, or any habitations at all. I could only see mountains covered with rocks and woods so thick and tangled that there was nothing to be seen there but the life of a lush wilderness. What should I do? I was direly perplexed.

I didn't lose courage, though, and sought to get my bearings as best I could. For that purpose, I increased my altitude slightly, and aimed my telescope to see what I could find in the distance…and a long way off, I eventually saw the sea.

"God be praised!" I cried—for at the edge of the sea I hoped to find people and information. If there were no towns, I thought, there would at least be villages—a few huts, perhaps some debris, at which I could seek information.

I therefore increased my speed. It was a fortunate inspiration, for I soon found myself in the midst of a few fishermen's huts. The poor savages fled at my approach, and then prostrated themselves at my knees when I had reached them, doubtless taking me for a god and my balloon, in all probability, for one of the stars they saw shining by night in the firmament.

I was unable to get any information out of those poor people. They didn't understand my language and I understood nothing of theirs—but we indicated by signs everything that we could say. I went with them to their huts, where they offered me fish and a few remains from their hunting.

After that modest meal, of which I had great need and which put me in a good mood, I set about examining the huts, which, like all the huts of savage peoples, were simple and hardly contrived; they were shelters half shaped by nature and half by endeavor. A few tree trunks disposed around a few caverns in the rocks, then branches, pieces of driftwood and the skins of a few animals killed while hunting formed the entirety of their architecture.

All that was simple but comfortably disposed, and I was admiring it when one of my hosts, after leaving in a hurry, came back a moment later holding in his arms a head and arm of perfectly-finished marble, which he obligingly showed to me.

Those pieces of statuary, my friend, I had no doubt, were the debris of an ancient statue—from the remotest antiquity, for it has already been many centuries since our sculptors have given up working in marble, prepared and hardened wood lending itself much better to our modern ideas of sentimental civilization.

I marveled at them, and my eyes testified to that, if not my words—which would have been wasted. So my host, understanding the pleasure I would experience in possessing what he was showing me, offered it to me, and I accepted, with extravagant demonstrations of gratitude.

I know where to find that beautiful debris, my friend; you shall see them, and appreciate them in your turn.

But where had all that come from? The pleasure that I had just manifested in receiving the present from one of my hosts excited the one whose home I was in. He took me by the hand and had me examine in his hut, which as large and had several compartments, various objects that I had not noticed at first. There were fragments of luxurious items of furniture, pieces of statues, antique vases and coins: an entire collection, for which our own museums would have paid dearly.

My astonishment was at its peak, and I wondered again where it had all come from, what country I was in and what excavations had revealed the treasures. It did not take me long to find out. By their gestures, my hosts made me understand that all these riches, whose value they were far from understanding, came from the sea, where they proposed that I should go with them.

The offer could not have been more agreeable to me, and I accepted, with great demonstrations of joy. I let them get into their boats, which did not inspire me with great confidence, and climbed into my own, which supported and steered my balloon. We traveled for quite a long time together through shallow watered furrowed with countless reefs, arid islets and bizarrely-shaped spurs of rock. Then my guides stopped, looking at me, and pointing at a rock that was almost at water level, and which big waves would have prevented me noticing any more than the rest.

It was a singular rock, my friend; the summit was unevenly rounded by the erosion of the waves, but it formed a point that grew larger as it extended until it was lost to sight. It was certainly not a natural rock formation; it was the work of human hands, which had constructed it, for I could clearly distinguish that it was composed of stones fixed together. The joints were perfectly distinct, like those it is said the ancients made—less perfect in that respect than our monuments, which appear to have been cast in a mould so perfectly are the materials adapted to one another.

Do you recall, my friend, an old decrepit engraving, devoid of authority, which we found one day on the stall of a bric-à-brac seller, which we threw aside with disgust, so coarsely was it made? Well, we were wrong to treat it with so much scorn. It was badly drawn, it's true, doubtless the work of a student, but it represented an authentic scene of antiquity, as it claimed. In that scene there was a temple, like none of those seen in our country but like those the ancients built, as the ugly engraving said: a temple with a portal of fluted columns, surmounted by pyramids of various sorts. What stupidity it was to have rejected that engraving, whose unappreciable price I now recognize! Well, my rock was that temple. The portal I couldn't see, for my eyes, in spite of all my efforts, could not penetrate the water to that depth. But the pyramid I saw, and saw perfectly.

Oh, how I regretted then not having my diving apparatus!

I roamed around the region for a good part of the day, in the company of my guides, who never left me and appeared to be taking considerable pleasure in discovering a host of curiosities, which they pointed out to me and which I admired like an envious child. The sea was so calm and the water so transparent that day that my eyes were able to plunge to an unusual depth...

If I didn't fear being taken for a visionary, my friend, I would tell you what I thought I saw...thought! No, no, I saw it; I really saw it. I saw monuments, the monuments of a city swallowed up by the sea. Oh, don't laugh—it's true. Anyway, I shall tell you something more astonishing still.

At a moment when I was occupied in contemplating something that my imagination told me was an equestrian statue raised on a rock at the bottom of the sea, I suddenly saw one of my savages jump out of his boat. I was about to hasten to his rescue, for I thought he had fallen into the sea, when he companions restrained me, laughing, and signaling to me to keep my eyes on him. He dived, so effectively that he came back after a few moments with a small plaque of laminated iron clenched between his teeth, which he offered to me.

That plaque was partly corroded by rust, but because it had been coated with some kind of inoxidizable enamel, which had only been partly destroyed, I was able to decipher a few letters of the plaque: letters like those in Père Franco's book, and therefore in French.

Oh, how glad I was at that moment to have known Père Franco! How I blessed his memory and his book. How glad I was to have studied it, to have been able to decipher, or very nearly, that alphabet, those letters, that language, relative to which we previously had made so many conjectures, in spite of all the tireless debates and declarations of modern savants.

On that plaque, my dear friend, I was able to read: *...tel...Alger*. Oh, all the letters of Alger were there. It was not difficult to see that only two letters were missing from the first word. When I know more about the French language, I will try to replace them.[34]

"Alger!" I exclaimed, contemplating my plaque, my eyes sparkling with joy. "Alger!" My traveling companions were bewildered by my exclamations. They certainly did not understand what had give rise to the great excitement that I was feeling at that moment. What was Alger to them?

Alger was nothing to those people but good or poor soil, while to me, it was an entire history, an entire misunderstood past that was revealing itself to me, an entire people being reborn before my eyes, an entire calumniated epoch that I was able to rehabilitate, an extinct light that I was able to reignite and cause to shine in all eyes. It was an illusion taking on a body, a myth reclothed in the forms of reality; it was, in sum, the great doubt of the past becoming clear before my eyes.

For Alger...what was Alger, then, after all? The most brilliant of the French colonies, some say; the richest and most fecund of the republics of the olden days, say others; the most unknown, I may say in my turn—for what do we know about Alger, if we know anything, before Hilarion Cokberg, its king, its president or its governor, according to the choice of modern historians...if, that is, Hilarion Cokberg had ever governed Algeria.

I spend a good quarter of an hour, my friend, contemplating that iron plaque, in utter ecstasy, talking to it mentally with an effusion that my savages respected religiously.

Poor Algeria! It's great city is there, under the water, well out to sea, forming reefs, rocks inhabited solely by marine monsters, forgotten—so completely forgotten, in fact, that

---

[34] Mettais' readers would have little difficulty jumping to the conclusion that the missing letters were *Hô* and that the full inscription must have been *Hôtel Alger*—i.e. Algiers Hotel. As well as being the name of the capital of Algérie [Algeria], Alger was also the name of one of its three administrative divisions in the colonial era, located between Oran and Constantine.

there are only a few very profound scholars who can say anything about it...the very little that they know. And yet, do not those pieces of debris that I held, those ruins that I saw, indicate a very active life, a very great science, a civilization once very advanced? Yes, but...for how many centuries had that life, that science and that civilization been extinct? How many peoples had come and gone since, occupying the attention of the world?

Poor people! Poor city! What catastrophe, then, had swallowed it up? Was it earthquakes, or volcanic eruptions? Or had the sea devoured it stone by stone, in centuries-long invasions? A question insoluble today, my friend. It's hard to admit for scientists like us, but that's the way it is.

The discovery of Alger was for me, at that moment, an important mater, doubly agreeable as a savant and as a traveler. You will understand how important it was to the savant, but as a traveler, I saw with great pleasure that the accident to my compass had not been fatal and that hazard, if it was hazard, had served me very well in putting my on the road that I wanted to follow, on the road to ancient France, the road to New Cosaquia.

I therefore said farewell to my hosts, and then set out over the open sea, but keeping my balloon at a low altitude in order to be able to study, to the extent that I could, the territory I was about to traverse.

That sea, my friend—which I took, with considerable confidence, for the sea that once separated France from Algeria—is very uneven. It is strewn with islands, evidently of volcanic origin, vast rocks that I was quite ready, remembering Alger, to call by the name of some ancient people or city. But there was no longer anything there, no inhabitants and no habitations, not even savage huts. There was, however, still a lush vegetation—olive-trees, fig-trees, orange-trees, all sorts of cereals, even vines climbing and clinging freely everywhere—as well as game in abundance.

Humans must therefore have been there—but what humans? In what era?

My balloon was moving slowly; I had so many things to see, both with my bodily eyes and my mind's eye. I don't know how long the crossing took, but it was evidently a long time for I suddenly perceived that it was getting dark. I was alarmed by that, because I didn't want to sleep over the sea, and I was annoyed at not having made preparations to spend the night elsewhere.

I had therefore stopped my balloon and begun to look around in all directions, seeking inspiration as to where to direct my course, when I was suddenly enveloped in the veils of the blackest darkness.

XIX. THE ANDROGENES

I am not timorous, my friend, but I confess that I was gripped by fear at that moment, for I did not know what that black veil was. It was not night, I was sure. I was trying to work it out when I saw it begin to clear gradually, and soon let through reddish glimmers, which increased by degrees and finally appeared to me as the reflections of a vast blaze.

An intense vapor and a sulfurous odor was rising from the sea, drawing with it myriads of insects, which formed thick clouds above and around me. The sun seemed to be covered by them. The sea was agitated, but within a very restricted area; the water was seething and roaring; humid mountains were rising up below me to a great height—so high that I was forced to take my balloon higher. Then submarine rumbles, thunderclaps, terrible inexplicable noises groaned in the depths of the sea.

What was about to happen? I was asking myself that when, all of a sudden, a horrible storm, such as I had never encountered, and such as I could not have imagined, burst forth—but beneath abysms of water. It was so frightful that I blocked my ears and closed my eyes, lying down in my gondola.

Then it all ceased. I looked...

I saw beneath me a small verdant island, covered with grass and bushes, on which strange beings were swarming that I had never seen during my submarine excursions. They all seemed to be of the same family, although various in their development. Some were so small and so shapeless that it would have been necessary to study them at close range to see whether they formed a branch of the same species as the others, or whether they belonged to a different species.

What a prodigy, my friend! The creatures did not seem to me to be malevolent, so I went down to the island, cautiously, because I wasn't sure that its ground was solid. It was.

As I approached, a part of that singular population fled into the water, where it disappeared; another fraction, too weak, too lacking in agility or too deeply sunk into the mud to escape, looked at me with all the fear of intelligence.

Only one of the larger beings, stronger and more highly developed than the rest—so it seemed to me through the long grass and bushes behind which I could scarcely make it out—was looking at me without trembling. I advanced toward it. Its torso and the lower part of its body was buried in the mud. At first, I could only see the head—but the head! What a head! The head, my friend had a human face, unmistakably—not, it is true, the human face with all its characteristic beauties, for it was more angular, with slightly more protruding organs, but it was nevertheless what can sometimes be found in more than one variety of the human species.

I was gripped by emotion.

I advanced further and extended my hand toward that strange being. It had arms, hands and the upper body of a woman. I spoke to her, my friend, for, fool that I was. I spoke to her, I took her by the hand. A few hoarse croaks emerging from her throat replied to me, or so it seemed.

Poor woman! I said to myself. *She's a shipwreck-victim.* And I reached down in order to seize her in my arms and lift her into my gondola. Before I could extract her completely from the mud that had trapped her, however, I felt the ground yield beneath my feet, and my efforts became impotent, and even dangerous, for I was sinking deeper and deeper. The woman suddenly escaped me; she disappeared along with her island, and I only just had time to cling to my gondola...

Then, I saw nothing but the surface of the water.

I was amazed and stunned, keenly distressed by the loss of that unfortunate woman, whom I would have liked to saved, for all the world. I therefore waited for a while, looking around in all directions—but nothing reappeared.

In the distance, however, it seemed to me that I could see something—perhaps a little islet or a rock. My telescope told me that it was, in fact, a rock—but on that rock there was a man: a man who was also looking at me, with the aid of a telescope like mine.

I therefore headed in that direction, in order to bring him help if he needed it—and I didn't doubt for an instant that he did need it.

I found a large rock—very large in fact, and easy of access. The man I had perceived was still there, telescope in hand, naked, watching me approach with an expression of great pleasure. To my great astonishment, however, my balloon didn't appear to make any impression on him, and he was calmer than I would have expected a castaway to be.

"Forgive me, sir," he said, offering me his hand to help me get down on to his rick, "for appearing naked before you. It would be difficult for me, for the moment, to do otherwise, given that I've deposited my garments on the sea shore, in order to get as close as possible to the place where I thought that something was about to happen. How unfortunate it is, sir, that you didn't understand me—for since the beginning of the submarine storm I've been making signs to you, asking you to come and pick me up."

"I didn't see you, sir," I replied, amazed by my interlocutor's self-composure.

"I would have done better to swim to it," he continued, "but the island...I thought that it wouldn't be prudent to get stuck there, in the midst of the waters, while you...anyway, it's gone now—but I'm deeply sorry, for I've been waiting for that phenomenon for fifty years, and I haven't seen it, or seen it very poorly."

"You astonish me, sir," I said to him, "or I don't understand. I took you for a castaway to whom I've come to render assistance."

"Thank you—but I'm not a castaway. I'm an amateur, a curiosity-seeker, somewhat knowledgeable in scientific research and emotion, that's all."

"And I assumed," I added, "that you were of the society of that unfortunate woman who escaped me, disappearing into the water with her island."

"Oh, what bad luck!" cried my interlocutor, slapping himself on the forehead. "There was an Androgene,[35] and I didn't see it! There was a woman there, you say?"

"There was a woman there."

"And you really saw her?"

"I touched her."

"Oh, sir—that was an Androgene!"

"An Androgene?"

My interlocutor looked at me in astonishment. "You've come a long way, sir?" he queried.

"From Caucasia."

"From Caucasia! A land of science! And yet you're not, it seems, familiar with the affairs of our islands. I am myself from the Island of the Androgenes, which you can see over there..." He pointed in a direction in which I could not see anything. "Well, sir, I repeat, the woman you saw was not a castaway but an Androgene." He raised his eyes to the heavens. "An Androgene! What a fine spectacle—and I missed it! What a fine object of study, and I missed it! Finally…!"

---

[35] In 1865 the Greek-derived word *androgène*, for which I have improvised an equivalent here, did not exist as a noun in French, although it does now, applied to the male hormone [androgen]. It did exist as an adjective, equivalent to the English androgenous [male-producing], but Mettais and his readers were thoroughly accustomed to language in which the male tacitly "embraces the female" (language that I have modified slightly in this translation, routinely translating *homme*, when intended to refer to the whole species rather than a male individual, as "human beings" or "humankind" rather than "man" or "mankind") and were thus vulnerable to construing *androgène*, mistakenly, as "human-producing," much as "android" is nowadays applied to hypothetical artificial humans of either sex. I have resisted the temptation to substitute Anthropogene, which would be the accurate Greek-derived term for "human-producing."

I was utterly amazed. I listened to my interlocutor open-mouthed and wide-eyed. I truly did not understand what he was saying, nor his despair.

"I can see that you don't know anything, sir," he said, looking at me with considerable interest. "Moor your aerostat to this rock, then, I beg you, and let us talk, if you would like to."

I did as I was bid, very curious to hear what the man had to tell me, having revealed himself as a victim of hallucination or an initiate of a science completely unknown to me.

"Well, sir," said my interlocutor, uttering a profound sigh, "all those beings you have had the good fortune to see are Androgenes, "from the smallest embryo—the tiniest fetal fiber, which you could not have seen—to that *woman*, which is the most perfect development, as it is also the rarest, of the species, for I have never seen one myself, my father never saw one and I do not know anyone at all who has ever seen one…and I wanted to see one.

"I am, sir, as I told you, an inhabitant of the Island of the Androgenes. Among us there is a religious belief that our ancestors emerged from the sea-bed—fully armed, according our forefathers—quitting a realm that no longer pleased them in order to settle on our island.

"The idea is charming and poetic, but it is not entirely true. Our ancestors certainly came from the sea-bed—science says so[36]—but how? They were certainly not fully armed."

---

[36] It is nowadays a given of evolutionary theory that life originated in the sea and invaded the land in a slow manner that extended over millions of years. Thanks to the work of Benoît de Maillet and the Comte du Buffon, Mettais' readers would have been familiar with the notion that Earthly life had originated in the sea and subsequently emerged on to land, but would have had no little or idea of the mechanism or time-scale process. The notion of "Androgenes"—which presumably have analogues producing other animals—ought not, therefore, to have seemed quite as inherently bizarre to them

I was listening to my philosopher with a smile on my lips, which annoyed him, I think. "Do you know, sir," he went on, excitedly, "what the sky, the land and the sea once were, what principles and what palpable and impalpable bodies caused them to change and live? Once! I mean 15,000, 20,000, 30,000 years ago, or more!"

My only response was a smile.

"It is, however, necessary to know," my master retorted, "for all the secrets, all the mysteries of the religion of our forefathers and the primal generation are therein."

"Of what happened several thousand years ago, we know very little," I replied. "What there is today, we can see."

"Yes. But what was there before, I ask you? Were the heavens and the earth always as they are today? Did they have the same temperature? Did they produce the same phenomena? Have they not lost some of their properties? Have they not acquired others?

"Our scientists say so, but what they also tell us is that we are gradually reverting to the atmospheric and terrestrial constitution of ancient times, and have been for some time.

"Now, if their calculations are accurate, and we really are returning to the past, we need to know what things were like in the past. That's precisely what I wanted to see. And if the Androgenes once made human beings, they must still be doing so, if the same conditions still exist...or if the same conditions recur, of course.

"What are those conditions? Are they constant or temporary? Are they in the nature of things, or are they prodigies? I don't know. All that I know is that a nugget of gold has sometimes been found where no nugget has been found before or ever will be again. I know that a phenomenon can be produced once, and only once. That is why I spend my life at sea, searching for that nugget, on the lookout for that phenomenon...because I believe, sir, that an Androgene might become

_____

as it does to us; hence the substance of the argument that follows.

a human being, as you have had the good fortune to see...what do you think, sir?" My interlocutor asked me the last question point-blank.

"I've listened to you, sir, but I don't believe it."

"You don't believe it! But you must be shutting our eyes in order not to see. You can't see, and therefore don't appreciate the gentle and constant gradation that exists between all things, from the polyp that is the primary vegetable to the last of the animals—to human beings, which are the model of animate and living perfection! You don't see how all living things are! You've never studied their constitution, their organs, their principles, which are the same for all of them, with the variation indispensable to their needs, in the environments for which and with which they must live.

"Given that, tell me, what is astonishing about an exuberance of life sometimes developing extraordinary forms that are only rudimentary, and appear to engender a new being, which only improves, and, by virtue of that improvement, brings forth an incomplete model in which reason is dormant, in order to transport it to its normal constitution, indispensable to the full exercise of an intelligence for which it does not seem to have been born?

"Given that, what is astonishing about the Androgene, whose head and face are very nearly human, whose aborted limbs are the embryos of those of humans—and what is astonishing about the Androgenes, developing extraordinarily under some unknown influence, forming the model that we are seeking?" However, my philosopher added: "But you don't believe me."

Indeed, I did not believe him, and he perceived it.

"Well, sir, so much the worse for you! Personally, I believe it because I have studied it. As for you—why don't you believe it? You probably don't believe it because your education instructs you not to, perhaps because your religion instructs you not to." My philosopher was becoming increasingly animated: "And yet, you believe things much more incredible than mine!

"An acorn becomes an oak tree by assimilating something of the substance of the earth—which, however, bears no resemblance to the acorn or the oak. A drop of blood enclosed in an egg produces a bird, incubated by gentle heat. A child becomes a man, transforming what he eats into blood, flesh and bone; furthermore, that child is born from I don't know what—a putrefaction, a tiny organic body that resembles nothing at all, according to some, an animalcule, according to others, but a formless animalcule in that case, spontaneously generated.

"How does all that come about? Tell me! Oh, if I proposed those incredible truths to you, you wouldn't believe me."

"Pardon me, but if I believe, it's because I see, and that is sufficient for me."

"Oh, if you only want to believe what you see, you won't believe very much...but does your reason, in any case, also tell you that human beings cannot be born in any other way than they are? Does it tell you that the origin of humans from Androgens is more incredible than yours? Does it tell you that humans did not emerge one day—when, I don't know, under what influence, I don't know—in the manner than I have described to you?"

"I don't know, sir," I replied, wearying somewhat of that kind of discussion, "but I repeat: I can see the oak emerge from the acorn."

"And that is very fortunate, sir," he retorted, hotly, "for the species would be doomed, just as the human species would be doomed if human beings could not produce human beings. So I'm not talking about reproduction, but about primal generation. Now it doesn't offend my reason to think that an Androgene might have formed a human by means of a generative process that I do not see, but which I understand."

And to me, sir, it is offensive to believe that a monster like your Androgene could have produced a being as perfect as a human."

My interlocutor burst out laughing.

"And are the putrefaction, or the formless animalcule of your reproduction," he said, "any more worthy of human generation? Oh, you're more credulous than me, sir." Maliciously, he added: "It's true that you see, while I'm only reasoning—but you didn't see the primal generation. How can you test my reasoning?"

"By telling you that intelligence can only arise in a being conformed for it," I replied, slightly annoyed by my adversary's persistence.

"Perfect! But I didn't tell you that my Androgene had human intelligence while it remained an Androgene; when it develops, however, as it acquires the beautiful human mechanism, of which it has all the rudiments, it can function from then on as a human. And your animalcule, sir, does it think? Has it intelligence, so long as it has not emerged from its embryonic state? No, it hasn't. It's like my Androgene, then." With a great expression of contentment, he added: "You won't get ahead of me, sir, because I'm right, while your reasoning, I fear, is nothing but your education, or perhaps, I repeat, your religion."

"But sir," I replied, firmly. "Why do you want me to deny my religion on this point? Has God nothing to do with our beliefs, especially this one?"

"I beg your pardon, but God has everything to do with this—that's my belief, at least. But what do you mean by God? What is the God of Caucasia? Do you think, like *good people*, that God is a patriarch with a white beard and a bald forehead, who commands a numerous family, a king on a throne who governs like the kings of earth? For us, God is a principle; he is the sovereign principle, life itself; for us he is the creator of human beings, whether human beings originate from Androgenes or from worms, as you contend.

"You see, sir, that we are all believers, as you are, on our island." He smiled with all the tenacity of a philosopher consolidating his theses, and added: "You also see that although you have proved to me, as I never doubted, that humans are reproduced by humans, you have not proved to me that the first humans were not born of Androgenes...who themselves, say some of our savants, are sometimes born spontaneously of a fetal putrefaction, just like your animalcule of reproduction..."

I was dealing with a strong party, as you can see, my friend. The man was probably a savant in his own island, and he had all the tenacity of a savant, as well as a fierce appetite for debate. So he transformed me into a combatant, although I had said almost nothing to him, doubtless in order to have the honor of defeating me. I was a trifle annoyed, I confess, but what I had just seen and could see did not disturb my philosophy overmuch. I therefore let my antagonist triumph at his ease. Besides which, the daylight was fading and I had no trouble remembering that this was not the goal of my voyage. I therefore started looking around, in order to get my bearings for my departure.

I don't know, in any case, whether, in spite of all that he had said, my interlocutor was firmly convinced, for after a moment's silence, he suddenly began laughing wholeheartedly. At what? I don't know. Then, shaking me by the hand profusely, he reminded me about his island, which he had invited me to visit, and dived into the sea, doubtless to go in search of his clothes.

My first impulse was to follow him, but reflection held me back. I was afraid of going further than I wished. I deferred the possibility of meeting up with him again one day on his island in order to study it at my ease. If I'm not able to do that, I abandon the possibility to you, my friend, knowing your great desire to learn.

My God, I merely said to myself, on seeing him cleave the waves so briskly. *In truth, I'm not entirely certain whether that is a man!*

He was, in any case, an individual who could have informed me about the sea where I was, the places in the vicinity that it was important to know about, and the route I needed to follow to arrive in New Cosaquia. And I had not asked him about that! Poor fool that I was, I had discussed armchair philosophy with him, and had forgotten the philosophy of the voyager.

I was able to repent of that at my leisure, for I looked everywhere, and could no longer see anything of my savant, and could not see the shore of the sea anywhere.

I therefore returned to the point at which I had seen the floating island appear, and the Androgenes, in order to resume my initial itinerary—and I did well, for, taking my aerostat up to a great height, I was able, on aiming my telescope in the direction I had been following to begin with, to discover land some distance way, or at least an island of considerable extent—perhaps New Cosaquia. I wasn't sure of anything, however, not even where I was, in spite of what the metal plaque that had mentioned Alger had told me—which might, after all, have led me into error.

Nevertheless, I drove my balloon bravely toward the land I had just discovered, and which I reached in a short time. My joy was soon complete; the country was inhabited, and, what seemed even more appreciable was that it seemed to be inhabited by a very hospitable people—for at the sight of my balloon, loud and joyful cheers rose up below me, and then a host of small balloons leapt nimbly into the air to come to meet me.

XX. THE QUEEN'S PALACE

I mingled with my escort of honor, to whom I waved very graciously, and accompanied them proudly. The cheers ceased as they drew closer; no words were addressed to me. They probably did not believe that they would understand my language, so I was not surprised.

We went forward in that fashion for nearly half an hour, and then I saw the balloons of my escort descend to the ground. I did likewise, but I could not guess where I was. At any rate, what seemed to me to be most certain was that I was not far from the sea. The time I had taken to arrive there with my balloon was sufficient indication of that.

We had landed on a gently-sloping hill, the earth of which was horribly afflicted with rents and ravines, sometimes very deep, running bizarrely in all directions, leaving fragments of earth and boulders suspended as if magically. On several of these islets the pillars of a bridge were majestically embedded, whose vault, holed and crumbling in many places, only seemed to be held together by the tangle of grasses and shrubs that almost hid it from view.

I could not see any trace of a river in the vicinity—only a few trickles of water running through the depths of the ravines. Whence came the bridge, then? Who had put it there? To serve what purpose?

What was no small subject of astonishment for me was to find such a monument on a hill, and I strove to understand what upheaval could have altered the aspect of the place to the extent of transporting to the summit of a mountain a construction whose usage ordinarily places it in the depths of a valley, or what imperious necessity had constructed there an artificial level that is only ever erected much lower down.

The bridge, moreover, was evidently not of modern construction; I can assure you of that, my friend, and you can take my word for it, for it was certainly not necessary to be a expert

179

architect to deduce it. Who had built it, then? I dare not say what I thought, and I had no hope of learning anything from my hosts, for the moment, because my hosts were not speaking to me. They were hardly saying anything to one another.

While I yielded to my reveries, they were entirely occupied in emptying their balloons, and they appeared disposed to make up a caravan by themselves. One of them, however, soon detached himself from the others and, extracting me from my dream, took my by the hand in order to invite me to follow him. We went back the way we had come and, in a few minutes arrived, by a horribly pitted road, in front of a kind of fortress, whose walls, which were nothing but a heap of stone slabs linked together by branches and rising up to a considerable height, loomed up to our right. A few narrow pathways excavated into the thickness of that fort by the removal of rubble, and almost invisible beneath the thicket of plants and trees, served to connect the inside to the outside.

What was that mass? To my eyes, a ruin among ruins. It was doubtless a ruin, but an inhabited ruin. I soon saw that it was an entire village, for I was introduced into it, preceded and followed by my guides; or, rather, it was a collection of huts of different shapes and dimensions, which were huddled in a vast enclosure. The enclosure was sealed by the vast mass of dry stones that had initially caught my attention.

One habitation more beautiful and grandiose than the rest rose up in their midst with some pretention of luxury. It was surrounded by courtyards and gardens. It looked bizarre, but it was not without elegance in the midst of the crude primitivism of the village. Its borders were protected by an iron gate that had certainly not been manufactured by the inhabitants of the place. It must have dated back a long away, if my memories did not deceive me, for it resembled in every particular a unique gate that we have in the Museum of Caucasipol, for which our government paid a high price, as a specimen off the workmanship of the remotest antiquity.

That artistic richness seemed strange in the midst of that savage chaos, but what seemed stranger still was that the bottom halves of the walls of the edifice were different in their construction, reminiscent of an ancient building, let us say frankly, in the style that a few excavations have revealed to us as that of the peoples we recognize as the oldest in the world. The rest of the building was the work of modern hands— probably those of my guides or their forebears.

Above the entrance door of the habitation a little metal plaque was nailed, on which I could read, with the aid of the knowledge I had acquired from Père Franco's book, but without being able to understand the French: Boulevard du Maine.[37] Even though that sign of sorts made no sense to me, it made me shiver with joy nevertheless, because it reminded me of some of my most cherished memories.

A black mark, however, still hung over my train of thought, throwing shadows of doubt and anxiety over it—for, after all, where was I?

I was asking myself that when one of my guides—the one who seemed to have taken particular responsibility for me—took me by the arm and took me into a hut a few paces away.

That hut was more spacious than the others, and divided into several compartments. I was introduced into the rearmost compartment, where I found myself confronted by several men assembled there to receive me.

The men were gravely seated around a table of raw wood. Their costume like that of my guides, was simple, and

---

[37] Mettais' readers would have known that *le* Maine (as opposed to *la* Maine, the river) was an ancient province of France, which gave its name to a Boulevard du Maine in Cholet and—far more significantly in this instance—to the Avenue du Maine in Paris, on which the Gare Montparnasse is located. They would, by now, having grown used to the prodigies accomplished by Daghestan's aerostat, would not have been unduly skeptical about the possibility of its having traveled from Algiers to Paris in a single day, including two stopovers.

could hardly have been more primitive. A sort of loincloth made of animal-skin, varied—probably according to individual taste—covered their spine instead of a cloak. The rest of the body as enveloped by similar hides, cut according to need. On the head they had a kind of fur bonnet, made of the same fabric, I thought, as their footwear.

I do not know whether there was any fashion in favor among those people, but I what I saw scarcely made my suspect it. A fortunate people, able to stick to the necessities, who did not seek to imprison their form and the strength of their limbs in cumbersome garments.

All my hosts were grim-faced, and received me gravely. Personally, I was smiling, confident at heart. The man I assumed to be the most important in the company seemed to have all the strength and energy of second youth, about sixty years old. I say sixty, in our language, although it would be necessary to say forty at the most, according to theirs, for I learned later that their year is about thirteen moons.[38] His ebony-black hair fell in long undulations over his neck. His beard covered his entire face; it as very smooth and cut to a length that did not extend as far s the breast. He had a handsome face, slightly harsh, to my mind, and with something that, it seemed to me, I would never have been able to make out—but there was undoubtedly intelligence there.

After studying me briefly, the individual I took for the president of the assembly—because he was seated in the mid-

_____

[38] This sudden indication that the Caucasian "year" is not as long as ours is so startling that many readers must have wondered whether they were misinterpreting Daghestan's allegation. Given that the year, unlike the week and the hour, is astronomically defined, one would expect it to be independent of cultural idiosyncrasy. Nor is the approximate ratio here implied adequate to explain such curiosities as the fact that Père Franco was said to have died at the age of 196, or that the reigns of the three Schlamyls were said to have spanned 300 years.

dle—got up and said to me, in a grave and tremulous voice, in a language that was not his own by custom, which I could grasp in part—which was, it appears, the language of the local savants: "Who are you? Where have you come from?"

"I am a citizen of the Republic of Caucasia," I replied, with as much gravity as my interrogator. "I am traveling in order to learn, and I have come from various places which you might not know, most recently from Timbuktu."

"But where did your balloon come from? Who gave it to you? It does not belong to you."

These words were spoken in a quavering voice that did not reassure me at all. My interlocutor was very pale; the muscles of his face were agitated, as if by a nervous tic, and his eyes were flashing.

I made no reply. In order to respond I would have liked to know what secret fire was burning my interrogator, in order not to irritate any further the anger that I could see rising to his face. I am no coward, as you know, my friend, but I don't know whether it would have been bravery or imprudence to say anything that might have caused a rage that was becoming more concentrated to overflow, which might put me in the gravest peril and cut short my voyage.

"Pardon me," I said, eventually, after having turned my tongue over in my mouth for some time, "but would you care to tell me, to begin with, where I am, in what country, and facing what judges?—for I can see that you are judges."

"Your balloon, your balloon," my interlocutor said, without answering my question. "Where did it come from? Where did you get it? You have stolen it."

That sentence, my friend—*you have stolen it*—was said so sharply that it struck me full in the chest, and I could see no suitable response to it other than in my pocket, where I had a fine ten-shot revolver, fully loaded. I wanted to take it out, but as I made the necessary half-turn I saw that I was surrounded by a multitude of men, armed to the teeth, who were filling the hut and its surroundings. They had slipped in there without my having noticed them.

To bring my revolver out of my pocket would have been folly; I contented myself with replying in a dignified manner that the word that had just been hurled in my face was a insult in my country, but I assumed that it must not be in the country where I was, for my honorable interlocutor, whom I took for a man of courage and heart, would not otherwise have said it to me in the midst of his army, while I was alone.

My speech appeared to make an impression, and I saw my judge—or my insulter, as you wish, my friend—grimace a smile at me. I took advantage of that problematic apology to declare myself satisfied and explained at length my possession of the balloon. I don't know what they thought of it, but I saw my interlocutor go even paler, if that were possible. He concluded the session, said a few words to his people, and left, escorted by the council that had assisted him with its mutism during my interrogation.

I stood there, very anxious about what had just happened to me, for I read the redoubling of my judge's pallor as a bad omen. I waited there for almost an hour, in the midst of an escort that no longer seemed to me to be an escort of honor. Then a messenger arrived. He opened a trapdoor that I had not previously noticed beneath my feet, and I was taken down into a dark cell.

My situation was direly complicated, as you can see, my friend, and I could not help taking it very seriously. What would become of me there? I had some suspicion. I had not yet been flayed alive, it is true, nor hung, nor impaled, nor run through with a sword-blade, but all of that might only have been postponed.

If I had had a clearer head, and especially if I had had light, perhaps I could have distracted myself from my anxieties by carrying out archeological research on the walls of my prison, its floor and its construction, for I might have been in some once-famous place, to judge by what I had already seen. But I did not think of that in the darkness. The past was no longer of any significance to me; I was only anxious about the present now, and especially the future. I knew full well, and also thought, that even the most celebrated prison—and the most enviable when one is in one's study, pen in hand—is still a prison, and sometimes the first step to the scaffold.

I don't know how long those reflections had lasted, rendered more painful by the complaints of my empty stomach, when the fatal trap-door opened, and something was dropped at my feet, which I picked up. It was evidently for my nourishment: an item of food, which I ate and found delicious. I was slightly consoled; if they intended to kill me, they had not yet made a firm decision, and were not treating me as a beast to be slaughtered or an enemy that one throws into an oubliette.

With my stomach settled, the funereal thoughts were somewhat distanced, allowing my mind to return to its normal state, recovering its passion for discovery. I could not do much for the moment, but I had discovered one thing, which might one day be more useful, I hope, than for a people to conquer a province. Let me tell you about that immediately, my friend.

The foodstuff that had been served to me so abruptly, is completely unknown to us and our neighbors, and in all the civilized countries I know. It might, however, be an immense boon to the entire world, and it is a fortunate supplement to wheat. It is a tuber, starchy, like wheat, but with a more savorous taste. It grows almost naturally in that uncultivated land, as I was later to learn. The people of the country call it by a name that is difficult to pronounce—difficult for me, that is—which means "ground-apple."[39]

If ever I get out of here, I said to myself, as I ate my ground-apple, *I shall gratify my homeland with this precious vegetable, and I shall try to immortalize myself by giving it my name.* And I shall, my friend, for I have brought some of these fruits back to Caucasia

---

[39] I have translated "*pomme de terre*" literally, as the context requires, although the reference is obviously to a potato. We must assume that the one thrown down to Daghestan was not raw.

185

I had, therefore eaten; that was good. The food that I had eaten might perhaps one day become, I thought, a source of glory; that was even better. A third matter, however, much more serious than the other two, presented itself to my desires: *when will I get of here?* I asked myself, very anxiously.

I was asking myself that terrible question when the trapdoor of my cell opened again. I heard a soft voice speak authoritatively above my head, and then a louder voice instructed me to come out. I did so without urgency, as without dread; I had all the resignation of a courageous victim yielding to brutal force.

I found myself face to face with a crowd that was doubtless not very benevolent, which was waiting for me there, but I paid it no heed. I only saw a young woman at their head: a woman who appeared to me to be more beautiful than all the women in the world, for she was looking at me with a great deal of interest, it seemed, and even—I believed so, at least—with a slight smile on her face. Her expression was, however, grave.

Was she the wife or daughter of some chief? Or was she the priestess of some anthropophagous divinity, come to feel an intended victim to see whether he was fat enough?

XXI. OUCHDA

I was soon reassured as to my situation. My gracious visitor made a hand gesture, said a few words and everyone vanished; we remained alone. She said down, and beckoned me to sit down beside her. She was very gracious for the daughter or wife of a barbarian, so I immediately decided to trust her completely and recovered my aplomb, which had been somewhat disturbed for a few hours.

"You are the citizen Daghestan?" my noble visitor said to me, in an accent and a language almost identical to ours.

Oh, on hearing my name I leapt from my seat. Who here knew me, then? I looked at my interlocutor with a bewildered gaze, which caused her to smile slightly, but I made no reply.

"You are the citizen Daghestan?" she asked me again, gesturing to me to sit down again.

"I am," I replied.

"You have come from Caucasia, passing through Zeeland, then…help me, I beg you."

"Through the Sudan. I have come directly from Timbuktu."

That's right—I'd forgotten." With perfect impassivity, she continued: "Well, you've been condemned to death."

"Ah!" I said, in a tone that carried so many meanings that my interlocutor seemed quite alarmed by it. "Is it to carry out that sentence," I continued, after a momentary pause, "that you have come to take me from my cell?"

"You weren't yet in a cell," she replied, with a coolness that terrified me.

"What! Madame is joking," I said, staring into the eyes of the priestess of the anthropophagous gods, "for that obviously was one; the vault of the cell is even stained with the blood of your victims."

At this point, my friend, my interlocutor burst into what seemed to me to be laughter of the most savage ferocity. "No,"

187

she told me, calming down somewhat, "you weren't in a cell; you were in a cellar; and the blood that you saw so clearly on the ceiling is the color of a sort of stone, which we call *brick*, of which we have found no quarry anywhere." In a tone that seemed to me to be mocking, she added: "Perhaps you, who are more knowledgeable than us, know where antiquity obtained those red blocks, for you were in a cellar that neither our people not the Cosaques who preceded us in this land for many centuries built. It dates back much earlier—to the French of olden times, say the people who surround us and want you dead."

I was listening to that beautiful woman with all the pleasure of an antiquary who is on the track of a discovery when the final word that had just escaped her lips reminded me of the sad reality of my situation.

"Well, if they want me dead," I said, sharply, "let them kill me and get it over with; for I don't know whether you've come on their behalf like a cat toward a mouse."

My interlocutor shivered, not with anger—oh, I could see that clearly—but with dolor, on hearing those words. So I hastened to take back the brutality of my invective.

"Forgive me, Madame," I said to her, with the gallantry of a fop attempting to soften a hard heart. "I didn't mean to say to you what I just said, but I wanted you to understand how much I regretted hearing such bad news from such a pretty mouth."

I don't know whether my words had the desired effect, but it established a moment of silence between us, after which we chatted like two friends. This is what I learned.

I learned from the young woman that I was definitely in New Cosaquia, that her name was Ouchda[40] and that she was the daughter of the king, Rhaman X. I'm conceited enough to admit that I had guessed almost all of that, and thought that I had grown a few centimeters taller. So I made myself even more amiable and gracious than ever, for I found at that mo-

---

[40] There is a city in Morocco called Oujda.

ment an infinite charm in conversing with that beautiful daughter of savages, even though I was still sitting on the executioner's chopping-block.

In fact, the conversation soon took such an interesting turn from my point of view that I almost forgot completely where I was and gave myself over entirely to Ouchda's stories.

When I say "conversation," my friend, that's an error, for we weren't conversing. Ouchda talked, almost on her own, and soon got carried away to such an extent that I saw that her mind, too, was a long way from the place where we were, and especially from the ax that was hanging over my neck. The present no longer mattered to us; we were like two lovers of knowledge talking about history and the fine arts—with the difference that I was almost always listening.

It seemed evident to me that King Rhaman's daughter was aware of my mania for learning, and that she wanted to satisfy it before arriving at the reality of my situation. Was that cruelty? I don't believe so. In any case, for me, her speech was so seductive that no such thought entered my head, and I let her speak at her ease.

I shall never forget that day's conversation, my friend, especially the scant information that Ouchda gave me, which I do not feel humiliated in taking for the truth, about the history of her homeland, even though that history is very different from the one we earnestly teach to our children as the only plausible and authentic one...

Thus, I proclaim loudly and sincerely now that we do not know the history of New Cosaquia. Furthermore, that no longer astonishes me, now that I know that the people in question have no written history, and that no one has ever penetrated their homeland. It is history is only found, in fact, in its popular traditions.

The people do, however, have a few books, which are regarded by them as sacred. The books must certainly be old—extremely old, in fact—for I don't know whether the Cosaques have ever gone in for printing, or, at any rate, in what epoch that might have been. It must certainly have been

189

unknown for centuries, not to say millennia. Unfortunately, no one is allowed access to these books, which thus remain locked treasures, so historical information is confined to tradition alone.

It appears, according to the tradition of these people, that the place where I was really had been a great city once, and that the city in question had been destroyed thousands of years ago—20,000, they said, with the popular exaggeration that it is necessary to disregard. It was God, religious devotees said—probably according to their sacred books, corrupted by their mores—unable to tolerate its excesses any longer, who sent against it the fires of volcanoes, civil wars, and invasions, first of neighboring peoples and then of peoples from further away.

No trace of the name of the destroyed city remained in my pretty companion's memories. She only knew the general history of the region, and within that history she only knew about the invasion of the Cosaques, who had retained it in their possession for several centuries, and that of the Moroccans, her ancestors—who, she said, no longer being able to contain their immense civilization and even more immense population in lands that the sea was incessantly diminishing by continual inundations, could find no better solution than to attack the Cosaques, whom they submitted to their domination and their laws, while conserving for the land the name of its ancient masters. For Ouchda, the ancient masters were the Cosaques; she was completely unaware that the country had had another name before them, and other possessors.

The Moroccan invasion had found the country divided into two distinct tribes, one dominating the other enslaved. It enslaved both tribes, so the land was subsequently divided into three tribes, the dominant one henceforth being the Moroccans.

The first two tribes had once enjoyed great power, which had rendered them redoubtable to their neighbors, but by the epoch of the Moroccan invasion they were singularly enfeebled. They had been weakened by continual revolts by the

190

slaves, who were seeking to recover a liberty that they had surely never known, and by the bloody victories of the dominators, who paid for their triumphs with the loss of their forces. From these struggles was born a strange hatred that only seemed likely to end with the death of the last of the vanquished. Domination by a third master, a common enemy, did not appear to have weakened it at all. These two tribes were the Cosaques—the stronger, sovereign tribe—and the French. That, at least, was their pretention.

The honorable judges who had condemned me to death were the children of the latter tribe; like them, they also claimed to have emerged from the blood of the French of olden times. I would have needed to study the physiognomy of the people in more detail and the physical type in order to take what my beautiful storyteller was saying seriously, for, in truth, the savagery of their conduct toward me scarcely disposed me to grant them a title that I regarded as a badge of honor. I contented myself for the moment with refusing them my approval by means of a pitying smile.

Ouchda guessed what I was thinking.

"You can think what you like," she told me. "The fact is that our city, which our forefathers called Figuig, in memory of a city of old Morocco, is called Paris by these French, your enemies, and the Cosaques have never protested about it. Personally, I prefer to say that I don't know what city was here..."

The Moroccans had not had much trouble implanting themselves in the midst of New Cosaquia, according to my charming Ouchda's history, but they had had a great deal of trouble, at first, in maintaining themselves there, and especially in keeping the peace there. The French, since it is necessary to call them by that name, were restless and conspiratorial, always on the lookout, as they had been under the domination of the Cosaques, to reconquer the imaginary domination that had only ever been, for them, a memory of tradition. The Cosaques, for their part, were not content to be submissive, to be slaves, and they frequently revolted.

The king of New Cosaquia was thus obliged to live, nowadays, in the midst of his new subjects, whose turbulence caused him great anxiety, dreading that he might succumb to the incessantly-renewed attacks of the two parties. He would certainly have succumbed, Ouchda said, if he had not had the cunning of a serpent—if he had not been more prudent than could be expected of a *barbarian*. I emphasize that word, my friend, because Ouchda emphasized it sarcastically in her narration.

Personally, I would certainly not have given the name barbarian to the great Rhaman I, perhaps the most erudite of the Moroccan race, according to history, in a time when that race was so advanced in the civilization of the Middle Ages. Perhaps I would not have said as much of his descendant, the present king, Rhaman X. That was evidently what his charming daughter feared, who was anticipating my thoughts in order to combat them. My thoughts could not be hostile to him, since I did not know him, but the fine and delicate mind of the young woman had divined that I was nevertheless not likely to be inclined to see him as a great man.

Thus, she was untiring in a eulogy that I desired to be true, attributing to her father a major role in the fortunate machinations that had sustained the prosperity of the kingdom in the midst of two troublesome tribes. To him alone that excellent daughter gave all the glory of a politics of which the ancients had had no inkling, and which was far from revealing an inept sovereign.

The politics of Rhaman X were, in fact, very clever; that was evidence of an extraordinary man, if the politics were indeed his.

In his time, the lands situated to the north of the city were assigned to the Cosaques, those to the south to the French; the king, his government and the majority of his subjects held the middle ground. There was, evidently, no fusion and no unity.

Everything indicates that these respective situations were not recent, and that they had always subsisted in that fashion since Rhaman I—but what was recent, according to Ouchda, and was therefore rightly attributable to her father, was the skill with which King Rhaman X had been able to profit from the hatred that divided the two vanquished tribes and maintain them in obedience by setting the Cosaques against the French and the French against the Cosaques whenever the need arose.

This strategy is quite simple, but it required to be found. Although it is habitual among a few people of our day, who maintain their domination thereby, holding in check the various passions that ferment in empires, it is not credible that the Cosaque monarch had obtained his inspiration from them. Thus, all the glory reverts to him, along with all the benefits—for, with those politics, he had no need of vast armies to maintain equilibrium in his homeland.

Thus, I sincerely admired that governmental skill—which had, moreover, achieved an excellent result, that of peace. The armed uprisings of rebels were, in fact, becoming increasingly rare, and by the time of my voyage it appeared that resignation was so complete that everyone was living in peace, while some were nevertheless still dominant and the others still salves.

Although Ouchda and her father attributed this calm to their wisdom, not everyone saw it that way. It appeared that the nation's sages attributed all the honor of the peace that they had already enjoyed for some time to an exceedingly rigorous law, to which many curiosity-seekers and imprudent individuals had fallen victim—a very ancient and fundamental law, which forbade entry to the region to any stranger, on pain of death.

At this point I shook my head sadly, criticizing that law and what it had permitted with respect to me. Ouchda noticed the gesture.

"You don't approve," she said, "And you're right, for you're a civilized man, while we're only savages, or at least *barbarians*..." In the same ironic tone, she added: "My father is a barbarian, and he was reasoning like a barbarian when he swore to observe that law, and said to us, in swearing it:

193

'Children, we're not on the earth to learn many things; we're only interested in learning one alone: the art of being happy. Now, to be happy, it's sufficient to be content, but we can only be content if we don't extend out gaze beyond our frontiers, if we're completely ignorant of what is happening there.'"

It appears, however, that Rhaman X had failed in that oath, for Ouchda told me that, driven by some mysterious influence, he had just repealed that law. She even added, very graciously, that he had repealed it in my favor; that his decree had been issued in Trevig, in the kingdom of Zeeland, where he was presently visiting King Belt, a crowned philosopher—who might, in my opinion, have had something to do with that decree…if the decree existed; for, after a moment's reflection, I did not believe it. So I lowered my head and smiled anxiously, trying to divine where the king's daughter was heading.

"But Madame," I said to her, "Have I understood you correctly? How could your father, the king, who is in Trevig in Zeeland, know that I'm here in a cell?"

"He knows," she replied, with all the naivety of conviction.

"That I've been condemned to death? Who told the king all that?" I raised my head and fixed the young woman with an interrogative stare that meant: "Aren't you joking at my expense?"

Ouchda understood my unspoken question and frowned.

"I have no desire to deceive you," she replied. "Everything is as I have said." Her expression opened up, and she added: "But how can you not understand, you who come from a land of savants? Are you not acquainted, as we are, with the power of spiritism?"

"Spiritism!" I replied, opening my eyes wide with astonishment. "What's that, Madame?"

"It's a science that I would certainly like to teach you," Ouchda told me, looking at me shrewdly and shrugging her shoulders slightly, "but I only know its effects; I'm not an initiate. It's a mystery to me; only the Queen…"

At that point she stopped short, and looked at me anxiously.

"The Queen, your mother, Madame?" I said, interestedly.

Ouchda pinched her lips; she was as red as a rising sun. "No," she replied, after a momentary hesitation. "No, my mother is in heaven."

"Oh, forgive me, Madame," I said, emotionally, "if I've been indiscreet." After a momentary pause, I added, with the effrontery of curiosity, for which I had no other excuse than a desire to know at any price: "It's just that I thought I had seen her in the king's cortege in Trevig."

"Ah! You've seen her," Ouchda said, in a tone that might well have been bitter irony. In a whisper, as though talking to herself alone, she added: "That's true, since he's in Zeeland and *she* is protecting him."

Then she stood up, with the abruptness of a petulant child and began walking back and forth in the room. Then she came back toward me, as I remained there, bewildered, with a question hanging on my lips. Her face was pale but calm.

"Who, then, is protecting me, Madame?" I asked, with more impetuosity than prudence.

"Who?" the daughter of the king replied, disdainfully. "That woman, our slave—the Queen, since they call her the Queen in her tribe, the French. She's the fiancée of the chief of that tribe, whom she ought to marry, according to the law...and as it is their most sacred law that orders it, she must obey under pain of death...unless she takes a vow of perpetual celibacy."

Ouchda appeared to take great pleasure in telling me about that savage law, which ought not to have been of any interest to her. Personally, I was devastated, and maintained the most profound silence.

"Yes, I can see that all that's of no interest to you," she went on, "and that it's cruel to talk to you at such length about so many things that are indifferent to you while you're there, at the foot of the scaffold..." She darted a covert glance at me, and added: "For you have been condemned to death by the Queen's fiancé."

"The Queen's fiancé! Him! That man!" I said, in a menacing tone.

"Oh, don't worry," Ouchda hastened to say, with a sardonic smile, which revealed to me that she had not misinterpreted the significance of my threat, although she appeared to accept it as a cry of resentment. "Don't worry: the man who has reopened the gates of his kingdom in your favor has also sent you a reprieve. My father has thus granted you mercy, Citizen Daghestan, and has ordered that an aerostat be placed at your disposal in order that you may continue your voyages." She bowed profoundly, and suddenly said, in a voice more broken than I had expected, to which I could not attach any significance: "Farewell, sir."

"Until we meet again, Madame!" I exclaimed, in my turn, wanting to hurry after her—for she had just gone out with the rapidity of a hunted deer.

A wall of armed men suddenly formed in front of me, however, which I could not get through. I could see nothing beyond it, but I heard the sounds of great activity around the hut. I guessed without difficulty that the king's daughter was still there, giving orders, but it was impossible for me to take a forward step in order to confirm it, for those who were guarding me obviously had no intention of letting me go free.

I was soon left in no doubt about that, on seeing the trapdoor of my ridiculous but fatal cell open once again beneath my feet, and then close again above my head.

"Ouchda! Ouchda!" I shouted then, with the rage of despair. "Oh! She has deceived me! I'm going to die here, miserably, in this cellar..."

Oh, my fatherland, how beautiful you seemed to me then. Oh, my friends, how ardently I would have thrown myself into your bosom. How I invoked your memory, your aid... But what as the point, poor fool that I was? I was there, alone, on inhospitable soil, devoid of civilization, rationality, justice...and the plaything of a coquette's cruelty, I thought at the time.

A few moments later I heard my judges come back into the hut, talking excitedly to one another. It seemed to me that they were not alone. It even seemed that they were accompanied by someone whom I judged to be a highly-placed dignitary by his insignia, who appeared to listen more than he talked. I was all ears at that moment, but I could not understand any of it—the language they were speaking was entirely unknown to me.

How long did they stay there? I don't know—an eternity, it seemed to me. They finally fell silent; then the trap-door opened again, and I saw I don't know how many men come down, some armed to the teeth, others carrying torches in their hands, which inundated my prison with lugubrious gleams. The men were silent.

At the sight of them, I did not strike a combative pose, which would have been futile; nor did I affect the arrogance of a man who fears nothing. I retreated to the furthest corner of the cell, and commended my head and my soul to God alone.

The armed men advanced toward me resolutely, their yataghans raised for an attack, but—O prodigy!—they suddenly recoiled, fearfully, and hastened to get out of the cell, uttering frightful howls...

What had just happened, my friend, was something strange and incredible, which I scarcely dare relate here, but which I saw—really saw, with my own eyes.

At the moment when my executioners were about to strike me—for they were only a few paces away from me—a cloud, which I took at first for a trick of the torchlight, suddenly rose up between them and me; and from that cloud I saw, as they doubtless also saw, a white shadow emerge, representing perfectly, beyond all doubt, even for a man of the highest civilization, an old man with a long beard, emitting fiery flames from his eyes, and advancing over my head a long fleshless hand, as if to protect me.

Al that, my friend, I saw—saw perfectly clearly, while wide awake, for you will understand that I was not sleeping at that moment—and better still, my executioners had also seen it. That was what saved me from their blows.

But it was not over. The shade of the old man was still there, motionless, while my executioners fled, gripped by terror, back to the judges who had sent them. I soon saw the latter descend into the cell, accompanied by the important functionary. They did not seem to be afraid, though; they all bowed to the old man, without saying a word, and immediately turned round.

The trap-door of my prison remained open. The shade of the old man disappeared, and it only remained for me to escape, but I stood there petrified—I don't know for how long—in an ecstatic state. I didn't go out until I felt the contact of a gentle hand, which took hold of mine and drew me outside.

It was Ouchda.

A considerable crowd of men and women seemed to be waiting for us there, in front of the hut.

"Wretches!" cried the king's daughter. "What did you expect? What were you going to do? This man is a friend of the king, my father, and is under God's protection. Did I not entrust his life to you? Why have you disobeyed my orders? You'll answer to me for that with your heads. Prepare an aerostat for him, so that he may leave, if he wishes." She kissed me on the cheek, and said: "Farewell, sir."

I was henceforth inviolable to those people. The king's daughter had marked me with that kiss, which instructed everyone respect my person. I immediately perceived that, for all the faces surrounding me instantly took on a benevolent expression. Everyone hastened to obey Ouchda's orders, and within minutes an aerostat was prepared, in the midst of the most profound silence.

The young woman herself said nothing more, although she presided over the preparations for my departure. When everything was ready, she said: "Where would you like to go, friend Daghestan?"

"To Zeeland, Madame," I replied, in a voice fill of emotion.

"Very well," she said, paling more than I would have expected.

"I must at least go to thank your father the king," I said, with a gaze full of gratitude.

"And thank your benefactress, the Queen," she retorted, through clenched teeth. "That's only just."

Everyone overheard this conversation, but no one, assuredly, understood it.

Did I understand it myself? How could I say, without temerity, that I had divined the cord that was causing Ouchda's voice to vibrate?

My balloon being ready, I bowed profoundly to Ouchda, who took my hand and shook it very firmly. Then I climbed into my gondola.

The Queen's fiancé had orders to set up the machine, making its maneuvering easy enough for me to be able to steer it as I wished, effortlessly. He set to work without making any reply, but did so with such ill grace and with movements that seemed to me to be so convulsive that I was frightened.

I departed nevertheless, commending my soul to the God of voyagers, and bidding another farewell to the king's daughter.

"No—until we meet again," she replied, with a most gracious smile…and a tear too, I believe, in the corner of her eye. "Think about me sometimes."

"Oh, always, always!" I cried, with the enthusiasm of gratitude.

And I left.

XXII. THE GRADUATE ARACH

I was not as calm as I wanted to appear to everyone's gaze. So, when I found myself alone, I felt my false vigor suddenly abandon me, and succumbed to the weight of discouragement. Why? Do I know, my friend? The memory of that young woman, those judges, that prison and its apparition, the fact of my departure in such singular circumstances, and perhaps other memories still, were all oppressing me.

I lay down in my gondola in order to yield more easily to the sensations of a vague and unreflective dolor; but that, fortunately, was only a matter of minutes—or so, at least, I believed. I soon got up again, ashamed of my weakness, and recovered all my human strength.

But my balloon was moving rapidly, and I had no difficulty in observing, contrary to what I had believed, that I had covered a considerable distance already. How long ago was I since I had departed, then? I had no idea. I no longer had a compass that would have allowed me to determine the direction in which I was heading, nor an hourglass that would have permitted me to measure time. I no longer knew where I was; I had nothing but my heart to guide me to Zeeland—a poor compass in a land that was utterly unknown to me.

I set about examining my machine then, but the aerostat was new to me; it was not the Queen's, with which I had familiarized myself somewhat. Unfortunately, while I was examining it and trying to steer it as I wished, it was still moving, and moving in spite of me. Its movements were so insistent and so difficult to control that I made the decision to leave it to its own devices.

I wasn't overly anxious at first, for I believed that I really was on the way to Zeeland, toward which I knew my aerostat had been launched.

After a journey that seemed to me to have been very long, my aerostat finally came to a stop. The machine was no longer functioning, its mechanism had jammed; I was only maintained in the air by my balloon, which was still fully inflated, but which was threatening to speed away at random. I therefore descended to the ground.

But where was I! Alas, I was not in Zeeland. Oh, I should have suspected it. The queen's fiancé had done me a bad turn, sending me to the extremity of the earth. I was still fortunate that his malevolence had had no other objective than that.

I was, at any rate, in a civilized land, for I could see neither ruins, nor desiccated rocks, not uncultivated wilderness. All around me, on the contrary, was the breath of life and social wellbeing.

The vegetation was lush, fill of sap and labor; all the crops surrounding me radiated intelligence and good fortune. I had come down in the midst of fields, but in front of me there was a splendid city, so far as I could judge at a distance, of considerable extent. The noise of the most active civilization, which was circulating in its streets, was clearly audible to me. Great rivers evidently went through it, for I could see the waves emerging from the fields to penetrate into animated flanks in several places.

The place where I had come down was delightful in its freshness and revealed to all my senses the life of fortunate people. Habitations were scarce there, but had an appearance that caused me to regard them as an abode of peace-loving philosophers, or a meeting place of business-men seeking an occasional escape from the racket of overactive life.

A deep and wide stream was running at my feet, on the bank of which I secured my balloon, in order to have the liberty of going to investigate the surroundings. I had noticed a small isolated house a short distance away, half-hidden by a clump of trees, above which its roof and chimneys rose coquettishly. I was about to go in search of information there when I perceived a small boat carrying a lone man being rowed upriver to where I was. I waited.

"I beg your pardon, sir," I said to the oarsman, when he was close enough, while he was pulling his boat out of the stream in order to fold it up.

"Aha!" he said to me, looking sideways at me without pausing in his task, adding, in my own language, but with a strange accent: "It's you, sir."

"Do you know me, sir?" I asked him.

"No, of course not—but I saw your balloon up in the sky just now, and I haven't come to pay you my compliments."

"Really?" I replied, a trifle piqued.

"Really," he said, "for I can see that you haven't had any more success than the others."

"What others, if you please?"

"All those who have been landing here for six months, claiming that they were steering their balloons at will."

"Ah!"

"And that's quite understandable of course; $200,000 have been offered by a society, which will perhaps never have to pay out, to the man who discovers that secret. So, everyone in the world is in quest of the secret—and I might even say, if I had any pretention to wit, that everyone is up in the air, chasing the $200,000, they all come down somewhere, though—many of them here."

"Well, sir," I replied, confidently. "I can have that $200,000."

"You! Ha ha ha!" my interlocutor laughed, heartily. "You! But no one shall have them, my dear sir, for it's impossible to control that"—he pointed up at the sky—"and that." He pointed at my balloon.

"And what society has promised these $200,000?" I asked, opening my ears wide.

"The Philanthropic Society of Borneo, of course!"

"We're in Borneo!" I cried, in astonishment.

"Where the devil do you come from, then, to ask me such a question? In fact, your costume…I took it for fancy dress."

"I'm a citizen of Caucasia, sir, and…"

"One might certainly think so from your language," my interlocutor replied, interrupting me, "but as it's the custom here to demonstrate that one is an erudite person by speaking a foreign language. I thought that you wanted to prove that, and, believe me, I'm speaking Caucasian as best I can, although, to tell you the truth, I'm getting sick of it—but go on, I beg you. I'll make every effort to answer you."

"…And I've come from Timbuktu, in the Sudan," I added, after having listened respectfully to the Bornean's explanations. "On the way, I stopped for a few hours in New Cosaquia, where I experienced emotions I wouldn't wish on you."

The native of Borneo looked me up and down, and, having considered me carefully, replied gravely and almost respectfully: "I beg your pardon, sir. At first, I frankly admit, I took you for one of those poor jokers who have been flooding our fields for some time. It didn't occur to me that you were a serious man, as I know that the people of Caucasia are. I don't understand, but I believe you; I shall therefore give you the address of the secretary of the Philanthropic Society, and wish you god luck."

"I beg your pardon, sir," I replied, "but I would prefer that you gave me the address of a good hotel, where I can get a room—for, as I told you, I've come a long way and I need lodgings. I don't know anyone here, and I have no recommendation to anyone."

"Caucasia is not a country that is completely unknown to me," my Bornean told me, without answering my question, "although it's a very long way from here. I visited it once, and left a few friends there, I believe. I've even conserved such a good memory of them as not to remain a stranger to their interests. I subscribe to one of their periodicals, the *Caucasian Gazette*."

"I'm a contributor to it, sir," I said, with a certain pride.

"What is your name, if you please, if it's not indiscreet to ask?" my interlocutor said to me, with an interest that was considerably flattering to me. "I'm the graduate Arach."

"My name is Daghestan," I replied, lowering my eyes modestly.

"Daghestan!" cried the graduate Arach, his eyes sparkling with an amiable vivacity. "Oh, I know you, sir—and permit me to tell you that I admire and like you. You shall be my guest, if you please—this is my house." And he pointed to the little house in front of me, where I had intended to go in search of information.

I could not accept right away, so I hesitated, but just enough to ensure that I did not seem like an ill-bred individual; then I gave in. While he folded up the canvas boat that he had left at his feet in order to talk to me, therefore. I folded up my balloon, and we departed thus, each carrying our vehicle.

The Bornean citizen's house was delightful seen from outside, as I have already told you, my friend, but I cannot say as much of the interior, where I found all the comfort of ease, and even a touch of luxury, but no order in the furniture, and a carelessness that did not inspire much confidence in the economic preoccupations of my host, even though I'm not in the habit of judging a person by first impressions.

When we were inside my host came toward me, took me by the hand and said: "Welcome to my home. I believe that it was God who sent you to this house, to console me a little for the cares of life, for you're a philosopher, and one I hold in high esteem."

"I bowed to acknowledge the compliment. "Sir," I said to him, "life is only what one makes it. It has no value save for that which one attributes to it. I thought that you must be fond of philosophy, for I see you in the full flower of age, the age at which a man becomes a man, because he has experience, a knowledge of people and things, the age at which he acquires a strength that renders him infinitely precious to society, and yet you live here, among the fields."

"And alone," my host replied, "disenchanted with the life of which you speak, embittered against a world that values nothing, humans who are perverse and society, which is badly organized."

I had nothing to say about that, because I knew very little about Borneo. All I knew about the country was what modern history tells us—not much—for one always knows very little about counties in which one has not loved. I therefore listened without replying to that sally—which might, after all, have been the caprice of an honest man.

"If you only knew the kingdom and city of Borneo," the graduate added," by what books and periodicals told you, sir, you wouldn't know it. You'd know, it's true, that Borneo is a vast kingdom, bounded by the kingdoms of Ceylon and Cambodia in one direction, and the sea on all the others—which makes it a marvelously-situated peninsula, not far from the illustrious Republic of New Holland, from which it is only separated by a narrow arm of the Indian Sea, over which one of your compatriots is in the process of making his name immortal by constructing a phenomenal bridge that will connect the two nations. You'd also know that the Borneans are full of valor and glory, that they at the forefront of modern civilization, that they're rich and industrious, with polite and elegant mores—in sum, models in every respect. You'd know all that, because that's what people say, and you'd know nothing.

"To me, who knows them intimately, Borneans have polite mores, if you do as they wish, but harsh mores if you oppose their interests. They are suspicious, proud—even arrogant—ambitious and egotistical, and malevolent in all those vices. Their tongues are poisoned daggers, which will slay you under the pretext of joviality; their morality…is that of a cornered rat; and they do not believe in virtue. Their virtue is a hint of sentimentality, which they sometimes feel and proclaim very loudly. Every citizen of Borneo is very much aware of everyone else's duties, and no one surpasses him in the consciousness of his rights...

"There you are, sir: the Bornean, as he is at home, by his fireside. In public, too, he is no different. Follow him everywhere; in every job, in every administration that you find him, you will always find the same man. His vices, however, he will modify, for he is skillful; he will adapt them to the different wheels that he causes to turn. So, don't be surprised if the man in question is a petty tyrant everywhere, glorying in the power that he wants to make felt, a slave to the passions that he wants to satisfy. May God protect you from Borneans, sir!"

At this point, my graduate smiled bitterly, darting a glance full of spite at the window of his room, as if the enemy were there; then he got up and began laying a table, which he loaded with various fruits, presumably for our supper. He said nothing to me, though; he maintained the most profound silence, and I was able to reflect at leisure on the mores of the Borneans, which were not good, if they were not slightly exaggerated by my host's spite.

"I beg your pardon, sir," I said, softly, smiling at him as graciously as I could, "But I don't recognize the Borneans from that description. Are you not looking at them, Mr. Arach, through a prism that might perhaps show them in a more favorable light if you rotated it in another direction?"

"Not at all, not at all," my host replied, sitting down at the table in a casual manner that gave me pleasure, and gesturing to me to do likewise. "I don't rotate my prism, because I see people as they are. If, moreover, I have put a certain exaggeration into my conversation with you, it's not there, but rather when I mentioned the cares of life. Don't, I beg you, take what that I said literally, for I am, myself, very philosophical in that respect. The cares of life don't affect me. All I need is a place to live, a little bread and water, and I have all that; in fact, I have more, for I'm rich. Furthermore, the fiber of sensitivity has withered in me; the malicious can't make it vibrate at will. My resignation, in any case, is great; it's all the greater because I despise the world, and I'm convinced that honest men cannot maltreat a honest man. You see, sir, that the cares of life are nothing to me."

"I should like to have arrived at that degree of perfection," I told the graduate, "for its philosophical perfection to be insensitive to the darts of malice. Permit me to admire you; your philosophy is better than mine."

"Perhaps mine is unnecessary in Caucasia, but it is here. You'll see for yourself when you're more familiar with our mores, our habits and our laws." The effervescent graduate continued: "Look, here are some facts—a few facts, a little corner of the picture; let's look at them squarely. I had a house in Borneo, a big house; it was a fortune. That fortune I had acquired by hard work, one dollar at a time, in order to have rest and food in my old age, for our society makes no provision for the needs of old age or the infirmities of the unfortunate So much the worse for a man who has been improvident or unlucky in his work! So, I had this fortune, every single coin of which was covered with my sweat and blood. I had paid for it; it was mine—I believed so, at least." My host asked me point-blank: "In Caucasian properties that you have bought are yours, aren't they, sir?"

"Yes, sir," I replied. "Subject to certain conditions."

"Ah!" said Mr. Arach, bitterly. "Well, in Borneo we also have certain conditions." The Bornean put his elbows on the table, raised his fingers in front of his face and began to count them. "Here are our conditions. We buy a house, we pay the person who sold it to us—that's fair; but we don't buy it for ourselves alone; the Treasury wants it share, and it takes it off the top. Is that fair? I don't know; in any case, it's a good deal, for it takes it every time the property is sold or every time the owner does. The Treasury puts its crooked finger every-where..."

I smiled at my host, who was surely looking at me with-out seeing me. His lips grimaced an uncertain smile, which seemed to be demanding some comment from me.

I only replied with a wink and a shrug, which were meaningless because I really didn't know what to say.

"Well, that's not all," he continued. "That house, when you have bought it, paid for it and given the *other one* its share, is still not yours. The Treasury takes possession of it then, and subjects it to the tribunal of its inquisition. There, it is weighed, calculated, dissected, put to the question—

tortured, in sum—by all the hot irons of eyes and numbers, and finally taxed with an annual payment in perpetuity..."

"What do you say to that, sir? You can see that I'm right when I tell you that the house is still not yours when you've bought it. I ought to have said that it will never be yours—never! You will only be its administrator or shareholder, and an unlucky shareholder, for your house will be sucked dry by an army of vampires, which I shall not mention..."

Mr. Arach was truly indignant in speaking thus. It was, therefore, hazardous to interrupt him. I was, however, about to venture a few words about his house and the income it brought him when he stopped me by replying to my question in advance.

"Yes, I know what you're going to say," he said. "You want to talk to me about income, and especially about the income from my house, while I'm only talking about charges. Well, I tell you frankly—and this is what irritates me—that the income from my house is far from responding reasonably to its expenses. Add that its expenses are often increased by the bad faith of some of those who live in it—and, in order to understand me, you ought to know, Citizen Daghestan, that in Borneo, people pay the rent as they wish. It's not necessary to be clever to avoid it; it's sufficient not to want to, and many people don't want to. The law, moreover, is flexible enough to favor them somewhat in that case, by imposing onerous conditions and difficult steps on the creditor if he wishes to safeguard his rights.

"You see, given that, how hypothetical the income from a house is here; nothing is certain but the expenses.

"Hold on—there's another charge that I haven't told you about, which I forgot, doubtless like many others. The street that passes alongside my house isn't mine. I have no other rights in that regard than a passer-by. I scarcely use it, moreover, because I always go on foot. Well, it's me who has to maintain it, maintain it for everyone, or pay the Treasury a few that it taxes arbitrarily, and which isn't cheap, if I wish to exonerate myself from that obligation.

"And then again—but no, I don't want to say any more about that. The anecdote would be piquant, but only for a Bornean. No more do I want to talk about that swarm of employees of all sorts, rascals of every age, which protective administrations launch upon us and devour us laughing...

"Well, would you believe, Citizen Daghestan," the graduate continued, advancing his inflamed face toward me and folding his arms over his chest, "Would you believe that, in spite of all that, there are Borneans who imagine that property is a paradise—a poor paradise!—and that those who are excluded from it have the right to vociferate against it, like peevish children, or, like thieves, want to send its favorites to the hangman?

Mr. Arach's anger caused me to smile sincerely, but as my smile was seasoned with a stereotyped grimace of satisfaction, my host thought that I was horrified and that I doubtless thought that I had fallen into a thieves' den.

"Oh, don't worry," he said, laughing humorlessly. "Thieves are rare here. Besides which, the only thieves are the owners of houses. All the rest are honest men, and they're the more numerous. Just read our newspapers, and they'll tell you the same: they'll tell you that property—that of houses, of course—is an infamy, a privilege, an insult to the rights of the public, in sum, theft; but that property in newspapers, ownership of a business, income, literary property, the property of any industry, is sacred and that the public interest demands...

"Well, I understood all that, sir, and I said to myself one day: 'Come on, let's go with the flow; the wind's getting stormy, let's head for port; let's get out of brigandage altogether. Let who will build houses for those honest folk; let who will administer that industry, useful as it is if one doesn't want the lovely star to set, but so ill-reputed. Anyway, that wretched house in which I'm only a shareholder, which isn't mine, with which I can't do as I wish, which can be stolen any time it pleases the caprice of an administrator , which has been declared injurious to the public interest, is corroding me, devouring me—let's sell it.' And I sold it.

"Do you see now what property has become here, what our modern civilization has made it? Oh, our forefathers were much more just! But let's not talk about the past; let's stick to the present. Well, the present in bad here, sir; we're decadent, our empire has gone. I don't know, but I suspect some ogre will devour us: envy...envy, the mother of all crimes, because it's the mother of all vices."

Here my host uttered a profound sigh, and raised his head, for we were no longer eating. He was, I think, less philosophical than he claimed, but I couldn't reproach him for it, even mentally, for, if he had suffered, he had every right to complain.

"Oh, I'm not complaining," my host said, all of a sudden, as if he were replying to my present preoccupation, although he was obviously replying to his own, which was presumably running in parallel with mine. "No, I'm not complaining. I sold my house for $50,000; I'll be rich, when I was in straitened circumstances, and what's more, I'll be an honest man, worthy of the public interest, instead of being fit for hanging..."

Arach fell silent then; he was almost certainly having a profound thought, which he did not express to me.

"But you've invested this money," I said to him, "And you're doubtless still paying the Treasury?"

"Oh, paying the Treasury doesn't frighten me," he replied. "The Treasury has to live, if we wasn't to live, for the Treasury is us, to some extent. But no, I've only invested it...in my cellar."

I stared at my host, as if I hadn't understood; one might, however, have had a suspicion that the excellent man was a trifle crazy. He understood me perfectly, however.

"Oh, I'm not mad," he told me. "At the most, I seem a little odd to you. My one goal is to live in peace, since I'm condemned to live,."

"But that money might be useful," I said, "not only to you but to society."

"To society!" he replied, hotly. "Yes, I'd like that—but I think it would be more useful to the administrative purse than the social purse. Well, what has the administrative purse done for me? Let it be just, paternal—social, in fact—and I'll come to its aid; if not, no, I'll only think of myself.

"This is my reasoning: I have fifty years to live, at the most: I'll take $1000 a year from my investment and I shall thus arrive, quietly and peacefully, without any fuss, at the end of my life and my dollars, leaving nothing to the Treasury but my crumbs—which it will scrape up, I know, but without bothering me in the least. That, sir, is my reasoning, and it's sound; too bad for the administrations whose cupidity and tyranny have rendered me an eccentric!"

"But if everyone reasoned thus," I told him, "What would become of your government, and, in consequence, you?"

"It would become like me: wise and economical. Anyway, have I said that administrations ought to be abandoned, that they have no good laws or decrees? No. I only say that administrations are only operated by people, and that the people of today are greedy, envious, interfering and tyrannical—in Borneo at least, for I don't know about other countries—and that I want to resist those people."

I did not continue that discussion, for it would have been futile with a man who reasoned so bluntly, outside of social needs, about the innate imperfection of human beings, which he would not forgive. Arach, moreover, did not appear to want to change his opinion, nor, or so I believed, to continue an argument that he probably only thought good in his present spiteful disposition.

We therefore both kept silent, him profoundly absorbed in thoughts that I could not divine, but which I respected. The man was evidently not mad; at the most, he was, as he had said, an eccentric. To be eccentric in that manner, however, I thought, he must be in a great torment, which was affecting the clarity of his intelligence.

XXIII. MR. ARACH'S FAMILY

We were no longer at table. Mr. Arach, after having wandered around the room briefly, breathing with difficulty and sometime loudly, came back toward me. Taking me by the hand, he led me to a door and put his hand on the key to open it. Then he looked at me with a tear in his eye, which made a considerable impression on me.

"You thought I was alone here," he said. "You were mistaken; I have a family. My family is here!"

At the same time, he opened the door and preceded me into the room. He advanced toward a bed of state. "This is my wife," he said, lifting up a veil that covered the bed.

Mrs. Arach had been dead for several years, but one might have thought she was asleep in her bed, there was so much apparent life in her face. Even her eyes, when my host lifted up her eyelids, seemed to me to be shining with health.

"I knew," I said to my host, "that the Borneans were very skilled in the art of embalming, but I did not know that they had attained perfection..."

Oh, my friend, that embalming process was far superior to that of Caucasia of which we are so proud. Our necropolises, grand and magnificent as they are, are far from giving us the happy illusion to which the art of the Borneans is able to give rise in families. When we have desiccated our dead, when we have mummified them, what remains to us? Skeletons, dead things: nothing or almost nothing...while in Borneo, one does not die!

Mrs. Arach's bedroom could have passed for a museum. Not only was she there herself, almost alive, but her portrait— a perfect resemblance it seemed—as well as those of several children, was also there, hung on the wall and repeated several times. In accordance with the fashion in Borneo—which is, in my opinion, in perfect taste—it was in relief, protruding from the central three quarters of a painting, whose subject, also in relief, reproduced family scenes painted from life.

The Borneans make skillful used for these scenic portraits, and even for their statues, on occasion, I'm told, of a kind of paste that sets hard when they desire and then acquires the hardness of stone.

While I was admiring all those portraits, my host pulled the edge of a curtain that was the same color as the wallpaper, disguising a kind of alcove that it was impossible to make out, for it disturbed the regularity of the room, which the curtain restored perfectly.

There was a work-table therein, around which several young women were sitting, occupied with needlework, while young children appeared to be playing around them.

"This is my wife and my children, sir," my host said to me, taking a seat in order to sit down beside the eldest of the group, who was indeed Mrs. Arach. "Would you care to join me?"

I could not do it; I remained motionless. My surprise was gripping, for the illusion was complete. I thought I was looking at a group of living beings although I as only confronted by a group of statues.

I confess, my friend, that in spite of the desire I have to proclaim the supremacy of the arts of Caucasia over those of all other peoples, we concede a great deal in this regard present to the Borneans, and even to the inhabitants of Timbuktu, who have almost the same practices as the Borneans.

We think ourselves very meritorious, and very skillful, when we have carved a person's features, sometimes in stone like the ancients, or in common wood, or prepared and hardened wood. I have no wish to play the eccentric by denying the merit that our artists might acquire in this kind of work, but alas, how far those bleak and colorless features, those eyes devoid of vivacity, those mouths that says nothing, are from the speaking statues of Borneo!

In Borneo, too, all statues are painted; and the love of reality is so strong in them that do not have a talent in painting adequate to the subject they represent, still have recourse to the most skilful palettes to give their subject the life that is lacking.

I was vividly impressed by that spectacle.

"I understand now the care that you take of your dead, Mr. Arach," I said to the graduate. "I understand your statuary, and the love that you lavish upon the objects of your affection. I did not know Mrs. Arach, nor your children, but I see them still alive here, and I would be quite astonished if the resemblance were not perfect, so perfectly natural is the art that you have given to this group. But permit me to say"—I pointed to the eldest of the children—"how beautiful this young woman is! If I'm not mistaken, she's several years older than the eldest of your remaining children."

"Oh, do you find her beautiful too?" he said to me, with great emotion. "I've never noticed that, but I loved her like my own children, without finding her more beautiful than them."

"She's not a member of your family?"

"No, she was an orphan, the daughter of my best friend."

"And…she's dead too?" I added, with a painful effort.

"Oh, she's not dead for everyone, although she's dead for me," he replied, with burning tears in his eyes.

Then, his face was veiled with somber shadows, which indicated a bitterness that I respected, for I thought I understood it; sad suspicions had passed through my mind.

"No, she's not dead," he went on. "She's in Borneo…they have killed me."

I did not question these words, convinced that there are griefs that it is necessary never to fathom.

"Listen to me," my host continued, "and see if I'm wrong to curse human beings and to tell you everything I have about Borneans. I had a childhood friend, a true friend. He was dying; his wife was dead; and he had no other relatives; there was no one but me, his friend. On his deathbed, he entrusted his daughter to me, whom I adopted. She was young, still very young; she grew up in my home and became beautiful, as you see. She was my daughter, the cherished child of

214

my wife, who loved her all the more because the poor child was an orphan and might have been unhappy.

"We lost all our children, whom the poor girl loved like her brothers; and then I lost my wife. I was therefore left alone, and became the sole guardian and support of Tarnawalis, as she was called. She was also my only family, and my sole consolation.

"Several years passed thus, both of us happy to the extent that we could be, she consoling her adoptive father with the gentle voice, me consoling my daughter by means of my attention and kindness. There eventually came a day, however, when I saw Tarnawalis' serenity cloud over, her caresses become more reserved and her soft voice more tremulous when speaking to me. If we went out for a walk, her arm only leaned on mine distantly; she became mute, excessively embarrassed with me, and her eye were always anxious and wandering. One might have thought that she was afraid beside me when we walked through the streets, or met someone in the fields. It got to the point where she no longer wanted to go out. Her health deteriorated in consequence. I was no less anxious, but I could not divine that cause of the change. It was an enigma to me.

"One day, finally, I found the key to the puzzle. A friend—one of those friends of whom one has so many; which is to say, a man who was not my enemy and had some concern for my consideration—said to me one morning, confidentially: 'My friend, why don't you marry Tarnawalis?'

"It was a thunderbolt for me. Who, me? Marry my daughter! But you can't think that, my friend! My daughter! 'But Tarnawalis is my daughter,' I replied to him, 'and I shall give her in marriage gladly to the honest man who asks me for her, and of whom my daughter's heart approves.'

"'Oh, well...it's just...' my friend went on, 'it's just that...' He was embarrassed to respond to my outburst. 'It's that I thought...I thought! That is, no I didn't think, because I know you, like you and hold you in esteem as the most honest

215

man in Borneo; but it's said…it's said that you'd do better to marry her,'

"'Yes, I understand,' I replied. 'Borneans are vile, vile, vile.'

"I couldn't say anything else to that friend, who wanted to console me, to wipe away the tears that were burning me eyes, and then said to me, as he left; 'Think about what I said, my friend, and be sensible.'

"He too, then, believed that hideous calumny! He too did not believe in the devotion of a friend. He too did not believe in virtue. He too! Oh, the cowards, the cowards! Infamous Borneo!"

My host turned to me. "And you would like me to love these people! You don't want me to say that these people know nothing but evil! Those caresses I gave to Tarnawalis were lust; the care with which I surrounded her was lust; the protection I gave to the poor orphan, the daughter of my best friend, who had entrusted her to me on his deathbed—all that was lust. Oh, the swine! The swine!"

My host wiped his forehead, which was streaming with sweat as red as blood; he rubbed his eyes, which were oozing bloody tears. I didn't say anything—what was there to say?—but I was sad, and I admired the man, whose principles until then had seemed so bizarre, and I understood his eccentricity.

"Well," said Mr. Arach, after a moment's silence, "if they wanted to ruin the debris of my happiness by slandering my good deed—for it was one, Mr. Daghestan—they succeeded." My host was speaking with an honorable conviction, which I thought worthy. "Tarnawalis had heard what my officious friend had said, and she disappeared from my home that evening, leaving me a letter, which is there, in front of her." He showed me a letter that he picked up from in front of the young woman's statue. "See here: she admits, the poor child, that she will die of grief, but that for some time she has been aware of the most odious suspicions pursuing her everywhere she goes with me, and even without me; that she has been subjected more than once to the odious gibes of passers-by

216

and even our neighbors; that, finally, she has just heard the conversation I had had with my friend, and that she does not want to expose me any longer to the ignoble sarcasms of malevolence; that she no longer wants to punish me for my generosity to her; that she has supported the mocking laughter that welcomes her everywhere for some time, because she hoped that it would not reach my ears, but that now she has seen me fall victim to it she can no longer hesitate, that she is leaving...

"And she had gone...and I'm alone now, and unhappy, yes, unhappy, for whatever I say, their wounding laughter is there, always there, in my heart...and my daughter...

"Oh, is my daughter any happier than I am? May she also have more courage! If she had only told me in person what she has written here! I would have said to her: 'No, stay! What does this odious slander matter to me? What has this cowardly lie to do with you? You need me in order to live—stay! I need you, in order to forget, a little, the mortal pains of life—stay! Let us be good, and let us say: God will judge us; down here, we accept but one judge, our conscience...'

"But no, she had gone.

"And you haven't seen her since?" I ventured to say.

"I haven't seen her since! It would have been necessary to kill me to stop me seeing her again. Yes, I've seen her, but like a corrupter, like a guilty man, like a coward; I've seen her, hiding myself from everyone's eyes. Yes, I've seen her; it was necessary, in order that she should live, to keep her safe from the evil counsels of poverty. But I have seen her by slipping into her home like a thief, like an outlaw tracked by the most suspicious police. But don't reproach me for that cowardice, sir—no, I'm not cowardly on my own behalf, for what can it do to me, the venom of that viper called society? It's for her, the poor child, who is dying slowly of the shame of having been suspected...

"When I tell you, sir, that in Borneo, morals are degraded, so degraded that no one even suspects that there might be a little virtue here..."

My host fell silent then; he seemed to collect himself. I was deeply impressed by the grief that had just overflowed from his soul, and I did not venture to offer him advice that could only be futile, and which, moreover, he did not seem to desire for the moment.

He squeezed my hand, doubtless to thank me for the interest I had taken in his stories; then, as night had fallen, he showed me to the room where I was to stay and installed me there—not to sleep, but to recall to mind everything that I had seen and heard.

XXIV. IN BORNEO

The next morning, the previous evening's storm seemed to have calmed completely. When I woke up, I saw Mr. Arach, who put his head round my door, smiling, said good morning, and brought me breakfast.

"Sir," he said to me, after having breakfasted with me at the foot of my bed, "we talked about me, and nothing but me yesterday; let's talk a little about you today. I will introduce you, if you think it appropriate, to the Philanthropic Society, where you can demonstrate your aerostat and your system—for I no longer have any doubt, personally, that you've found the secret for which everyone has been searching."

"Thank you, sir," I replied. "The secret isn't mine; I acquired it from another country, which we people of advanced civilization call barbaric. My own secret isn't yet ripe, and when it is, I shall donate it to my homeland, which will transmit it gratuitously to yours—for what use are millions to us? We already have, without money—without much money, at least—the happiness of life. But I shall gratefully accept your arm to visit your city and study your mores—mores that don't delight me, it's true, but about which it is good to know, if only to find myself happier with ours."

My host smiled and offered me his arm, and we went out together.

We headed out into the fields because, for the moment, I planned to study the land of Borneo rather than its inhabitants.

The land of Borneo is very picturesque in appearance; it is strewn with mountains and hills of all heights and shapes, evidently volcanic, and profound valleys covered in bogs, certainly filed by water that the sea has left behind in its various retreats. From that I was able to conclude—at first glance, it's true, but incontestably for me—that the sea was once there and that Borneo, at a time that I cannot specify as yet, was merely an island surrounded by islands of different dimensions.

That was a precious discovery for me, my friend, for it confirmed my calculations and permitted me to base more solidly those that I had made on the successive transformations of seas and continents, and on various revolutions and the relationships between them. It permitted me, above all, to suspect the age of the globe, that respectable but flirtatious old lady who continually seeks to rejuvenate herself by effacing her birth date from her face

Mr. Arach and I spent several hours a day inspecting the surroundings and the city of Borneo. Mr. Arach was charming company, although he often had bitter words on his lips for his compatriots. Eventually, one day, we went into the houses. My host took me to visit all his friends; they were numerous, and I could see that he was held in esteem, in spite of everything he had told me. I visited the courtrooms, all the scientific societies and I saw the theaters always in Mr. Arach's company, who silenced his hatred of the world for my sake. Perhaps he was not displeased to bring me face to face with all the vices he had described to me so harshly.

I was received everywhere with considerable benevolence; perhaps my status as a foreigner and a Caucasian opened all doors and drawing-rooms to me. When I wasn't visiting, I read the Bornean newspapers and new literary works. My host didn't leave me to that; he helped me to read and to comment on what we had read.

Newspapers are numerous in Borneo, for the press is free, as it is here, in the Sudan, in Zeeland and, in sum in all civilized countries. They are also subject to very severe laws, but no one complains about that, for it is only the imprudent or the evil-minded who allow themselves to infringe the duties of polite society or the contract they have signed voluntarily.

In Caucasia, the newspapers are purely literary or social; in the Sudan they are literary, social and administrative; but in Borneo, they are almost uniquely political; they aim to become a power within the government. I fear that they might crush it one day—the day when that redoubtable instrument falls into the hands of people in agreement, who bring all their strength to bear against the throne that they have founded.

Their present prince probably senses that, for he is a man of great intelligence and rare vision; he it was who declared the freedom of the press, which only dates from his reign. During his reign, too, Borneo has never seen so many periodicals, so many political dissertations of every hue and so many pamphlets debating different opinions, when they are not disputing them.

That very liberty is excessive, and the conflicts that it engenders sometimes offer very little courtesy—but the government, which might often take offense and apply laws of repression, never does so. The newspapers and other publications of the same sort take responsibility for that concern very freely, and the government reciprocates, sometimes more energetically than the law probably would.

All that is noisy, it's true, but it isn't dangerous. It's probably that the King of Borneo is aware of the principle that is of all countries and probably of all times: Divide and rule. Thus, he divides the press in order to reign in peace, and his reign is, in fact, quite calm.

As for the literature of Borneo, I don't like it, even though the present trend is being set by a man of Caucasian origin, the illustrious Kouban. It's very imaginative, very romantic, even fantastic and impossible—empty, in sum. It's said that the Borneo, fine minds have given themselves the mission to write in order to amuse children and sentimental women, or eccentric or blasé minds with it is necessary to stir by the extravagance of narratives.

To be fair, however, I ought to say that there is at present a faint reaction against that highly-spiced literature, which is revealed by a few volumes deeply steeped in the social duties and the virtues that reign over a people.

"Is Borneo becoming serious?" I asked my host one day, having read one of these works.

Mr. Arach smiled, shaking his head, and then went out.

221

Poor people! The people of Borneo really are a poor people!

I was writing those last words, my dear friend, in the notebook in which I record my travel notes, when Mr. Arach came back into my room. You will understand how embarrassed I was to see him. To treat my host's compatriots so badly! That might be permissible for him, but on my part, it was a crime, for it was an insult to my host. It could, at least, be taken s such, although that was far from my intention. So I blushed to the roots of my hair and hastened to close the culpable notebook.

"Oh, don't bother," the excellent man said to me, having divined my thought. "You'll never say as many bad things about Borneans as I think. Show me your note, I beg you, so that I can add to it what you don't know, for you don't know Borneo as I do."

I apologized with good grace and reopened my notebook.

"Is that all?" exclaimed Mr. Arach, after having read it. "But I'm the one who told you that—why worry? Here, I'll tell you a little anecdote that won't make you change your opinion.

"Do you remember that yesterday, we went into a courtroom briefly, and heard a case argued and judged, which made you yawn, although it hadn't gone on long, and was cut short because the presiding judge interrupted it mid-way, suddenly declaring that he was sufficiently enlightened?

"The case was, in fact, of no great interest to you or me—but it was for the two adversaries: two merchants, two competitors, one of whom must have been ruined by the pronouncement of the judgment. The merchant who was condemned and ruined was, according to public rumor, the one who was in the right, but it also appears that his adversary had something in his favor.

"The advocate who was successful did not argue much, but he had talent enough to communicate his victorious argument in time in a letter to the judge. That letter is being hawked all over Borneo today; it appears that the judge, thinking he was putting it in his pocket, had dropped it. Here it is: 'Old c..., I expect you for dinner this evening, but try to bring my good news if you don't want to be f... at the door. Your darling, who adores you...'[41]

"Put that in your notes, sir," added the graduate," and don't hide any more. Oh, you think we're not civilized? You think we can't prove with fine words that a thief is an honest man? That we can't assassinate our overconfident neighbors, not with a dagger, which might compromise our reputation, but with a word, a judgment, a well-contrived slander? That we can't steal, from the cabinet as from the tribunal, in a perfectly legal fashion? You're mistaken, sir—we're civilized enough for that..."

---

[41] I have left the initial letters of the two censored words as they are in the original, although it is highly unlikely that the English equivalents would have the same ones; they are obviously not the words most commonly represented in euphemistic English by the same two letters.

XXV. THE GRADUATE'S CIVILIZATION

My host then burst into infernal laughter.

"Vile Borneo!" he suddenly cried. "There's your civilization!"

"Civilization is the art of being happy put into practice," I said to my host, very calmly, desiring to deflect him gently away from the excitement I could see rising within him. "It's the social condition sufficiently well organized for each individual not to find any serious obstacle in his path to his existence as God's creature and a member of human society."

"Oh, don't say that, Mr. Daghestan," Mr. Arach retorted, sharply, his mental state not having recovered its tranquility. "That's your civilization, in Caucasia, but not that of Borneo. How people here would laugh if they heard the naivety of your philosophy!"

"Among us, a man does not come into society to embarrass us," I replied to my host, with as much self-composure as I could, seeking to reason with him, convinced that reasoning ought to reduce the irritation that I saw in him. "A father, on seeing his son born, need not worry about the bread that will nourish him. Society has thought of that; all its members have bread assured until their last sigh. Since society has received them, since it has given them the responsibilities of association, it gives them its benefits. It thinks about them; it acts on their behalf. All is foreseen. That, Monsieur Arach, is our civilization, which progresses by means of a very simple mechanism, for it has but two wheels: *do not do unto others as you would not have them do unto you; do unto others as you would have them do unto you.*"

"If your civilization progresses on two wheels," my host said to me, with an ironic smile that caused me to expect a further sarcasm, "ours is more perfect, for the simplicity of a machine determines its perfection, and our civilization only progresses on one wheel: the love of money. Money is the God of Borneo."

"Among us," I said, "it is intelligence that is the God of our civilization, but intelligence does not render us proud. The man of great intelligence makes use of his mind as the wise rich man makes use of his money, for his own wellbeing and the wellbeing of all; and if he puts himself to work, he throws himself into the search for truths; he does not seek to know in order to have clothes fringed with gold or the luxury of the proud, but to honor himself, and to obey the will of God, which has created us and given us a vast and sublime enigma to solve down here."

"Oh, yes," said my host, "I found out a long time ago that in Caucasia, it was mind that made civilization, while here it was matter."

"No," I replied, "that's an error; it's mind that makes civilization everywhere, even when the means of civilization is matter. For example, is there anything in your society more beautiful as a material thing, and also as perhaps the latest word in the most advanced civilization, than your railways? Well..."

"Oh, yes, our railways!" cried Mr. Arach, with jeering laughter. "Tell me about our railways. Tell me about steam, the blind and irresistible force that has turned everything up-side-down, and ruined thousands of families, pitilessly taking the wealth of one to give it to another. Tell me about the ferocious beast that so often removes its muzzle in order to devour us. But to whom, then, have our railways brought benefits? Who have they enriched, save for a fortunate few? Oh, the beautiful invention that conducts us straight to famine by stealing immense lands from agriculture, industry and commerce! Oh, the beautiful invention of a free people, which puts shackles on public circulation everywhere! And why? In order to go a little faster...

"Oh you don't make so much fuss about your travels in Caucasia. You told me yesterday, I recall, that if you travel, you have at home, in your shed or your room, instead of our steam, our wagons and our machines, a piece of wood shaped as you please, set moving by a mechanisms that you have found—and that piece of wood, animated by very simple mechanisms, runs through the fields, along ordinary roads, over mountains, at your behest. Yes, talk to us about our railways after that! Glorify our inventors!

"Glorify them too for having invented—what? The art of heating and lighting with the gas of which they're so proud? But what gas? A gas of which they're obliged to go in search by digging down into the entrails of the earth. Their civilization has been unable to procure it in any other way.

"What do you glorify, then, in their civilization? Having guided rivers into city-centers by means that could frighten the imagination? But who hasn't done that? What people, young or old, hasn't done similar things?

"And we call ourselves civilized! And we call other peoples...yes, do we not call them barbarians?

"They've invented...what else? Unsinkable ships, portable rowing-boats. A fine thing! Haven't you told me that you've seen savages traveling over the water, staff in hand, as on earth, with the aid of wings that they attach to their shoulders, to sustain them lightly in the air? Have you not traveled in that manner yourself?"

"Yes, but Mr. Arach, I'd like to say..."

"No, no!" he cried, cutting me off. "No, we're not civilized. We won't be, so long as we only travel in the wake of others, and our inventions are inferior to those of other peoples..."

"But sir, you're confusing..."

"I'm not confusing anything—no, I tell you, our inventions are nothing; our civilization is nothing, either in their inventions you see or in its mores. Its mores! Oh, yes, tell me about a city, a people, in which one man is esteemed more highly than another according to whether he is rich or poor; where matter is valued more highly than intelligence, clothes, carriages and wealth more than human beings. No, no, no, I repeat, we're not civilized..."

I gave up trying to give my host other ideas than his own on the subject of civilization, for his fury was reaching its extreme. I felt sorry for him, but I no longer sought to refute his argument. I gave him time to achieve by himself the necessary calmness for him to see with more justice and truth that which he was decrying at present.

I was, in any case, soon able to comprehend what viper was biting his heart at that moment and envenoming his words—and, in truth, his furious exasperation and irrationality could not be explained otherwise, for Mr. Arach was perfectly sensible. At the height of his fit, I saw him suddenly calm down, as if, warned by a mysterious voice, he had been obliged to make an unanticipated but firmly decisive resolution. At least, the somber sadness of his face, and a few tics that were creasing his features, gave me that impression.

"We'll go out together, if you like, sir," he said, in a halting voice. "You haven't seen all of Borneo by any means."

XXVI. TARNAWALIS

We went out and headed toward a quarter that I had not yet seen, located on the outskirts of the far side of the city. It was rather strange to behold, unless one wanted to do so philosophically, for it was repulsive in its poverty and dirtiness.

I don't know, my friend, how Borneo, which is a highly civilized city—although my host and I had two opinions about that—or at least very elegant, can tolerate the appearance of that quarter. It's true that all the human filth of the household—everything that the society, not merely elegant but honest and proper, of the city does not want to retain—is to be found there. It is, after all, necessary that the dregs of a city be located somewhere.

As we entered that lair of a thousand faces, I looked at my host, who remained silent. My gaze seemed to make him uncomfortable, but did not break his silence. He stopped outside a building with several stories, but cracked and overhanging, daubed throughout its lower part with grotesque paintings, which probably indicated, for I could not decipher them, the variety of trades that were based there, and perhaps disguised unadmitted trades.

Mr. Arach looked round, and then, making a heroic gesture of determination, took me by the hand and took me into the hovel.

"It's here...." he said, then. "*She*'s here..."

I understood everything, and shook his hand benevolently; his hand squeezed mine again by way of thanks. We went up to the top of the house. Our footsteps had been heard. A door opened to await us, and on the threshold of that doorway, someone was indeed waiting for us—or at least waiting for my host, for on seeing me, Tarnawalis retreated to the back of her room, ashamed of her urgency, which might have seemed incriminating.

"He's a friend, Daughter, a true friend," my host said to the young woman she he introduced me to her. "He loves us, and feels sorry for us."

Tarnawalis looked at me confusedly, lowering her head slightly. Her bow had been most gracious, like a thank you at the announcement of good news.

"Permit me, Miss," I said, offering her my hand, in which she placed two fingers, which I kissed with the most profound respect. I knew that in Borneo I could not expect any better response to what Mr. Arach had just said. He was almost in tears, for I had just testified by that respectful kiss against all the slanders that the city had leveled against Tarnawalis.

In consequence, the young woman did not hold back any more, and threw her arms around Mr. Arach's neck, hugging him tightly and weeping profusely, calling him "Father." The poor father was suffocating; he could no longer say anything but: "Daughter, Daughter..."

The scene was heart-rending; that mute embrace spoke of a torment that was unprecedented for me. I understood everything at that moment.

"Tarnawalis," said Mr. Arach then, "we're mad. We're sacrificing our peace and our happiness on the altar of opinion—and whose opinion? The opinion of wretches, of good-for-nothings, or at least thoughtless, sniggering people. We're mad! Come back home; you're my life and I'm yours. Yes, you're my life, for your absence renders me unjust, stupid, malign—and, in consequence, unhappy. Ask my friend Daghestan whether I haven't been saying foolish things since he's been staying with me. I must be your life too, for I can see you dying slowly, Daughter; your face frightens me; it no longer has the freshness of youth and happiness; your eyes are hollowed out by tears; your face is wrinkled. Come back, Daughter! There will no longer be anything for us in Borneo but God, you and me. What does the rest matter? The rest, we'll burn in the flames of our conscience. Come back, come back, come back, Daughter!"

And the poor father looked at his daughter with eyes moist with tears. Tarnawalis was breathless; she lowered her eyes and her lips were moving continuously, but without making any sound. The poor father, however, never stopped repeating: "Come back, come back, Daughter!"

Tarnawalis did indeed come back—partly thanks to me, thanks to my reasoning, I hope. I was able to install her in her father's house before my departure. I was glad about that; I had, therefore, been able to pay to pay for my hospitality by returning happiness to my host's house...

My arrival in Borneo had only been an accident for me; if I had remained there for a few days, it had only been to obey the orders of hazard and the unexpected, which had retained me here involuntarily. I had never had any intention, however, of staying long, although it would have been very agreeable to study the mores that I had probably not appreciated very accurately, and which I still planned to study some day.

After the reconciliation of Tarnawalis and her father, therefore, I thought seriously about my departure. Something—a presentiment of some sort—was summoning me elsewhere, and I began to regret the fatality that continually drove me away from Zeeland. So, all my host's attempts to persuade me to stay could not break my resolve.

I therefore set about repairing my aerostat with as much zeal and expertise as I could. I even recruited Mr. Arach's assistance in that matter, explaining the mechanism of my balloon to him. I wanted to be as agreeable to him as he was to me, and was not at all displeased to leave him, in his land of money, with the means to make an immense amount of it if he wished. I did not hide my desire from him, and urged him strongly to profit from the secret I held in my hand, and which I abandoned to him with all my heart.

"Thank you, Mr. Daghestan," he replied, shaking my hand affectionately. "I only had need of one good fortune, and you have procured it for me—thank you! In exchange, I should like to offer you and give you some good advice—more than that, a treasure, a very precious treasure, especially for a traveler like you who sometimes lives in the midst of the savages of barbarism, and might sometimes also encounter in your travels the savages of civilization. That treasure is a new invention. Freshly emerged from the womb of our Borneo...of fire and gas."

"Aha!" I replied to the graduate. "So you do hold your civilization in some esteem."

He smiled, and replied, with eyes radiant with pleasure: "Yes, a little...more than that at this moment, but let's not talk about that any more. Let's talk about my treasure, my weapon—for it will be a weapon for you. With your balloon you can go far and you can go rapidly; with our secret, for it's still a secret, you'll no longer have anything to dread on your journey. Your revolvers can misfire, your daggers can break in your hand, but my weapon will never fail in your defense. Take it, and believe in me, as I believe in you.

Mr. Arach then gave me several hermetically-sealed boxes, instructing me not to be so curious as to open one without need, and above all without precaution. Some enclosed thunderbolts, without the noise, but thunderbolts nevertheless, with their lightning. On opening them, I had to direct their interior at my enemy, maneuvering it as he indicated to me, and my enemy would then be blinded by the glare that I was projecting into his face. The blindness, it is true, would not be permanent—and that was, in truth, for the best—but it would last long enough for my defense.

In the other boxes was a stupefying gas, which it was sufficient to release into the enemy's atmosphere to be protected against any attack. The essential thing was to escape asphyxia oneself by fleeing promptly, which is always easy when one is forewarned.

Evidently, all that might be very useful, if it was all true. I didn't have much confidence, but what did that matter? I thought I would give my host pleasure by accepting his present, and I did so with abundant demonstrations of delight. For me, my real treasure and my real weapon was my balloon; there were also my trusty revolvers, but especially my balloon.

231

For Mr. Arach, his treasure as something else; it was assuredly not my balloon, for I had learned before my departure that he would not take any advantage of it, and that my secret would die with him. Fortunate is the man, the blissful philosopher, who needs nothing but a sentiment for his happiness.

When everything was ready, I fixed the day of my departure. On that day, Mr. Arach prepared a triumph for me. I made my final preparations in the courtyard, between the house and the trees that hid it from external gazes; I didn't see anyone, thinking that I was alone. My friend, in the meantime, ballasted my gondola with thousand of various objects that might be useful to me during my voyage.

When I had taken off and surpassed the treetops, I perceived a numerous but select company beneath me. I went back down to the ground then, into the midst of that curious crowd, whose members hasten to gather around me.

My friend and Tarnawalis ran toward me first, and then, with one foot in the gondola and the other on the ground, I shook Mr. Arach's hand effusively. Taking Tarnawalis' two fingers. I kissed them in front of everyone, and then bowed to the others. I made a few turns in my aerostat at low altitude, in order to prove the intelligence of my steering, and the bowed again and departed in the direction of Zeeland.

My machine was in good working order this time; my compass was in position; all necessary measures had been taken; I could therefore expect a good journey.

I passed rapidly over the great empire of Cambodia, Borneo's nearest neighbor, flying over a sea of ruins, dotted with charming oases—a vast area where, it's said the China of the old world was located, the highly civilized China in which no art was unknown, to which no discovery was foreign, and the least of whose citizens could pass for a savant in neighboring lands.

I did not stop anywhere, in haste as I was to reach my goal, for something was driving me instinctively, so I paid no heed to the beautiful oases that form the brilliant China of our own days, nor to the vast and curious deserts that surround them.

When I arrived over the soil of the beautiful, wise and happy Republic of Poland, however—which includes, as you know, my friend, the greater part of ancient Russia and extends its possessions to close proximity with the kingdom of Zeeland, from which it is only separated by a few petty states of scant importance and the arid and uncultivated lands that form a desert on its borders—I paused for an hour, but only for an hour.

I knew Poland slightly, and liked it, but it was not to testify to my sympathy for it that I took my aerostat there. I needed to touch down and obtain news of the neighborhood, for, I don't know why, but I was suffering from an anxiety that had only increased since my departure from Borneo.

I learned very little about Zeeland; I could only pick up a few vague rumors that were in the air, which only served to increase my torment. Thus, I shall not say anything about the Republic of Poland here, about which I shall talk to you at leisure later, except to record the good impression I experienced of the wisdom of the people in hearing everyone speak.

Everyone says that their government is perfect. That unanimity of opinion, my friend, seems miraculous to me, for I have not found it anywhere but that blissful land, and I strongly doubt that it has ever been observed in another people. So they flatter themselves on having found the sole governmental plan that can effectively unite all the voters.

They have no emperor, sultan, king or president. Their government is composed of five individuals, equal in title and in power, who divide up the administrative concerns. The government is eternal, the Poles say, but it is modified and improved according to need, and is continually rejuvenated. Every year, one of its members leaves, to be replaced by another, and can only be re-elected after five years of absence, when the entire government has been renewed, or rejuvenated, as they say. The government is elected, and anyone may be a candidate.

All that, my friend, I find very good, since it works. The fact is that Poland is said to be content, happy and prosperous—but I did not seek any further assurance of that, for I felt increasingly afflicted by a dread that was becoming very sharp, and reminded me obstinately of the dream I had had in my aerostat during my escape from Lining.

I left, therefore, after having picked up a little information, without occupying myself in the study of a republic of which we know very little, in spite of its proximity to our country, and which seems to me to be well worthy of our attention. I was in a hurry to arrive in Zeeland, at Trevig.

It was high time, if it was not already too late.

XXVII. CONVERSATIONS IN A BALLOON

Everything I had dreamed was nothing but a dream. The most horrible tumult reigned in the city of Trevig, which seemed to have sunk into the most frantic disorder. The soldiers were there, assembled around a scaffold erected in the city's largest square. Two gibbets stood on the scaffold. Had they already devoured their victims? I had no idea.

My heart was palpitating violently; my chest was so tight that I could no longer breathe, so anxious and emotional was I. Why? Yes, why? I did not know these people at all; I had nothing for which to reproach them; they evidently had nothing against me—but I had a friend there, perhaps two, and who could tell? Was I not struck by the idea that all this disorder was against them? That those gibbets were for them?

I was stationed at a high altitude; I could see with my telescope, but I could not hear anything, and I wanted to hear. I therefore descended some way, but prudently, in order not to be noticed—although it seemed to me that I had nothing much to fear.

I distinctly heard shouting then, and the impatient stamping of feet—and in the midst of all that was the cry: "The Mouraviev! The Mouraviev! Give us the Mouraviev! Where's the Mouraviev?"[42]

---

[42] Mettais renders this name "Mourawiew"; it would have been familiar to his readers whatever its spelling, as that of a highly significant Russian military family. There was more than one Nicolas Mouraviev, but the one that Mettais has in mind is probably Nicolai Mouraviev-Amourski (1809-1891), who eventually capped a glittering career by becoming Governor General of Siberia but had earlier become notorious for a massacre carried out in 1840 on the shore of the Black Sea.

I understood, for I had learned while passing through Poland who was called by that name in this region: he is the equivalent of our executioner.

The executioner was not yet there. *So much the better!* I thought, and felt suitably relieved—but my joy did not last long, for the mouraviev was not far away. He arrived in the square to loud cries of joy from a crowd thirsty for blood. By a refinement of cruelty or precaution, he was sitting at the front of the carriage that was bringing his victims, in order to be ever ready to execute them, in transit if necessary.

The precaution was unnecessary; the victims were not putting up any resistance, and no one was making any attempt to help them; they were able, therefore, to arrive at the foot of the scaffold without difficulty,

The mouraviev left his post then; gravely, he climbed the funereal steps and began preparing the ropes on the two gallows, in the midst of the silence and attention of the crowd.

I did not know whether the two victims were thoroughly guilty and universally hated, but it seemed to me that the silence enveloping them was that of a tiger about to pounce on its prey. I shivered at the sight of all those wide open and ferocious eyes, those gaping mouths extended toward a single goal, smiling with savage stupidity.

The door of the carriage finally opened. There was no woman, but there were two victims. One of them—oh, my friend! it was my cicerone from Lining, the king's brother. The other was probably the king of Zeeland, but I didn't know him.

My first impulse was to rush to my controls, to release its brakes to render my aerostat more impetuous, and to launch forth like a thunderbolt into the midst of that bloodthirsty rabble—but I stopped myself in time. What could I do there, alone and unnamed—or very nearly? I would have been torn to pieces along with my balloon before being able to snatch the two victims that I wanted to save.

But what could I do? A thousand various thoughts and plans went through my head, but I did not settle on any of them. Time was pressing, though. The preparation of the gallows had not taken long; the mouraviev seemed quite expert, and in no time at al the first victim had been shoved to the foot of the scaffold to await his moment. His moment was not long delayed, for at the same moment I saw the mouraviev's hand take hold of the fatal cord in order to put it around the victim's neck.

Oh, at that sight, I could not contain myself. The memory of Mr. Arach's boxes came to mind like a sudden inspiration, and I picked them up, determined to make use of them, while making a superhuman effort, for I did not have complete confidence in the gas, with whose effects I was unfamiliar.

I therefore hurtled down like lightning, shaking and hurling around open boxes. Their effect was instantaneous and terrifying; one might have thought that the furious crowd had been magnetized I was thus able to seize the two half-asphyxiated victims without anxiety, place them in my gondola and flee with them without anyone being able, or even make any attempt, to interrupt me.

My triumph was complete. I remained utterly amazed by it, but I was then, I must confess, my friend, a trifle anxious. I had saved two men, and was very glad of that, but at what cost? I wanted to know. I therefore rose up some distance above the square, to an altitude at which I had nothing to fear, took up my telescope, and watched the effect of my gas.

Then I let out an irresistible burst of involuntary laughter at the sight of the disorder I had produced. No serious accident seemed to me to have occurred, but all the faces were so bizarre, everyone's movements appeared to be so strange and comical, that my busts of laughter became inextinguishable, to the point that they became a nervous crisis that I regretted, but could not stop.

So, in order not to be laughing on my own, I passed my telescope to my guests, who were beginning to breathe easily. They could not help forgetting their misfortune momentarily in laughter, although they soon repressed it.

Finally, I felt happy that no serious consequence had been occasioned by my gas, and I thanked Mr. Arach with all my heart, who had truly given me a very valuable present. Of those that had been so blithely asphyxiated, some were shaking their fists at my gondola and others laughing wholeheartedly. I was then able to shake hands with my friend, who had thrown himself into my arms with an effusion that touched me deeply.

The king too shook my hand with all the force of his wrist, but he remained mute; he was absorbed in profound thoughts full of sadness. When he raised his head again to look at me, his eyes were red, although he had not been weeping.

"I know you, Mr. Daghestan," he said to me, then. "My brother has told me such good things about you that I'm not astonished by your great devotion."

"And yet, Master," I said to him, "if my memory serves me well, it would have taken very little for me to have been unable to come to your aid. I was only able to do so because this balloon, which has so fortunately saved you, also saved me one day from the stupidity of your police."

"Is that a reproach, Mr. Daghestan?" said the king, sadly.

"No, Master," I replied, humbly, "it's an observation, but an observation that has a certain value, for you evidently wanted to arrest me, and yet you didn't know me."

"What do you expect?" the king replied, dolefully. "A report had been made against you. Poor kings are often led into error."

"I believe so, Master, and I also believed that it is these oft-repeated errors that give birth to revolutions. Because one had strength around one—I'm not talking about you, Master—because one has thousands of soldiers under one's orders, a great deal of money, a great empire, one thinks oneself invincible. Flatterers say so: the envious, the ambitious, the arrogant—tyrants of all classes in sum; one believes them, acts via their hands and acts harshly; but the day of disillusionment finally comes. Popular disaffection has arrived; it has been a long time coming, it's true, but it has finally come, and with it rage and fury, and dangers of every sort…and the king finds himself alone on a scaffold, at the foot of the gallows, without any cry being raised in his support, without any arm taking up a weapon on his behalf."

"That's true sir," said the king, mournfully, hiding his face in his hands.

"Oh, yes, it's true, Master—believe me, for I've seen the world and I know people, But, forgive me for telling you, your advisers don't know them, your senior administrators don't know them. They're too highly-placed, they only see what's on their own level: a sky always blue, meteors and mirages. They never seen the reality on the ground, and yet it's that reality on the ground that gives birth to revolutions. Don't look for them elsewhere, Master! And if I tell you not to look for them elsewhere, it's not, Master it's not because I'm unfamiliar with your principles, or because I don't know that there are viewpoints of local knowledge in governments—and entire system of savant administration, lofty thoughts on every question; a code, in sum, from which one cannot deviate for a single instant—it's because I'm trying to tell you that your governments are mistaken, that their viewpoints are false, that their code is false, and that when the storm rumbles, they're wrong to look upwards, to see what clouds are threatening to break overhead; I mean that the clouds are down below, and that the storm is coming from volcanoes that open beneath your feet and engulf you."

"You're harsh, Mr. Daghestan," the king said to me, placing a hand on my arm, which he gripped nervously.

"Harsh, Master? Oh, I don't mean to be, but I want to tell you what I think and the whole truth—but I'd like you to understand how thrones collapse. I can even tell you that I've seen a few cast down by violent storms, that the majority, in my opinion, sink, silently undermined by ants. The ants are the arbitrary acts, the injustices…"

"Oh, I loved my people, sir!" the king exclaimed, sharply, interrupting me, "and I never wanted to subject them to injustice or arbitrariness."

"Not you, Master," I replied to the king. "Oh, I believe that—but your people, from the first of your ministers to the least of your functionaries, have been guilty. And what is more terrible for you, Master, which is perhaps logical, is that the smallest denial of justice, the meanest chicanery and the slightest administrative severity are not held against them but against you. It is not them who are punished in consequence, Master, but you."

The king looked at me in bewilderment; one might have thought that a great conviction ha just penetrated his mind. His brother was kind enough to say to him: "Mr. Daghestan is a philosopher; did I not tell you that, Brother? And a true friend, as well."

"You must be right, Mr. Daghestan," the king said, who seemed to be listening to me very attentively; that's the only way that I can comprehend the revolution in my realm, for how can Zeeland hate me? Everything reasonable that my people have asked of me, have I not granted them? Have I not satisfied them on all the major questions of the day? My heart does so with pleasure, and the wisest and most progressive of my counselors have told me that the salvation of my fatherland, and my own, was there...and yet, I'm in flight; and you can see how I'm fleeing. Without Mr. Daghestan, we'd both be swinging at the end of a hangman's rope now, Brother... Yes, my brother too, and why? If I belonged to the conservative party—a charming terms with which people tried to insult me—my brother, my poor Falster, belonged the progressive party, and a very advanced progressive. He was the man of the people, the thought of the people, the voice of the people, the arm of the people; he was more often sitting in workshops, in clubs, in cottages than in our palaces...and yet...and yet..."

"Yes," Falster replied, sadly, "and here I find myself at fault; my reasoning went astray. I've done everything for the people; I traveled everywhere; I wanted to see all their needs, study their grievances, in order to report them to the king. And I've done so, Brother, as you know; I've done what Mr. Daghestan has done, with great conviction."

"Yes," said the king, shaking his brother's hand, "and I didn't always believe you, my friend. Too often, I believed my savant counselors, as our friend said just now." The king looked at me affectionately. "But at least, Brother, people ought to have been grateful for your solicitude."

"And they would have been, I'm convinced," Falster replied, with his eyes flamboyant with hated and scorn, "but for a few accomplished conspirators, who have no profession but overturning empires."

"Oh, I beg your pardon, my friend, but you're wrong!" I replied. "The conspirators of whom you speak are always somewhat to be feared in a great nation; they're dangerous agitators it's true; they're very energetic leaders when the day comes; but if they were alone, if they did not have that innumerable army of the discontented behind them in support, what could they do? And if you or your functionaries had been able to act in time to make that army of the discontented into an army of satisfied men, satisfied with your impartial justice, satisfied with the leniency of your administration, nothing but the falling sky could have crushed you. Look elsewhere for the motives for your condemnation, my friend."

Falster made a gesture with his head, which signified forcefully that he had not yet abandoned his own opinion.

"My God!" I said. "Why not accept a simple but disagreeable argument to find the truth, instead of looking so far afield? People in Zeeland love you—I believe so, at least, for I had proof of it in Lining. The whole oasis sang your praises, but, for reasons unknown to me, they wanted to destroy your reign. It then became necessary also to destroy everything that might revive it one day; that was logical. With your brother dead, and you dead, there would be no more pretenders to the throne of Zeeland, and thus no more muted efforts in that direction, no more efforts and campaigns on your behalf, no more assassinations, no more revolutions, no more civil was for your restoration. And who knows whether the people of Zeeland did not say, on looking at you and complaining about you both: 'Better that two men die than kill thousands for their cause.' Are there not times, Master, when the people must be judge and king?"

"Oh, oh!" said the king, muttering in a voice tremulous with doubt.

"Yes, Brother, I believe myself that the people have that right," Falster replied, firmly. Then he addressed himself to me and said: "But demonstrate to me, Mr. Daghestan, that there were no intrigues against us, nor errors, at least, nor ambition, nor democratic sentimentalism. Demonstrate to me that it was not interested or turbulent factions that led your discontented people on a leash, who enrolled the nonchalant, the timidly ambitious, the people without faith, without heart, without reflection…oh, whereas I would say: let us rely on the justice of the people, for the people is judge and king."

"Let's stop there, my friend," I said to Falster, "for you're opening the door too wide to suspicions, recriminations, and I don't want to go that way. When I see popular power passing in the street, when I sense it is edicts, I obey and I don't raise suspicions, in order to see whether its orders are good. If they're good, they're just. It's the king and the judge who is speaking…

"Forgive me for my principles, gentlemen; they're those of a citizen of Caucasia, those of a republic that nursed me in my infancy and nourishes me in the prime of life with the dogma of civic equality. I've said nothing, and know nothing, besides, that relates to you personally."

"I any case," said the king, uttering a profound sight and extending his hand toward the city of Trevig, "may God grant them peace, and may they be happy!"

"Happy, Master?" I replied, with a degree of courtesy. "If they haven't been happy with you, will they be happy with others? Perhaps the Zeelanders lack the wisdom that makes people happy. To be happy, I don't believe, myself, that it's sufficient to bring down a throne, and to raise the seat of a republic on its debris. All governments are good, in my opinion, whatever name they have, if they are just, mild and paternal, for the governed are happy then. But will the government that comes to Zeeland be paternal? Will not the same men who have administered it until now still be found there, in different clothing but with the same errors as before? If, on the contrary, new people are established in the councils of government, who knows whether those men will be able to get rid of the old bad, men, the petty tyrants, in order to make their republic loved?"

"So," said the king, "is it because I'm convinced of what I should have done before that I regret my departure somewhat, and said just now: 'May God grant them peace and render them happy...as happy as I wanted to make them?'" After a moment's pause for thought, however, the king added: "I have only two regrets in my heart, though: not having had time to put our plan for corporations into practice, and having been too hasty in implementing the project of universal suffrage. Universal suffrage, is, in my opinion, a fount of discord."

"No, no, Brother, don't reproach yourself for that law," said Falster, enthusiastically. "You did a good deed there, even a great act of generosity, for you did it against yourself. With his vote in hand, every citizen judges you; he absolves or condemns you. With universal suffrage properly understood, Zeeland will have no more revolts; it will only have revolutions..."

This whole conversation took place above the city of Trevig or in its vicinity. My balloon was out of range of any attack, and I had no fear of staying there. I don't know whether I was mistaken, but I thought it gave the king pleasure, Although he was banished from his kingdom, and had been condemned to death by his subjects—his fellow citizens, as one says in Caucasia—he appeared to be experiencing some satisfaction in not leaving as yet. Thus, I had had no fear of prolonging our conversation beyond what was perhaps appropriate to its present position, and I had done so, believe me, in

243

the manner of a Caucasian who, which respecting misfortune, does not seek to hide the face of the truth. I was, moreover, emboldened in my democratic predictions by the tacit approval of Falster.

After our comment on universal suffrage, silence suddenly fell among us. Each of us directed his gaze where he pleased. The king kept his constantly on the city, but he was surely unable to distinguish anything, for we were at too great an altitude. Then came a moment when all three of us looked at one another, perhaps slightly embarrassed by a thought that had occurred to each of us.

The king broke the silence first. "We can't stay here forever, my friends," he said. "We need to decide what to do."

"That's what I was thinking too," said Falster.

"There's only one thing we can do," the king went on, in a heart-rending tone of dolor and resignation. "That's to abandon the city and the kingdom, which we can't save from the disasters of the revolution, and wait in a safe place for divine and human justice."

"Speak, Master," I said to the king. "I'll take you anywhere you want to go."

"I expected no less of your courtesy, Mr. Daghestan, "but I only ask you to get us out of Zeeland; my brother and I will confer afterwards."

"I beg your pardon, Master. I won't abandon you until you're where you want to be. Besides, where will you find a better sailing-ship than mine? So give your orders, Master! Unless my offer is indiscreet."

"Indiscreet! Oh, you can't think so, my friend!" exclaimed the king, squeezing my hands affectionately. "It's me who would be indiscreet in asking any more of you. My intention is to go to somewhere friendly, I hope, where there would be good to do, but a distant and savage land where I would not wish to exile my most relentless enemies. I'd like to go to New Cosaquia, which is separated from us by deserts, ruins, poverty, barbarism. It is a home of poor people, but there's a king there who recently came to ask me for my friendship and my advice. Do you understand why I'm refusing your offer now, Mr. Daghestan?"

"No, Master," I told him, firmly.

"Look at our friend Daghestan's face, Brother," said Falster, smiling. "It will tell you whether our friend will accept your plan, and even with gratitude." He held his hand out to me. "Isn't that so, Daghestan?"

"You've read my mind, my friend."

"Oh, I've read more than your thoughts," Falster said, looking at me fixedly with a subtle smile.

I blushed involuntarily, and my heart beat violently, in spite of all my efforts to restrain it.

"Because you love the science of antiquity," he immediately added, generously, as if to give the lie to my emotion, "and you have, I know, made plans to go scratch around in New Cosaquia, in order to rediscover the ruins of ancient France."

"Well, then, let's go, Mr. Daghestan," said the king, then. "We shan't go our separate ways, if you wish—that suits me very well." With a soft and sad smile that he meant as a testament of amity, the king added: "As we're a society, then, and we now have to found a government, I nominate you as dictator. Take charge, sir; we shall obey blindly."

I went swiftly to my controls, and, consulting my chronometer and my compass, saw that we could leave in total tranquility. I therefore set a heading for New Cosaquia, and accelerated to top speed.

We soon reached the frontier of Zeeland, to enter into a vast desert that opened up before us, which borders Zeeland in that direction. We saw nothing thereafter but sand, rocks, large muddy pools covered with aquatic plants and a few stunted forests, edged by a few groups of huts inhabited by savages, the sad forerunners of the barbarity of the West.

After leaving Zeeland I took my aerostat down to a lower altitude, in order to be able to direct my course as I wished and stop if necessary, for it was moving so rapidly that I had no doubt that we would soon arrive at our destination. In any case, I needed to keep an eye on the ground, if only to satisfy a voyager's curiosity.

The king was thoughtful, but his brother gladly looked around, occasionally darting an amicable glance at me. Nobody said a word. We continued thus for several hours, without knowing exactly where we were, for I know nothing about the territory we were crossing, but my compass was guiding us well; I was sure of that.

"Master," I said to the king, eventually, "we need to hold council, for we can't be far from our goal now."

"What, here?" said the king's brother, standing up in the gondola and looking around, fearfully. To the king, he said: "Oh, that's not possible, Brother—it's not possible that the goal of our voyage was to come here! Look at it!"

"My friend," I said to Falster, "you're forgetting that Zeeland is the highway of civilization in this part of the inhabited world, and that beyond this desert is barbarity. Why do you expect to find anything here but what you see: brutal and savage nature?"

"It's just I can see more than that," Falster said, "For I see a nature turned upside-down, wrecked and ruined. I see the disorder of a lightning-strike—and what a lightning-strike!"

"Thus, we must be close to our goal," I replied, smiling, "for where we are going, I assure you that we shall find nothing else."

"No, we won't find anything else here," said the king, taking a little book from his pocket which he must often have leafed through, to judge by its worn condition. He showed me the book, having opened it. "Have we time to read a page?" he asked. "This is one I value greatly, although I'm not as devout as I ought to me. I have great confidence in these books, which are our sacred texts, for I always find true images therein, and lessons of divine wisdom. They're the prophecies of the greatest of our prophets—prophecies that bear a strong resemblance to history."

"We'll listen, Master," I replied, with an enthusiasm that pleased the king.

"It's not for you that I'm reading, Brother, the king added, smiling, for you're a skeptic, but I'll read for our friend and me."

"If your prophecies concern these places, Master—which is to say, those that were perhaps the most civilized and most beautiful in the ancient world, we'll surely be better able to understand them here than elsewhere."

"And perhaps we'll also be able to console ourselves better for our fallen grandeur in seeing all this," the king replied, uttering a profound sigh.

The king read, therefore, while our balloon progressed so slowly that one might have thought it motionless.

"This is the prophecy of Feröe, the last servant that God sent into the world to instruct it to mend its ways. 'I have sent you an army of faithful servants,' said the Al-Powerful, 'to speak to you about me, justice and your evil ways, and you have put them to death.

"'I have sent you a further army, which has told you about your crimes and reproached you for the death of God's servants, and what did you do? You have scorned, abused and mistreated them. And you have thought that the day of my vengeance would not come, because it came slowly.

"'Well, I tell you through the mouth of my prophet Feröe, you are not far from the year 2000—the year 2000 of the old world'—the year 2000 of the old world," observed the king, who continued: "'you are not far from the year 2000; well, perhaps you shall perish in that year.

"'Go, Feröe,' said God, 'travel the world and say to people, to cities and empires, that their last day is nigh. I have decided to destroy the world that I have created.

"'I created humans good, and they have become wicked; pride, ambition and egotism are devouring them. This earth and its wealth, which I organized to be useful to all, has become the prey of a few, the strongest or the most cunning. Humans, so tiny before me, have amassed beneath their feet mire upon mire, and have thought themselves greater for it, and have insulted their equals. They have insulted me...

247

"'Go, go, Feröe! Go around the world. Say to each people: You shall perish. Say to France: You shall perish. Say to Paris: You shall perish; your last day is at hand. Neither your profound ramparts with the hundred gates, nor your cleverly-constructed fortresses, nor your ships that cover the seas, nor your battle-hardened and numerous soldiers, nor your heaps of gold, nor your magical squares, nor your luxury, nor your riches, nor anything else, will protect you from my wrath.

"'It is necessary that you should be destroyed, because you know neither law, nor duty, nor virtue. You have created a law, duties and a virtue for yourself. You have denied your God and you have made gods of yourselves; you have bowed down before your vices...

"'I will therefore fill in your ditches; I will hide your monuments in the bowels of the earth; I will break your ships, your soldiers, all your cities and your empire; and over all of that I will hurl ricks, woods, stinking waters and poisonous herbs. I will make a desert where there as an evil civilization, and I will send ignorant and barbaric peoples who will be at home there, who will eat the bread and lie down in the beds of the proud people of Paris...'"

The king closed his book and looked at us with a satisfied expression.

"We must be in Paris, Brother," said Falster, then, "For there is certainly all of that here—minus the savages, whom I can't see."

"There they are, my friend," I replied to Falster, pointing at several little aerostats that were advancing toward us. In a whisper, I went on: "Yes, we're really in Paris, for it's only in Paris, I believe, that aerostats serve as vehicles."

"Paris, Paris," muttered the king, shaking his head. "You're talking about it as a savant, Mr. Daghestan. Personally, I can only see Figuig." He suddenly came to his feet, looking in the same direction as me. "'Oh!" he exclaimed. "But if I'm not mistaken...!"

XXVIII. IN THE KING'S PALACE

The king's exclamation had been provoked by a strange spectacle that had just become manifest in front of us, and which was truly beautiful—as beautiful as the enchantment of a dream. At first, I had only seen a few aerostats, barely perceptible in the distance, like birds of prey cleaving the clouds. Scarcely had I drawn them to the attention of my guests, however, than they had grown prodigiously by virtue of drawing nearer to us, and also multiplied to the point that the small advance guard that I expected soon looked more like a powerful army: an army of magnificent aerostats, my friend, magnificent in structure, equipment and flexibility. In the midst of them flew an aerostat of colossal dimensions and a luxurious appearance that surpassed anything I could imagine. It was the king's balloon.

It was the King of New Cosaquia, Rhaman X, and his court that was coming toward us. How had he known about our arrival? A Caucasian obviously could not have known, but I suspected immediately, on remembering the past. I only knew one person capable of divining the misfortune of the King of Zeeland, and his approach to Figuig.

The King of New Cosaquia's escort soon reached us. All the aerostats then descended to the ground. We followed suit. The two kings were able to embrace like brothers, and the king's brother and I had the honor and the advantage—especially the advantage, for it was a sign of the warm friendship and protection that we has been given in the face of a people who would probably have liked nothing better than to abuse their hospitality—of kissing the hand of the King of Cosaquia.

The king really was the man that I had seen in my dream.

The two kings had scarcely given one another the fraternal accolade and exchanged a few words than all the aerostats took off again in order to travel to the capital of New

Cosaquia—for, in spite of what I had thought, we were not there yet.

We took our place in the king's cortege, which advanced at full speed. In a very short time, therefore, we finally reached the Paris that I desired so much to see—but it was late; night was falling, and we could not see anything. My heart was afflicted, though; I could hardly breathe. My eyes could not widen sufficiently, even though I could not see anything, and my feet dared not step on to the ground for fear of breaking some magnificence of the Paris in which I hoped to find so much.

"Oh, my friend," Falster said to me, looking back at our aerostat, which he seemed to regret leaving, "this is the desolation of desolation!"

My illusions and dreams flew away at that remark, and began, in fact, to feel something like an icy hand about my heart, squeezing it. I don't know, however, whether it really was Falster's remark that brought me back to reality or the sight of a man I had not seen until then, but whom I suddenly perceived: the queen's fiancé, who looked at me grimly and ironically.

Ah! I thought. *That's annoying; I believe I have an enemy there. So much the better that he has seen the king offer me the back of his hand to kiss. In any case, I'll take care that he always remembers that I'm a guest in his land.*

He was, at any rate, the only person I knew that I could see, in spite of all the attention I devoted to looking—but he was also the only one that I thought I had reason to fear.

We had no difficulty in observing that we were not expected in Figuig, for no preparations had been made to greet us. As palaces are rare in the city, as well as available private habitations, we were taken directly to the royal palace, in order to spend the right there. The king offered us his gracious apologies, and promised us a palace for the following day—even if it had to be constructed, he added.

The remark was charming, but it caused me to open my eyes and ears wide. Were there still in Figuig, I asked myself, magicians powerful enough to strike the ground with their foot and make palaces spring forth therefrom in one piece? The king spoke so casually about such construction that I was ready to suppose it, especially in a land where I had come to see marvels. I was soon to understand what the king meant, however, when I saw the palaces of Figuig.

The king's palace—the one in which we were temporarily installed—is situated on the edge of a pool, adjacent to the water, from which it is defended by a mass of stones, very artistically carved, which were certainly not put in place by the Cosaques or their descendants. It is composed of a few huts made from tree-trunks perfectly fitted together and covered with reeds, probably gathered from the neighboring pool, woven with considerable artistry.

The hut dedicated to the residence and service of the king is large, beautiful and surmounted by embellishments of all kinds—various kinds of curious objects, of inestimable value for a savant, found in the local ruins. Other huts, less beautiful but still precious in the same way as the king's, surround the royal hut. They are occupied by important dignitaries and the king's particular friends.

People cannot approach the royal abode at will; it is well-defended by a fortress that surrounds it on all sides and forms a pleasant enclosure, planted with a few trees and shrubs that have grown there of their own accord, but are nevertheless given a little care. The great work of the palace is evidently that fortress, which is only formed of dry stones, cemented by a little earth in which ivy and all kinds of climbing plants grow, linking together the different parts of that singular wall.

Masonry is utterly unknown in that region, but the people excel in the art of fitting stones together, and that's very fortunate, for I don't know how, even with the aid of their luxuriant vegetation and the prodigious breadth they give to the feet of their walls, that mass of rubble could have any solidity.

It's immense. It's a veritable mountain—a circular mountain formed of stones that don't come from any quarry but for which the barbarians search in all directions, which they have removed, with great difficulty and investment of time, from the old and beautiful monuments whose value they are unaware, in neatly-shaped and chiseled masses, which they are able to extract and throw at the feet of their lairs like ornaments.

All their labor and all their art is there. Their only concern is to find some beautiful piece of debris and then to place it in their construction, with an eye to the picturesque, always provided that the accommodation of their materials permits it; if not, the picturesque is pitilessly sacrificed. I have seen, in the wall of the royal palace, marvels of art, perfectly-finished statues that were mutilated, evidently by the barbarians, when a head, an arm or a leg interfered with the desired stratification of their fortress.

Oh, the monsters!

Forgive me, my friend, for that exclamation of a scholar at bay, forgetful of the duties of hospitality. It's certainly not the exclamation of a philosopher, I confess. The philosopher lives in the present and adapts himself to everything. Perhaps, after all, the Cosaques whose guest I was are more philosophical than I am; they have but one concern, that of living, and who knows whether that is not where wisdom lies? With all our fine sentiments, dreams, illusions and memories—and all our knowledge too—are we any happier than them?

We were, therefore, given shelter in the Royal Palace. Although the roof wasn't beautiful, the bed was good. It was loosely made up of two main components, one of wool, the other of a very fine cotton that is grown locally, all enveloped in the hides of wild beasts killed in hunts, prepared for that purpose. But I could not sleep.

My over-full heart overflowed under the pressure of the thousands of various thoughts that besieged it, and were not all thoughts of joy. The life that was beginning for us there promised nothing very disagreeable for a philosopher, however, especially a Caucasian republican—for if there were social inequalities in that country, we were scarcely able to perceive them. The king, our host, had a frank and cordial simplicity and out marks of respect seemed to weary him more than our familiarity. His habits, moreover, were not troublesome for us, and I had not seen thus far that the habits of his close associates could be any more inconvenient—an immense privilege that one does not find in the prudish confines of our civilization! I was thus as free, and perhaps even freer, than in Caucasia—and yet I dreamed about torments.

The following morning, quite early, the king sent words to us that he expected us at breakfast, and that the table was laid. The people of Figuig are early risers; we highly civilized folk are much less so. We got up immediately, therefore, and joined King Rhaman, who greeted us with broad and hearty laughter, embracing his guest, the king, and presenting the back of his hand to Falster and me, which we kissed cordially. Then we sat down sat table.

We have habits of sobriety in Caucasia of which I approve strongly, but the Cosaques could give us a stern lesson in that regard. The table was set up next to one of the windows of the hut; on the opposite side of the room the royal bed, which was as good, though no better, than ours, was encased in a kind of alcove in which it remained visible to everyone, and unmovable. The table was also fixed to the ground, standing up in the midst of large tree-trunks that were fixed in the ground and served the guests as seats. It could not have been more primitive, but it was sufficient for our needs, and there is wisdom in being able to be content with the necessary.

The menu of our meal was no more complicated than the rest; it comprised milk of various sorts—cow's milk, goat's milk, ewe's milk—to satisfy different tastes, eggs variously cooked, and a few vegetables, especially the famous ground-apple that I had already encountered, and which appears to be the nourishment of kings as well as prisoners in that country.

Wine is unknown to that people; grapes are never served at table, except in nature. Thus, we drank water, and an insipid water that I do not like. Our host sharpened it with a strong liquor that I would have preferred, personally, to drink neat, although it was not entirely to my taste.

We had no need of anyone to serve us such a meal; it was a perfect free-for-all, at least as far as service was concerned. There were, however, servants around us, doubtless to do us honor, for nothing was required of them. We could have made requests, and they were ready to answer them, but I preferred, myself, not to invoke their collaboration in anything whatsoever, because I had observed at their head my intimate enemy, who was watching me, and seemed to me to have the attitude of a tiger ready to pounce on its prey.

"Gentlemen," said King Rhaman, graciously, sitting down at the table, "forgive me for serving you like a savage. It was only recently that I learned in Zeeland how one treats friends in civilized countries. If, however, I had known that you were about to arrive in my realm, I would have made every effort to replicate some of the good customs of the Eastern lands. Until I can give orders on that subject and educate my subjects somewhat, if that is possible, please accept with a good heart what the savages of New Cosaquia give you with a good heart."

This little speech was very tasteful, so the King of Zeeland replied to our host with a well-wrought toast, which gave King Rhaman pleasure, for he replied with hearty laughter that made the table and the hut tremble.

No one ate with us but the king; that was the etiquette, it seemed—but all the inhabitants of the royal enclosure appeared after the end of the meal to partake with us of a reddish-brown ambrosiac beverage, which they called coffee.

Coffee is produced by a bush that grows in the region without much cultivation, thanks to the warmth of the climate, and which appears to me to originate from there, for I have not seen it anywhere else during all my travels. The taste of the fruit is slightly bitter, but one softens it with a liquid sugar that these peoples extract from various shrubs, and which they prepare with a great deal of skill.

All things considered, the liquor has an exquisite taste, good for the digestion, and leaves you with an agreeable sensation that relaxes the nervous system and banishes dark thoughts. Thus I felt more cheerful after having drunk it, and even experienced a moment of sympathy and confidence that bore me toward the man I detested more than any other in the world just then, the Queen's fiancé.

I felt that I ought to say something to him—just a few words—for, since my arrival, I had not seen the Queen, nor heard anything that might indicate that she was not far away. Another absence also worried me slightly—that of Ouchda—but I told myself to be patient, for I could not fail to see her soon, or at least hear news of her.

I therefore took a step toward the unfortunate fiancé, who swiftly came to meet me with a brighter expression than I expected. He listened to me attentively but made no reply. Had he understood my question? I thought so, and saw his lips curl in a dubious smile, when I pronounced the Queen's name. Still, he made no reply, although he was still listening to me without impatience.

I therefore decided to take my leave of him, and did so with all the grace I could muster, in order not to envenom an enemy than I knew to be ardent, as I had been able to see. I waited for another opportunity.

"Now, my brother," said Rhaman to the King of Zeeland, after having drunk and savored his coffee, "I'll leave you at liberty." He turned toward his entourage, whose members were listening attentively—doubtless primarily out of respect, but also out of respect for the Herculean force that he was able to employ if necessary—and added: "Gentlemen, these gentlemen are out guests; woe betide anyone who does not respect them, or does not accord them a respect equal to mine."

His eyes were menacing, and his clenched fists allowed the sight of muscles that would have delighted a painter, but whose effects must be frightful to feel.

"So, gentleman, I leave you at liberty until this evening," he repeated, turning back to us, "when I shall come to dine with you; I'm inviting myself. You'll be taken to the palace I've allocated to you." He turned to the Queen's fiancé. "Johan-Ali-Schahpohtink," he said, "take our guests to the Palace of Administration, which you must have got ready, as I ordered you to..."

We therefore departed for the Palace of Administration, smiling privately at the pompous designation of such a paltry place, for we did not expect it to resemble the Royal Palace. I was far from being saddened by that, for my goal as a voyager and antiquary had been attained. The king seemed resigned, like a true philosopher, but Falster had difficulty straightening his face in order to smile at the graciousness of our crowned host. His habitual philosophy was completely lacking, and I no longer found in him the freethinker of Lining.

It's true that if Falster saw nothing ahead of him than the prospect of inhabiting that place of exile permanently, it was certainly not a cheerful prospect, while his brother, the king, could console himself by resigning himself to becoming the apostle of Figuig.

We walked along the edge of a marsh that was bordered on both sides by ruins that I devoured with my eyes, for my imagination gave them a hidden value that their appearance was far from divulging. That marsh is interminable in its length; I could not even say exactly where it stopped. Nor did it seem to be unique; its course, interrupted by rubble covered with trees and plants of all kinds, which form lateral dikes, sometimes very broad, seems to give birth to a host of successive ponds. It was not difficult for the imagination to make a whole of it, though, for those pools have a common bed that always follows the same slope, except that the bed is interrupted at intervals...

"Could this," I said to Falster, thinking aloud what I had already thought silently, "be the famous River Seine of which history speaks?"

Falster shrugged his shoulders, raising his eyes to the heavens.

"Poor fellow," he said to me, "your mind is really too well-made. I'll wager that you don't see this as a filthy marsh with murky, stinking waters, but as a beautiful river spanned by magnificent bridges, bordered by broad and carefully-maintained quays, splendid houses and palaces populated with all that the most advanced civilization can offer to Caucasian eyes."

I smiled, opened satisfied eyes that meant to say: you've seen through me.

"But where are we, then?" he exclaimed, louder than I could have wished, stopping and then drawing his head back within his shoulders and folding his arms, in order to look at me.

"In Paris," I told him.

"In Figuig," he replied, throwing the word in my face disdainfully and continuing on his way, for we were going on foot; we had not wanted to get into the aerostat that had been offered to us.

Having walked for some time, still following the banks of the marsh, we arrived in front of the Palace of Administration, which was also called the Island Palace.

XXIX. THE PALACE OF ADMINISTRATION

The Palace of Administration looked no different from all the other palaces in Figuig; to the first glance it appeared as an enormous mass of rubble enveloping a space that could be estimated s very large. That space was dotted with huts that scarcely differed from one another except in size and a few slight details required by their purpose. They were not visible from outside, but we were sufficiently well-acquainted with the local architecture to tell what they might be from there. In any case, they were veritably admirable to my imagination, which saw them laden with incredible riches—which no one else noticed, however, not even the philosopher Falster, who walked over them while puling faces at me. Perhaps he wanted to protest against my enthusiasm for a place that was, for him, a land of desolation.

The palace was also known as the Island Palace because it stood at the center of a small stream, which enveloped it on all sides, the stream being no more than an arm of the eternal marsh, to which I hoped one day to be able to give another name.

One might have thought, on looking at the entire impos-ing mass that formed the fortress of the palace, that it was a mountain formed centuries before by ruins of all sorts, and that subsequently, in an era that I could not specify at first glance, human hands had hollowed it out with care and perse-verance. Then they had cleared it out, nevertheless respecting the crust that, being pierced vertically, no longer offered any-thing but a ring of walls built and consolidated by the weather,

Such was the effect that the Island Palace had on me, es-pecially after having inspected all its parts minutely—and I had guessed correctly, as I heard later from the mouth of King Rhaman himself. He it was who had been hollowing out the palace in a mountain of debris for years, and had raised the bed of the surrounding marsh by having some of the earth and

258

trees that his digging produced thrown into it. It seemed that a large number of statues, bas-reliefs, sculpted stones and art-works of every sort had been found there, but everything that had not caught the eye of that new species of builder, to be enclosed in his museum, had served in the past to consolidate the walls of the palace, and partly in the construction of other palaces. Profanation!

Profanation, I said, my friend! But am I right to say that? May I be allowed to condemn the King of New Cosaquia, pitilessly, without at least admitting the extenuating circum-stances for his devastations?

Even though Rhaman X was far from employing in his excavations all the intelligence of a Caucasian savant, it would really be an injustice to say that he misunderstood them com-pletely and squandered them stupidly. The proof that one would be mistaken is that he had created a museum for them. That museum was in a special corner of the palace, in the treasure section. There, the king had gathered everything that had excited some interest or curiosity, and everything that appeared to him to be useful, for the present or the future.

It is in that museum, my friend, that I have found the model for our Caucasian rifles, veritable rifle-barrels…yes, yes, rifle-barrels, which we glory in having invented only a few centuries ago, laughing at the ancients who probably only knew how to make war with clubs, we said…

Well, I repeat, I've seen rifle-barrels there, and in large numbers, connected end to end, to take water from the roofs into reservoirs—and what reservoirs! Guess, if you can. Mor-tars: bronze mortars, for the invention of which our ancestors called General Bakou illustrious.

Blissful ignorance! These men have only found mortars and rifles useful for storing and carrying water. Alas, my friend, perhaps some traveler strayed into Caucasia a few thousand years hence will find our rifles, mortars and cannon serving even more ignoble uses, among people even more barbaric than the Cosaques of Figuig. Poor world! Poor peo-ples, so proud of themselves! O humankind!

The space enclosed by the palace wall was vast; it comprised the whole of the rest of the island, and that was not too much for its purpose, for, as I've already said, it was the Palace of Administration.

The king's steward in a very important person in Figuig; he is responsible for guarding the king's treasures and provided food to the court.

The treasures of the King of New Cosaquia are not comparable with those of the sovereigns of our civilization. They comprise all the objects that the king takes pleasure in possessing, whatever value they have: products of all sorts, gold and silver jewelry, and silver coins from all nations.

Silver money is of little use in Cosaquia, so it is rarely seen, except in the king's palace. He makes no use of it, but locks it away as something precious and an object of curiosity. Jewels are something else; they're much sought-after, especially by the great ladies of the region. The king being a widower for the time being, his jewels are very little used, so I have been able to admire almost all of them in their cases, although not all of them would be admirable for us, and some display a great naivety of artistry and taste.

The king's treasures do not only consist of objects of intrinsic but dead value. They also include objects of commerce derived from taxation or come from other sources. The commerce of the Cosaques of New Cosaquia is neither very varied nor greatly lucrative. That is easily comprehensible, when one has seen the people in question and understood their needs. The people are simple, primitive in their tastes; their needs are easily satisfied—so very easily that the soil of the land can supply them fully, or very nearly. I say nearly, because there is probably no people on earth, however barbaric, that does not have some desire and cannot create some need.

The Cosaques—who, in my opinion, are something better than barbarians—have not completely escaped that innate human vice. They ask for little, it's true, but they nevertheless ask for something, and that something is jewelry, of which they are very fond, a few fabrics, and some of the materials that enter into the construction of their aerostats, notably iron and copper. Those metals are only sought, it's true, by the French tribe, who are the only ones to devote themselves to the construction of aerostats, which they do in great secrecy.

I haven't seen money in Figuig, so commerce can only take place by barter. That exchange isn't entirely free; it only takes place at certain points on the frontier at certain times of the year, and always in the presence of government agents. The Cosaques bring the produce of their hunting, which is always abundant. Their forests and their vast wildernesses teem with big and small game, which wanders in herds: horses, red deer, gazelles, fallow deer, and wild dogs and cats.

Their flocks of sheep and goats also provide wool that is much sought-after. It appears, in addition, that for some time, large quantities of coffee have been exported, for which neighboring regions are beginning to acquire an avid taste, and might perhaps reach us in Caucasia, God willing. The king does not engage in commerce himself, but he is not forbidden by etiquette to seek its benefits, so he seeks them very actively, though only through the intermediate of his steward. A part of the treasure section of the Palace of Administration is used to store trade goods.

In another section, which is no less vast, are found the foodstuffs that the steward must always have to hand in sufficient quantity for the needs of the court, which is not an easy task, for he is not allowed to keep living animals there, awaiting the hour of slaughter to aliment the royal table.

The Cosaques never kill animals, wild or domestic, in order to eat them, except be hunting them. They think it inexcusably cowardly and cruel to kill a defenseless creature. Even sheep, which we raise for slaughter in spite of the utility of their fleeces, their milk and their fecundity, in spite of their gentle mores and their familiarity with us, those savages will not slaughter. When their flocks are too numerous, they release a few of them from time to time in their vast forests, where they survive without difficulty, ultimately forming semi-wild flocks that no one then has any scruple about hunting and eating.

There remains a third section in the palace, which is reserved for the steward and his family, and the guards responsible for maintaining good order. The huts in the enclosure are large, decorated, as they are everywhere else, and perhaps a little more than elsewhere, with antique objects found during the excavation of the mountain that became a palace.

The huts of the food section differ essentially from the others. They resemble what we would call covered markets. They have vast roofs formed by the combination of lots of small roofs perfectly fitted together. As those small roofs need ground-supports, however, they are naturally formed by the intermediary of columns of stones sculpted with an infinite artistry that is certainly not known either to the Moroccans, the Cosaques or the barbarians that preceded them. What are these columns, then? What were they? What monument did they support? For they evidently supported a monument, and only one; their disposition, the uniformity of their design and their sculptures indicate as much.

Oh, if I could only overturn those ignoble huts, slice through those seemingly miserable walls, excavate them and separate from its matrix the ancient gold that is there, what fine problem would I solve? How easily I would then reconstruct the palace that must be there, and which would speak a language to me much clearer than that of Père Franco's book. God grant that modern civilization can one day set foot in that den of savages! Antiquity would then no longer be a myth for us, and perhaps we would find beyond these ruins other ruins, just as rich, which preceded them. What a prospect! It's enough to confound human ideas and desires.

One cannot go directly to the Palace of Administration, since it's an island. There is, in consequence, an arm of the marsh to cross. The arm isn't very wide, but wide enough for a tree-trunk to be unable to serve to cross it. It has therefore been necessary to take other measures and construct a bridge—but what kind of bridge can one demand of such a resourceful people?

Bridges in Figuig are formed by debris of wood and rubble, such as one finds everywhere, with varying degrees of solidity, on the ground and, alas, in the excavations. The constructors throw all their materials into the steam over which they need a passage, and heap them up as best they can up to the water-level. They have understood, however, doubtless by virtue of experience, that these primitive bridges, however useful they might be for passage, can become deleterious is blocking the watercourse and flooding habitations. So they engineer small gaps to allow the water to run through. It is understood, and it was explained to me, that these miniature arches of a sort are formed during the construction of the bridging causeway.

It was, therefore, over one of these bridges that we passed in order to enter the Island Palace, in which we were to reside. It wasn't broad, perhaps by strategy, in view of the importance of the palace, and had had an unparalleled originality and beauty: a veritable jewel of antiquity.

The first point of solid support that it had on the bank was the rump of a bronze horse that was hidden under the water, but which the eye of the imagination could easily follow. I don't know for sure, but I believe, in truth, that there is also a bronze rider mounted on the horse; although I could only see the upper body of the man and the head of the horse, the pose indicated as much. That is assuredly strange for us, who only know the horse as game in our forests, but I can respond to the skeptics that it ought not to astonish us, since the Sheikh of Timbuktu has assured me that the people of a tribe in his neighborhood have tried to domesticate horses and have succeeded. What is astonishing, given that, about believing that the French of antiquity made use of horses as mounts, at least sometimes?

The rider's head, which I shall consider for a few moments with all the attention of a justly-enthusiastic amateur, was superb in its frankness. The beard grew as it liked and

263

covered the whole face; it was cut short; the hair was close-cropped, the nose aquiline, the mouth smiling, the eyes keen and wide open.[43]

That statue had not been placed at the head of the bridge as an ornament; it was there to serve a function. It was, indeed, very useful, at the entrance to a passage that, in spite of all the care taken, had remained a trifle muddy, to have a solid point of support for the hand. Well, that point was provided by the horseman's head; the rump of the horse itself served as a base for the apron of the bridge. It was luxurious.

The apron itself was a marvel, if not a luxury, at least of interest. It was formed by two long granite stone, squares and inscribed with hieroglyphs. They were obviously two separate pieces of a single block, broken—by the malevolence of time, I hope, but perhaps also by the barbarians, who only saw it as a suitable surface to form the lack of a bridge.

I had no reason to admire that fragmented block, but the hieroglyphic symbols that were engraved on its faces strongly intrigued my curiosity. What was that stone? What did the engravings signify? Was it a residue of the old Cosaques, the old Moroccans of New Cosaquia, or did it date further back? It evidently had a more distant origin, but where? From whom? And what did it say? Oh, if I had only been able to put it into my traveling bag and bring it here to my study, in order to interrogate it at my ease! What fine secrets, I'm sure, that stone and its hieroglyphs would have revealed to me! What fine lessons it would have taught me about the practices of the ancients, their mores and their history! Those symbols, those symbols! Who can tell me what those symbols are? What alphabet would they reveal to me? They're hieroglyphic symbols, I can see that, of course, because I have the writing of the French here in Père Franco's book, but...unless it's only a

---

[43] Mettais' readers would have had no difficulty recognizing the equestrian statue of Henri IV which had stood at the entrance to the Pont-Neuf since 1818, replacing a previous one that had been destroyed during the Revolution.

savant script, such as many of the peoples of our time have…or a special script for public monuments…or...[44]

Perhaps the future will tell me.

Oh, if only I had Franco, I said to myself as I passed over that stone—but thought furtively: *Or rather, if I had my beautiful witch…!*

---

[44] Mettais' readers would have recognized the Luxor Obelisk, but might have wondered how it had been transported all the way from the Place de la Concorde to the eastern end of the Île de la Cité, where Louis-Philippe had set it in 1833.

XXX. A MUSEUM IN THE PALACE
OF ADMINISTRATION

Such, my friend, was the palace where we were to reside.
We installed ourselves there: me joyful, finding it richer and
more beautiful than all the palaces in the world; the King of
Zeeland with the resignation of a fully-determined philosopher; and Falster with the resignation of a philosopher at bay.
The steward, of course, had moved out; the treasure and the
royal food-supplies had been taken elsewhere to make room
for us.

We installed ourselves without any difficulty, our bag-
gage not being extensive and our furniture, for its part, being
neither cumbersome not luxurious. We had the necessary,
however, even the superfluous, if one considers what others
had.

The king accommodated himself to what was put at his
disposal; his brother did the same, being unable to do any
better. As for me, I thought myself the happiest man in the
world. At that moment, I was far from regretting the comforts
of Caucasia.

I organized myself lodgings that the most difficult of an-
tiquaries would have envied, immediately setting out in search
debris of inestimable value, which I piled up all around me.
My hut was soon no longer anything but a small museum,
apart from my bed, which was a blot thereon.

I could not, however, change anything about the bed,
which was solidly mounted on four wooden pylons fixed to
the floor—but I compensated for my impotence by planning a
metamorphosis of my table, which, like my bed, was far from
being elegant. Anyway, it was very nearly the sole item of
furniture at my disposal, which I did not regret at all, for my
habits as a traveler had taught me to reduce my needs considerably. Since it was there, though, the table seemed to me to
be genuinely necessary for writing my travel notes, and I

would have plenty of those to record in that enchanted land where it as sufficient to scratch the ground with a finger to find marvels. So I decided to write them in luxury, since I could.

I had noticed in a corner of the courtyard a large square marble tablet covering a damp sewer collecting the rainwater falling from several roofs. It had been placed there as a precaution, to carry the water away and thus preserve the foodstores. I suspected—accurately, I believe—where that tablet came from, but I said nothing to begin with, in order to avoid Falster's gibes and jokes.

One day, however, I said to him: "The Cosaques did not carve that marble in the past, much less the Moroccan Cosaques who are here today; so..."

"So?" said Falster, bursting into laughter, although he had no desire to laugh.

"So, I'm carrying it away," I replied, abruptly, to my friend's attack. Then I did my best to lift up the marble slab, looking at Falster—who, seeing my difficulty, came to my aid, and the two of us transported it to my hut. It was a magnificent piece of sculpture, perhaps the bas-relief of some historical monument, for it was not difficult to see that it represented some event.

"Well?" I said to Falster, widening my eyes to give better proof of my interrogative admiration.

"It's a poor table," Falster replied, maliciously, "for you can't write on those reliefs, and I'll wager that you won't get any information out of the Cosaques of this bazaar." He emphasized the last word disdainfully. "Did you notice that they put the flat side of the tablet uppermost and the reliefs on the underside—in the sewer, in fact? Why? To make the water run more easily. Do the same, if you want the tablet to be a good table."

I had hardly installed my table than I thought of procuring another household necessity, which had been completely forgotten. I don't know whether the Cosaques wash their hands and faces other than in streams and rivers, but we Caucasians, who have different habits, experience other desires. I therefore made myself a wash-basin with a fragment of marble artistically hollowed out in the form of a seashell, which had been relegated to a corner of the courtyard and was used by the steward's slaves for washing clothes.

What else can I tell you about our palace, my friend? My own hut—my apartment, as we say in Caucasia—was not the most comfortable, but I can assure you that it was, in truth, luxurious, because I had filled it with all the magnificence of antiquity, of a people who were certainly the most civilized in antiquity, whatever our savants might say. I had around me there, close at hand, broken arms, legs and heads, some in marble, others in stone—but what arms, what legs and what heads! Masterpieces, such as our finest sculptors could never make. Except that all of it was lifeless, for all of it, although sculpted from life, was devoid of paint—or perhaps it never had been painted, contrary to the customs of people like us, who paint all our sculptures.

I installed myself there like a mistress in her boudoir, or, rather, like a miser amid his treasures—yes, my friend, like a miser. I no longer had any but one dread: that of being dispossessed of my riches, either by virtue of my unforeseen departure or that of the king and his brother, which I feared greatly, because it would render mine necessary. So I never ceased extolling to them the pleasantness of our abode, which I rendered as agreeable as possible for them with all sorts of generous gestures—but I had difficulty persuading Falster.

One day, however, when he came to see me early in the morning he found that I had already gone out. I was seriously occupied in digging, in order to extract a magnificent specimen of art, which I began to praised to him more highly than anything else, although I couldn't yet see enough of it. My verve was excited by the artistic attention that I surprised on Falster's face.

So, I launched into an enthusiastic historical excursion on ancient France, on the magical Paris in whose soil we were most certainly digging, and on the good fortune and glory that we would certainly obtain by deciphering the enigma of the remotest antiquity, by remaining long enough on the most beautiful land that we could study: on the virgin territory of France, which had only every been trodden by the feet of barbarians and excavated by the hands of ignorant savages.

Oh, I talked with a great deal of fire. I was eloquent and persuasive. Thus, I saw Falster smile supportively. He had understood me, and I believed that I also understood him perfectly; for I knew that, although he might regret the enjoyments of Zeeland, and the good that he hoped to do there, he was also a philosopher, and a sound philosopher, to whom the glory of which I had spoken wasn't indifferent.

I had, after all, no intention of staying there forever, and I told Falster that frankly, in case he had read that desire in my excitement. From then on, therefore, I saw that he was less depressed, and more active in enjoying the life that I was enjoying. For the moment, he even helped me in my labor, and by combining our efforts, we were able to bring out of our excavation the object I had been working on since the day before.[45]

It was a marble statue of a woman holding a child in her arms—at least, I was able to deduce that by her pose, for nothing any longer remained of the child than two legs. She had a snake beneath her feet and a crown on her head, slightly broken, it's true, but perfectly recognizable. The statue was well-preserved; the figure was intact. We found nothing else of the child in the same excavation, except for a crown much smaller than the woman's, which I attributed without hesitation to the child.

Who, then, my friend, was that woman? My ignorance— I can even say, without wounding anyone, our ignorance—of

---

[45] When he wrote this passage Mettais seems to have been anticipating that Daghestan would have a less eventful and more leisurely stay in Figuig than the next few chapters describe, into the chronology of which this "one day" cannot be readily slotted.

the past is too deep for me to make any pronouncement. Beneath her feet was written: MARIA.

Maria! Was she a queen, a regent, a famous woman—and in what era? Was she a goddess, an allegory?

We can suppose anything we wish here, for the name tells us nothing; history is mute with respect to her, and yet the statue indicates an important person, or an allegory of the highest interest. If history had taken the trouble to tell us something about the religion of the French, I think that we might perhaps have been able to find the explanation of my statue there, but it tells us nothing, or almost nothing, about that religion. Did the French even have one?

The religion of the ancients—not the ancients of the remotest antiquity but those about whom we know something—was, it appears, very demonstrative. Like us, they believed in God—what people, in fact, does not?—but while religious worship among us is very simple, among them it was very complicated.

The ancients had temples that were sumptuous in their architecture and their decoration, lavish funding for their maintenance, highly-organized religious corporations for service—in sum, an entire government for the administration of the large-scale business of religion.

Our historians vary as to the date of the catastrophe that caused the government in question to crumble, but at any rate, it did crumble, to such an extent that nothing of it remains in our mores, our practices or our memories. Only belief remains: belief in God.

Among us, religious observance is very different from that from that of the ancients, as everyone knows. We have no religious corporations, everyone offering his homage to God in his own way—no priests or high priests, as ancient terminology had it. Among us, the "priest" is the head of the family, who speaks to God on behalf of the entire household, and in public we have no other priest than the leader of each commune, who represents governmental authority. Our temples are everywhere that a crowd might assemble.

It's very simple, and it is, I believe, just as respectful and recognizant toward the deity as making a great deal of noise and displaying a luxury insulting to the poor. That, at least, is what all modern people think, for it's not only in Caucasia that the belief is accepted.

Our ancestors thought differently: may God protect me from holding it against them and criticizing them! To every century its own mores and beliefs, to every century its needs!

But if our ancestors had the religious organization of which the historians inform us, who can tell whether they might have inherited it from their own ancestors? Who can tell whether the remotest antiquity might also have had its luxurious temples, its priests and its sacred government? Who can tell whether the France of the primary era might have also had all that organization? Who can tell whether I might, in the middle of the Palace of Administration, have been in the ruins of a temple of that era, and that might statue might have been the statue of a goddess or a sacred individual of the time?

I said a goddess, my friend, but don't be scandalized by that. How do I know whether the French worshiped one or several gods, in spite of all that's said about them? They worshiped a cross; we know that from legends, and history has been able to hand down to us, almost certainly, that item of ancient knowledge. But what worship did they render to that cross? What worship did they render to all the individuals their statues represent? Why a cross? To whom were their altars dedicated?

It's said that they worshiped saints—which is to say, good men, benevolent in life, two whom they raised altars as well as to God. We are asked, in consequence, whether they were idolaters. Idolaters! Oh, I'll never believe that. Idolaters, them?—the French! No one will ever make me believe that such a civilized people worshiped their peers as equals of God. No, no! I know nothing about France, but I know what it is to be civilized, and that's sufficient for me.

Patience, though! Patience, at any rate! If I know nothing today, I shall know in due course. Let me only spend a year,

271

only a year, in Figuig, and I will then know what no one has ever known about ancient France, its mores and his history, as well as its religion...

You can see, my friend, that I'm getting ahead of myself. We've only just arrived in Figuig; we've only just installed ourselves in the Palace of Administration, and already I'm giving you an account of all the work I did there. Forget that for a while, I beg you, and don't remember anything but our arrival in the palace, and my entry into my hut.

We had only been there for a few hours—and very busy, I can assure you, exploring our new domain, which was, take my word for it, large, even very large, dotted here and there with natural arbors, somewhat cultivated gardens, and especially with huts—when our host, King Rhaman, arrived, on his own, like an ordinary citizen, to visit us.

When I say "on his own," that's an error, for he was accompanied by a slave weighted down by the burden of a mountain of papers, which the king had come to offer to our curiosity, out of courtesy. It was the history of his nation, written by some unknown hand, probably reviewed and corrected by interested parties.

At any rate, it was a pleasant pastime that was being offered to us, and we thanked our host in sincere terms. My own curiosity was keenly excited thereby. I, who had been so much occupied with history, was finally about to be able to study unpublished historical documents relating to a country of which we knew so little in the East, and about which we had probably told many fables.

Our disappointment was not trivial, however, when we perceived that the history in question was written by hand, and by a rather unskillful hand. We were not overly astonished by that, since printing was probably unknown there, but we were inconvenienced by it.

"You will, I hope," our host said, "be interested to learn the origins of this country and our race, and you will doubtless see the truth, for we do not know to be deceptive." He tapped the voluminous manuscripts with his plump hand. "In here," he added, "there is nothing but facts. We are scarcely philosophers here, and we don't know how to dress facts up in brilliant frippery that blind you and prevent you seeing the truth."

King Rhaman is not, in fact, entirely a barbarian; there is even the cloth of a civilized man within him, as you can see, my friend, from his speech. Personally, I would have preferred it if he had not told us anything about his history, for I was no longer sure that it would be impartial, given that the king understood the advantages, and doubtless also the inconveniences, of historical impartiality.

At any rate, as he had not written everything himself, and as, in any case, we were only talking about the antiquity of New Cosaquia, I hoped to find a fine work, from which I would at least be able to disentangle something useful. So I asked permission enthusiastically to open the precious wad, in order to make an immediate start.

"Oh, not yet, not yet!" King Rhaman said to me, laughing heartily, as if to soften the rudeness of his prohibition, and catching hold of the arm that had gone to work too quickly. "Not yet! Later. For the moment, we have to talk. Come!" To the slave, he said: "You stay here. You'll answer to me for those papers with your head..."

XXXI. KING RHAMAN'S CONFIDENCES

Then Rhaman X took the King of Zeeland by the arm. Falster and I followed them, but at a distance, for I didn't want to be overheard if the desire came upon me to talk—and I noticed that Rhaman, who wasn't talking, could easily hear me. He wasn't talking, presumably thinking about what he had to say; he remained silent until he had arrived at the place where he wanted to sit down in order to open the conversation he desired. The conversation had, therefore, to be serious, for those people only discuss serious matters while sitting down; if they speak while walking, it's to say trivial things; they only like talking at rest.

"I shall be curious," I said to Falster, not restricting myself to the customs of our new hoists, "to discover how such savants write history, and what history they can have."

"Yes," Falster replied, with a sigh, "what history? The history of their palaces, no doubt, of the architecture of their bridges of their commerce. Poor people! Everything is dead here." And he shook his head sadly.

I saw that I had made a mistake, for I should only have spoken to Falster about joys and pleasures. "Oh, don't talk that way about death," I said, as cheerfully as I could, "for death speaks here more eloquently that life, and that's precisely what ought to render this place enchanting for us. What use is philosophy, if it can't cheer us up among ruins?"

"Your philosophy, Daghestan, isn't mine," my friend retorted. "Your philosophy lives in the ruins of the past; mine lives in the present."

"Well, for the present, then, admire the royal contentment and tranquility that our host enjoys in his city. Look—he comes and goes, without anxiety; public opinion does not tyrannize him. That man is free, and freer than the powerful kings of our civilized nations, who make everyone around them tremble, for he can walk here like an ordinary citizen of

274

Lining or Caucasia. So, as he has nothing to fear, as you can see, he need not be accompanied by noisy and gaudily-clad police, nor secret police. Oh, barbarism certainly has something to be said for it."

"Aren't you mistaken, though?" said Falster, after darting a glance around to see whether what I had just said was true. "Look!"

I looked, and saw what my friend had seen: the head of a soldier or a slave, showing itself at intervals with much precaution, following all our movements—which is to say, King Rhaman's movements.

"That's the police, my poor friend," I said to Falster, disconcerted. "Yes, that's definitely the police..."

I couldn't say any more, for the two kings had just come to a halt, and were looking at us as they waited for us. We had reached the end of our stroll.

The place where we had stopped was not an arbor, but a thicket of trees and bushes, which had sprouted and grown in the midst of rubble and ruins of all sorts, covered with thick moss. It was evidently a strollers' meeting-place for the inhabitants of the palace, for the path that led to it seemed well-trodden and upper bodies of statues lying on the ground and conveniently disposed served as seats for them. Behind us, there was only the clump of trees, then the enclosing wall, behind which was an arm of the pond—which, seen from this position, acquired the name of Administration Pond.

"King Belt, my brother," said Rhaman X to the King of Zeeland, sitting down on the torso of a statue and gesturing to us to do likewise, "You brought bad news on your arrival yesterday. I didn't say anything more about it because I thought I ought not to; I didn't want our first conversation to make us weep together. I do, however, feel a need to console you, so I've come to ask you what misfortune has overtaken you since my departure from Trevig."

"I'm no longer king, my brother," King Belt replied. "The Zeelanders have dethroned me, and they condemned me and my brother to death—and if our friend Daghestan"—he pointed at me—"hadn't arrived, we would be dead now."

King Rhaman stood up and came toward me as graciously as he could. Then putting his hands on my shoulders, he kissed me on the forehead. "You are our friend," he said.

A man of our high civilization would doubtless have said it better, but he would never have said it with such sincerity. The simplicity and frankness of the barbarian king touched me deeply. He said nothing more; he seemed nonplussed, and remained pensive for a few moments.

Then he stood up again and, placing himself in front of King Belt, said to him: "My brother, I have no consolations to offer you for such a great misfortune. You will find your consolation in your great heart and the resignation of a true philosopher; but I have a refuge to offer you, and I offer it to you...until I too am condemned to death by my subjects."

Rhaman added the last remark with a painful effort that communicated itself to us. "Yes," he continued, "condemned to death; that's what I said. I don't know whether that time is very distant, but I wish that it were more distant still. That's why I wanted to visit you in Zeeland, where I wanted to learn the art of governing and conquering the love of my subjects, and that's why I've brought you the history of our nation, which we must not communicate to anyone. That's why I wanted to talk to you here.

"The history of our nation will inform you, my brother, that we did not arrive here yesterday, but that a long time ago God created one of our ancestors to come and conquer New Cosaquia. Our ancestors were originally from Morocco, a vast country that extends beyond distant seas, a long way from here, of which I no longer hear any mention today.

"Abd-el-Moussa, the first of our ancestors, guided by the hand of God, crossed the vast sea, accompanied by a numerous people, heavily armed, and came to take possession of the land that God had given him. That land was, however, inhabited by numerous and powerful tribes, come from I know not where, but composed in great part of Cosaques, who had given

276

it the name it still retains, which neither our ancestors nor we have changed. I believe, however, that the city of Figuig, where we are, was thus named by Abd-el-Moussa. It was known by another name before him, or perhaps did not exist. Our history says nothing very clear about that.

"At any rate, Abd-el-Moussa vanquished the peoples—all the peoples—of New Cosaquia, and submitted them to his laws. He had a numerous posterity, who reigned here, and took various names, each according to his whim. Personally, I have conserved the name of Rhaman—one of my ancestors—and I am the tenth of that name.

"Our history will tell you about my reign thus far: what measures I have always taken to have peace and good order, and to render my people happy. Have I succeeded? People will say so, for there was often internal strife in the past, whereas everything seems tranquil today—and yet, I'm not reassured.

"Of all the peoples vanquished by my ancestors, only two tribes remain, that of the Cosaques and that of the French. The members of the Cosaque tribe not longer occupy themselves with anything but hunting and fishing; once, they were solely occupied in pillage, but I have established good order there. The members of the French tribe—who claim that they were the region's original inhabitants, and believe themselves to have descended from the heavens, so remote is the tribe's birth in the obscurity of olden times—are more industrious. They also have more ambitious desires, and think themselves out of place in the slavery in which we hold them. What slavery, though! They have retained their own mores, and we have encouraged that, as well as secrets of all kinds, which we have not sought to extract from them.

"We allow them a measure of domination among us. If we have need of the services of an intelligent slave, we go to them; if we have a favor to grant to someone, we take it to them. In sum, we do more for them that for subjects of our own blood. It's also true to say that they have marvelous knowledge that we don't understand, but whose effects we can't help but admire. They claim that their knowledge has been handed down to them from remote antiquity.

"The tribe once revolted so frequently that we were obliged to decimate it, so that it became so few in number that we no longer had to fear it, but it has seemed submissive for a long time now, and its population has increased considerably. Their mores, being mild, have contributed a great deal to the peace.

"Their marriage customs are not like ours. Among us, custom does not allow a man to have more than two wives, but among them, one might say that there is no marriage, or that marriage is unlimited. A man and a woman only remain together as long as it suits them, except that the woman, while she is with the man, must not communicate with another man, although in any other case she is free. The man always is, unless he does not wish to release the woman he has chosen and she consents to stay with him.

"The children, moreover, do not suffer at all from the elasticity of these mores, for they are brought up in their earliest childhood by the tribe's nurses, if their mother does not keep them, and later in public schools that the tribe maintains at communal expense.

"There is, however, one exception to this marriage law, and that exception is for those they believe and designate to be of royal blood. In order that the blood in question should not be adulterated, their kings—those, at least, who are called by that name among them, for we do not recognize that pretention of our slaves ourselves—are not free to take a woman at whim. They are obliged only to marry among themselves, and to have but one wife. If the population of the royal family does not permit that, however, or there is only a single offspring, the elders of the tribe assemble and search in their midst for a branch on which to graft that shoot.

"For the moment, they only have a queen, Nhohelle Merihukeck, a young woman already past the age appointed for her marriage, I believe because the spouse chosen for her from among the members of the tribe most distinguished by their family and bravery, is not to her liking.

"Whether these mores are well-organized or not, I don't know, but I see nothing in them injurious to them; they are only harmful to us, for their population is very large today, and they are an enemy tribe, although they appear to serve us zealously. They hate us; they despise us; and they want to reign over us. That is our misfortune.

"Once, they were the enemies of the Cosaque tribe, but they fawn on them today. They also fawn on the people of our blood, whom they once detested. Why? It's because, you see, that the rigor of insubordination has never succeeded, and they now have recourse to submission and cunning.

"That's why I fear them more; that's why I went to request of your civilization the means of thwarting them; that's why I'm consulting you today, my brother. I keep the queen of the tribe close to me, whom I cover with flattery—which, in any case, she deserves—and I'm ready to marry her if you advise me to do so, my brother, in order to gain complete control of her tribe and reinforce my grip on the throne."

The barbarian's confession struck me in the heart. I don't know why, because, quite frankly, how could he be my rival? I had never had the foolish idea of marrying the queen; I had not yet been able to explain the attachment that bound me to her. Nevertheless, my heart beat faster on listening to his confidences; I would certainly have found it impossible to reply. Fortunately, although the question had been put to me as well as the others, since Rhaman had wanted to admit me to the council, it was not up to me to reply first, and I had time to pull myself together. No one, in any case, had observed my emotion.

"My brother," said King Belt, with a wisdom that could not compromise him, "if you are free, and if the queen is a woman worthy of you, as I have no doubt that she is, since you have deigned to cast your eyes upon her, if your throne is shaky and that union can consolidate it, I don't see why you shouldn't listen to the counsels of your reason."

"It could, moreover," said Falster, at whom Rhaman looked interrogatively, "only gain the good graces of the tribe's Council of Elders."

"And only distance, very considerably," I said in my tone, in response to the king's gaze, "the queen's fiancé."

"That's the sole point that makes me pause," said King Rhaman, "for that's the difficulty. Johan-Ali-Schahpohtink is at present, so far as the tribe is concerned, the husband of their queen, although it's only, as yet, by election—an election that even Nhohelle hasn't yet sanctioned with a formal consent—and to get rid of him appears to me to be impossible, at present. The entire tribe would be against me; it would perish, to the last of its children, in order to punish me for such a crime. I had thought, in order to placate Johan and his brothers, of raising him to a high rank in my kingdom and then giving him my daughter Ouchda, but Ouchda, who initially appeared to consent, has recently refused that proposition with all her might. What can I do?"

King Rhaman put his head in his hands and became pensive again. We could do nothing but imitate the king, so we each devoted ourselves silently to our own train of thought. Personally, I had such a strong aversion to Ali-Schahpohtink that I approved wholeheartedly of Ouchda's resolution, but I did not voice my opinion.

"That's what must be done, though," said Rhaman, abruptly raising his head again and looking at us in consternation.

"Well then, it must be, my brother," replied King Belt, "since it's your salvation—and we'll give you all the help we can."

"Yes, help me," Rhaman replied, swiftly, as he rose to his feet, "and you will render me a great service."

We got up with the king, who led us back to the bridge that I had thought of calling the Horseman's Bridge because of the equestrian statue that serves as a pillar, and we separated with profuse demonstrations of amity.

We did not discuss Rhaman X's confidences with one another, each of us doubtless having his reservations in that regard. So, to distance ourselves from a conversation that might surge forth at any moment before anyone had settled on a theme, we threw ourselves upon the king's papers, in which we thought we might find a useful and agreeable diversion.

XXXII. HOW RHAMAN X BECAME KING OF FRANCE

"Before we do anything else, my dear Daghestan," Falster said to me, "tell us, you who are a confessed historian and a very erudite savant in matters of history—especially ancient and foreign history—what you know about the history of these people." With a smile that signified that he had never known anything about it, he added: "Personally, I've completely forgotten it, and I wouldn't be displeased to be reminded before dipping my nose into this." He pointed disdainfully at good King Rhaman's historical manuscript.

"Yes, I understand," I replied. "You're not entirely satisfied with this Abd-el-Moussa created by God in ancient Morocco for the express purpose of coming to take possession of New Cosaquia. In fact, that's strange; history, at least so far as I've examined it in many books and deciphered it in many manuscripts, doesn't tell us that.

"In the year one of our era, it says, or perhaps a little before the year 2000 of the ancient era, the approximate era of your prophesies"—King Belt had taken his little book out of his pocket and tapped it in a satisfied manner—"the Empire of Morocco was flourishing. When I say 'flourishing,' it's out of habit, for the empire was not flourishing very much. In that era, Morocco might have been what New Cosaquia is today, or very nearly.

"The empire was large, however; its emperor, Almoravis,[46] was no greater for that, for he was not master in his own land; he obeyed more than he commanded. Each of his provinces had a governor at its head, some of whom were

---

[46] The Almoravid dynasty reigned over Morocco in its heyday, in the 11th and 12th centuries, ruling much of Spain as well as north-east Africa; this subsequent leader was doubtless echoing its august name.

members of his family, others important men whom he had gratified with honors.

"All these governors, however, relatives or not, only obeyed him if they wished; it would not have required much for them to be completely independent, for the links binding them to the imperial authority were so weak that they occasionally broke. Then, the emperor, in order to retie the knot, was obliged to send his armies out on campaign—and he usually achieved his objective, when the governors did not assist one another in their resistance.

"Abd-el-Moussa lived in that era, and he had not been created miraculously, whatever King Rhaman says; he was the emperor's brother—but he was also one of the most turbulent governors and the most jealous of imperial authority, just as he was, admittedly, one of the bravest and most intelligent warriors in Morocco.

"One day, he rebelled, this time seriously, against his brother. He led his enterprise so well that he was on the brink of dethroning Almoravis—but he didn't succeed; he was defeated and taken prisoner.

"The custom in Morocco on such occasions was to throw into the sea, tightly bound in a sack, any prisoner of the noble family, and to hang all the rest on an island, where they served as fodder for birds of prey. Almoravis was humane, however, and also loved his brother very dearly. He had him brought before him, as free as the prince was every time he came to the imperial palace, and said to him tearfully:

"'Brother, you ought not to die by my hand, for God and my mother would reproach me in this world and the next. Nor shall I punish the rebels you dragged into your revolt. They obeyed you, as they had to do. But you cannot stay here; you ought no longer to live by our laws, which you do not like, and which you have dishonored. Go over the sea; there the people are in discord; there is civil war, and those people are so weakened by pleasures and vices of all sorts that you'll reckon with them easily. Go! I'll give you as many soldiers as there are who want to go with you, and as much gold as you can carry.'

"Abd-el-Moussa made no reply, but he embraced his brother, his heart swollen by that generosity and his eyes full of tears. Then he left. He crossed the sea in his brother's ships, which disembarked him and his followers on the shore of ancient Spain, and returned to Morocco.

"The Spaniards, like the French, like all the people of the continent then, had been ruined by vices, as Almoravis had said. So Abd-el-Moussa had little difficulty in establishing himself among them, fighting facile battles against them which they only sustained out of pride, but in which they were almost all annihilated and their cities laid waste.

"It was not Abd-el-Moussa, as King Rhaman said, who then invaded France. He stayed in Spain, along with a considerable fraction of his posterity. France was invaded, at almost the same time, but the Cosaques, who descended like an avalanche from Caucasia and its neighboring regions, expelled by other peoples, as I can relate to you some day if you wish.

"Later, however—much later—the descendants of Abd-el-Moussa and his soldiers became so numerous, and so enterprising too, that the small land of Spain was no longer sufficient for them, and they hurled themselves upon France, which was known as New Cosaquia even though it was not entirely occupied by Cosaques, for other equally barbaric peoples had settled in different parts of the country.

"Moussa's descendants subdued all these regions, and, as their ancestors had done in Spain, destroyed everything, even that which had escaped the devastations of the Cosaques.

"That is how Rhaman X comes to reign today in New Cosaquia, whose name and barbarity he has conserved, too ill-educated himself to revive the beautiful name of France, which he does not know.

"As for Figuig, which was not formerly the capital of New Cosaquia, it is for me the Paris of ancient France, whatever anyone may say. The Cosaque invaders had destroyed it, had razed the capital of France and its neighboring habitations to the ground so completely, that they could no longer live there. Their own capital was more central.

"It was, I believe, Rhaman's ancestor—Rhaman I himself, so history says, this time with reason—who came to pitch his tent here on these ruins, because he liked the location. He it was who, to ornament the seat of his empire, created the palaces we see in Figuig; their style and architecture are his. If Rhaman X has added anything, it has only ever been a matter of repair. I don't contest the claim that he has added to the number of the palaces, but he has only done so by copying the ones that already existed..."

"I had no doubt that King Rhaman was mistaken," Falster said, then, rising to his feet and placing is hand on the king's papers. Looking at me with a mocking smile that was addressed more to himself than to me, he added: "But I was glad to learn it from your mouth, and I think it's clearer now."

Then he started riffling through, and read us some of the histories that seemed to be the most interesting. I didn't understand the language of our hosts very well; King Belt understood it a little better than I did, but Falster spoke it well enough for someone to be able to mistake his nationality, had it not been for the accent, which he could not imitate perfectly, so Falster took on the whole responsibility of that reading. As for me I took notes—very exact and very extensive notes, which I hope to publish some day.

That reading, and the conversation it stimulated between us, was our sole occupation until dinner time—a time that we awaited with all the patience of savants fully occupied in solving difficult but seductive problems. Thus, it took us by surprise when we least expected it. It was King Rhaman who, with all the punctuality of an invited guest with a healthy appetite, came at the appointed time to remind us that we were to receive him at our table, and also to inform us that dinner was served.

That meal, although it was held under our roof, was a royal feast. It was served with the customary etiquette of the court but, contrary to my expectations, all the dishes there were quite substantial—much more substantial that those of the morning meal.

At breakfast, we had not eaten meat, and that appeared to be the custom, but and diner, by contrast, it appears to be the custom that nothing but meat is eaten, and enough was served to us to make the most gluttonous eaters tremble.

The maxim of those people, which is assuredly not a bad maxim, is that, in order for the mind to be free, the stomach should not be overladen. Hence the frugal morning meal, in order that one might apply oneself to the day's business. As dinner is eaten at sunset, however, and as the evening and night are devoted to pleasure, feasting and digestion, never to work, they eat in the evening for twenty-four hours, and they eat well.

The first course—the one that was supposed to give us an appetite, because of the gamy aroma of the meat—comprised of cutlets of wild dog and cat; then there filed before us, successively, mutton chops, roe-deer fillets, fricasseed rats and, finally, for dessert, the national and royal dish: an enormous joint of horsemeat, which King Rhaman ate with an infinite pleasure because it was the produce of his own hunt.

In New Cosaquia, the horse is much sought-after game, and probably will be for a long time to come, for it's good and very productive, to the extent that some Cosaque cleverer than the rest has, as in the Sudan, demonstrated that horses can be domesticated, and that they ought to be preferred for various uses to the machines that are normally used everywhere.

Our meal lasted for a long time, and not a word was said there about serious business. It was the same all evening, the entirety of which we spent with the king and his court, which had, as usual, been invited for coffee, except for the ladies.

It is not customary in Figuig for ladies to sit down at the same dining-table as men. Is that for reasons of modesty or jealousy? Is it a matter of convention? I don't know, and the Cosaques themselves probably can't explain the custom, which has been handed down to them along with many others, and which they don't change out of habit. However, as the liberty of celebrations, especially among the rich—and for everyone, on feast-days—is very great; as people eat enormously and drink in the same fashion, especially a very intoxicating liquor that some mix with water and others drink neat, but which, in either case, never fails to trouble the intelligence when abused, it's probable that, in order to have more liberty, men have preferred in the main to set up the ladies' table in a different room, and to join them there long after their own meal is over.

In fact, that can't be a bad thing, in my opinion, if all their meals are like the one King Rhaman had us served in the Palace of Administration. When one emerges from such a meal, to with it is necessary to do honor with one's appetite if one wants to honor one's host, one really needs, for one's personal tranquility, not to have allowed any ladies to witness the enormous quantities of meat and drink one has consumed, and the bestiality that is subsequently reflected in one's face.

Our feast went very well, but I wasn't sorry when it was over. I hadn't gorged myself like a Cosaque, but I had eaten and drunk more than a Caucasian, and I found the time that the king stayed with us after dinner interminable.

XXXIII. A CATASTROPHIC NIGHT

It was dark when the king left; his court and his slaves accompanied him with lighted torches. He had wished us good night, and we really had need of one. My head was on fire; my ears were ringing deafeningly. I'd eaten a great deal, it's true, but I think the liquor I'd poured out, perhaps too frequently, in order to render Figuig's water drinkable, and which I had subsequently drunk neat in order to blot out the dessert roast, had more than a little to do with the disturbance provoke in my intelligence.

So, when the moment came, I went swiftly to my hut, where I lay down without casting the slightest glance over my magnificent antiques, which I never neglected to caress every time I went home. I fell asleep immediately, but it was an exceedingly tormented sleep, during which I had the most unusual dreams and experienced the most diverse sensations.

That agitation had scarcely lasted an hour when I felt a vigorous hand weighing upon my shoulder, which I resisted at first, but which shook me so violently that I ended up opening my eyes.

I couldn't see anyone, but my room appeared to me to be on fire. Convinced that the vision was a product of my deluded brain, I didn't worry about it—and, in truth, I don't know whether I had enough strength to do anything about it. I therefore closed my eyes and put me head back between two mountains of wool.

A further shaking weighed upon my shoulders, so urgent this time that I sat up in bed with a start and, stretching my neck and opening my eyes wide, sought to discover where the bright light that was enveloping me entirely was coming from.

The door of my hut opened just then; I saw and immediately recognized the old man with the long beard whom I had already seen on another occasion. He seemed to be trying to get out, but he stopped, and, turning his head toward me, ges-

288

tured to me to follow him. His eyes were so sharp and imperious that I dared not resist, even though I had a strong desire to do so.

I therefore followed him, all the way outside the palace, for he was still walking ahead of me; I couldn't make him out clearly, but I followed his pale form.

We went over the palace's only bridge, and then crossed the pond again by another bridge to reach the other bank. Having marched silently for several minutes, we arrived in the middle of the ruins, which I wasn't about to admire at that hour. Although I'm by no means timid, and have no fear of the dead—who are much less redoubtable, in my opinion, than the living—I was nevertheless not very reassured.

"Stay here for an hour," a soft voice said to me then—a voice so soft that it couldn't be the voice of the old man with the long bard and the vigorous wrist. It was, in fact, a woman's voice—a voice that I recognized perfectly, by virtue of hearing it every day in the depths of my soul. It was the Queen's voice.

I stood there nonplussed for a moment—only a moment—during which I could not make any reply, and when I was able to open my mouth, there was no longer anyone there; I was alone. Was it a dream? Or might I be suffering a bout of somnambulism?

I tried to convince myself that I was awake; I took a few steps through the ruins; I touched the old trees that covered them; I scratched the walls; I spoke, and spoke aloud...

No, I wasn't dreaming. I took a few more steps to make perfectly sure; I was still speaking...

A voice replied to me: a woman's voice.

"Who are you?" I asked.

"Ouchda," the king's daughter replied. "But how do you come to be here, Mr. Daghestan?"

"Wasn't it you who brought me here?"

"No," she told me, "but I wanted to bring you here."

"You! Oh, speak, speak, Madame!" I said, with an emotion that I couldn't master. "Speak—if only to tell me that all this isn't a dream."

"No, all this isn't a dream—but you speak first. How did you get here?"

I needed no persuasion; I told the king's daughter what had just happened to me.

"It's *her*," Ouchda said, then, in a whisper, as if talking to herself.

"Who?" I asked.

"The witch," she replied, disdainfully.

"What witch?" I said, without being put off by the tone of the young woman's voice, and in a slight tone of reproach that I wanted to inflict on her ill humor."

"The one they call the Queen." She added: "Johan's fiancée," in a tone in which there was as much scorn for the fiancée as malice for me.

A profound silence was then established between us. Each of us, no doubt, was thinking deeply. I was thinking about the Queen; perhaps Ouchda was thinking about her too, but assuredly not in the same way as me.

The young woman broke the silence first. "Listen to me, Mr. Daghestan," she said. "Your life is in danger."

"You think so, Madame?" I said, with an emotion that was very forgivable, it seems to me, even in a philosopher.

"I'm sure of it. You have a very bitter and redoubtable enemy in Johan-Ali-Schahpohtink."

"I've already perceived that; I haven't forgotten my first arrival in this country."

"He thought he'd never see you again; your unexpected return has only served to reanimate his hatred. I've been living for some time in a palace that's only a short distance from here, on to which these ruins back. There I learned about your arrival here; there too I learned about the malevolent schemes of which Johan is the soul. I sent you one of my slaves a short while ago to ask you to come here this evening."

"I didn't see him, Madame."

"I thought he was devoted to me, but I see now that he was even more so to Schahpohtink, for he hasn't carried out my orders. I wanted to warn you." She lowered her voice. "And I wanted to tell you a great secret."

"Speak, Madame," I said, taking her hands to encourage her confidence. "I'm a man of honor; your secret will not be betrayed."

"My father wants to marry Nhohelle Merlhukeck..."

I made no reply, because I didn't think it appropriate to reveal that I knew the secret already.

"But the Queen is promised to Johan; she must marry him under pain of death, for the Council of Elders has decided it, and the Council's decisions are sacred laws. Joha himself could not renounce that marriage. My father wants that, however, for political reasons, which he explained to me a little while ago. But to make this marriage it's necessary that the Council of Elders revoke their decision, and my father hopes to obtain that favor by giving compensation to Johan. That favor will be to raise him to high status—him, the vanquished stranger, to our blood—and then..."

Ouchda did not finish, but she put her arms around me and laid her forehead on my breast.

"Go on, Ouchda," I said, disturbed by the agony that I glimpsed in her voice and pressing her to my heard. "Go on!"

"My father wants me to marry Johan," she said, sobbing, and trying to muffle her sobs.

I already knew that, and yet the news made a deep impression on me, so touching did he young woman's distress seem. I would not have dared to say, however, whether the devotion she had shown to me previously, and the charms and graces of hr person, had not also given birth in me to some other sentiment of which I had not taken clear account.

I imprinted a kiss of her forehead that she did not refuse; but, suddenly drying up her tears, she straightened up: "Well, no!" she said, with grim determination. "I won't marry him. I—the daughter of a king, the future queen of New

Cosaquia—would rather become the slave of the least of the kings of the East."

At that moment I heard a noise—an indistinct noise—in the ruins. Swiftly, I took Ouchda by the arm and drew her behind me, in order to protect her if necessary. I would have become brave again to save the king's daughter, if she were threatened. But there was no threat. A voice that I recognized without difficulty, in spite of the note of irony that I thought I found therein, emerged from the darkness.

"The hour is up, Mr. Daghestan," the voice said. "Go back to the palace—your friends are looking for you with great anxiety."

And the Queen—for it was her—disappeared into the ruins.

"Farewell!—no, until we meet again, Mr. Daghestan!" Ouchda said to me then. "I shall watch over you..." She raised her voice slightly to add: "And I shall love the Queen like a sister, if she will continue to take you under her protection."

We separated, shaking hands affectionately

I had not gone far enough into the ruins to be unable to get out easily, but, not being familiar with the route I had followed in such a singular manner, and in the midst of the darkness of a dusk that was already well-advanced, I found myself in some difficulty as to how to find my way back to the palace on my own.

"Follow me!" said the Queen, who suddenly appeared in front of me, torch in hand.

I was about to speak when she put her finger to her lips bidding me to be silent.

"Think about what Ouchda said," was all that she said to me, "and don't speak to me."

That instruction was given without sharpness, but firmly. I didn't think I ought to disobey it. We walked thus as far as the bridge to the palace, where the Queen left me, smiling at me and saluting me with her hand, but without saying anything.

I was downcast; I wanted to talk to her; I had so many things to say to her—but she had ordered me to be silent, and she left me. Would I ever see her again, at least?

"Oh, I'll see her again," I said, decisively, but in a whisper.

Then I went back to my hut, more content with myself after that declaration..

I had scarcely taken a few steps into the enclosure of the palace when I met King Belt and his brother. Falster threw his arms around my neck and embraced me with all the vivacity of a man who has found a friend he believed to be dead.

"Come here!" he said to me, in a breathless voice that he could hardly articulate, dragging me toward my hut. "Look!"

My hut had been destroyed by the collapse of its roof, which had crushed it.

"I thought you were inside!" Falster added.

I threw my arms round Falster's neck in my turn and embraced him with all my strength, for I understood at that moment how deep his friendship was.

"I've been out of my hut and the palace for nearly two hours," I told him. "I'll tell you how and why."

"Well, my friend," Falster said to me, "it's been nearly two hours since my brother and I were suddenly woken up by the noise of your hut collapsing. We shouted, calling for help with all our might, but no one came at first. Later, however, some of the palace guard came running—but as slowly as possible, it seemed. We'd already made every effort to rescue you. They helped us then, but slowly, more as if they wanted to kill you than save you, if you hadn't been crushed. Finally, how terrified we were not to find any trace of you under the debris! 'They've killed him for sure,' I whispered to my brother. 'They've murdered him, and the collapse of the hut was only to cover up the cause of his death.' And I believed it, my friend...but, thank God, it isn't so..."

I was very glad that my life had been saved, but I bitterly regretted the riches that I had already amassed under my roof, which were badly damaged.

King Belt and his brother offered interminable commentaries when I had told them how I had left the palace, about finding the guilty party and the cause of the hatred that was driving him against me; for we could no longer doubt, the following day, having inspected the beams of my roof, that a malevolent hand had sawed through them—skillfully, it's true, in order to disguise the evil intention, but not sufficiently to hide the evidence completely from our eyes.

"Perhaps, after all," King Belt said, trying to reassure us, "chance was the guilty party."

No, I said to myself, *the guilty party is the Queen's fiancé*. But I did not say that out loud, for fear that King Belt might think it his duty to take the complaint to King Rhaman, who might perhaps have felt obliged to punish him—which would have rendered our position worse still, while not making that of our host the king any better.

From that day onward, Falster no longer wanted to leave me alone; the same hut accommodated both of us. That catastrophe, moreover, made me resolve to be more circumspect, by revealing to me that an indefatigable enemy on my heels, who would not stop at any means to kill me. I had already had grounds to suspect it, so I decided not to take another step without knowing where I was putting down my foot.

XXXIV. THE NEXT DAY

The night of the catastrophe passed rapidly for me; it was filled by a little sleep and a great deal of reflection. I had, in fact, seen and heard so many strange things that evening!

The next day, I only had one desire, which was to see in broad daylight the ruins that I had only suspected in the darkness of the night. Nature always reasserts itself, in spite of everything, my friend, and is more stubborn in an antiquary than anyone else. I believe, at least, that I had no other sentiment than that of antiquarian curiosity in desiring to go back to the place that I had visited to singularly a few hours before.

I did not go alone, however; Falster, who did not seem disposed to abandon me so soon to the chance of an encounter as dangerous as the previous night's, wanted to go with me. I was far from being annoyed by that concern, which promised to give me someone by my side to whom I could confide the impressions I expected to experience in the ruins near Ouchda's palace.

King Belt remained at the palace to receive King Rhaman, who certainly would not fail to come to bring him his compliments and condolences for the catastrophe that he had so fortunately escaped.

Falster and I, therefore, set out each of us unobtrusively armed with a good revolver, which could fire several shots if necessary. I followed the same route that I had followed the previous evening, as best I could. I knew, in any case, that I had to cross over the whole of the marsh and seek adventure on the opposite bank.

The trajectory was not difficult, and I easily found, downstream of the Administration Bridge, the bridge we had to take. As that bridge was of the same manufacture, it also had the same architecture as the others, but was perhaps more graceful, in that its back was formed by a layer of earth in which several bushes, and even trees, had sprouted and grown.

It had thus become a very pleasant shaded path. It was long-er—much longer—than the Administration Bridge, for it extended from one bank to the other without pausing on the island.

After traversing the marsh, we walked more hesitantly along paths that were sometimes not much used, which snaked in labyrinthine fashion through fragments of walls, sculpted stones, partly covered in moss, lichens and ivy, often hidden under thorny brushwood, all of it dominated by a forest of tall trees that I had scarcely glimpsed the previous evening.

It was, in consequence, very difficult for me to discover the ruins I sought in the midst of those dense thickets. Having walked for some time with my nose to the wind and my ears pricked, it seemed to me that I had gone astray, and we were about to turn round when the screech of an osprey stopped us short and gave us a frisson or two.

At that moment, Falster and I had more irresolute timidity that was appropriate to adventure-seekers, but we were not used to hearing that cry during the day.

"Is that really the cry of a bird?" I said to Falster. "Isn't it rather a malevolent signal given in our respect by some human bird-caller?"

"Bah!" said Falster, laughing at our hesitation. "The osprey is the bird of ruins, so the ruins are not far away. Let's go on."

And we went on, resolutely, like two fearful people plucking up their courage, but with our hands on our revolvers nevertheless. We had done well to go forward, for after a few more steps we found ourselves in front of our ruins.

The ruins were quite simple; they offered nothing very marvelous at first glance. At that moment we were on a narrow path, slightly more frequented than the others. An edifice of rather meager dimensions loomed up ahead of us, cracked at the summit in various directions. High walls rose up on either side, which came on toward us, leaving an empty space between them.

All these walls were pierced here and there with openings of various forms, some of which only penetrated to half the depth of the wall, and therefore did not let through any daylight. Under the walls of the central building was a rather vast opening that had probably once served as a passage, beyond which we perceived daylight—which told us that there was another empty space there.

The masonry of those walls offered nothing grandiose; there were none of those large carved and sculpted blocks that I had encountered so often elsewhere, and no ornaments. It was composed of a mass of extremely hard mortar, in which little stones had been embedded, coated with a uniform layer of little sharp stones, and sometimes of bricks very solidly fitted and cemented together.

There was no luxury there, but there was a solidity that appeared proof against anything. Ivy and all kinds of climbing plants carpeted the walls. The empty space that was facing us was filled with large trees, which a careful hand maintained in a state of considerable neatness; it was almost an arbor. It was not difficult to recognize the care of a woman's hand there, and I suspected that these ruins were probably the solitude to which Ouchda came to mediate from her palace nearby. There were luxurious seats formed from mutilated statues there, lying on the ground and artistically coated in mosses and grasses, as there were in the dependencies of every palace, at the service of strollers.

Falster and I tried hard to work out what might have been the purpose of such edifices in ancient France. We made endless reflections on the subject, appealed to all our historical memories—which were not very extensive, it's true—of the place where we were. We tried to compare it to all the ruins that we had already seen, which did not resemble it at all, but we could not deduce anything.

Everything indicated, however, that there must have been a national monument there, even though the construction demonstrated no luxury. Well, there, as everywhere else, we were obliged to lower our heads, admitting that we could not discover anything.

"Poor savants that we are!" I said to Falster. "I imagined, in my study in Caucasipol, that if I could only set foot on the ancient soil of France, I would know it by heart, reconstruct it in its entirety—and here I am, frustrated at every step." I threw myself down to sit on the back of a statue. "And to think," I continued, that there is a tribe here that claims to be descended from the old French, those heroes of ancient civilization—the barbarians, the savages, the idiots we know!"

"You're mistaken, my friend," Falster replied, sitting down facing me between the mutilated arms of another statue. "These people aren't idiots. We haven't yet seen many of them, it's true, but do those we have seen give you the right to judge them so severely? Do you recall their physiognomy, full of finesse—shrewdness, if you wish? What do you say? Do their souls not appear to you entirely in their faces? And are those faces the faces of human idiots? Is the Queen an idiot?"

"Oh, no!" I said, immediately raising my head, which I had lowered at Falster's first words, in order to listen more attentively.

"Is Johan a idiot? No—he's a man of modern civilization: he shuts up when he can't do anything; he speaks when he thinks he's the stronger. And how does he shut up? How does he talk? You've seen that. He came before us when we arrived; he smiled at you in the king's palace. He could not do otherwise, so he shut up—but he talked when he thought he had the advantage. Your ruined hut ought to remind you of what he said. He's a very civilized enemy, my dear Daghestan; he wants you dead and he might succeed...and you know why." My friend looked at me significantly. "He's the Queen's fiancé; you might be an obstacle that he needs to break before completing that marriage. What do you think of that, Daghestan?"

I made no reply.

"Don't you think, then," Falster went on, "that since he is what he is, and that nothing good can come of this fatal struggle, that we'd do better to give ourselves the courage of the truly brave, who always flee from an unequal combat? Then again, I don't know if I'm mistaken, but I've reflected a great deal since yesterday, and I think I've worked out many things. We've got out of a country where we nearly lost our loves; I don't know whether the place we've ended up in is any safer. My experience glimpses civil war here, and my instinct foresees it. Remember what you've seen and heard since our arrival.

"Remember what King Rhaman told us yesterday about the reconciliation of the two tribes, whose hostility has been his strength thus far. Who engineered that reconciliation? The Cosaques? No; they're not intelligent enough for that. The Moroccans? No; what would be the point? It's the French tribe. And why? To subdue the Cosaques and the Moroccans in their turn; to regain the superiority they say that they have lost, and which belongs to them—in sum, to rule. And if you want to know what I think, yes, they will rule, but after having fought a battle that won't do us any good at all."

Falster rapped me on the knee, as if to awaken me from the distraction into which I had been plunged by profound thoughts, which were, however, following my friend's conversation avidly. "And why would you doubt their victory? The Cosaques and the Moroccans, and all the other mongrel races that have no other name here than inhabitants of New Cosaquia, what are they? What do they do? Go out hunting, fishing, pillaging. What are they good for? What monuments have they constructed? What culture have they contrived? What amelioration have they sought? What industry do they have? Look—look around you. Perhaps King Rhaman has some inclination to do good; his mind, I think, is open to enlightenment—but so what?"

"And Ouchda?" I said, swiftly.

"Yes, Ouchda," said Falster, smiling maliciously. "Yes, Ouchda isn't the daughter of barbarians. Perhaps she's the one who has inspired her father. But so what? Whereas, in the French tribe...oh, there's everything: commerce, agriculture,

299

industry, physical and metaphysical sciences, everything. Look at them: how well their lands are cultivated, how fine their flocks are, how well-prepared their wool; how their institutions of family and hierarchy are flourishing; how beautiful their women are, especially in their souls; how richly and elegantly dressed they are!

"And their aerostats! Their aerostats, Master—what do you say about them? You, the man of the most advanced civilization, who has been searching for so long for the secret that is familiar to them and their endeavor? And the divinatory rod that the Queen once put into your hands, in a balloon, to serve you; and this Père Franco that she always has at her orders; and the eye that she always has on you, from near or far? What do you think of that, Master? What would they say to all that in Caucasia? Ignorance, superstition, magic; spiritism and conjuring…and they'd laugh, and shrug their shoulders. You, however, have seen…" Excitedly, Falster concluded: "You've seen clearly, my dear fellow, that intelligence is there—and it is where intelligence is that victory must come. Believe me, let's get out of this place!"

"What about science?" I said to Falster. "That divinity which devours its worshipers?"

"What about life?" he replied.

I was overwhelmed in my convictions. No longer having any reply to make, I made none. Taking my friend by the arm, however, I drew him away. He did not say anything more; I could see that he was anxious, and unconcerned with what we were looking at. I was touched by his resignation to my desires.

"A few more days," I said to him, then. "Just a few days, and we'll talk about all of this again—but in the meantime, my friend, help me to investigate this people, this great people."

Then, releasing Falster's arm, I took the lead, advancing under the tall trees and into a sort of ravine, at the end of which I found a doorway in the wall. Beyond it, we suddenly found ourselves in a little wood filled with a legion of almost-intact statues representing all kinds of bizarre images, of animals, of which each creature possessed the limbs of the entire animal kingdom. The heads of birds could be seen on the bodies of lions, a human torso on a horse's quarters, women's heads on the bodies of serpents. It was monstrous, but it was brilliantly imagined, although rather mediocre in execution.

"What is this?" I said to Falster, my gaze shining with hope.

"Follies," he replied. "Whims: the phantasmagorias of dreamers."

"Aren't they rather," I replied, smiling, with a strong desire to contradict him, "bizarrely-represented truths—but truths nevertheless? Who can tell whether the ruins where we are might be the ruins of a temple, and that we're in the presence here of the gods of ancient France? Don't your prophets tell us, in their imprecations, that France renounced the God of its fathers one day, to adopt a new religion? Don't ancient historians, the best-authenticated in the Sudan, Borneo, China, Zeeland itself, and Poland, as well as Caucasia, tell us the same thing, in the few words that have been handed down to us from antiquity?"

"I'm not a scholar, but I know that," Falster replied. "I even know that the new gods of France were gold, silver, luxury, pleasure, ambition and lust. I know, too, that many raised altars to inconsistency, calumny, mendacity, egotism, and even to theft—not the brutal robbery of the highways but the robbery of honest men, domestic theft and confidence trickery."

"Well, who can tell whether these might be the images of their gods?" I said to Falster, trembling in the hope of his contradiction.

But Falster suddenly became animated. "What!" he said. "You believe all those historians? You, the man of modern civilization, a scholar, a thinker? You believe historians who lived no one knows when, if they ever lived? You believe all these prophesies that come from no one knows where, which ten different pens and ten different epochs might have revised, corrected and probably augmented considerably? You believe that—you! You believe that a people like the French, whose civilization you hold in such great honor, could have worshiped vices other than within their hearts; that they could have raised altars in order to kneel before them seriously! Do you think those people were stupid, then? No, my friend, no, they weren't stupid—and your prophecies, your histories, if they are real, are only allegories, believe me: allegories that we idlers of today have taken literally."

Falster's energetic tirade was what I wanted; he has said everything that I thought. By a bizarre mental caprice, however, I thought him a trifle bold to scratch out with a single stroke the information of so many centuries. It's true to say, too, that I felt a little ashamed—me, a scholar, a philosopher, and antiquary with reformist pretentions—in finding myself thus overtaken and found at fault by a man who had written nothing, and whom I would not have been sorry to teach. So I did not want to give in right away. I certainly was not inclined to sustain seriously what I had only put forward initially as a playful suggestion, but I wanted to take my time. Perhaps a hint of pride held me back.

"Who knows," I said to Falster, "what we ought to think about this? Let me see for a few more days, and then we'll decide..."

XXXV. A VISIT TO OUCHDA'S PALACE

I did not look at Falster while speaking to him in that fashion. It seemed to me that I ought to be blushing, for I had just deviated from my habitual honesty. There was a moment's silence between us; we appeared to be fully occupied with the ancient art that was there, beneath our hands. Drawn from one object to another, we advanced thus, taking a tour of the ruins we had entered—but we were soon halted by a wall that we had no difficulty recognizing as a modern construction, and even as a Cosaque construction.

It was, in fact, the wall of Ouchda's palace. There was a postern in front of us, connecting the palace to the ruins, but we dared not go through it, however desirous we were of so doing. We were looking at it curiously, seeking to see or divine what was on the other side, when we saw an apparition suddenly surge forth on the threshold, the memory of which petrified me, but which gave confidence to Falster. It was my bear from Lining, whom Falster had no reason to hate, as I did. He gave us a sign to follow him.

"No," I said to my friend, retaining him by the arm, "it's a trap. Isn't it true that the abodes of women, especially royal women, are forbidden to men? The women of New Cosaquia, I believe, have gynaecea into which we have not yet penetrated; they weren't invited to any of our feasts. They are, therefore, sequestered, so we ought not to visit them, at least without competent authority. That's my opinion, and I'm not authorized to have another. I don't trust the people of that tribe, and with reason; I'm particularly suspicions of that fellow who's summoning us. Be prudent, my friend; let's not put our heads at risk. There's probably some law of which we're unaware, that will render us liable to the gallows. Stay here, my friend!"

"Who sent you to us, Cheorchek?" asked Falster, advancing toward my enemy with the iron grip, who had turned

303

back toward us without ceasing to invite us to follow him, making a horrible grimace that he evidently mistook for a smile.

"The king's daughter," he replied. "She's waiting for you."

I still resisted, but Falster went through the postern deliberately, making an admirable gesture of boldness, and I followed him.

And I did well, my friend. We found ourselves in a little courtyard, in a veritable museum, resplendent with artistic riches of the first order of an incontestable antiquity, which I did not have time to inspect for the moment, it's true, but which made me forget the gallows I had feared so much completely. Everything there was admirably arranged; the order testified to intelligence.

We were evidently no longer in Cosaquia, and, in order for the illusion to be complete, we no longer had before us savage huts, but a palace, a veritable palace of civilized human beings—a palace like none in Caucasia.

That palace, my friend, was probably a monument unique in that country; it could not have been built by the hands of our hosts, nor by those of their predecessors, Cosaques, Moroccans or otherwise. There was nothing in it reminiscent of their architecture. It dated back much further.

For me, and without any doubt, it was a monument of ancient France. That later peoples had added to it was easy to see, for the monument had been subjected, like all the rest, to the insults of time, wars and barbarism. The more recent barbarians had, however, apparently been ashamed of their ancestors' devastations, for they had made some repairs—in their own fashion, it's true, but they had repaired it, which rendered them almost dear to me.

I shall not tell you anything for the moment, my friend, about that monument, its sculptures, its towers, and that splendid treasure of arts. All of it was scratched, mutilated, badly damaged—and, what's worse, it had all been rebuilt, ineptly and hideously, by the architects of huts and royal palaces, the constructors of the bridges about which you know. They had put heads and arms found in their excavations on torsos that would certainly have been astonished to receive them, but so what? The torsos had no heads, and needed them, no legs, and needed them—and no one to make them. Poor artists!

The monument was habitable, however, and it was, indeed, inhabited—inhabited by a woman of sentiment, a woman of taste, whom I shall no longer call barbarian because of her good intentions. I could not cast an eye over the palace at that moment; I had no time to examine it further because Cheorchek was still walking, and Falster was drawing me along by the hand, as a mother does with her child. He suspected that I could spend an eternity there in contemplation.

We went up a magnificent staircase to the first floor, which was terminated in its upper part by tree-trunks fitted together as best they could be the restorative workers. On the first-floor landing we were met by Ouchda, who looked at us in amazement, and whom I was on the point of embracing unceremoniously, so much did I admire her good taste.

"Oh, this is wonderful!" she exclaimed immediately, turning to the interior of the apartment, whose door was still opened. "You've divined accurately, Nhohelle; here are the gentlemen!"

And the young woman, as nimble as a hind, clapping her hands naively, launched herself toward Nhohelle, whom she seized around the neck in order to embrace her.

Nhohelle, the Queen—for it was her—remained grave and silent. She doubtless did not understand that effervescent demonstration of gaiety, or perhaps understood it from her own viewpoint. Her viewpoint, in that case, could not be the one that Ouchda wanted to be apparent to us, for the Queen understood perfectly well that the divination of which she had just given proof was neither a miracle nor a novelty for the king's daughter. Ouchda had thus given herself away by her outburst of joy, but not to us. However, the Queen received the young woman's kisses patiently, and then rose to her feet to greet us.

"Excuse *our* joy, gentlemen," she said to us with a thin smile. "It's quite natural at *our* age. Madame has been devoting herself for some time to the study of magnetism, under my direction. I'm her tutor, but her unhappy tutor, for I have only half-succeeded in the object of my lessons. Madame understands the secrets of magnetism very well; I've revealed them to her—but her fluid is resistant to all my efforts; I have not yet been able to put her into a somnambulistic trance, which is why her convictions are a trifle resentful of my theories. She would like to see and feel for herself the divine effects of the fluid.

"It's not the same with me, however; the magnetic fluid develops of its own accord, or very nearly. So, just now, to convince my royal pupil, I put myself to sleep, instructing her to interrogate me, to ask for some item of information that might interest her, and which she could verify immediately. Madame asked me..."

Ouchda blushed like a child caught being naughty, and put her finger to her lips, exclaiming: "Oh, it wasn't that! It wasn't that!"

The Queen continued, in a tone full of malice, probably modifying the question that had been asked: "Madame asked me where King Rhaman's guests were. 'In the ruins of your palace,' I told her...and immediately woke up. Cheorchek was immediately summoned, then sent to you, to invite you, on Madame's behalf, to come and visit her palace."

Having all the intelligence of a woman of modern civilization, the Queen added: "That, gentlemen, is why Madame gave evidence of such great joy on your arrival, part of it being due to the pleasure of seeing the guests of her father, the king, in her home, and part of it to the recognition of the accuracy of my vision."

Ouchda seemed quite satisfied with the Queen's interpretation, and testified that by squeezing her hand in a convulsion of joy. Falster was smiling at the Queen's subtle and delicate intelligence. As for me, I admired that incomparable woman with all my heart.

"But Madame," I said, after a moment's silence, "you speak to me about animal magnetism as people speak of it in our Academies in Caucasia, where they attribute the glory of the revelation of that spiritualism to one of our compatriots, who is still alive."

"I'm sorry for your Academies," the Queen relied, with a fascinating smile, "but our tribe—some of our tribe, at least—have always possessed those secrets, which have been handed down to us by our forefathers, perhaps eternally. At the moment, I am their sole depository here—in their practice, at least, for the principles of magnetism are no longer secret here. We teach them to anyone in our tribe who wishes to know them. Unfortunately, they are disdained, and as they are disdained, it is required for the tribal leaders to know them and to study them constantly, in order to conserve them as we have received them.

"Our leaders must also be initiated into all the knowledge that our forefathers have bequeathed to us. They are its natural depositories. We must not lose any of that which comes from our ancestors; it is an item of religion for us."

"I understand that, and I admire your ancestors even more in consequence, if that is possible, as well as your tribe, Madame," I said, darting a curious glance around me, which was not the first.

We were, in fact, in a vast room filled with marvels, magnificent works of art originating from excavations made under Ouchda's orders. All that, however, no longer received anything but a glance from me, so accustomed had I already become to the prodigies of that ancient land—or perhaps I had some other preoccupation. There was, in fact, heaped up amid all the jewels of that artistic treasure, all the equipment of a first-rate chemist. *My God!* I said to myself, *where am I, then? I thought I was arriving here in the fullness of barbarity!*

Falster had doubtless divined my preoccupation some time before, and understood what my heart and mind were saying, for he smiled at my astonishment like a man who could no longer be astonished by anything.

"This is our chemistry laboratory," the Queen told us, probably having also guessed what I was thinking. "Madame desired some days ago to participate in my experiments, and I installed myself in her palace, but in truth, I'm not very knowledgeable in that science, and I'm a very poor teacher, who has not succeeded in communicating to the intelligence of her pupil the little that she knows."

"I'd dearly like to know, though," said Ouchda, with great enthusiasm. "Science is such a beautiful thing." Looking at us, she added: "It makes a savage into a civilized person, isn't that so, gentlemen?"

"You're right, Madame," Falster and I replied.

"It's true," said the Queen, "but perhaps we're trying to learn too much at once. Perhaps we'd do better to devote ourselves to one thing, to begin with: chemistry, or magnetism, or..."

"Well, let's stick to magnetism," Ouchda replied, swiftly. "It's more attractive, and I believe in it so firmly now that I'm sure I won't be resistant to its mysterious fluid any longer. Do you believe in that science, gentlemen?" Her eyes were sparkling with curiosity.

"I believe in it sincerely," Falster replied, quite seriously.

"Me too," I replied, for my part, under the interrogative gaze of Ouchda and the Queen. "I've taught the science, with some success, in Caucasipol, and, moreover, I've always been, thus far, a very lucid subject—except that I can't put myself to sleep. I haven't yet arrived at that perfection."

"But you go to sleep very easily under the gaze and touch of a magnetizer?" said the Queen, who advanced towards we with the casual manner of a scholar who is oblivious to sex, took me by the hands according to the sacramental rite, and subjected me to a gaze under which I immediately fell asleep.

"Perfect, Madame!" exclaimed Falster, amazed. "I've never seen it done better."

"Interrogate him now," said the Queen to Falster. "He'll reply to you, for I wish it, and I assure you that my magnetic power is irresistible."

"I can do no better, then," Falster replied, "than to ask him where he is. I'm sure that if, when asleep, he has the same desires as when awake, he'll see many things that will give him pleasure."

"A fine idea!" said the Queen. "I'll do everything I can to help you."

Then, placing a finger on my forehead, she made a sign to my friend to interrogate me, which he did with great curiosity.

A thick veil before my eyes was suddenly ripped apart. I was no longer in Figuig. I was no longer in the midst of ruins. I no longer saw Cosaques, or huts. I found myself confronted by the most marvelous spectacle. My admiration was incapable of describing anything calmly; it burst out in exclamations and sibylline declarations.

"Paris!" I cried. "But this is Paris!"

"Did you doubt it, man of little faith?" said the Queen, with satisfaction. "I too have seen it, for a long time; did I not tell you so once?"

I was so breathless that I could no longer say anything. The Queen passed her finger over my forehead again, and I became calmer.

"Be calm," she said, "and see."

"And that marsh! Oh, I knew full well that it was not a marsh, that it was the Seine. What a beautiful river! Quays, bridges...what life! What activity! What fine people!"

The Queen, it seemed was radiant with joy.

"But...they're your ancestors Madam?" I said, emotionally.

"Yes," she replied, with a profound sigh. "Those beautiful people, those powerful people, were our ancestors, the ancestors of that petty tribe, lodged today in a narrow corner of the great capital of old; that petty tribe which no longer has any honor, no power, no men, no children, no palaces..."

"No palaces!" I repeated slowly, after the Queen, bringing my mind back to the palace in which she usually resided, where I had nearly lost my life on my first entry into Paris, after my condemnation by the Council of Elders. "No palaces!" I said aloud. "And yet...no, there's no memory there, save for me alone... It was nothing, nothing but an ordinary little house...an ordinary little house! And yet...but no, no...originally... Oh, what joy! What vivacity! What pleasures! It's funny..."

Then I remained mute; I was savoring eccentric images that pleased me infinitely, by retracing for me mores with which I was unfamiliar. I expressed my joy from time to time by exclamations inconsequential for anyone but me.

"That's all right," said Falster, doubtless annoyed by the incoherence of my speech, which wasn't telling him anything. "But talk to us so that we can understand you. Look—tell us about the Palace of Administration."

"The Palace of Administration!" I continued, after a moment's hesitation. "But...what do I see? What! It was a temple! A temple...with admirable monuments all around. What beautiful palaces! And King Rhaman's palace...what! It was the palace of the old kings! What a city! What a city! And then...look! Here, where we are, a palace! A museum! And beside it...beside it...what? Where does that come from? Ruins, always ruins? Oh! No, no, it was...but how can that be? Another people built it, lived in it—great men, heroes, who were not French..."

"Leave it," said the Queen, passing her finger over my forehead. "You, who are avid to know, continue to see France, further back, much further..."

"Yes, yes—forests, always forests, vast forests, and barbarity too, but..."

"And beyond?" said the Queen.

"Oh, beyond!" I replied. "I can't see very well...cities, more cities, I think...civilization, but very obscure to me...other peoples, it seems to me...yet other peoples...and I believed that the world was so new! Oh, weakness of the human mind! Oh, ignorance! All that goes back to an incredible unknown antiquity..."

"But France, France!" the Queen said, greatly animated.

"France! Its historic cradle...forests, half-naked savages, more huts...but heroes, giants...what battles! Always battles...then invasions of barbarians, invasions of civilized men... Then...then rivers of blood, to shake off the yoke of slavery...then more rivers of blood, subsequently. Oh, what a history! Poor France! Poor people! Great men, however...and then...oh, my God! Civil wars...brutalization, degradation...earthquakes, volcanic eruptions everywhere; floods everywhere, ravages; invasions of the sea, all the way to here...ruined cities, swallowed up; mountains collapsing, valleys becoming mountains...then, finally, savages irrupting from all directions, who complete the total destruction. Ah!" I cried out in horror.

"Enough," the Queen said, placing her finger once again on my eyes, to prevent me seeing what seemed to be frightening me so much, perhaps also for fear of hearing what I was about to say, which might have betrayed secrets that she was keeping to herself, and whose entire range it was impossible for me to understand, since I was no longer living an ordinary existence.

Then she woke me up.

I looked at them all, in amazement. It seemed to me that I had emerged from a dream in which I had experienced great joys and great pains. Thus, I remained dazed for some time. I eventually recovered my senses.

"I don't know, in truth, Madame," I said to the Queen, then, "whether I ought to be grateful to you for having extracted me so abruptly from the pains that I was enduring, and the many indescribable emotions I found therein. I saw so many things that I had never seen before, and I still had so many things to see that I would have liked to know!"

"What do you expect?" the Queen replied, smiling her most malicious smile. "I saw you so unhappy that I took pity on you. If you want to see more, however, I can, whenever

311

you wish, return you to the path from which you emerged. For the moment, you ought to be satisfied to have seen all that you have seen; at least you can get your bearings on this terrain now, and make better comparisons." She bowed toward Ouchda, and added: "Tomorrow, moreover, with Madame's permission, I will offer you a cicerone with whom you may begin your peregrinations and your studies. You have only to be, at sunrise, on the ruined bridge that you must have seen in your magnetic sleep, near to which you came down when you first arrived in Figuig. There you'll find a man waiting for you." With all the affectation of a highly-placed lady of our civilization who wishes to imply more than she is saying, she added: "I advise you to obey him as you would me."

I was far from wanting to conclude that visit, so agreeable was it to me, but Falster thought that it would not be decorous to prolong it further. He therefore rose to his feet in order to give me a signal to withdraw. I was disappointed; I don't know whether I was the only one. It was necessary to obey, though.

"You'll come back, gentlemen," Ouchda said to us, with much amity, "for you have a great deal to see in this palace that I've raised from the ruins as best I could, and have done my best to embellish. Your advice regarding its complete restoration will be very useful, I hope."

No invitation could have been more agreeable to me; I would even have established my residence there, if that had been allowed...

Finally, we left.

We did not go out of the postern to the ruins, however. Ouchda wanted to reserve a pleasant surprise for us, in sending us through a little courtyard in which we found the façade of the palace, which we had not yet seen: a true jewel, my friend, all the beauty that it is possible to contrive in sculpture. I'll make a sketch of it for you. Then we passed through a final doorway, which opened on to a little path shaded by the leafy branches of centuries-old trees. That door was worthy of the façade. Oh, what beautiful things I had seen there!

"Are you going to the Queen's rendezvous tomorrow?" Falster asked me, once we were out of the palace.

"Yes, why not?" I replied.

"Your innocence is charming, my dear friend," Falster replied, folding his arms and looking me in the eyes. "You know that you're an enemy to that tribe, since you're an enemy to one of its chiefs; you barely escaped one of his ambushes yesterday, and tomorrow…you're mad!"

"Why?" I retorted, with complete self-confidence, folding my own arms. "The Queen has not seduced you, then, with her grace, her knowledge and her soul, as elevated above the people of Figuig as the sky is above the earth?"

"Yes, talk to me about the Queen," Falster replied, striding away. "A siren…a seeress…probably the priestess of the goddess Vengeance. You mustn't go."

We continued walking and arguing in that fashion until we reached the Palace of Administration, which I was in haste to reach in order to admire what I had seen in my trance. My imagination, still seething with my beautiful dream, no longer saw a marsh, or huts, and my enthusiasm was tireless in its exaltation, as it reconstructed for Falster the temple and the palaces, and the animation of their surroundings, which I could still see in gazing at that hideous wilderness.

XXXVI. THE RENDEZVOUS

At sunrise the next morning I was no longer asleep. Falster was sleeping profoundly. So I got up, making as little noise as possible, and went out of our hut the same way—but I had scarcely set foot on the palace bridge when I found him on my heels.

"You're mad, Daghestan," he told me, his eyes full of anger. "What you're doing now isn't courage—neither the courage of the fatalistic philosopher, not the courage of the devoted scholar—it's madness."

"You believe, then," I replied, in a convinced tone, "that the Queen has set a trap for me? She would no longer have that intelligence which you admired so much! What! You believe her so unskillful as to extend her net in front of you, in front of Ouchda? You believe that she has so little fear of the king that she would provoke his vengeance by murdering his guests? Oh, no, no…you can see, my dear friend, that I'm not mad, and that I would be much more so if I didn't go to the rendezvous, refusing to learn what no one but me can learn, and manifesting mistrust of a woman who has until now watched over me as a mother watches over her child.

"Remember Lining and its deserts; remember yesterday evening—and I'll remind you about my imprisonment and condemnation to death in the Queen's palace. Believe me, I have nothing to fear. Besides, I'll come back in three hours; if I haven't arrived by then, ask the Queen where I am, and have your brother the king protest to King Rhaman."

Falster was almost convinced of the soundness of my reasoning—at least, I think so, for he looked at me with eyes full of amity and made no reply. I took advantage of his silence, which I accepted as permission to go. I shook his hand and left as quickly as I could, in order not to be subjected to a further round of objections.

When I had gone far enough to think that I was about to go out of sight I looked back at him. He was still in the same place, following me with his eyes, in an attitude that I took to be one of discouragement. I waved to him, and fled into the forest of tall trees; the forest is everywhere in that region.

It did not take me long to reach the ruined bridge that the Queen had mentioned to me, and which remained so sadly engraved in my memory. Having traversed the numerous deep cracks in the ground that surrounded it, sometimes on tree-trunks thrown across them, sometimes by placing my feet on the tips of rocks that served as stepping-stones, I found myself at the designated spot on the far side of the bridge.

There I did indeed find a man toward whom I advanced, and whom I recognized immediately. It was Cheorchek.

With his hand, Cheorchek indicated the path that I was to follow. "Go that way," he added, in a dialect that I could scarcely comprehend, and yet I already knew, "and to the first man of our tribe you meet, say 'Jehovah'—and then follow him."

I did as Cheorchek had told me to do.

I was certainly not afraid, but the mystery was disturbing, and I found it strange, at least, that the Queen had confided my fate to a man who had already tormented me so much. Thus, while following Cheorchek's instruction, I never ceased to be on the lookout and to examine the places I passed by, as distantly as I could.

My first concern, when I had taken a few steps beyond the bridge, after leaving Cheorchek, was to look behind me, to see what attitude he had adopted. I could no longer see him. Searching with my eyes, with an anxiety that was not stupid, for he could not stay in the same place indefinitely, I perceived him at the top of a tall tree, where he was manipulating an iron wire that I had not noticed. That wire continued above my head, attached at intervals to trees alongside the path I was following.

A telegraph! I exclaimed, silently, with what seemed to me to be a perfectly natural surprise. *An electric telegraph here in New Cosaquia, among barbarians, when it has only been operating for a few years at home, in the heart of civilization!* Smiling disdainfully, I repeated: *No, no.* After a moment's reflection, though, I added: *I seen the marvels of animal magnetism here, though; I've seen a chemistry laboratory; why should I not also find the mysteries of physics in action in the Queen's realm?*

I had stopped in order to make these reflections, and I was gazing like a idler at the unmoving wire, which appeared to continue its route along the one I was to follow. Then, instinctively, I looked back at the tree where I had seen Cheorchek—but Cheorchek was no longer there. I soon spotted him striding away on his long legs beneath the trees, heading toward the Queen's palace, at which I couldn't look without shivering slightly. It was the first time I had seen it since my second arrival, and in my present state of mind I was incapable of finding it a very pleasant sight.

I soon found myself in front of it, but I didn't attempt to go in; that was not my objective.

In spite of the shadows that the sight of that palace cast in my mind, I didn't stop, much less feel any desire t retrace my steps. On the contrary, my heart was suddenly animated by an unreflective courage—perhaps the courage of the desperate who throw themselves head first into an abyss—and I hastened my steps in order to arrive more rapidly at the place where I had been told that I was expected.

My curiosity was overexcited; it was the frenzy of the scholar, or, perhaps, the curiosity of a reader avid to reach the denouement of a highly intriguing book. I wasn't walking as quickly as I desired, though, for the ground was so extensively torn up by landslips—which I could only attribute to volcanic eruptions, over the traces of which furious torrents must have been subsequently unleashed at intervals—that my steps were continually interrupted.

It didn't take me long to find the man I sought, however. He was standing next to a large thorn-bush, only his head being visible—which caused me to doubt his mission at first.

But he looked at me with such an expressively interrogative gaze that I understood very quickly.

"Jehovah," I said to him, stopping opposite him.

"Come," he replied, emerging from his bush. "Walk ahead of me."

We didn't change our itinerary; we were still walking in the direction of the iron wire attached to the trees. My observations increasingly confirmed the suspicion I had had that it was an electric telegraph. I will admit frankly that I was so accustomed to that idea that I no longer found it strange.

We walked thus for about a quarter of an hour in the most profound silence. We were still under the trees of a forest, in which I seemed to recognize ruins at intervals, for there were blocks of stone scattered everywhere, which had evidently served some purpose, but I had neither the time nor the inclination to examine anything more closely. I had but one idea: to follow my guide and keep an attentive eye on the places that we passed.

We finally arrived in a large clearing. There we saw no palace, but there were huts in large enough number to take on the aspect of a village. The huts were similar in all respects to those in the royal palaces, with the difference, however, that their dimensions were more restricted and the materials employed more modest, for no sculptures or other art-works extracted from excavations entered into their construction, luxury being entirely reserved for the palaces.

We were at the end of our journey; my guide did not tell me that, but he led me to a hut whose door opened in front of us without our having any need to knock. On the threshold I saw a man suddenly appear who seemed to be there to receive me. The sight of him made me shiver involuntarily; it was Johan-Ali-Schahpohtink, my eternal enemy. Instinctively, I sought the eyes of my guide, but he had disappeared. We were alone.

"Come in," said Johan, trying to smile as graciously as he could, letting me into the hut.

I hesitated. All Falster's remonstrances came back to mind at that moment, and I looked around for something that might restore the confidence I no longer had.

"You've been entrusted to me to instruct you," Johan went on, not appearing to understand the motives for my hesitation. "I shall fulfill my mission as a gallant man. If, therefore, you desire to see our Little Paris first"—he waved his hands at the surrounding huts—"I'm at your disposal. Speak, Mr. Daghestan."

Without waiting for my reply, Johan emerged from his house and walked in front of me into the middle of the village. I followed him, my confidence returning slightly. I moved to his side, deciding to have no fear henceforth, while remaining prudent, and to take advantage of his good will to interrogate him at my ease.

XXXVII. LITTLE PARIS

The village of Little Paris seemed quite tidy to me; it was redolent with the comfort of order and good will. That's all I can say by way of a eulogy. Unlike the villages of our country, the smallest of which has streets, and houses regularly aligned along them, the houses of Little Paris were planted according to the whim of their owners and isolated from one another. Each one was surrounded by a little orchard without a fence, composed of fruit trees; a few combined that with a little garden ornamented with flowers of the fields, which cultivation had embellished.

They were all similarly structured, almost identical in size. One would not have been able to say, on seeing them, whether any of their inhabitants were richer than the others. None of the huts had doors that could be locked. I manifested my surprise to Johan, who gave me to understand that in this fortunate corner of the earth, thieves were not much to be feared.

Print that news in your paper, my friend, in letters of gold, to make moralists reflect on the advantages and disadvantages of civilization.

After all, though, what could one steal there? One cannot take anything from someone who has nothing—and yet, since it's necessary to say everything—I saw prisons some distance from the village. It's true that although there is no money to steal there, there are, as I learned from what Johan told me, ground-apples. It is, it appears, that fortune which sometimes tempts the filchers, and renders them culpable.

Fortunate, in any case, I said to Johan, are the people who can find nothing to take in their treasures but a few fruits! Fortunate are the people who are unfamiliar with all the refined thefts that so cleverly evade the reach of the law in our land, when they are not made sufficiently skillfully to win honor and praise!

I don't want to say, however, that those are a god-like people; no, they're human beings, and human beings are always human. They have their vices, therefore, and they commit crimes; and as they live in society, the law creates misdemeanors for them. At that moment, however, it appeared that crimes and misdemeanors were at a low ebb in Little Paris, for the prisons were empty.

"So much the better!" I exclaimed, fearfully, at the sight of the horrible prisons that my guide showed me.

Those prisons, my friend—listen to me without shivering, if you can—are deep wells, very deep, into which the convict is lowered by means of a rope, to be raised up again at the expiry of his sentence. Oh, the law is not gentle in Little Paris, and the Council of Elders, which judges everything and without appeal, never compromises with any consideration. Every crime or misdemeanor that is denounced to it or that it discovers, is under its exclusive jurisdiction, and it pursues reparation actively and relentlessly, without occupying itself with the intervention of the parties concerned.

That jurisdiction is the sole concern of the tribe; the government, persuaded that it is well-exercised, does not pay any heed to it. It does not lose in consequence the rights that remain to it, but it only reserves to itself the investigation and repression of crimes and misdemeanors that attack society as a whole, not the tribe alone.

All that seemed reasonable to me, and I listened attentively to Johan, who gave me all those details in an obliging manner.

We didn't see anyone in the village—not even one of the children that one encounters in such large numbers in ours. I remarked on that to Johan.

"Remember," my guide said, "that children are not under the supervision of their parents, who always do so badly; they're confided to the guardianship of the tribe, which is careful not to let them wander the roads. Children are not free here; that's our policy; they ought not to be, until they have learned to make use of liberty. So, from early age until twenty,

320

for girls, twenty-five for boys, they should only obey. They're brought up and work under the orders of these that the Council of Elders has deemed capable."

Johan went on: "We have always found that national institution good. I have no doubt, personally, that most parents are prepared to give a good and solid education to children, but what education? Everyone understands it in his own fashion, and it will assuredly be too various, even if it were not often poor. It does not, therefore, achieve its goal, the vigor for which our tribe is ambitious..."

Quite innocently, he added: "Then again, as you doubtless know, marriage is completely free here. How do you expect us to entrust children to a girl under twenty and a young man under twenty-five? We want to keep our girls and women strong and healthy; we want to have children whose health will do honor to our blood. By taking our children into tutelage until that age, we attain our goal. You can judge for yourself, anyway, if you'd care to follow me."

I followed Johan gladly, who led me out of the village, where I saw cultivated fields admirable in their order and neatness. All the cereals there were more beautiful than those I had seen in any other part of the world. The ground-apple, of which I shall only cease to speak when I cease to write, the unique fruit that I had not encountered in any of my voyages, and is completely unknown in Caucasia, is a marvelous crop there. It is a precious supplement to cereals, if it is not their peer.

Well, that cultivation is in large part the work of women and children; the men are more specifically occupied with hunting, a few works of art—an activity that is thriving in the tribe—and commerce.

We soon found ourselves in a vast plain, which I only saw when I came into it, for it had been hidden from me until the by a curtain of trees. It was covered at that moment by a legion of laborers of all the ages of childhood and youth, who seemed to be actively occupied under the guidance of older people, the boys on one side and he girls on the other, far enough apart that there could not be any communication between the two camps.

"Do you believe," I said to Johan, "that these young people never deceive your surveillance and never infringe your rules?"

"Never," he said. "Not in human memory, at least. Personally, I've never seen any of these young people in our prisons, where the guilty party would certainly be condemned to attain maturity. Why, in any case, should they break our rules? What would lead them to do it? Us? A guilty party would not be excused by anyone in the tribe. Their passions? The law represses them, and prudence keeps them away from temptation."

"That's perfect," I said. "All the more so as I can see that your pupils confirm the wisdom of your law by their sturdiness and apparent good health." I had, in fact, drawn nearer to the children and had been able to confirm what my guide said with my own eyes.

"Those are our children, as you see sir," John said, satisfied with the impression made on me by the sight of his tribe's pupils. "Come and see our women now."

We left the double army of little laborers and went back through the curtain of trees in order go forward in another direction, without going very far from the village. Before leaving the little farm definitively, however, I darted one last glance at it, for a thought had just occurred to me.

"And when the children emerge from your tutelage," I said to Johan, looking at him fixedly—without him turning a hair, like a man conserving some hidden agenda beneath the evidence of frankness that he was giving me—"what do you do with them?"

"They become what they wish," he replied. "They can follow their own inclinations from then on, for all our careers are open to them. The first thing they usually do, though, is to marry, and no one raises any obstacle to it. All our girls are at the disposition of the boys; there is no difficulty for them but that of choice. Marriage and its preliminaries are simple here.

Once the choice is made, the family sanctions it, and the sanction is always given at a friendly meal. The union of the couple lasts as long as they please; it can only be dissolved with certain reservations and conditions, but it is, at any rate, transitory if desired, perpetual if that is desired."

"So there's no dowry in your society," I said, swiftly, expressing a thought that had occurred to me a few moments earlier, which I had not expressed sooner in order not to interrupt his narration. "How do the newlyweds live, then?"

"By working with all the members of the tribe," Johan replied. "There's always work for the wife to do. The man, as you know, becomes a hunter, a trader or an artist. Wealth, among us, does not belong to individuals; it belongs to the tribe. There is, in consequence, work and produce for all. Death, unfortunately, creates gaps in families from time to time; that makes room for new arrivals. When the cultivated lands appear, in spite of everything, to be too small in their extent to suffice for the probable needs of the cultivators— which is exceedingly rare—we clear a corner of the woods and thus extend our crops. The result of this is that there is little envy here, little jealousy and little theft, since goods are communal, and work too."

"What about the slothful?" I asked. "What do you do with them?"

"Sloth is almost unknown here," he replied, "but it does exist. Idlers are given bread and alms at our gates, but we do not encourage to their humiliations. They are banished from our gatherings and our pleasures; our daughters do not want to see them; our families only speak to them to send them to work; they're stigmatized as beggars. It is rare, in the midst of all those torments, that they don't renounce their errant ways to enter into communal life again."

I made no further reply to Johan, but I silently admired the wisdom of his tribe's laws. I left the children's farm behind then to go into the common terrains of the village of Little Paris. There were several groups of woman of all ages there, working with all the activity of happy people avid for good results.

The complexions of all the women were tanned by the open air of the fields; a generous and highly colored blood appeared to be running in their veins. Their bodies were firm and muscular; without being immeasurably developed like the Herculean women of certain lands, they seemed well-constituted to me. All the workers were chatting in the midst of their occupations, and I could hear the admirably enthusiastic conversations at a distance. There was no lack of laughter to give them animation.

Those women, even the youngest, were very casual in their costume; although they weren't naked, as I have seen in other countries, they required very little. Modesty didn't appear to be an issue, for they didn't seem to worry much about the slightness of their clothing.

For those women, in any case, nudity is merely the uniform of labor; on feast days and in hours of rest they cover themselves with garments that testify to a certain coquetry of taste. They only allow their faces to show then, and the tips of their fingers, the rest of the hand remaining imprisoned in a kind of fabric glove, almost as elegant as those of beautiful Caucasian women.

Their most refined clothing only differs from ordinary dress in the more exquisite neatness of the fabric. That fabric is always very simple, and offers no great choice; it comes from their commerce with their neighbors, who appear to have agreed between themselves not to spoil their clients' taste. But no fabric, however beautiful or luxurious it might be, is ever employed in the national costume, which is always the costume of feast-days. That clothing, whose form is still similar to other clothes, is composed of animal skins, which they tan in their own manner, while conserving the animal's external pelt. The upper body is very graciously enclosed in a kind of jacket, which hangs well and clings to the figure with the aid of a broad ribbon of hide. The jacket is made of the skin of a short-haired animal in summer, a long-haired one in winter.

The rest of the body is clad in trousers, sometimes matching and sometimes different in color, which descend to the base of the leg, where they're secured by narrow thongs, which all the art of coquetry attempts to disguise. A broadly-pleated skirt, still in animal-hide, but which is required to be different in color, covers the trousers down to the knees. Only the Queen and her family have the right and duty to lower that skirt to ankle-length.

The head-dress consists of a little cap made from the skin of a short-haired animal, on which they mount feathers, each to her own taste—the brightest they can find, whose colors they know how to combine with considerable artistry. Only the Queen has the right to cover her hat with white feathers.

That costume is very picturesque, my friend, as it will seem from its description, and I've always seen it arranged and worn with exquisite distinction.

Our arrival in the middle of the fields did not fail to attract the attention of the workers, who looked at me with a curiosity at least as great as I put into my own gaze. I don't know what they thought of me, but I thought that although they hadn't couldn't all have been called beautiful, they could certainly all be called pretty, for the features of their faces were usually graceful, and when they lacked artistic regularity they seemed to be animated by such a sparkle that one was tempted to prefer it to linear regularity. There was soul therein, a great deal of soul, and when an honest soul is reflected in a face, the face is never ugly.

"Have you seen enough?" Johan asked, while I was admiring the beautiful spectacle that was before me as if in ecstasy, which was causing my philosophy to dream profoundly.

"Yes," I replied, suddenly thinking about Falster, and looking at my watch, which told me that I still had an hour of liberty before me without awakening my friend's anxieties. "If it's acceptable to you, we can go rest for a while in your home."

Johan made no reply, but he hastened to lead me to his hut. The urgency with which he did so was sufficient testimony to the pleasure my confidence gave him.

XXXVII. A DESCENT INTO THE CATACOMBS

The door to Johan's hut, which he had left open on our departure, as I remembered clearly, was closed.

"Do you live alone here?" I asked my guide.

"Alone," he said.

"Your door was open when we left, though," I said, looking at him hard.

"That's true," he replied, "and that was imprudent. I'm not afraid of thieves, but I ought to have been fearful of the indiscreet; there are secrets in my home that no one ought to know…except you, perhaps." He stared at me in his turn. "Someone has doubtless done me the favor of closing the door to my hut. Even on the latch, I'm sure that no one would open my door of it were closed."

He lifted the latch then, and the door opened.

Johan had said that there were secrets inside that he wanted to hide from everyone except me; I therefore opened my eyes wide as I went into his dwelling—but those secrets were well hidden, for I saw nothing of the sort in spite of the attention I devoted to it.

His room was by no means cluttered, though; one might even have said that it was completely bare had it not been for a bed almost identical to the one I had in the palace, and two tree trunks that apparently served as seats.

Johan's secret, as you can see, my friend, was well-guarded. However, my attention did not take long to be alerted by the glances my guide darted, as he moved around, at a corner of the hut's walls, at which I looked in my turn as intently as I could. I ended up detecting an iron wire that led in the direction of the door, above which it went out through a little opening.

My attention had not been covert; Johan noticed it.

"It's an electric wire," he said. "You must have noticed the commencement near the ruined ridge where you met

Cheorchek. It was Cheorchek who notified me of your arrival. But what you don't seem to have noticed is this." With his hand, he indicated the direction of another wire running vertically down the wall behind his bed to disappear underground. "Look," he said, pointing out signs on the wall that could only just have been engraved there, beneath the end of the subterranean iron wire "They're waiting for us. Are you courageous, Mr. Daghestan?"

"Yes, I think so," I replied.

"Trustworthy?"

"Yes."

"Honorable? I'm not asking; I've already been told that you are. Well, before we go any further, swear to me that you will not tell anyone—anyone whatsoever, you understand—what you are about to see and hear."

I hesitated; his tone and that oath seemed strange to me. Demanded by Johan, they made me shiver.

"I'm asking nothing of you myself," my guide added. "I'm carrying out the Queen's orders."

"I swear!" I said then, firmly.

Johan then braced a piece of wood against the door of the hut, although he had told me that he had no fear that anyone might lift the latch in his absence. Then he went to the bed, which he dragged into the middle of the room with his muscular arms—without difficulty, for, unlike ordinary beds, that one was not fixed to the ground.

An iron crowbar was hidden between the different sections of his bed; he picked it up, and with its aid he swiftly lifted up a stone slab blocking the opening of a tunnel whose depth I couldn't fathom, but which seemed immense. There was an odor escaping from it that could only have come from a very deep cavity.

Johan went down first, offering me his hand to draw me after him. "Follow me," he said. "There's a staircase we have to go down—be careful. I'll speak to you from time to time so that you don't lose track of me, until we've reached the light..."

We descended thus for nearly a quarter of a hour, not without difficulty—for me, at least, who could not see anything and did not know where I was. I felt damp beneath my sliding feet, and sought continually to steady myself with my hands on surrounding objects, but could find no support anywhere; my hands only encountered sticky moisture, which sent a chill into my heart.

We finally set foot on level ground. The Johan took me by the hand, and we walked like that for some time, still in darkness. Then he stopped. I heard him tap his foot in a cadenced manner, and a door suddenly opened in front of us.

An old man, whom I recognized immediately by his costume as a member of the Council of Elders, came toward us with a lighted torch in his hand. "Mr. Daghestan," he said to me, "you are free—completely free, appearances notwithstanding. Swear that you will not reveal to anyone in the world, at least so long as you are in this country, what you are about to see and hear."

"I so swear," I said, without trembling, in spite of the solemnity with which the oath had been demanded of me.

"Enter, then," the old man said, pointing at the door from which he had emerged. "Here, you are in our catacombs."

The door gave entrance to a vaulted cellar, closed on all sides by masonry whose regularity and solidity astonished me. It was vast; in the middle was a marble table supported by a single foot. The foot and the table were charged with exquisite reliefs that were perfectly preserved.

Perfectly conserved, did I say? I spoke accurately, because, for me, it was evidently an antique piece—and I say it with all the more certainty because that cellar was like a precious museum buried underground. It was filled with statues, large medallions and sculptures of every kind, restored at least by cleanliness, if not the science of artists.

Around the table, all the members of the tribe's Council of Elders were seated. No one got up when I came in, but they all stared at me, and greeted me with a gesture of the hand and head that touched me with its gravity, replete with nobility.

Nothing was said to me; nor was I to stop there. Johan repeated the cadence of his foot, then opened a door toward which he invited me with his hand to advance—which I did, taking note of the profound silence that reigned around me.

I was, I confess, severely shaken in my confidence; a heavy weight oppressed my heart. *Where am I?* I asked myself. *Where am I going?* I remembered the tribunal that had once condemned me to death, in the hands of which I found myself again at that moment. I could no longer stop, though; I could no longer even hesitate. I therefore went through the doorway that had been so silently indicated to me.

Oh! The icy hand that had gripped my heart so forcefully suddenly relaxed. I was facing the Queen—the Queen, who was coming toward me with a smile on her lips, extending a friendly hand to me with which she shook mine.

My confidence had returned in its entirety, and my gallantry with it. I was deep in the bowels of the earth, but what did that matter? I was there with the Queen. So I held on to her hand, which I raised to my lips, palpitating with pleasure and good memories.

"No, no," she said to me, withdrawing her hand swiftly. "Since you want to give me a kiss, give it to me on the cheek, Brother."

I kissed the Queen's cheek, but with less pleasure than I had kissed her hand. The word "brother" had chilled me.

"Brother!" I said, with a languorous sadness, emboldened by the fact that we were alone. "Oh, you afflict me, Madame!"

The Queen did not reply, but she smiled at me with a grace that completed my fascination. I was vanquished; I had lost my head; I was ready to swear the most incendiary oaths. Fortunately, she did not ask me for any.

"Do you know," the Queen said to me, sitting down on an artistically disposed stone seat and drawing me toward her in order to sit me down by her side, as she had in the cemetery in Copenhagen, "that you are a courageous man."

"Did you doubt it, Madame?"

"No—but you might have been afraid of coming here, where you doubtless didn't know that you would find me."

"That's true—but I had a presentiment that you would be here...and I'm overjoyed to find you here in comfort such as I observe here." I cast a glance around me.

The second cavern was about the same size but infinitely richer than the first. Art and wealth were represented there in all their forms.

"It's my royal boudoir," the Queen told me, smiling, "and these riches are the work of our forefathers. When hazard, and sometimes also our research, causes some souvenir of our ancestors to fall into our hands, some debris of their vast knowledge and great power, we bring them here in secret. We do our best to restore them, and make them into trophies of glory—of a past glory, it's true, but one that means a great deal to us. You may work here when you please, Mr. Daghestan, studying our history and the history of the old world. This museum will always be at your disposal."

I was stunned; I was admiring silently, not only what the Queen was saying to me but what I could see.

"No!" I suddenly exclaimed. "No, never has Caucasia, that land of fine arts and sciences, never has the Sudan, our rival, never has any country produced anything so beautiful!" With a sentiment that approached delirium, I added: "But Madame, your France was thus the perfection before us! And they talk about the world of yesterday! And they talk about the civilization of today! Ha ha! The scholars are ignorant fools."

I laughed disdainfully. I no longer had the calm of a philosopher, and the Queen exulted in my exaltation. She was listening to me and looking at me avidly.

I calmed down eventually and, taking her hands in mine, said: "Why, Madame," when you have so many riches that you know how to appreciate, do you lurk here like conspirators?"

The Queen's expression darkened at that word; she lowered her eyes sadly.

"What a word you've just thrown in my face, Mr. Daghestan," she said, raising her eyes to look at me again. "I expected it, but feared it from your mouth, for it expresses a horror in any country. A conspirator is a person who seeks by means that are only good for him the realization of what is often a utopia. Do you believe that we are conspirators?"

"Oh no, Madame, no!" I said, in a tone that attempted consolation, but which was not a retraction sufficient to deceive a woman like the one who was talking to me.

"No politeness or sentimentality with me, sir," the Queen retorted, sharply. "I can hear the truth, however harsh one cares to make it. Are we conspirators?"

"Yes Madame," I replied, firmly this time, "if you wish to trouble a society legitimately and honestly established; no, if you wish to reclaim your rights."

The Queen got to her feet then, with a radiant surge, then went to a corner of the cellar, where I perceived a little iron door that screeched on its rusty hinges.

That door enclosed a long and broad cupboard, lined with marble tablets, fitted together so well that I could not see any joints. She took out a wooden box, lined externally, for the most part, with iron plates, and internally by tanned hides, which seemed to me to be admirably well conserved.

The box was full of books, before which I stood in ecstasy. The Queen took several of them out and presented them to me. "You shall read these books," she told me, "And you shall be our judge thereafter. Our history is there—our authentic history, you may be certain, Mr. Daghestan, for those books come from an antiquity unknown to us. They have been handed down through the ages from our forefathers to us, who will hand them on to our children, God willing, with all the care that you observe. Only I, the Elders of our Council and you know that they exist."

I took the books from the Queen's hands and put them to my lips with a profound sentiment of respect. Then I opened one of them—but I stopped suddenly. My radiant thought had just recalled Falster, the memory of whom suddenly recalled me to the reality of my situation, and the recommendation I had given to him. I was distressed, and reached precipitately for my watch.

The Queen caught my arm. "I understand," she said. "You're anxious, for your three hours of leave have elapsed—but I anticipated that." She smiled, and added: "You have sent word to Mr. Falster asking him for two hours respite, in order to complete the interesting observations to which you are devoting yourself."

"What!" I said, dazedly, looking attentively at the Queen, to see whether she might be delirious, or whether she might, for some unknown reason, be amusing herself cruelly at my expense.

"Oh, what nasty thoughts you have!" she said, sadly, reading my heart like an open book. "Don't you recall the past, then? Why don't you want to understand that it was Franco who saw you leave the Palace of Administration and gave me the information? And that, in accordance with that advice, I've just made use of our electric telegraph, which you admired near the ruined bridge where Cheorchek was? Well, in accordance with my orders—and your consent, I assume—Cheorchek has gone to the Palace of Administration and, by way of our telegraph, he tells you that Mr. Falster will wait for you for another two hours; I shall even say that he will wait for you impatiently—at least, that is what he said."

"I beg your pardon, Madame!" I said, falling at the Queen's feet. "I'm a great fool—but admit, too, that I'm living a life here that isn't mine, which surpasses all my science and conviction, and you'll then excuse me, I hope."

"Child!" said the Queen, putting out her hand to help me get up. After a moment's silence, she added: "How I want to see you here again. "Put the books back in the box, close the iron door again, and come sit down beside me, for we need to talk."

I did as the Queen desired, obeying her with the naivety of a child, delighted as I was by the gentle familiarity with which she was treating me.

"Brother," she said to me then, taking one of my hands in both of hers, which she rested on her knees, "you will read our history tomorrow, if you wish; today, I want to tell it to you briefly myself, such as it is written in those books, which I know by heart, for I am in haste to tell you who we are in coming to our subterranean refuge; I want you to know that we are not conspirators."

XXXIX. THE YEAR 5865
ACCORDING TO THE QUEEN

"Our present masters," the Queen continued, "were not born in this land, and this land has not been given to them. Nor were those who preceded them born here, and as with the others, this land has not been given to them. We must go further back to discover the indigenes of this country. You know all that, Mr. Daghestan, as well as I do.

"Well, those indigenes were the French—us. Our traditions say so, and our history is also written. You will read it, and judge it as a scholar; we have no fear of that.

"But how does it come about that a small tribe like ours is directly descended from a powerful nation like ancient France? Or, rather, how did the powerful France of old come to fall so low as to no longer be anything but a weak tribe lost in the desert of barbarity, reduced to a few thousand individuals?

"That is for you to answer, Mr. Daghestan. A savant historian like you, a philosopher like you, ought not to be embarrassed to teach the ignorant how the most heroic and strongest people fall, how mighty peoples have doubtless fallen since the origin of the world."

"Philosophers who have the habit of studying causes and effects, Madame," I replied to the Queen's interpellation, "say that when luxury arrives at its peak in a people, when money no longer serves any purpose but to find the road to pleasure and to sow it with flowers and perfumes, that people is on the eve of ruination."

"I believe that peoples fall like that, Mr. Daghestan, since you say so," the Queen said, "but I don't know anything about that. All that I know is that we have indeed fallen, perhaps by virtue of the same causes that make all peoples fall.

"I don't know what you've written about France, Mr. Daghestan, and I don't know what your historians have written. Certainly, they haven't written everything we know, thanks to our books, for you've told me yourself that in your history France plays a very small role, and the little that you know seems to you to be so uncertain that a serious historian scarcely dares to rely on it.

"Our books will tell you what you don't know, then, but I want to tell you, briefly, why our forefathers fell so destructively from the altars on which the old world adored them.

"In the year 2000, according to the ancient era—which calendar is still ours, with regard to years that are, as in the time of our forefathers, approximately thirteen lunar cycles, and with regard to the calculations of the centuries, which we have also retained..."

"With the result," I said to the Queen, interrupting her by virtue of the desire I had to know, "that instead of being at present, as in Caucasia, in the year 5001..."

"We're in the year 5865."

"Why the year 5865?" I said to her. "From what starting-point are you counting? Or, rather, from what starting-point did your forefathers count?"

"From the origin of France," replied the Queen, unhesitatingly.

I said nothing; I was able to believe, given her assurance, that she was right. I was, in addition, more disposed to believe it because we also use the origin of Caucasia—its historical origin, at least—as a starting date; which, I shall say in passing, corresponds roughly to the ruination of ancient France in the year 2000 the Queen had mentioned to me.[47]

"Well, then, in the year 2000," the Queen continued, "the colossus that was our France collapsed. It's necessary to say,

---

[47] This passage makes no sense unless the Caucasian "year" is, in fact, different in length from the sidereal year, being only 3865/5001 (0.772) as long—i.e. approximately 282 days, presumably being calculated as ten lunar months. No such process of decimalization has been carried out with respect to the hours of the day, however.

too, that France had already been undermined for a long time by the vices that had grown within it, like weeds in the fields, and which, when the avalanche of savages rolled over its flanks, had already defeated itself.

"I am not criticizing our ancestors, sir, but nor am I making excuses for them. I am not saying, in any case, that they had all become wicked and were all guilty of that ruination. No, I'm not saying that—but you know very well that the good are often too circumspect, or perhaps too indolent, and that vicious people are full of boldness. The harm was surely only done by the latter, who, in spite of their small number, must have dragged their brethren down with them.

"You, who are a scholar, know that France, before the year 2000, had been a monarchy and a republic by turns. Well, as the year 2000 approached it was a republic.

"The President of the Republic, Mogador, was a very learned man, our history says, and a very intelligent man, know and loved throughout the world for his intellectual works, but he had a boundless ambition, and only ever dreamed of the impossible. Accustomed to finding everything easy of execution when he was in his study, when he came to power he wanted to organize a government according to his rash illusions. Then he found himself alone.

"Although he had only been a writer, the spirit of contradiction had gathered a legion of friends around him, who set out with him bravely to make war, pens in hand. But his elevation to power had sown seeds of jealousy whose germination dissolved his cohort of friends, and the President's folly had made him enemies. The most violent thrusts of the boar's tusks that the republic received, in fact, came from journalists. So the presidential chair did not take long to become unsteady; it collapsed after barely two years of his term of office.

"What the pen had begun the sword completed. Army generals succeeded, or rather joined forces with the writers. Ashamed of being commanded by a utopian with that governmental authority, the boldest and the cleverest refused their collaboration, and as France was large then, and some of its

337

provinces were far away from the capital where the government was seated, they found it easy to render themselves independent and to round out small republics, which they governed as they wishes.

"That example was, as always, contagious. In no time at all, other generals imitated the first, and France was then divided into as many republics as there were provinces—départements, as they were called then.

"The central government, brought down by the outrages that it received from all sides, and further abased by its own incapability, found itself impotent to reclaim the authority that had escaped it. Mogador therefore fell, and fell so completely that history doesn't tell us what became of him. He was replaced by a king, whose history you'll find in the books. I shan't rob you of that pleasure..."

"I beg your pardon, Madame," I said to the Queen, interrupting her, with a smile that was not entirely full of confidence in her story, "but France must have been deeply corrupted to be dismembered so easily."

"It was indeed, as I have already told you, I think," the Queen retorted, sharply, with a tone off assurance that was intended to dispel my doubts. "It was a field sown with all the evil passions; how could it be expected to harvest anything but shame and ruin? The government itself was no longer the council of surveillance of the people, nor its aegis, nor its protector; in sum, it was no longer the head of a family; it had made itself into the owner of a flock, which it sheared and slaughtered for its own needs.

"When I say the government, you doubtless understand what I mean—I don't only mean its leader, but all those who worked in that vast mine. All of them, in fact, had become tyrants, each in his own sphere, all the way down to the inferior employees, who found themselves in contact with the citizens every minute of every day, rendering residence in France harsh and impossible—with the result that honest people were at their wits' end, quietly desiring an end to their troubles, no matter by what catastrophe it might arrive. Thus, when a few men wanted to dismember France, France was ready to submit to that misfortune..."

"All that I knew, Madame; the books of our prophets say so," I replied, smiling incredulously, but hiding my smile somewhat, for I was probably wrong.

"Well, they're correct," the Queen retorted, with a tone of conviction that contrasted with my smile of incredulity, "because it's all true. But do they also tell you that the dislocation gave birth to envy and a love of grandeur, and then to civil war, and to the enfeeblement of the entire country, which founding itself dying when foreigners invaded?"

"They say that to, Madame."

"Your prophets are true, then, and I bless them, for they agree with our history books, which will tell you all this better than me. It's to then that I leave the care of retracing those times and our misfortunes for you, the epoch of that last ill-bred republic, which descended into the mire of crime. You'll see how it made itself illustrious, the individuals that it dragged through the mud, the vices that gave it life and the crimes that killed it—and how royalty then emerged once again from its ashes.

"It was in that period of our history that you will find my own origin, the origin of my royal ancestors. What they were before that time, I don't know, but I know that they rose to the throne in that era, summoned by the wishes of good citizens. Alas, what could they do? To bring the cadaver back to life was impossible.

"A few days of glory, however, surged forth once again for France under their reign—a few very rare days. One might have thought that it had been condemned, that it required a punishment, that it was God's will. God could not have wanted us to be doomed, however—that's impossible. God recalls people to him either by recompense or by punishment, but he doesn't want the death of the sinner. No, it wasn't God—it was the barbarians who killed us...

"And at this point, Mr. Daghestan, our history becomes entangled with yours. Tell us the origins of your homeland, and we will know the end of ours."

"Speak, Madame," I said to the Queen, to whom I was listening avidly, for she was speaking like a philosopher of advanced civilization. "Speak—don't, I beg you, take away the pleasure of savoring the charms of your speech."

"Well then," said the Queen, squeezing my hands in hers even harder as she became more animated, "I'll go on speaking, and I'll tell you that in that same era, so our history says, the peoples of Caucasia, composed of a host of tribes that misfortune and a desire for vengeance had bound tightly together, finally weary of the long and cruel despotism to which all-powerful Russia had inflicted on the for centuries, shook off the iron yoke that they could no longer bear, and had already shaken many times.

"One unhappy nation among many—as unhappy as it was possible to be—which had been martyrized for many years under the pitiless hand of the Russians, but had finally ended up casting them out, lent them effective aid; that nation was Poland.

"Russia, pressured from every side—for other neighboring peoples that it had tyrannized too much, also agitated against it—was vanquished and stifled in its turn. The twenty various peoples making up its empire were restricted to their own soil, where they trembled like cowards awaiting the hour of the torture they had merited.

"But Caucasia was not a land of pitiless barbarians; Poland too was at the forefront of the civilization of the time; and the other peoples did not want anyone's death, but only peace at home. Humankind thus entered into universal council. The victors exiled the Russians into the wildernesses from which they had apparently come, a very long time before, in the depths of Asia. Some other parts of that tyrannical people remained dispersed in the new circumscription that Caucasia and Poland formed around those countries; the rest were ignobly expelled from their kingdom.

"It was those bands, with Cosaque pillagers at their head, which came to descend upon France and the lands that they encountered before reaching it, which were no longer able to do anything but receive them. Instead of uniting to repel these savage hordes, everyone clapped their hands in seeing them come down so harshly on their enemies—but everyone's turn came, and when they realized the stupidity of their egotism, it was too late; they no longer had the strength to oppose the invaders.

"France was therefore vanquished, sacked, pillaged, put to the torch; the French were hanged along the highways, when they did not fall under the executioner's ax. What remained of them was so small in number that our history is content to talk about them, without daring to say how many the Cosaques killed."

The Queen fixed her dark eyes on mine, and added: "Do you believe, Daghestan, that those men had legitimately acquired our country?"

"No, Madame," I replied, with a profound emotion that was, in truth, not at all simulated, "for I did not know that history in this fashion, and for my part, I had learned it quite differently. This appears to me to be at least as plausible as mine—or, rather, the one that our scholars have taught us for centuries."

"Do you believe, too, that the Moroccans and others who have invaded our country since then, which they disputed with and seized from the Cosaques, in order to spread ruin and desolation in their turn, have legitimately acquired France?"

"No, Madame, I don't believe so."

"I knew that you wouldn't believe it, as a man of sound philosophy and justice," said the Queen, squeezing my hands with all the ardor of her exaltation. "Embrace me, Brother."

"But Madame," I said, then, "since your rights are incontestable, since you have the right to the wealth that have been stolen from you by force, and have been retained by force and cunning, why do you remain submissive?"

The Queen looked at me with a strange expression—because I had, indeed, said something strange, as the guest and friend of Rhaman X. I bit my lip, but I gazed unflinchingly at the Queen, who never ceased to meet my eyes.

"Because we're the weaker," she said to me, after a momentary pause.

"The weaker, Madame! But isn't all of France in your tribe, then?" I replied, without hesitation, and without fear of appearing to be a man seeking to penetrate a secret that he ought not to know.

"No," the Queen replied, "Our tribe isn't entirely confined to the village of Little Paris; it's dispersed over the entire land, which is possessed in part by Rhaman X, and in part by the other peoples surrounding him, and it's now numerous again—but not all keep the sacred memory of the fatherland intact. Many have mingled with the victorious peoples, whose laws and customs they've adopted; many remain indifferent and only live in their egotism. Cosaques with the Cosaques, Moroccans with the Moroccans, Mongrels with the Mongrels, Tunisians with the Tunisians, French with is, they don't belong to any people; they are only linked to us by blood. Their king, their duty and their fatherland is their self-interest. For their self-interest, they all betray their brothers. The number of the faithful, of true believers, is tiny.

"That's why we've always been defeated in our attempts to revolt; that's why we're still serfs and slaves; that's why we hide ourselves here. This is the government of France; you know that now, Mr. Daghestan, for you have seen it—but that government has been unable until now to do anything but maintain the traditions of our forefathers in the tunnels beneath Little Paris, in the catacombs...at the gates of Figuig."

The Queen added the last remark with superb disdain. I had lowered my head at that moment, listening with a religious silence to the Queen's words, which charmed me.

"It's time to go, my friend," she said, pointing with her finger at a small hourglass that I had not yet noticed.

"Already, Madame!" I replied, swiftly looking at my watch, which told me that the Queen was right.

"Oh, you'll come back," she added. "You'll come back here—but only when I ask you to, because, in order to receive you, we need to take precautions. The future of an entire people is at stake. I fear that your movements might be noticed and followed—but I won't let your curiosity languish for long, be sure of that.

"As, moreover, you want to learn, and I also want you to be informed. Johan will be at your disposal to take you, not only around Figuig, which is not difficult to explore, but throughout ancient France, if you wish. You'll remember then the visions of your magnetic trance, and you'll be able to reconstruct on all the ruins you see what you've seen in dreams, and that which your ancestors built in their time."

She offered her forehead for me to kiss and squeezed my hand, "Go, my friend. Mr. Falster is beginning to get impatient; he's waiting for you on the Administration bridge."

I opened the door to the cellar then—but a little too quickly, it seemed, for I perceived that I had almost bumped into Johan-Ali-Schahpohtink, who was standing directly outside. He looked at me with a piercing gaze that was not at all reassuring, revealing an abyss of anguish in the depths of his heart that sent black vapors all the way to his facial features. The Queen undoubtedly perceived it, for her eyes darted a spark at him that caused him to lower his head and set his face straight.

"Johan," she said to him, "you have the confidence of the Queen and the Council; would you please escort the friend of the tribe to the palace and then come back. We'll wait for you." She turned back to me. "Mr. Daghestan, our Council and our brother Johan offer you their services whenever and for as much time as you please. Tomorrow if you wish, my aerostat will be at your disposal to make your scientific expeditions—which, we hope, will work to the advantage of our tribe..."

Nhohelle was a truly a Queen is speaking thus: great dignity and an authoritative tone adorned all her words. I was gripped by it; I was also vividly impressed by the memory of what I have heard in the Queen's cellar, and the fine spectacle of the old men that I had before my eyes, in national costume—the picturesque costume with its jacket of shaggy hide, tightened at the waist, and the trousers, also made of hide but short-haired, and broad, tightened by something akin to gaiters of the same cloth up to the knees. Their heads were coiffed in fox-fur bonnets, on which long tails had been left, which hung down their backs. They had full beards, and almost all of them were as white as snow.

I bowed profoundly to the Queen, then to the Council, and left, following Johan.

We didn't take the same route that we had followed the first time, but, as Nhohelle had instructed, we took the route to the Queen's palace, which led us via indescribable detours, illuminated by the lugubrious light of the torch that my guide was carrying.

We finally came into the sunlight; we were in the middle of the palace that I knew so well by virtue of having been offered, on my first arrival, the cruel hospitality of its prison.

"Thank you, Johan," I said to my guide then. "I believe that I can find my way on my own now, and rejoin my friends."

XL. MHOSKOW

I arrived just in time, for Falster was in mortal anguish. The time for my return had passed; he was, as the Queen had said, standing on the Administration Bridge, peering into the distance as far as he could, cursing the stupidity of my confidence. As soon as he perceived me he ran toward me.

"Ah, finally!" he cried, with a profound sigh of relief, accosting me and squeezing my hands as if to crush them.

"No reproaches, my friend," I said. "My stroll has been very pleasant, and the people of that tribe are not the barbarians you think."

Then I told him about all the incidents of my excursion—omitting, of course, anything that might compromise the secret I had sworn to keep, whose gravity I fully understood. Such as it was, however, my narration appeared to give infinite pleasure to Falster, for Falster is a true philosopher, who likes to study the mores of all peoples.

"Tomorrow," I said to him, "I shall recommence my travels and my studies, if you have no objection."

"Be wise and prudent," he replied. "No, I have no other objection to your voyages than anxiety for your safety, which does not appear to me to be very solidly based on the hood faith of your new friends. However, as I know that you're desirous of learning, and I also know that all the discoveries you make will be in very good hands, I admit that I'd be very sorry to see some danger arising to stop you on your route."

"If these voyages, my friend," trembling internally that he might accept, because of his excessive prudence, which might have been a hindrance to me, "aren't agreeable to you..."

"Oh, no, no!" he replied, swiftly, interrupting the invitation I was about to make. "I'm not afraid...you can't suspect that, at least?" He looked at me with flashing eyes. "But I'd rather hear you talk. Ruins have no other attractions for me than those of memories. I don't like digging in the ground to find old broken pots, bits of rusty iron and a few stumps of statues. It's sufficient for me to know that all that is, and has been something, to set my philosophy to work...

"Then again, what holds me back even more—the true motive, my friend, that keeps me here, abandoning you to yourself—is my brother. I owe him my society, my advice and the consolations of my friendship in his misfortune. I don't want to leave him for an instant in the pain that he's trying to disguise, but must have in the depths of his heart. You go, go alone, whenever and as many times as you wish; I'll take responsibility for justifying your excursions to King Rhaman's court and to my brother."

"Tomorrow, then, my friend," I told Falster, "I'll depart again at daybreak. I have a rendezvous for tomorrow—but this time, don't worry; peace has been made, even with Johan, and I'll come back when I've seen what I want to see. In any case, I'll never be absent for more than a day."

The rest of the day was employed in paying my respects to King Belt, in chatting with him and Falster about the country we were living in, and the various little adventures that had befallen us. We had a long discussion about history and antiquity, especially about France, and we offered the king more than one occasion to open his book of prophecies.

I made my notes afterwards, and the time that remained to me was employed in ferreting around in all the nooks and crannies of the palace, to find what Falster called old broken pots, old pieces of iron and the stumps of statues.

The next day, I was not the last to rise in the Palace of Administration, but this time Falster was not asleep, and had not seemed to be asleep when I woke up. When I went to open the door, very quietly in order not to disturb him, he looked at me, and, putting his arms out of bed, extended his hands toward me, in which he pressed mine.

"Have a good trip, my friend," he said. "Come back as soon as possible, your heart full of what you've seen, and your lips as fluent as usual. See you soon!"

And I went out.

A great embarrassment stopped me at the doorway of the palace, however. Where should I go? We had agreed to make a few excursions, but I didn't recall having fixed a meeting-place.

"Bah!" I said, shaking my head determinedly. "Let's go. Since it's Johan who has to guide me, let's go to Johan's house." And I took the same route that I had taken the previous day, intending to go knock on Johan's door. I didn't need to do that, though; when I arrived at the bridge where I had found Cheorchek, I found Johan, who was finishing setting up the balloon that was to transport us. At first, however, I doubted that it was for us.

"Ah!" I said to him, with a hint of disappointment. "I was just coming to fetch you from your hut, in order to take the voyage we planed yesterday."

"Well, I'm waiting for you," he replied, a trifle dryly, "in accordance with the information you gave the Queen."

"Me, Johan! But I haven't seen the Queen since yesterday, and I haven't said anything to her."

"The Queen told me yesterday evening, however, that you'd be here at sunrise," Johan replied, softening his voice slightly.

I didn't want to argue with him anymore; my only response was summarized in a gesture of surprise that seemed to convince him, so natural was it. For myself, I understood perfectly that my pretty witch always had an eye and an ear open to discover the most hidden secrets, and that it was not impossible that her Père Franco had overheard my conversation the with Falster the day before and had relayed it to his protégée. Quite naturally, then, the Queen had deduced that I was bound to go to the center of her tribe to meet the cicerone she had put at my disposal.

In response to Johan's invitation I climbed into his balloon, and we departed. We traversed Figuig in a flash. I understood from our speed that my guide had a destination in mind, at which he wanted to arrive as soon as possible.

My own objective as not to go quickly but to see, so I stopped him. "Johan, my friend," I said to him, with all the mildness of a supplicant, "would it displease you to hold your balloon over Figuig—in the center of the city, if you can? I'd like to see the city as a whole."

Johan obliged with good grace, and retraced his steps. "Here it is," he said to me, maintaining his aerostat immobile.

"Here!" I said, amazed, although I ought to have expected such a panorama. "This is the capital of New Cosaquia, Figuig! But where's the city, then?"

"Look hard," Johan replied, ironically, "and you'll see what the Cosaques make of cities." And he waved his hand to indicate the vast forest that extended beneath us.

I perceived clearings filled with huts at intervals in the midst of the tall trees. All the clearings were linked to one another by roads, on the edges of which there were a few huts—not counting those that I could not see and which were, my guide told me, dispersed in the woods.

From that height I could embrace in a single glance the various palaces that I knew and a few others that I had not yet seen. I could also follow the course of the long pond that I had crossed several times, and which I saw extending into the distance, in the woods and fields above and below the capital of New Cosaquia. But I could see nothing else, nothing that advertised the life of an inhabited city, nothing that advertised anything but annihilation and desolation.

The ground was not entirely level; the disposition of the trees and the undulation of their foliage indicated as much. There were mountains, valleys and hills, probably formed by the debris of the old Paris that had to be there, covered by a little more or a little less earth, according to the caprices of its devastation by the barbarians, time and the intestinal revolutions of the ground.

I was sad and downcast, as in the face of a catastrophe that had struck my property. In order to console myself a little I strove to excavate the memories of my magnetic visions, but I could not reconstruct anything in the midst of that chaos.

"Let's go," I said to Johan, sadly, when I emerged from my funereal contemplations. What is there to do here?"

Our balloon immediately resumed the route that he had interrupted, and in the blink of an eye we found ourselves above a village in which I understood that Johan wanted to stop, fort he slowed the balloon down and caused it to circle indecisively, as if he were waiting for my assent.

"Where are we?" I asked him.

"A few leagues from Figuig: the village of Moskhow, the principal Cosaque village in the vicinity of the capital."

"Can we land here?" I asked.

"We can if you wish, Mr. Daghestan," Johan replied, with a disguised joy that I could read in his eyes, "for we're at peace with the Cosaques of this village."

We landed, therefore.

Moskhow is, as my guide had said, a few leagues from Figuig, on the opposite side to Little Paris, from which it is separated by the capital. The village seemed quite considerable to me, but the huts did not have the naïve elegance or even the tidiness of the huts of the French tribe. Some of them were separated from one another by bushes and trees, but most of them were made up very simply of long wooden hangars covered with brushwood and heather. At intervals, partitions divided up the length of the hangar and formed compartments appropriate to the needs of each family. They were long caravanserais divided up as everyone desired but devoid of artistry and taste—and wretched in their effect.

The most horrible untidiness reigned everywhere, and spread unhealthy odors far and wide. The population was puny, sickly and feverish. The children—who were not, as in Little Paris, busy with the cares of the tribe—were mostly scrofulous and deformed.

In that tribe, work is not, as among the French, in honor and flourishing, so the fields are badly cultivated, with poor yields. The Cosaques, in any case, live by hunting and marauding rather than work. Commerce is not, however entirely neglected by them; they trade with neighboring tribes and the nearest peoples, but it is of scant importance, like the products they have to exchange.

Their marriage, unlike that of the French, is indissoluble. Each man may marry several wives, which does not prevent the sanctity of marriage from not being respected. Neither the husbands nor their wives hold tight to the fidelity of their contract, but the most savage conflicts are seen among them on such occasions, and the cruelest murders.

"They have laws," Johan told me, who very obligingly informed me as to these mores, "but people observe them as they wish. Their chiefs are impotent to compel respect for them. Their crimes and misdemeanors are, moreover, the responsibility of their tribunals, as among us, so long as they do not infringe any communal laws, and I can assure you"—Johan smiled disdainfully—"that very few are referred to Figuig, so little does good King Rhaman care about them."

"Is that a reproach or a compliment that you're addressing to your king?" I asked Johan. "Is he a hard master to you?"

"No," Johan relied, seriously. "I admit that, conscientiously. The king is a gentle master to us, and we wouldn't complain about him if we weren't his slaves."

"His slaves, you say? But don't you have your own laws, your own mores, even your own government?"

"That's true, but we're slaves; we're obliged to give the king a part of our produce and our labor. If he needs domestic help, he demands it from us, and we can't refuse. The service of his palaces, his lands, we owe to him by virtue of our serfdom. We owe him everything for his person: our arms, our food, our rest, our lives, still be virtue of our serfdom. He has the right of life and death over us, because we're vanquished, and enslaved..."

Johan became animated as he talked, and I saw his words becoming hateful and malevolent. I wanted to draw him on to another topic of conversation, more interesting to me, and I succeeded in that, in uttering an exclamation that was quite natural, which had been provoked by the sight of a monument that I certainly had not expected to find there.

We had taken a few steps on the ground while chatting, as Johan was searching for a place to attach his balloon. On going around a clump of trees and bushes, which had until then hid the scene that appeared before us at that moment, I had just seen the portal of an artistically magnificent monument, well-preserved in spite of the degradations to which the stupidity of the Cosaques had subjected it in order to adapt it to their needs.

The portal in question was vast, grandiose and charged with a sculpture admirable in its purity and elegance. It was filled up to about a third of its height with debris of various sorts, but remained allowed the deduction of the height it must once have attained. The edifice to which it gave entrance was no longer tall; destruction had afflicted it, but as the buildings were useful to the Cosaques they had repaired it after their fashion. Pieces of wood, bizarrely interwoven, continued the building to a certain height. The summit was enclosed by the eternal covering of the tribe's habitations: brushwood, heather and the branches of all kinds of flexible trees. Two other portals of lesser dimension most have existed on either side of the principal one, but nothing remained of them but fragments of the superior arches.

"It's magnificent," I said to Johan, who had said nothing, and was smiling in satisfaction as he watched me admiring that almost divine architecture.

"That's how our ancestors built," he replied, with flashing eyes. "Let's go in—this is where we're going."

"What! This is where we're going?" I said to him, with astonishment.

He bit his lip. He understood that he had allowed me to divine too easily that he had premeditated our voyage.

I followed him without anxiety, however, curious to see the interior of a monument that displayed the remains of such artistic richness externally. Alas, there was nothing to be seen inside for a lover of the fine arts.

The monument served as the abode of the principal chiefs of the Cosaques, who had appropriated it for their service—which is to say that they had despoiled it utterly. They had established an upper floor there. The ground floor was for them and their mounts; the upper floor served as a granary, where they stored the results of their foraging, their crops and objects designated for trade.

In the French tribe, people travel by means of aerostats; among the Cosaques, the Moroccans and the other peoples of the region, they make use of red deer and reindeer, which they domesticate with a great deal of patience and skill. Bulls and cows serve for heavy haulage, as among us.

Johan introduced himself into the abode of the Cosaque chiefs with all the familiarity of a regular visitor. We were received with great cordiality, but my entire person was inspected minutely. A brief discussion, in a language I did not understand, was established between them, after which, each of them smiled at me in amity—which gave me to understand that I had been its subject.

One of the chiefs detached himself from the little circle then and, coming to stand in front of me, bowed his head profoundly. He was the supreme chief. His costume was similar to that of the others, his supremacy only being indicated by the three horses' tails that were attached to the back of his head-dress. Some of the other chiefs sported two, others only one, according to their rank; those who were not ranked had none.

The head-dresses worn by all those men are round and made of animal-hide, thus resembling a perfectly-rounded toque. The most ornate are bordered by a little strip of fur, variable according to taste. The edging of the chiefs is always made from brightly-colored feathers interwoven with sufficient artistry not to be unpleasant to the eyes, even of a foreigner. That edging is forbidden to all the other members of the tribe.

Their upper body is covered by a small mantle with broad sleeves, tightened at the wrist. The rest of the body is clad in trousers, intensively creased about the legs, at the bottom of which it is tightened by a hem. The garment comes up to the armpits, where they are fastened by two straps that serve as braces.

The costume of the women is slightly different; the trousers only come up to the waist and the mantle is replaced by a long and broad piece of cloth, in which they envelop themselves rather gracefully. On their heads they wear tall pointed bonnets, which they decorate with flowers, leaves, tree-branches or even herbs, according to the season and their caprices.

That, at least, is what I learned from Johan, for I did not have the good luck to see any women at close range. I didn't see any at all in the chiefs' dwelling; they had probably been sent away—which proved to me that we were expected, as I strongly suspected, and that our visit was significant, for it appears that the people of the West have a habit of sending their women away when there is serious business to conduct.

All of that seemed so trivial to me that I did not seek to get to be bottom of it at the time. I was fully occupied mourning the profanation of the beautiful monument that I had just entered, while trying to discover some architectural beauty that the devastation had neglected.

Meanwhile, Johan was examining me very attentively; my preoccupation seemed to please him. So he invited me, in the name of his hosts, to visit all the parts of the monument without any hindrance. I did so, in their company, but I saw nothing, or almost nothing, but stables full of animals, granaries filled with hay and dry leaves and lodgings little better than the stables. The architecture was fractured and disfigured, and what appeared to remain was hidden under straw and household utensils.

My visit did not last long. It was slightly prolonged, however, when we reached the extremity of the building, for I took a great deal of pleasure in what I saw there. There was a small platform that had not been soiled by the ineptitude of the Cosaques; perhaps that was because they needed it to remain as it was. The debris of some marble statues was heaped up in one corner, where it served as a point of support for wooden beams, which propped up a few stones in danger of falling. Those items of debris were still beautiful, and above all, very visible. They were near what were evidently tombs, for the little monuments there had the form that ancient history tells us. Portions of funerary inscriptions could still be seen on the stone. As they were fairly well conserved, The Cosaques had found it convenient to store the grains of their harvest therein.

These precious relics being of no interest to my cicerone, he left me to my admiring inspection in order to go further on and engage in a very animated conversation with our hosts. When I glanced in that direction momentarily I perceived Johan disappearing gradually, as if he were descending into a cellar.

My curiosity was keenly excited, so, abandoning my statues and my tombs, I went toward him. He was indeed going down; there was a cellar ahead of him, but a very deep cellar, into which I followed him.

Johan immediately turned to face me, without being surprised by my presence—which, on the contrary, he seemed to desire. The Cosaque chiefs were also looking at me with a hint of anxiety. And yet, there was nothing extraordinary there. Personally, I could only see what seemed to me to be a few remains of tombs, and remains devoid of sufficient splendor to make anything vibrate in my heart but the philosophical fiber.

"What individuals are sleeping here?" I asked myself, and asked Johan. "Were they kings, powerful and rich men, benefactors of society, scholars or proud men, heroes of crime and titled ignoramuses?"

Johan could not say.

O humankind! This is where your vanity ends: in oblivion, in forgetfulness. The tombs had surely not been constructed with such an objective.

Were the Cosaques and Moroccans of the early days capable of building such mausolea? I wondered.

I did not have time to resolve that question because, while I was meditating most profoundly, Johan and the Cosaque chiefs suddenly lifted a curtain that hung in front of us and hid the greater part of the cellar's depth, which I had not suspected until then.

It was an arsenal that appeared before us: an arsenal filled with weapons of every sort. There were, in good condition, axes, halberds, scythes of some sort, wooden pikes with iron heads, iron-tipped arrows in vast quantity, bows, slingshots for launching stones; in sum, all the apparatus of war.

"Men who possess all these weapons are invincible," Johan told me, his eyes sparkling with courage and confidence, "if they are brave men. There are more weapons here than there have ever been in all of Figuig."

"And why all these weapons?" I asked him, with a dazed smile full of anxiety.

"Why?" he replied. "Don't far-sighted men create reserves of grain when it's abundant."

"But why amass weapons in such large quantity when one is at peace, and nothing suggests that war is imminent?" I asked, persistently.

"Misers hide their treasures, slaves disguise their strength," he replied, pulling the curtain that prevented me from seeing any more. "Of men of honor," he added, staring at me, "one does not ask an oath that they have seen nothing."

And we went out.

XLI. THE SEBOU

My mind was confused by a thousand different thought. What did Johan want of me? Why had he taken me so precipitately to the Cosaque tribe—once an enemy tribe on which he was now fawning? What was I doing there? What trap was the man still trying to set for me? Having not succeeded in killing me, was he trying to get me killed by the laws of his country? Did he want to render me odious to King Rhaman, my host and protector, by giving me all the appearances of a conspirator?

Johan had doubtless achieved his goal, for he testified a desire to leave that place. I was not opposed to that, so, after having bowed most respectfully and as amicably as possible to our hosts, while Johan said a few words to the that I didn't understand, we returned to our aerostat, into which I climbed, without desiring to see anything more for the moment, and quite ready to return to the Palace of Administration in order to have a discussion with Falster, and the Queen, if possible.

When we were in the balloon, however, Johan said: "You have no desire to see the Cosaque tribe, it seems, Mr. Daghestan, nor the curiosities of their country, so I didn't want to keep you here any longer. As the weather is fine, though, and as we have plenty of time ahead of us, would you like to take advantage of it to go as far the extremities of the kingdom of New Cosaquia? We can go and come back in a matter of hours, thanks to the agility of our balloon."

The proposition was tempting; I accepted. I was curious to know what the extent and strength of the country in question might be, and where its soil was covered in ruins, like Figuig.

The aerostat made rapid progress; I did not call any halt. I was meditating more than gazing. I saw nothing during our journey but collapsed houses at intervals—towns in ruins and forests almost everywhere.

"But where are the inhabitants?" I asked Johan. "Cosaquia isn't deserted, is it?"

"Not entirely," he replied, "but nearly. You can't see the inhabitants because they're lodged in those ruins that you see in every direction, which they've appropriated for their own use. Some have built huts, though, like us, in the middle of forests or on the banks of rivers."

Poor France, I said, silently, leaning my elbows on the rim of the gondola and my head in my hand. *This, then, is what you have become! It was well worth the trouble of building your cities with so much luxury, of extending your commerce so far, of amassing so much wealth, of raising yourself up so high, of being so proud of your name, your glory—in sum, to have worked so hard, suffered so much—for such a future! Hardly anyone knows your name today, nor knows any longer where you were; your king, so great and magnificent, are forgotten; your inhabitants, so luxurious and proud, who dreamed of such a sweet repose, there they are…there! Their bones are there, underneath those disgusting ruins; their wealth is there, underneath those rags; their sensuality is there, in that mud…O France, France! But is it really you?*

"We've arrived," said Johan suddenly, his voice snatching me from my reverie. "Here are the limits of New Cosaquia."

"Oh!" I said, looking around, astonished to see the animation of an inhabited country, especially a frontier region. "And what do you call this city?" I asked Johan.

"It's not a city," he replied, "it's a village—a poor village, in fact, although it's the headquarters of the frontier patrol. It's Sebou.[48]

He stopped the balloon then, and we descended to ground level.

We found ourselves on the bank of a river, whose current was very broad and dotted with sandbanks covered with osier-beds and the stout trunks of poplars. The encasement of the

---

[48] The Sebou is a river in Morocco, the longest in the country.

bed was split at intervals by profound cracks, which had allowed streams of water to establish themselves at their ease in the vicinity, forming ponds that were often dry, or very nearly, in which detritus of all sorts was fermenting in the damp mud. In consequence, the atmosphere is charged throughout the surrounding area, and even some distance away, with fetid and pestilential odors, which occasionally decimate the frail population that inhabits the banks.

That population, moreover, is not very numerous—and also, it must be said, no more industrious than in all the other corners of the region. The ruins of the city, which appear to have existed in olden times—but when?—serve as their retreat, and they are, in truth, well disposed to spare the pains of those idle and ignorant architects.

I don't know whether that city descended as far as the banks of the river where we were; reason says yes but no evidence of it remains today. A short distance behind us, on the other hand, everything indicated that a city had existed there, on a hill, whose slope had a truly picturesque appearance, facing the river. The habitations were grouped in the midst of rocks and hillocks of different heights with the help of an admirable savant art.

Nothing more remains of all that than a few half-collapsed rooms stacked one above another, retained in mid-air by some unknown magic. It is in there that the inhabitants of that new kind of city have found their niche, which they reach sometimes by climbing and sometimes by long and sinuous circuits.

It seemed, moreover, that the people are hardly encouraged to make their dwelling more elegant, harassed as they are by the other peoples of the region, who, no more laborious than they, gladly devote themselves to raiding and pillaging, in order to make a living that they do not take the trouble to obtain in any other way.

"Are there a few members of your tribe here?" I asked Johan.

"A few," he replied, "as there are everywhere, even beyond the frontier; but they're people of our blood, not of the fatherland. If they are pillaged, they also pillage, even their brothers; that barrier makes them enemies."

I shrugged my shoulders disdainfully.

"Let's leave it," I said to Johan. "We have nothing more to see here but the landscape, and these eternal ruins we continually tread beneath our feet. These people are savage, and will probably never be civilized. Let's look instead at the river, which flows with such majesty, carrying its waters to everyone, even beyond the frontiers of your New Cosaquia, as if to give us all a lesson in benevolence and fraternity."

Desirous of extracting my guide from the taciturnity into which he had plunged, I continued: "But what was here? Has the Queen told you anything about that?"

"The Queen," he replied in a tremulous voice. "The Queen...yes, the Queen has told me that there was once a city here, but which has been ruined for centuries, since the invasion of the Cosaques. It was very beautiful, the Queen says, and extended everywhere all around." Johan indicated both banks of the river. "Look—one can still see the remains of walls on the river bed."

My guide was right, as I had already noticed; there were considerable ruins under the water. A few paces from the place where we were standing, the piles of a bridge were visible, disposed symmetrically across the river bed. They were still solidly based, and a great quantity of artistically-carved stoned had accumulated around them, which were undoubtedly the remains of the bridge. In the middle, half-hidden by the sand, blocks of stone and the parasitic plants that had grown everywhere, there was a tall column lying on its side.

I examined that column attentively—as attentively as the continual swaying of our balloon permitted, which Johan, skillful as he was, had difficulty maintaining immobile. Although I could not decipher anything, it did have an inscription on its base—or at least the traces of an inscription, for I could no longer see anything but the grooves of the engraver's chisel.

I had better luck with another block of stone, which did not appear to me to belong to the column, but I wasn't much further forward. The block seemed to be the pedestal of a statue. I was able to transcribe in my notebook, in the order of their inscription, a few letters that it bore, but they taught me nothing more, in spite of the attention I have since devoted to studying them. Here they are:

Den.. ..pin
Invent...r d. .a va.eur,
Né à Bl..s . . 16.7[49]

I would have given ten years of my life to understand that inscription. Such as it was, though, what could it tell me, with an ignorant guide and memories like those we have of France, its history and its language? I interrogated Johan, I interrogated the river and all the debris it inundated...nothing. I could find out anything—and what saddens me the most is that I still know nothing today.

Even the Queen has not told me anything. Why? Magnetism itself has not wanted to tell me anything more. Why?

Being unable to discover anything, I became as sullen as a sulky child, and no longer wanted to occupy myself with the

---

[49] Mettais' readers would have had no difficulty filling in the blanks to spell out the inscription: *Denis Papin, inventeur de la vapeur, né à Blois, 22 août 1647* [Denis Papin, inventor of the steam engine, born in Blois, 22 August 1647]. The statue informs the reader that the village of Sebou is what remains of Blois and that the Sebou used to be known as the Loire. Mettais' desire to incorporate his home town into his future scenario is understandable, but seems inconsistent with the new geography he has established, in which the sea is now not far south of Paris; it is difficult to imagine how that could be the case without the Loire valley being submerged.

inscription, nor with science, nor with research. I abandoned myself entirely to the pleasure of the voyager who looks without thinking.

I no longer occupied myself with anything but contemplating the picturesque spectacle that the river Sebou offered at that place. Its waters, impeded by the almost mountainous barrage of the ruins amassed on its bed, climbed magnificently over their back on one side, to fall in a cascade on the other. It was delightful and grandiose.

"It's beautiful," I said to Johan, peevishly, "but let's go. We only have unintelligible ruins to look at here, and everywhere: everywhere, the degradation of people and things, and no key to open the book. Let's go. I can, at least, say in my memoirs that I've seen the frontier of the kingdom of New Cosaquia; I ask for no more today."

I was mistaken, however, for, in spite of what I said, I was very desirous of seeing more than I had seen. I was only too well aware that there is always much to see and learn on ground as unfortunate as that where we were.

I should have been especially desirous of wandering over the inhabited hills, the rocks that rose up behind us, where I perceived the petrified roots of old giant trees that snaked through the bedrock, foundations of ancient monuments whose remains allowed the divination of a primitive beauty. I should have become even more desirous of touring that picturesque and savage location when Johan had told me that there were more beautiful ruins on the Sebou, the ruins of a palace magical in its position and its decoration, in which the captain of the border guard lived—but nothing retained me, and I suppressed my desires.

Something serious had been on my mind, obsessing me, since our departure from Moskhow. It seemed to me that since then, Johan had become even more thoughtful than usual, and that his reverie was becoming increasingly morose—and that made me anxious.

Without being inappropriately fearful, I nevertheless felt the need to get back to Figuig. A sentiment that I could not

361

define, to which I could attribute no cause, told me that I needed to be there.

"Let's go," Johan said to me resolutely, stepping back into the balloon, which we had left momentarily. "Let's return to Figuig, since that's what you want."

I installed myself precipitately by his side.

"We'll pause for another two minutes a short distance from here, though," my guide added, "in a celebrated place of pilgrimage that I never pass over without stopping."

"All right," I said, briefly, "but that will be our last stop."

XLII. THE PLACE OF PILGRIMAGE

Johan made no reply, but he pressed his machine forcefully, and in ten minutes, still following the river, we arrived in a village composed of a small number of huts set some distance from the water, for fear of floods, which are very frequent. That village is very soundly situated in the middle of several small hills, which are crowned, as everywhere is the region, by forests extending in all directions. A few clearings have been created at intervals for the habitations and cultivated fields necessary to the population's requirements.

Drawing away from the river, after passing over the debris of houses overwhelmed and overloaded with all the evil imprints of time and devastation, we arrived beside a stone wall—yes, I swear, a stone wall!—which was a great rarity and a great magnificence for the village. The blocks were bound together by a mortar of earth.

That wall surrounded a patch of land into which one penetrated by means of an opening that was only closed by a tree-trunk thrown across it. The tree was certainly not there to block a passage that remained almost open in spite of it, but doubtless merely to testify that the patch of land was reserved, and perhaps also to prevent large animals from entering the sacred ground. It was the place of pilgrimage that Johan had mentioned.

That place of pilgrimage has, it appears, been held in great veneration throughout the country, perhaps for centuries. That veneration rests on a legend that certainly has its touching aspect, and which is an article of incontestable faith in the beliefs of the French tribe.

According to the tradition that everyone knows and repeats, a Cosaque once wanted to build his hut there. Scarcely had it been built than it collapsed of its own accord although it seemed solid. He was not deterred; he rebuilt it a second time,

363

and a third, but it always fell, the final time uttering plaintive cries. The Cosaque was afraid then, and went away forever.

A half-breed, and then a Moroccan, both strong-minded, resumed the task, laughing at the Cosaque; they experienced the same catastrophe.

Finally, a Frenchman, mocking the stupid credulity of his predecessors, pitched his tent there resolutely, declaring loudly that he would never build elsewhere. Scarcely was it finished than the hut collapsed very noisily, and its ruins, as if hurled by a furious hand, almost crushed the miscreant, covering him with debris.

The Frenchman's boasting had attracted a crowd while he worked; the crowd proved useful in saving him from almost certain death. From then on he was convinced—and so was everyone else—that the finger of God was there, and that the place ought to be sacred. The king of the French tribe, consulted on that point, told them that the place had once been a cemetery of their ancestors, and told them to restore the tombs and pray for their dead.

The tombs were restored, and on the first evening of their repair all the inhabitants of the village presented themselves there in order to pray—but they stopped some distance away, stupefied by terror and admiration. On each tomb several people were sitting, some dressed in light white robes, others in black ones; they were silent, in an attitude of the most profound meditation. They all had black or white crowns on their heads.

When the inhabitants of the village, having recovered a little boldness, approached to greet the specters, the specters disappeared; then a sound was heard, like that of a stone lid falling back upon them, although no movement could be seen in the tombs.

Since that epoch the terrain had been surrounded by a wall, and few days passed without a woman, young or old, bringing a black or white crown to place on the tombs.

"I've never seen any supernatural apparition here," Johan told me, "but I know that they sometimes still occur. All the people of the village can tell you as much."

At the moment when we went into the funereal terrain, a young woman was depositing a white crown on a tomb, in front of which she remained for some time, with her hands crossed over her breast and her head bowed. She seemed to be praying with the most profound concentration, for the sound of our footfalls did not cause her to turn her head.

I had no crown sat my disposal; I collected a few flowers from the field, which I braided. I made one white crown, and then another of dark hue, and I placed both of them on the same tomb.

"To you, poor father," I whispered, "who have lived in probity for all and love or your own!

"To you, poor maid, who have fallen before your time before the icy breath of death, like a tender flower before the winter wind…you who were the delight of the family and the hope of its old age!

"Rest in peace, and pray for us…for us, who do not know whether we shall ever have a peaceful tomb, to which friends and pious people may come in pilgrimage!"

Johan seemed deeply touched by my sensitivity, but I was mortally sad.

We left, without even glancing at the young woman who was praying, and soon arrived in Figuig. I had not seen anything during the journey; I had left my eyes and my soul in the cemetery at the place of pilgrimage.

XLIII. THE IMPOSSIBLE DEPARTURE

Johan set me down at the Palace of Administration, where I was anxiously awaited. Falster ran to greet me.

"There's news," he said, "and it's serious!"

What Falster told me was, indeed, serious. My visits to the French tribe, which I had not thought I needed to hide from anyone, because they were honest and solely motivated by my curiosity as a voyager and writer, had been denounced as criminal to King Rhaman. The King was in such a state of mind that he was entirely ready to receive the evil impressions of suspicion, and the journey I had just undertaken with Johan had certainly not been calculated to introduce a calming influence into the affair.

Thus, King Belt and his brother had been obliged to argue ardently on my behalf, and thanks to their kindly eloquence, they had contrived—at least, they believed so—to dissipate the storm that had threatened to burst forth. That was good, but it was a stern lesson for me, which Falster made no attempt to soften.

He assured me, however, that the explanations had been frank on both sides, and that at the end of the conversation, the king, in order to demonstrate his satisfaction and confidence in his guests, had invited them to accompany him to his daughter's palace, where he was expected.

That entire scene had taken place immediately after my departure with Johan, and had take place at the Palace of Administration, where King Rhaman had come to visit his guests. Another scene, however—more troubling, in my opinion—had taken place in Ouchda's palace.

The young woman had invited her father to come and take his morning meal with her, with an intention that soon became clear—but there were two witnesses she had not expected, and whom the king did not seem displeased to have.

At the end of the meal, which was brief, since it consisted of nothing but a cup of the precious coffee, in which everyone dipped a few morsels of a hard, dry cake made of ground-apple flour and cooked under ashes, Ouchda suddenly rose to her feet. She went to sit like a spoiled child on her father's knees, embracing him convulsively, indubitably to obtain a favor that would not easily be granted.

The good father, who had doubtless expected some demand of that sort in coming to Ouchda's palace, knew exactly what game his daughter was playing. He started laughing heartily, returning the caresses he received—which seemed a good omen to everyone.

"Speak, Daughter," said Rhaman X to Ouhda. "What you have to ask of your father you may request before his friends." Falster old me that he added, while looking at them with a frank expression: "My friends know all my secrets."

"Even your plans for Johan-Ali-Schahpohtink?" said Ouchda, hesitantly.

"Even my plans for Johan and you."

"Well, Father," the young woman continued, taking her father's head in her hands and planting a long kiss on his forehead, "if you want your little Ouchda to die, marry her to Johan."

The king pushed his daughter gently—very gently—off his knees, then got up and placed his plump hands on the young woman's shoulders. "And if my daughter," he said, "wants to see her father fall from his throne and die under the yataghans of his subjects, she won't marry Johan."

Then, turning to King Belt and his brother, Rhaman X seemed to be asking with his gaze for them to approve what he said. The situation was delicate; King Belt and his brother replied with a ambiguous pantomime that attempted to satisfy everyone.

Ouchda said nothing more; she remained sad and thoughtful. No one, in fact, replied, so a profound silence fell within the little assembly. King Belt was the first to break it, with a proposition that was completely expected at that moment.

"My brother," he said to King Rhaman, "we know all your plans, since you have done us the honor of communicating them to us. I hope that they will satisfy everyone. It would be good, in any case, if you were to have the sole merit for your resolutions in everyone's eyes; I would be very sorry, personally, if anyone were to suspect that we had suggested them to you. Do you not think, therefore, my brother, that it would be good if we, your guests, were to make a short voyage, either in your own lands, or those of your neighbors, while you do what needs to be done here?"

"You may do as you wish, my brother," King Rhaman replied. "Since you wish to leave, I will give orders for an aerostat to be placed at your disposal, and men to guide it."

King Belt's proposal, unexpected as it was, did not appear to be unwelcome, since it was accepted immediately. King Rhaman has received too brilliant a hospitality in Zeeland for him not to strive to render his own as gracious, and he had done that thus far; in spite of his reconciliation with me, however, my visits to the French, and the amity with which they had welcomed me, were undoubtedly still on his mind. He knew that he could only gain their support by making unprecedented concessions to them.

Falster and I could see no other motive that might explain the king's eagerness to seize upon that proposal, which had fallen into his lap so unexpectedly, for it was clearly understood that, even though I was not there at that moment, the permission to travel was for all three of us.

Ouchda seemed distressed by that. Perhaps it seemed to her, Falster suggested to me, maliciously, that she was losing intelligent protectors in us, on whose support she might have been counting greatly in her difficult position. She remained mute; she had completely lost the graciousness and assurance that she had shown a moment before.

"So," said Falster after he had told me the whole story, "we're going to leave Figuig; it's settled."

That news, I confess, was devastating for me. Although I had been obliged to expect it someday, I had not expected it so soon, and I was not at all prepared for it.

"Well then, we'll leave," I replied to Falster, with a little ill-humor that was critical of King Belt. "We'll go to the ends of the earth, if you wish, since your brother has made the decision."

"Voyages don't please you any more, then?" said Falster, shaking my hand, to calm the fit of irritation that emerged in my words. "Or have you forgotten that we're only traveling within New Cosaquia—your France—and will probably return here in a few days?"

"When are we leaving?" I asked Falster, with all the anxiety of a questioner who fears bed news.

"Tomorrow," he replied.

"Tomorrow it is, then!" I said, dryly. "I'll be ready."

The precipitation of that departure, arranged without my knowledge, had pricked my sensitivity to the quick. Falster was not so blind as not to have seen that; so, from then on, he was perfectly amiable toward me—even obsessive, for he affected not to want to abandon me, even though I wanted to be left alone.

Alone, I would have wandered in the direction of Little Paris; I would have summoned up my memories there; I would have sought new impressions, and perhaps I would have hoped to see individuals in that vicinity that it would have been very agreeable to me to see, since we were leaving.

We were leaving on a little journey, a journey of short duration, Falster said—but who knows where one is going, when one is going into a desert? Who can tell when one will return, or is one will return, when one is traveling in the midst of barbarians? Thus, I wanted to say my farewells.

We were received that evening at the Royal Palace, where we went to take our leave of the king. We were received with all the usual cordiality, and there was only a single glance more doubtful than the rest in which I thought I could detect that I was under suspicion. That glance was, however, informative to me.

So, when I got back to my hut, I made my preparations to leave as if I were never to return, and sat down to write a letter of farewell to the Queen.

Falster left me to it; he leaned nonchalantly in the doorway of the hut, on the threshold of which he was breathing in the perfumed evening air.

My letter to the Queen was scarcely begun when I felt a tap on my shoulder. I turned round, but Falster was still in the same position; he was not moving, and did not appear to have moved. I returned to work, convinced that my friend was in a good mood and wanted to tease me with some mischief. That was not the case, for a second tap on my shoulder caused me to turn my head swiftly, and this time I saw quite clearly a hand emerge from a light white cloud and invite me to follow it.

I recognized the hand without difficulty, although I could not see the old man's white-haired head, and I therefore followed it.

"I'll be back shortly." I said to Falster, with an emotion that I had difficulty in mastering.

I left the Palace of Administration, and marched straight ahead, without knowing where I was going, but convinced that as long as I didn't feel the old man's hand weighing upon me to stop me, I should keep walking. I still couldn't see him.

The air was calm, and a profound silence reigned around me throughout the forest. The moon sent enough light through the tall trees for me not to be in complete darkness. I didn't go across the pond; nothing pushed me that way. I went forward, without knowing why, through the trees I found to my right, searching for an unknown for which I was hoping with all the faculties of my heart.

I did not have to go far before reaching my goal, for at a bend in the path I was following I suddenly found myself face to face with the Queen.

"I'll wait for you tomorrow," she said, "at the eighth hour of the morning, at the telegraph post. You know it. You also know the password: Jehovah."

"But tomorrow, Madame," I replied, in a voice quavering with emotion, "We'll be leaving earlier than that."

"You shan't leave tomorrow!" she said.

She disappeared as she spoke those words, with lightning rapidity. And I had said nothing to her! But I had wanted to talk to her…there were so many things I had to say to her! So I launched myself after her—but I could not follow her far.

I plunged into the trees where I thought I had seen her disappear. My efforts were not in vain—at least, I thought so—for I soon caught sight of her again, advancing through the bushes, in the midst of which she was walking on a barely-perceptible path, but which she was following with perfect assurance. I hastened my steps, and in response the noise I made, she turned toward me, uttering a little cry.

It wasn't the Queen; it was Ouchda.

"Are you avoiding me?" Ouchda said.

"Why do you say that, Madam?" I replied, gripping the hand that she offered to me in both of mine.

"I learned that you had come back, and immediately sent a slave to tell you that I was waiting for you in my palace, but you didn't come."

"I haven't seen your slave, Madame; I swear it on my honor!"

"If no one obeys me any longer, it's because I've been betrayed," the young woman said. "I didn't think that my slave had betrayed me, though—I thought you had forgotten me, Mr. Daghestan…and I was wandering here on my own, seeking a means to see you, for I wanted to see you."

She raised her head abruptly, after a momentary pause, and said, abruptly: "In Caucasia, sir, is a woman who offers herself to a man as a slave despised? Here, it's a courage that is admired, often a virtue that is respected."

"Among us, that woman is not despised, Madame," I relied to the king's daughter, without thinking about the gravity
of what I was saying.

"Well then, let's go," she said, resolutely. "I'm your
slave."

Ouchda was speaking frankly; I had great difficulty replying in the same way. So I stood there momentarily as if
stunned by that point-blank gunshot. I pulled myself together,
though, after a brief silence.

"Madame, I said to her, "your proposal touches me intimately and honors me, but you know that I'm not free; I'm
under an obligation to King Belt, who has accepted my services in his great misfortune, and I'm only free to leave this
land with him, and with the aid of the king, your father."

"You're mistaken, sir," Ouchda replied, firmly. "You're
no longer under any obligation to King Belt, who will be traveling under my father's auspices, and we can leave without the
aid of King Rhaman. I have two fine mounts at home—
exceedingly rapid gazelles, which are waiting for us. I had not
counted on an aerostat, which might not be available to me. A
few leagues from here we'll reach the sea, and then a ship that
will take us wherever you wish. I have enough jewels to pay
for our transport."

"I'm no longer hesitant, Madame," I replied, with ever-
increasing embarrassment, "but permit me to think tonight
about the preparations for our flight."

"But you're leaving tomorrow!" Ouchda cried, despair-
ingly, "and I'll be married to Johan in a matter of days."

"I won't leave tomorrow, even if King Belt leaves, and
Johan will never be your husband!" I said, with a firmness that
convinced the young woman.

She threw herself at my feet like a devoted slave then, in
order to kiss them, but I raised her to her feet immediately,
and, confused by the fervor of her abnegation, I hugged her to
my bosom and covered her with ardent kisses, which were
perhaps not solely inspired by the amity resulting from her
confidence.

We separated then, she apparently satisfied by my promise, while I was extremely discontented with the impossible situation in which she had placed me. How, in fact, could I get out of it? I had no idea, in truth. I had probably promised more than it was I my power to deliver. I was counting to some extent, it's true, on unforeseen circumstances, and it was permissible for me to count on them, since the Queen had said that I would not be leaving the following day.

XLIV. THE MORNING OF A REVOLUTION

The next day, however, shortly after we got up, a magnificent aerostat, crewed by two men, descended into the courtyard of the Palace of Administration. It was small, though—so small that only three people could be easily accommodated within it, and it required a steersman. The larger aerostats were not in working order, the French workers told us—the only thing they had been instructed to say.

At that moment, I began to acquire a confidence in the Queen's assertion that I had almost lost—but I lost it again when I saw another balloon arriving, the same size as the first,

It was settled, then; I was about to leave. Poor Ouchda! What would she think of me? As for me, what was I to think of the Queen at that moment? She had deceived me, deceived me basely—but why? *Oh!* I said to myself, with the discontentment of an ousted fop. *She's jealous!*

I looked around for Ouchda; I could not see her. Nor could I see the Queen. There was nothing to prevent my departure. Slowly, I climbed into my balloon...but I did climb into it...nothing caused us to pause.

We took off.

King Belt's balloon flew away rapidly; ours was following close behind when we suddenly heard our machine emit a dry click. An important spring had just snapped, and our aerostat veered sideways. I shouted to Falster, whose balloon rapidly came back to ours, anxiously.

"Oh, it's nothing," my guide told me, "but I can no longer steer the balloon because the machine's broken down. We'll repair it."

"We'll wait for you, my friend," said King Belt.

"No, Master," I replied. "Continue your journey, as far as the frontier of you wish, and we'll rendezvous at the town of Sebou."

"Very well, we'll wait for you there," said King Belt, while we retraced our steps.

We didn't go into the Palace of Administration, however; in spite of its broken spring, our balloon headed straight for Little Paris, where we came down.

It was eight o'clock in the morning. The Queen had not deceived me, therefore, and I began to hope that I might not have deceived Ouchda either.

"Johan-Ali-Schahpohtink is waiting for you," my guide said, pointing to Johan's hut, which I recognized easily, while the aerostat took off again.

At that moment, Johan appeared before me, smiling at me as graciously as he could.

"The Queen was right, was she not, Mr. Daghestan," he said, "when she told you that you wouldn't be leaving us to-day. She's waiting for you...."

Meanwhile, we took the same route as before, and I was escorted into the same cellars in the catacombs.

The first of the cellars was full of armed men, and when the door opened, the light that spilled out into the neighboring corridors showed me that I had passed between two ranks of men armed to the teeth, like those in the cellar.

This time, my friend, I was afraid, for I understood that there was a terrible threat of death there. The same old men that I had already seen, the Elders of the Council, in full national costume, like those surrounding them, were there again, around the marble table, on which an iron cross, the symbol of their God, was lying—the only sign of religion that I had been able to glimpse among them.

The deepest silence reigned in the midst of that crowd. I could see that they were anxiously awaiting some great event.

If I had been less overwhelmed by that strange spectacle, perhaps I would have been able to be less afraid, for profound nods of the head were made to me by all the Elders.

I had scarcely arrived at the door of the second cellar— the royal cellar—than the door opened. It was resplendent with light. The Queen was there, alone, also clad in her na-

375

tional costume, with a beautiful white plume on her hat, as on feast-days. She had a golden cross on her breast, as a badge of dignity.

When I arrived, she came toward me and said to me, in a tone of indescribable affability, while offering me her hand: "Be welcome, Mr. Daghestan. We've been waiting for you with great anxiety."

"Me, Madame?" I said, in astonishment.

"Yes, you," the Queen replied, sitting down and drawing me toward her. "Listen to me; I have important things to tell you. The elite of our tribe is here; you've seen them; others are in their huts, in the tunnels, all armed as those are.

"Well, all those men no longer want to be slaves; they want to cultivate their land, which is theirs, freely, and wrench it from foreign hands. They can do it; the Cosaque tribe is with us. You've seen them; they know you too, and at the present moment, they're ready, as we are.

"Our forces are therefore considerable, and our weapons..." The Queen suddenly opened a door that I had not seen before, which let me see a vast cavern filled with ancient weapons—cannon, mortars, helmets and breastplates—before which I stood, utterly amazed, for I was seeing what I had not seen before, and for which I had not dared to hope.

"What a wealth of art and antique curiosities!" I exclaimed, involuntarily. "The French of old must, therefore, have had these terrible engines of destruction, which our modern times believed they had invented! No, no—there's nothing new under the sun; the wisdom of our proverbs is correct."

"Well, sir," the Queen ad to me, "these arms have been left to us by our ancestors in order to break our slavery. But how are they used?" The Queen's tone became coaxing. "You know that, Mr. Daghestan—you, a scholar, a man of the same civilization as our ancestors. Tell us how to operate the weapons that shoot thunderbolts. Just one of those cannon would suffice, one of our oracles has said, to destroy an entire army of Cosaques."

"Madame," I replied, smiling at her naivety, "these weapons can't be used instantaneously. They're old, probably corroded by rust; they're no longer good for anything but a museum."

"You're mistaken, sir; we've found them in the excavations, badly damaged, it's true, but our workers have cleaned them and repaired them as best they could they can still be used, believe me."

"Even if they were usable, Madame, they couldn't function alone. Their thunderbolts won't explode without the aid of gunpowder. You have no gunpowder, and I can't manufacture it."

"Very well," said the Queen, bitterly, closing the door of her arsenal discontentedly. "You're right, Mr. Daghestan; we'll put these weapons in our museums. Our own weapons will doubtless suffice for the brave..."

Her features softened, having been briefly darkened by disappointment. "You doubtless understand me, Mr. Daghestan; you understand that the day of reparation and justice has arrived for us, and that we're armed to take back our wealth. Would you like to join us? Would you like to help us to expel the enemy that oppresses us, to cast down those miserable huts that dishonor our soil, to dig down in the earth to rediscover the foundations of our monuments and our palaces, and rebuild them, to seek out the bones of our ancestors and renew the tombs that barbarity has soiled? Would you, a civilized man, like to lend us the illumination of your science and your strength for the reconstitution of our fatherland?" With a dignity and a authoritarian tone that made me feel very small, the Queen continued: "Would you like to be King of France, Mr. Daghestan?" After a moment's silence, as if talking to herself, she added: "Johan is unworthy of me."

I did not reply immediately. I was wondering what response to make.

"Think about it, Mr. Daghestan," the Queen said to me, gravely. "You're free, at any rate."

The permission to withdraw seemed very welcome to me at that moment, because I needed to get my thoughts in order. It seemed monstrous to me to have come to Figuig to dethrone my host and the friend of my friends, and yet the Queen...

Under the influence of that latter sentiment, I took her hand and kissed it very ardently.

The door of the cellar had just opened, and Johan was on the threshold, awaiting his sovereign's orders. I was momentarily distressed to have been caught in that attitude, which would have been perfectly permissible in Caucasia, but of whose significance in New Cosaquia I was unaware, especially in the presence of a jealous fiancé.

"Take Mr. Daghestan back, Johan," said the Queen, with a calm dignity that her fiancé did not appear to me to have.

The crowd opened before me silently, as on my arrival— except that I heard in the distance of the tunnels voices that were saying in a sinister tone: "We so swear!" They were swearing, no doubt, on the cross that I had seen on the Elders' table

I was not yet out of the tunnel when I saw the torches go out. Several hands seized me then from behind, others stifled my cries and I was stabbed by several thrusts of a yataghan. I fell, bathed in my own blood, and lost consciousness completely.

What happened around me then? Who came to my aid? I don't know...

I only came round again in my fatherland, on the shore of the Black Sea.

What about my friends? My beloved Falster, what became of him? And Ouchda? Poor Ouchda! And the Queen? And that beautiful land of France, so disfigured—what has become of it?

Oh, if only the Queen had given me time! If only the assassins hadn't interrupted my reflection with their brutal attack!

Well, what would I have done?

In truth, I have no idea...

XLV. THE LATEST NEWS

Caucasian Gazette
Caucasipol, 2 Messidor 5001

I regret to inform our readers that our friend Daghestan, in sending the last pages he has written about his voyage to New Cosaquia, has warned us that he will not be able to continue his story here for some time. His wounds, aggravated by the assiduous work to which he had devoted himself in order not to interrupt his narration, have become very painful again.

I have no reason to think that his aggravation of his suffering is dangerous. It is, however, a misfortune that I deplore sincerely, firstly for our friend, and secondly for ourselves, who will be unable to learn even more by listening to the confidences of our savant voyager—for I have no doubt, myself, that he would have revealed to us many of the marvels he has seen, of which we know nothing as yet.

Even though I do not expect a complete history of ancient France at present, given the limited time that our friend spent in the ruins, without digging, and the fact that he only obtained a bird's eye view of the region, I am convinced that his reliable gaze saw more than he has said, and that we have more to learn.

Let us be patient; it will, I hope, only be a delay, of which we can take advantage by turning our eyes and ears westwards. To see and hear what is coming and might yet come from that direction. The final words of Daghestan's story have greatly excited my curiosity, as, I think, they have excited everyone's...

I too am wondering, like our friend Daghestan, what has become of that beautiful land of ancient France, the ruin that is known as New Cosaquia. Was the revolution that was in preparation there carried through? Was it successful? Was it suppressed? Our communications with that country are too slow and too difficult for us to know anything yet. Then again, will we discover anything? That poor country counts for so little in the social balance, who will worry about it? It is so disagreeable to visit, if one is not a Daghestan, who will go there in order to tell us what is happening? No one, at any rate, is coming out...

Let us, then, wait and see...

Our newspaper was printed when we received the following important news, which we communicated immediately to our friend Mr. Daghestan, who will be more interested in it than anyone else, to judge from what we have read thus far.

Via Zeeland, night service.

Trevig, 30 Prairial

Figuig, the capital of New Cosaquia, is in full insurrection. The tribe of the French, which set itself at the head of the movement, has triumphed. King Rhaman X is in prison, awaiting judgment by the Council of Elders.

The news coming by way of Poland is more positive.

Warsaw, 3 a.m.

A revolution has taken place within the last few days in Figuig. Nhohelle Merlhukeck has been proclaimed queen under the name of Nhohelle II. New Cosaquia has resumed the name of France, and its capital that of Paris.

Warsaw, 30 Prairial, 10 p.m.

Nhohelle II, assisted by her Council of Elders, which supports her in all her actions, has just decreed that France will be open to all nations. She is appealing to foreign colonists to help raise from its ruins the country she has been called upon to administrate, and to cultivate it according to the rules of civilization.

A telegram that has just reached us by way of Zeeland informs us, additionally, that King Belt and his brother, who had retreated to New Cosaquia after their departure from Trevig, have obtained from the Queen and her council the release of their friend King Rhaman and his daughter Ouchda. It also informs us of a fact that denotes the barbarity of these people, who nevertheless seem to want to give birth to civilization.

Johan-Ali-Schahpohtink, who was far from being an old man, was nevertheless a member of the Council of Elders because of his capability and his energy. He was also the fiancé of the present Queen, whom he should have married some time ago, although, for reasons not originating from him, the union was continually postponed.

The hostility that he showed in the Council, from the earliest days of the revolution, to the reforms that the Queen proposed caused a rupture between them that had already been threatened, it appears, for some time. Doubtless in order to get rid of her suitor, the Queen exhumed an ancient law forbidding the throne to anyone soiled by the murder of an unarmed man, and it appears that Johan was guilty of such a crime.

Johan ceased to exercise any restraint then; he became the leader of a systematic and vindictive opposition; he criticized all the reforms that the Queen submitted to the Council. On leaving the Council meeting, in which he had been excessively violent, he was stabbed, virtually before the Queen's eyes.

The news from Poland confirms this fact.

Warsaw, 31 Prairial, 1 a.m.

Johan-Ali-Schahpohtink has just been stabbed in the royal palace, in a Council Meeting. It has been proven that he had assassinated the savant voyager Daghestan. The Queen granted an immediate pardon to his murderer.

If Queen Nhohelle did not know yet who had attempted to murder our friend, we have guessed it easily, given Daghestan's story; Daghestan did not doubt it for a single moment. However, when we told him this news, he generously shed a tear for the death of his enemy, whose patriotism, finesse and energy he appreciated, even though all those qualities had been turned against him.

Caucasipol, 3 Messidor

Our friend Daghestan's state of health is not improving. Far be it from us, however to think that it is getting worse. It is not possible that Heaven will not take the trouble to conserve in the world the science and amity of such an eminently useful man, who has risked his life so courageously on behalf of all of us. Public anxiety is at its peak. The wounded man's house never empties of visitors bringing him their most ardent good wishes.

These testaments of affection do not only come from the bosom of our capital; they are arriving from everywhere, from the remotest extremities of the circle of our social relations.

None of our readers will have forgotten, I assume, Daghestan's strangely accidental excursion to Borneo, and his encounter with the graduate Arach, whom we know as a subscriber to our newspaper, the only one in that distant land. Well, that eccentric philosopher with a heart of gold has just arrived in Caucasipol, accompanied by his ward Tarnawalis. They have brought their friend the expression of the great sympathy that all Borneo experienced for him when the news reached them of his odious attempted murder, while giving him the cares of their own profound amity.

How fine it is to be thus beloved!

Caucasipol, 4 Messidor.

The health of citizen Daghestan appears to have taken a turn for the better since yesterday. Our friend even got out of bed for a few hours today. He was able to rest sitting on the balcony of his window, where we were with him, and from which we could admire a spectacle that was not new to him but which surprised me strangely, as it must have surprised all the inhabitants of Caucasipol, even those who have read about Daghestan's voyage to New Cosaquia.

As we were looking up into the sky, whose pure atmosphere, graciously stamped with the most beautiful clouds, we were admiring, we suddenly saw a moving black dot appear in their distance, which made our friend shiver, for he had recognized it. The dot expanded and developed in a matter of minutes.

It was an aerostat—an aerostat coming, as we have learned and everyone now knows, from New Cosaquia, or France, steered by expert crewmen.

It carried King Rhaman and his daughter, King Belt and his brother, and two French crewmen.

That balloon will remain in our midst for several days; it can be admired by everyone and studied by our scientists, who have been investigating the art of steering balloons at will for a long time. Will that art, therefore, as Daghestan has said, really come to us from a land of barbarians? We shall see...

Caucasipol, 6 Messidor.

Daghestan's health is stable, so the physicians say; our friends even say that it is still improving. Thus, we feel able, today, to repeat here the rumors that are circulating in the city, and which, for our part, we would gladly see realized, because we have wished that it might be so several times. It is said that a marriage is planned, to take place imminently, between our friend Daghestan and King Rhaman's daughter, who will accredit as her husband's second wife Mr. Arach's ward.

Caucasipol, 10 Messidor, 10 a.m.

We have very sad news to announce to our friends; Daghestan is gravely ill. His wounds reopened last night; they present a disquieting aspect. His fever is not dissipating; it is even acquiring a character that doctors always dread. My God! My God!

3 p.m.

Daghestan has just died!!!

Caucasipol, 11 Messidor.

Our dear Daghestan died yesterday, at three o'clock in the afternoon, surrounded by as many of his friends as his room could contain. He died quietly, without complaining of his suffering, which must have been atrocious, in everyone's judgment. He did not curse hi murderers; he contented himself with smiling at the name of Johan-Ali-Schahpohtink, which one of us pronounced in a moment of malediction. Poor friend, one might have thought that he was leaving on a voyage from which he would soon return, for he seemed to be leaving without regret. Did he want to console us all with the placidity to his face? Did he want to dry our tears—the tears that we could not hide from him—with the softness of his smile?

Hazard, as if it wanted to mock us and insult our poor friend, caused a brilliant deputation to disembark an instant after his death, bringing him homage that would certainly have been very welcome to him. Nhohelle II had sent her royal aerostat, in order to bring our savant friend back to France, with the honors due to the most important persons. It was even said—in whispers, it's true—that the Queen of France wanted to offer her hand to Daghestan. Poor friend! Poor friend!

Caucasipol, 15 Messidor.

A telegram sent from France, by way of Poland, informs us that Queen Nhohelle II has abdicated, declaring that she will never marry. She had advised the Council of Elders not to appoint another king, but to retain royal authority in their own hands, and to govern the country alone. She will help them with her advice. The Queen has retired to an isolated house where she will live alone, devoting herself to study.

Caucasipol, 16 Messidor.

The last duties were rendered yesterday to the mortal remains of citizen Daghestan. The graduate Arach had embalmed and disposed his body according to the Bornean fashion, which we know from Daghestan's own story.

A small cell had been prepared, by the cares of all of us, in the city Necropolis, and we had deposited there the savant of whom Caucasia is so proud, the friend who was so dear to us. It is there that we hoped to see him every day, while we live, in order to contemplate his features, so well conserved by the admirable art of the Borneans, and to learn from that smiling mouth how one pardons the blindness of an enemy, after having sacrificed his repose and his life to the privations of science.

Well, a strange profanation, a sacrilege, has just been committed in that mortuary cell. Daghestan's body has disappeared. It was probably stolen last night, for yesterday, until nightfall, and this morning, from daybreak onwards, pious visitors never ceased to go to him, without interruption.

Is it really a sacrilege? Might it not rather be an excessive affection that was responsible? The police have been informed; everyone will assist in their investigation.

For myself, if I did not fear passing for feeble-minded, I would say that I expected that theft, or something similar. Yesterday, during the funeral procession, it seemed to me that something strange was happening in its midst. That something

I do not feel courageous enough to relate to strong minds, but I feel brave enough to confess here, on this occasion, that, like Daghestan, I am imbued with some ideas that are called prejudices, and others that are called follies, and many people will doubtless think me mistaken in believing that there is a world beyond ours, and that events occur in that world that we do not see, but of which it is not impossible that we sometimes feel the impact.

Here I ask but one grace, which is that people should not laugh at me, because I shall not laugh at others. Every thinking man, I tell myself, has his principles; mine, I think, are good, but I always respect those of others, for how can I be sure that only mine are good? Who can tell me whether this truth, which I do not understand, does not emerge from the principles of my contradictors? So, I have made myself a rule, which I recommend to laughers, which is to say, when I see an effect whose cause I cannot see: "Who knows?"

Who knows whether, outside my conceptions and my logical principles, there are not laws—a world, in sum—that move in an unknown milieu?

Who knows whether savage lands have not retained some shreds of an exotic science that comes to them from far away, very far away, of which we are ignorant?

Who knows whether New Cosaquia, where a tribe has conserved a small residue of the infinite science of our ancestors, does not have in its bosom notions that surpass ours?

Who will dare to say that there is nothing outside of us, nothing above us, nothing beyond our civilization and our philosophical knowledge?

Who will dare to say that the sciences we call occult sciences, at which we laugh so lightly, are not ones that we ought to study with particular care, because they are the sciences of immateriality in its relationships with matter—an admirable and necessary study if ever there was one?

Who will dare to say that a phenomenon outside of our ordinary physical laws was not produced in Daghestan's funeral procession, according to those laws? That there was not, for example, a supernatural apparition, and that the venerable Franco, with whom our friend had dealings several times, was not there, in his immortal cloud?

Who will dare to say that the disappearance of Daghestan's body was not due to the prodigies of that occult science, which was probably highly developed in antiquity, and which still appears to be in the French tribe of New Cosaquia, and which, I hope, will be taken seriously here some day?

Woe betide the man who believes that he holds the final knot of science in his hand!

Caucasipol, 1 Thermidor.

Perhaps I have the answer to some of the questions I asked in this paper on 16 Messidor last, in a letter that I have just received from a friend who has recently departed for Figuig.

I shall not say anything about the flood of workers and travelers who are coming from all directions to work on the resurrection of Paris; I shall not mention the charming hospitality that everyone receives there, the prodigious upheavals that have already been effected on the ground they wish to regenerate. My correspondent has told me about that briefly, and he will inform me more amply later; but I will talk about a fact that he relates to me with a great deal of interest, and which is the very response that I have just mentioned.

Queen Nhohelle my friend tells me, and as we already know, is living in the most profound retreat, in a small house, very comfortable and very pretty, surrounded by a vast garden that favors the silence of the habitation.

That house is situated to the south of the city, about a league from Paris, on the sea shore.

The Queen has not come to Paris since her abdication, but every day she receives the visit of some member of the Council of Elders, who has come to obtain her advice. A few friends who have remained faithful to her do not fail to make a pilgrimage to her retreat from time to time, where they are always made welcome. The door of the house, moreover, is no closed to anyone. It is the respect people have for her, more than the royal recluse's orders, which make the house a sacred place that one does not approach.

Lately, however, a certain animation appears to reign in the House of Retreat—which is the name by which the Queen's house is known. The Queen had asked for an aerostat and a crew from her ancient subjects, who had hastened to obey her wishes; but the aerostat was not for her. The crew departed alone over the sea, above which it traveled for a long distance, although no one knows exactly where it went. Then it returned to the little House of Retreat, accompanied by two travelers…whom I now know, my friend says.

One of them is Fittri, the Sheikh of Sudan; the other his first minister and friend, the same man that Daghestan's story represented to us as a mere warden of the great penitentiary of Tahiti. Having departed a few days ago from Timbuktu, they were going to Caucasia to see our illustrious scholar, their friend. The Queen had seen them, by means of her incredible science, crossing the sea in a ship that was far from having any intention to land on the shore of New Cosaquia, doubtless knowing nothing about the strange revolution that promised to change the face of that nation.

Furnished with precise instructions, the crew of the royal aerostat had no difficulty finding and introducing themselves to the two travelers they sought. They took them aboard—and the latter, it seems, climbed into the balloon without any mistrust, which took them to the Queen's house.

Then there was a strange occurrence; the first utterance of the Sheikh on entering the most secret room in the house, which no one except the queen had entered before, was a cry of joy.

"Daghestan!" the Sheikh cried, precipitating himself into the depths of the room, his arms extended toward someone. That was seen. Then a profound silence was established there, followed by a few stifled sobs...

The Sheikh and his friend stayed at the Retreat with the Queen for a few days. When they left, their eyes were red, as if they had been weeping.

"For myself," my friend added, "I've been admitted to the little house several times, where, from close at hand, I've heard the Queen talking in her mysterious room, even conversing…with whom? I don't know, for she was alone.

"Alone! No, my friend, no; and pardon me that reticence. I dare not speak the truth, which I know in its entirety, but which I learned by indiscretion, by an indiscretion of which I'm glad, but for which I nevertheless reproach myself. I darted a glance—only one, and covertly—into the mysterious room one day, and I saw…yes, yes, I really saw…I saw Daghestan…"

Daghestan! There, in Paris, in the Queen's house! I suspected as much.

Power of the occult sciences, how great you are!

Who will tell me, then, that Daghestan is not still living a strange life that I do not understand?

Who will tell me that the Queen, that celestial woman, that goddess, does not have among her secrets one that resurrects the dead, or at least give the dead an ability to communicate with the living?

One can smile with incredulity at those questions, but one can never refute them.

For myself, I am like Daghestan; I no longer have any doubt, and I admit without blushing, at this moment—at this moment most of all—that we are forced to recognize that were are ignorant of more scientific truths than we know.

But what we do not know can be learned; what we do not know doubtless will be learned, one day.

Who will dare to deny that? Who will dare to set limits on the science of the future?

SF & FANTASY

Henri Allorge. *The Great Cataclysm*
Guy d'Armen. *Doc Ardan: The City of Gold and Lepers*
G.-J. Arnaud. *The Ice Company*
Charles Asselineau. *The Double Life*
Cyprien Bérard. *The Vampire Lord Ruthwen*
Aloysius Bertrand. *Gaspard de la Nuit*
Richard Bessière. *The Gardens of the Apocalypse*
Albert Bleunard. *Ever Smaller*
Félix Bodin. *The Novel of the Future*
Alphonse Brown. *City of Glass*
André Caroff. *The Terror of Madame Atomos; Miss Atomos;*
The Return of Madame Atomos; The Mistake of Madame
Atomos; The Monsters of Madame Atomos
Félicien Champsaur. *The Human Arrow*
Didier de Chousy. *Ignis*
Captain Danrit. *Undersea Odyssey*
C. I. Defontenay. *Star (Psi Cassiopeia)*
Charles Derennes. *The People of the Pole*
Georges Dodds (anthologist). *The Missing Link*
Harry Dickson. *The Heir of Dracula*
Jules Dornay. *Lord Ruthven Begins*
Alfred Driou. *The Adventures of a Parisian Aeronaut*
Sâr Dubnotal *vs. Jack the Ripper*
Alexandre Dumas. *The Return of Lord Ruthven*
Renée Dunan. *Baal*
J.-C. Dunyach. *The Night Orchid; The Thieves of Silence*
Henri Duvernois. *The Man Who Found Himself*
Achille Eyraud. *Voyage to Venus*
Henri Falk. *The Age of Lead*
Paul Féval. *Anne of the Isles; Knightshade; Revenants; Vam-*
pire City; The Vampire Countess; The Wandering Jew's
Daughter
Paul Féval, *fils. Felifax, the Tiger-Man*
Charles de Fieux. *Lamékis*

Arnould Galopin. *Doctor Omega; Doctor Omega & The Shadowmen*

G.L. Gick. *Harry Dickson and the Werewolf of Rutherford Grange*

Edmond Haraucourt. *Illusions of Immortality*

Nathalie Henneberg. *The Green Gods*

V. Hugo, P. Foucher & P. Meurice. *The Hunchback of Notre-Dame*

Michel Jeury. *Chronolysis*

Gustave Kahn. *The Tale of Gold and Silence*

Gérard Klein. *The Mote in Time's Eye*

Jean de La Hire. *Enter the Nyctalope; The Nyctalope on Mars; The Nyctalope vs. Lucifer; The Nyctalope Steps In; Night of the Nyctalope*

Etienne-Léon de Lamothe-Langon. *The Virgin Vampire*

André Laurie. *Spiridon*

Gabriel de Lautrec. *The Vengeance of the Oval Portrait*

Georges Le Faure & Henri de Graffigny. *The Extraordinary Adventures of a Russian Scientist Across the Solar System* (2 vols.)

Gustave Le Rouge. *The Vampires of Mars The Dominion of the World* (w/Gustave Guitton) (4 vols.)

Jules Lermina. *Mysteryville; Panic in Paris; To-Ho and the Gold Destroyers; The Secret of Zippelius*

Jean-Marc & Randy Lofficier. *Edgar Allan Poe on Mars; The Katrina Protocol; Pacifica; Robonocchio; Tales of the Shadowmen 1-8*

Xavier Mauméjean. *The League of Heroes*

Joseph Méry. *The Tower of Destiny*

Hippolyte Mettais. *The Year 5865*

José Moselli. *Illa's End*

John-Antoine Nau. *Enemy Force*

Marie Nizet. *Captain Vampire*

C. Nodier, A. Beraud & Toussaint-Merle. *Frankenstein*

Henri de Parville. *An Inhabitant of the Planet Mars*

Gaston de Pawlowski. *Journey to the Land of the 4th Dimension*

Georges Pellerin. *The World in 2000 Years*
J. Polidori, C. Nodier, E. Scribe. *Lord Ruthven the Vampire*
P.-A. Ponson du Terrail. *The Vampire and the Devil's Son*
Henri de Régnier. *A Surfeit of Mirrors*
Maurice Renard. *The Blue Peril; Doctor Lerne; The Doctored Man; A Man Among the Microbes; The Master of Light*
Jean Richepin. *The Wing*
Albert Robida. *The Adventures of Saturnin Farandoul; The Clock of the Centuries; Chalet in the Sky*
J.-H. Rosny Aîné. *Helgvor of the Blue River; The Givreuse Enigma; The Mysterious Force; The Navigators of Space; Vamireh; The World of the Variants; The Young Vampire*
Marcel Rouff. *Journey to the Inverted World*
Han Ryner. *The Superhumans*
Brian Stableford. *The New Faust at the Tragicomique;The Empire of the Necromancers (The Shadow of Frankenstein; Frankenstein and the Vampire Countess; Frankenstein in London); Sherlock Holmes & The Vampires of Eternity; The Stones of Camelot; The Wayward Muse.* (anthologist) *The Germans on Venus; News from the Moon; The Supreme Progress; The World Above the World; Nemoville*
Jacques Spitz. *The Eye of Purgatory*
Kurt Steiner. *Ortog*
Eugène Thébault. *Radio-Terror*
C.-F. Tiphaigne de La Roche. *Amilec*
Théo Varlet. *The Xenobiotic Invasion; Timeslip Troopers* (w/André Blandin); *The Martian Epic* (w/Octave Joncquel)
Paul Vibert. *The Mysterious Fluid*
Villiers de l'Isle-Adam. *The Scaffold; The Vampire Soul*
Philippe Ward. *Artahe*
Philippe Ward & Sylvie Miller. *The Song of Montségur*

MYSTERIES & THRILLERS

M. Allain & P. Souvestre. *The Daughter of Fantômas*
A. Anicet-Bourgeois, Lucien Dabril. *Rocambole*
A. Bernède & L. Feuillade. *Judex*

A. Bisson & G. Livet. *Nick Carter vs. Fantômas*
V. Darlay & H. de Gorsse. *Lupin vs. Holmes: The Stage Play*
Paul Féval. *Gentlemen of the Night; John Devil; The Black Coats ('Salem Street; The Invisible Weapon; The Parisian Jungle; The Companions of the Treasure; Heart of Steel; The Cadet Gang; The Sword-Swallower)*
Emile Gaboriau. *Monsieur Lecoq*
Steve Leadley. *Sherlock Holmes: The Circle of Blood*
Maurice Leblanc. *Arsène Lupin vs. Countess Cagliostro; Lupin vs. Holmes (The Blonde Phantom; The Hollow Needle); The Many Faces of Arsène Lupin*
Gaston Leroux. *Chéri-Bibi; The Phantom of the Opera; Rouletabille & the Mystery of the Yellow Room*
Richard Marsh. *The Complete Adventures of Judith Lee*
William Patrick Maynard. *The Terror of Fu Manchu; The Destiny of Fu Manchu*
Frank J. Morlock. *Sherlock Holmes: The Grand Horizontals; Sherlock Holmes vs Jack the Ripper*
P. de Wattyne & Y. Walter. *Sherlock Holmes vs. Fantômas*
David White. *Fantômas in America*

SCREENPLAYS

Mike Baron. *The Iron Triangle*
Emma Bull & Will Shetterly. *Nightspeeder; War for the Oaks*
Gerry Conway & Roy Thomas. *Doc Dynamo*
Steve Englehart. *Majorca*
James Hudnall. *The Devastator*
Jean-Marc & Randy Lofficier. *Royal Flush*
J.-M. & R. Lofficier & Marc Agapit. *Despair*
J.-M. & R. Lofficier & Joël Houssin. *City*
Andrew Paquette. *Peripheral Vision*
R. Thomas, J. Hendler & L. Sprague de Camp. *Rivers of Time*

NON-FICTION

Stephen R. Bissette. *Blur 1-5. Green Mountain Cinema 1; Teen Angels*
Win Scott Eckert. *Crossovers* (2 vols.)
Jean-Marc & Randy Lofficier. *Shadowmen* (2 vols.)
Randy Lofficier. *Over Here*

HEXAGON COMICS

Franco Frescura & Luciano Bernasconi. *Wampus*
Franco Frescura & Giorgio Trevisan. *CLASH*
L. Bernasconi, J.-M. Lofficier & Juan Roncagliolo Berger. *Phenix*
Claude Legrand, J.-M. Lofficier & L. Bernasconi. *Kabur*
Franco Oneta. *Zembla*
L. Buffolente, Lofficier & J.-J. Dzialowski. *Strangers: Homicron*
Danilo Grossi. *Strangers: Jaydee*
Claude Legrand & Luciano Bernasconi. *Strangers: Starlock*

ART BOOKS

Jean-Pierre Normand. *Science Fiction Illustrations*
Raven Okeefe. *Raven's L'il Critters*
Randy Lofficier & Raven OKeefe. *If Your Possum Go Daylight...*
Daniele Serra. *Illusions*